WINDOW GODS

About the author

Born in Sydney, raised and educated in Canberra, and now living in Melbourne, Sally Morrison originally trained as a molecular biologist before beginning her writing career in the 1970s. Her work includes the play *Hag*, short story collection *I Am a Boat*, and novels *Who's Taking You to the Dance*, *Against Gravity*, *The Insatiable Desire of Injured Love* and the award-winning *Mad Meg*, which is set in the same world as *Window Gods*. Her last book was a biography of Clifton Pugh, *After Fire*.

www.sallymorrison.com
www.facebook.com/SallyMorrisonWriter

SALLY MORRISON
WINDOW GODS

Truth sleeps in the seed

hardie grant books
MELBOURNE · LONDON

Published in 2014 by Hardie Grant Books
Hardie Grant Books (Australia)
Ground Floor, Building 1
658 Church Street
Richmond, Victoria 3121
www.hardiegrant.com.au

Hardie Grant Books (UK)
5th & 6th Floor
52–54 Southwark Street
London SE1 1RU
www.hardiegrant.co.uk

A Cataloguing-in-Publication entry is available from the catalogue of the
National Library of Australia at www.nla.gov.au
Window Gods
ISBN 9781742709208

Cover and text design by Nada Backovic
Cover watercolour by Samuel Holden © Victoria and Albert Museum, London
Author photograph by Jacqueline Mitelman
Typeset in 12/15 pt Granjon by Cannon Typesetting

Printed in Australia by Griffin Press

The paper this book is printed on is certified against the Forest Stewardship
Council® Standards. Griffin Press holds FSC chain of custody certification
SGS-COC-005088. FSC promotes environmentally responsible, socially
beneficial and economically viable management of the world's forests.

FSC
www.fsc.org
MIX
Paper from
responsible sources
FSC® C009448

1

'God, who's that loser?' croons my recently made friend, Louise-who-wants-to-be-a-painter, her plump pink lips at my earlobe. She's down from Daylesford for my exhibition opening.

'You mean that one over there?' I say, pointing to where my son, who's come straight from the gym in his tracky daks, is sauntering past my big triptych, *Madonna, Madonnina*, sipping nonchalantly on a champagne he's swiped from the silver tray at the entrance.

'Someone ought to chuck him out,' says Louise-who-wants. 'He's just wandered in off the street and pinched a glass of bubbly! I'm going to tell the organiser.'

'Well, hang on,' I say and I call through a gap in the gathering that aligns my low-slung mouth with his high-slung ear, 'Eli!'

He hasn't heard. I'm about to tunnel through the crowd to grab hold of him, when Louise says, 'Do you *know* him? Who is he? Is he mentally ill or something?'

'No, he's just wearing his gym clothes.'

'To an *opening like this?*'

It's true the place looks plush with its Victorian decor and famed collection of Australiana. Marian, the organiser, and I have hung my work among it, hoping, with a long pull on the bow, that it won't look too out of place – after all, the images derive from monumental buildings of a similar era, only they belong to Milan, not Melbourne. Milan has history for me, being the place where my father spent his early life – besides, it's very paintable.

'Don't worry about him,' I say to Louise, 'come over and meet my partner, Mick.' And I haul her over to where Mick is standing, large and companionless in his best clobber, kind of circling round his champagne flute, no doubt looking for the top of my head in the throng. Poor chap has only been to one other exhibition opening and was so at sea that he kept swooping past the food table and bucketing up handfuls of hors d'oeuvre to bring me, thinking it was all we'd have for tea.

We push through the expensively perfumed guests, almost none of whom I know. There are those from my painting work-shops, like Louise, and those from my weekend classes and one or two dear stalwarts – I suppose I recognise about ten people. At short notice, because I was double-booked out of my original venue, Marian – gallery manager for the big business venture housed in this building – took me on and invited the company guest list, say-ing, 'It'll be a smash hit, just you wait and see!' Marian's a trouper, good-natured, funny and chaotically organised – nothing falls into the pit, although it looks as if it might, which is just the way I like it. The people here are by and large the owner's friends who've stayed back in the city after work to sit out an extraordinary weather alert in this safe and opulent place, with free and fancy food laid on. The weather bureau is tipping one hundred and fifty kph winds; there've already been some appallingly noisy blasts and the trams have stopped running. I yank Mick's coat bottom. He says, 'Oh, there you are!'

'Meet Louise, pet. I've just got to scoot off for a tick and...'

I've brought some clothes for Eli. They're in a backpack in the conference room behind the gallery. Unfortunately, the TV crew's in there and they aren't letting anyone in. That's why he's dressed the way he is. He's a journalist: he's returning to Afghanistan tomorrow, all his ordinary clothes are packed and I had to bring in his old wedding suit from its storage place in my wardrobe. I shuffle up to Marian, who's serving the wine, and she says, 'I'll get your son to hop into the gents, Isobel, and I'll whip his kit in there away from that ridiculous TV crew. Why they have to have it all to themselves, God knows.'

Half the gathering's already noticed Eli and people are forming temporary clumps to look him up and down in a mixture of mystification and distaste. He's arousing far more interest than my paintings. They've probably decided that he's a tramp or homeless, that he's come to sit out the disastrous storm that's supposed to be upon us within the hour and that the security on the door isn't up to scratch.

I take over from Marian, who walks purposefully up the corridor that leads away from the exhibition space, opens the forbidden door, retrieves the backpack and beckons Eli down another corridor where there is a gents and where he would have come in had it not been that the weather alert meant the side door had to be shut.

People come up to the table ignoring me as if I am a waitress. They ask each other questions like 'I've never seen any of this person's work before, have you?' and give each other answers like 'She's Henry Coretti's daughter, you can tell.' 'Yes, there's a problem with painting dynasties, the kids never seem to be able to get out of their parents' shadows.'

'Actually,' says one of my mother's many relatives who hasn't noticed that I have just become a menial, serving the wine at my own do to someone who doesn't know I'm the star turn, who thanks me for the champagne and takes my glass, 'she won some major award a few years ago. Can't remember the name of it, but the Art Gallery acquired the work. It's in the Australian collection.'

'Really?'

'They're a very artistic family. I'm related to her mother.'

'Not Viva Laurington? I thought she was dead.'

'Not Viva, no. She *is* dead. Stella Coretti, his first wife, is my second cousin.'

'There was another wife!'

'Oh yes. And two daughters. Isobel is the younger one. The older one, Allegra, committed suicide.'

'I thought Henry Coretti only had one daughter…I thought Cecilia was an only child…*Suicide*, you said?'

'Married the wrong chap. Terrible fellow. Isobel and Allegra had an art gallery – he got jealous and laid waste to a show of Isobel's work.'

'Oh, they should have called the police! Killing yourself's just letting someone like that get away with it!'

'Yes, well…The pity of it was that there was a child. A little girl. In the end, Isobel and Stella took her in hand.'

'And all along I thought Cecilia Laurington-Coretti was an only child!'

'Well, no. Which puts a spoke in the wheel of the inheritance. You'll have heard the kerfuffle over the Siècle Trust, I suppose?'

'I thought Cecilia ran the Siècle Trust?'

'She's on the board. Isobel and her niece, Nin, own some of the pictures but Cecilia and her mother wanted them in the Trust – the pictures, I mean, not Isobel and her niece. Cecilia and Isobel are at daggers drawn…'

(Really? Are we just? At daggers drawn! I don't own a dagger. I pass out more champagne to reaching hands, ears pricking.)

'Oh, you might be able to help me with something,' goes one of the women the relative is talking to. 'Somebody told me this and I've always wondered if it was true. They said that Henry Coretti was a spy in France during the war…'

Laughter… 'Oh no. No. Henry came to Australia before the war broke out. He came out from France…'

'I must have got it wrong…'

'No, no, not altogether. You see, his family were émigrés from Milan…' (How she loves that word émigré.) 'That'll be the Milanese connection in these paintings – they were anti-Mussolini and went to Paris when Henry was still a teenager. They lived in

4

Paris where the parents worked for the Italian underground. They ran a newspaper, or helped to run it. Henry was a courier.'

'I heard he met Viva in Paris.'

'Yes, well, that's it, you see. She was staying in the same apartment. She'd gone over as a guest of the Coretti's host family. They were living all-in-together. Imagine, in one of those poky Paris apartments. I stayed in one – you couldn't swing a cat! If you ask me, Melbourne's a much better place to live, these days at least.'

'Absolutely. And Paris is so expensive.'

'Didn't you get one of those travel card things? I did, but there you are, you see Viva was hardly more than a schoolgirl, although she'd known the host family's relatives back here and they more or less sent her off. Quite possibly…' chortle, 'to improve her French.'

'Like finishing school?'

'No, no, no, no! No! Not like finishing school. No, by all accounts, Viva had a pretty rough start. Guess who was her brother?'

'I've no idea.'

'Leslie Hallett!'

'Oh, wasn't his father a woodcutter or something? Wasn't that in the paper recently?'

'Yes. They've begun writing about him and that group of artists. *So* talented. If he'd lived they say he'd have been better known than Henry Coretti.'

'I've forgotten how he died…'

'Leslie Hallett? Another suicide. He was gay, you see. But that article in the paper didn't say who his lover was,' says the relative, knowingly.

'Who?'

'Harry Laurington!'

'*Really? No!* I thought he was Viva's brother.'

'No, dear. She was married to him for years before she married Henry Coretti. It was a cover. Oh, it suited Viva! There she was, you see, caught short with Henry's bun in the oven…'

'Oh, I thought Henry Coretti had always been with Viva.'

'Did you darling? Ha, ha, ha!'

'But why didn't they stay together if they'd known each other so long and she was pregnant? Oh, I'm on *her* side!'

'He was mad about someone else.'

'Your cousin?'

'Oh no. Not Stella, more's the pity. No, it was someone he knew in France. She died, you see. He was devastated. Maybe he had a one-night stand with Viva or they did have a brief affair, but he found out about this other woman's death and went walkabout, not knowing Viva was pregnant. When he came back, it was a fait accompli – wedding ring and baby.'

'Oh!' Swallowed shrieks. And, 'Gosh, how do you know so much? I mean, that article in the paper wasn't that revealing!'

'Angela Crawford's doing it for her mature-age PhD at Swinburne. Naturally I was fascinated because of Cousin Stella. I don't suppose it matters much to her now though. Another cousin, Audra Cordage…'

'Gosh, Audra and I were on the Scotch mothers' committee. It must be forty years ago. But go on.'

'Well, Audra told me that Isobel's had Stella put away in an old folks' home. Audra's livid!'

'Give her my best, won't you?'

'Certainly. Funny old thing, Audra, but loyal, you see. Anyway, who's for more champagne?' And she turns around and… '*Isobel!*' And then, to cover her tracks, she breathes a little smile that catches on her tonsils and while she's doing that, I give her a cold stare and skedaddle towards the loo past Marian, who is back, pulling herself up to her full-breasted, capable size, glasses round her neck on a lanyard.

Eli is scrubbing up and now I have to let my indignation cool and get ready to face the cameras.

The light in the lady's loo is kind to me, thank God. Nevertheless, splashing my face with cold water was a mistake and I have to keep dabbing my front while I screw up my eyes in search of the lashes with the mascara wand.

Last week, when I was in the middle of preparing for this launch, there was a knock on my door. When I opened it I had a paintbrush in my hand and spraypaint goggles pushed back on my head. 'What?' I growled. I hate being interrupted in the middle of work and I have to kick myself every time I allow it to happen. I had my mind on the physics and geography of my far-too-small studio and no free fingers to take hold of the sheaf of papers the interrupting bastard on the doorstep was proffering me. Mick was away. I was very, very busy, but the bastard kept on thrusting the papers at me, saying, 'You Isobel Coretti?'

'Yes.'

'Well, I've been ordered to serve these on you.'

'Serve?'

'Legal papers.'

'Fuck!'

'Sorry.' And he looked sorry, like a roadside weed in a hailstorm. So I took off the goggles and the rubber gloves I was wearing and while I was doing that, he said, 'It's not really that urgent, but you have to take the papers. It's a Statement of Claim and I have to verify that I've delivered it.'

And there on the top page of this statement was the name Cecilia V. Laurington-Coretti, as Checkie likes to style herself. In the claim she was described as the owner of Siècle Art Gallery and Director of the Board of Trustees for the Siècle Trust.

She was claiming ownership of an important group of paintings that my niece and I were awarded from Dadda's estate.

Why couldn't he have just saved his sperm for Allegra and me? Why did he have to test his proclivities for procreation with bloody Viva? Checkie claims that the estate has never been legally finalised and that since I appear not to have the means of maintaining them, the paintings should come to her as part of the Siècle Trust to which our father belonged.

I deeply resent having to waste time even thinking about Checkie, but she has announced publicly and loudly that she is the true owner of the paintings in my care, and now a blasted current affairs program has found enough mud in it to ring me and ask if they could televise my opinion on the matter tonight.

They're not here to talk about my paintings and the effort it's been to paint such big and intricate work in the tiny premises of my home – no! Not here to gauge the difficulties involved in painting large when you're knee high to an ant and have to tie your brushes onto the ends of giant sticks in order to get the sweep and the buzz going – no. Not here to talk about the years involved in planning things on this scale! Oh no! They're here to talk about what they call the Coretti dynasty and now I have to rehearse it all quickly in my head before I talk to them.

We all shuffle trivia to a greater or lesser degree to make the world reflect more glory on us, but Viva Laurington-Coretti did it par excellence. Viva had quite a story behind her: the story of a poor girl made good, even heroic with her flight from Mussolini's henchmen and a handsome young man tucked under her arm. She and Dadda had gone to Normandy to drop propaganda to two leaders of the Italian resistance just before the Cagoulards waylaid the leaders and murdered them.

Stella would never have been able to handle such a story. Political intrigue, murder and being on the run were outside her ken. At the time she met Dadda, Singapore had fallen and she was numbly trying to concoct a tale that would disguise from her suffering self the deaths abroad of all the dear young men in her life – her three brothers and her fiancé. It took all her energy just to save herself from the impact. If she was clever, that cleverness was never allowed to grow – all was covered in the luscious vines of charity which extended to envelop Dadda over the counter of the bank where she was his teller.

She did not know that Dadda had come to Melbourne with Viva; she barely knew that he was allowed in because he had a French passport and an uncle in Melbourne who was able to sponsor him. She did not know that in Melbourne, Dadda had a liaison with Viva for want of knowing anyone else. She did not know that Viva exulted in this relationship and saw it as the culmination of a high-minded adventure.

Viva's dream of landing Henry Coretti for herself came true once they arrived in Australia. She kept urging that dream to stay up where she'd put it, but the more she strove to empower it, the more she realised that she had in her arms a man who was grieving over someone else. She could not hide her bitterness. She was deeply, enduringly jealous. I don't know whether Dadda weakened before news of his beloved's death reached him. If it had been me, I dare say I might have weakened, fatalistic creep that I am: it was very doubtful that, once he left, Dadda would ever see her again. He must have been heartbroken and in need. Whatever happened, while he was off wandering, Viva had a better offer.

Harry Laurington's Siècle was one of the first private art galleries in Melbourne. It showed the work of young contemporaries. Dadda showed with Siècle at first, but, after Checkie arrived, decided against it because Harry was bringing her up as if she were his. But Leslie Hallett, the painterly brother, had always been a troubled person: add to that the fact that he was having an affair with his sister's husband and perhaps it was enough at the time to drive him over the edge. He committed suicide, so instead of the marriage liberating Viva, it meant that she lost both her lover and her brother and had a gay man for a partner.

She had to take on Leslie's death somehow so she began a myth that was one of the props of her existence – had he lived, Leslie would have been the greatest painter of his generation. A certain lore grew up around Leslie's name. He had mystique. He became the subject of research and writing. Harry Laurington formed a trust in which his work was preserved for posterity. But there wasn't enough of it for posterity. More painters of Leslie's generation had to be inveigled to add work to the Siècle Trust in return for lore to be established around their names as well. There were already some paintings of Dadda's that were included in the Trust – his thoughts were that they might end up with his daughter as a gift that Harry and Viva could explain.

One way of looking at his marriage to Stella was that it was his key to Australian citizenship, which, combined with his French passport, gave him a fictitious place of birth and kept him from being interned as an enemy alien. But I don't believe it was just the practicality – I think he actually fell for the hazel-eyed flirt in the bank with her sad story of dead soldiers and her desire to make good her losses in children. I think Dadda became willingly entangled in her vines. He did love her once. We all loved her: she was funny, warm, kind and soulful.

I didn't do Dadda any favours in the eyes of Stella's people, the Mottes, however, by being the second girl in the family. I was a mistake – one girl was adorable, but plenty. What they needed were men. They were on the land and Stella was their brood mare. They looked down on Dadda – he failed as an Australian. Lovely to look at, but he didn't cut his hair or polish his shoes and he painted pictures no one understood. All right if he'd painted heroes or horses or woolsheds but he painted naked women made out of vacuum cleaner parts!

Poor Dadda! He did his best to be pleasing to the Mottes but the Mottes thought themselves way above him and regarded him as a person without dignity or prospects.

I hate to say it, but it was little wonder that when Viva came back into his life and Dadda had two teenage daughters and was starved for intelligent company in the arts, he left Stella, and Viva left Harry, and they were married. It was then that his career took off.

While he was courting and marrying, Allegra and I, having inherited some money from Stella's big sister, began our gallery,

Mad Meg. We named it after Breughel's *Mad Meg*, a print of which we came across under the bed of our aunt's drunken husband. It seemed appropriate – both the way we found the print and the image itself.

I've since seen the painting, where it hangs in a dark museum in Antwerp. It's hard to see the whole thing all at once because the light glares variously from the old surface – but I suppose this is appropriate, too, because you can never see all of life at once, just parts of it – comic and tragic sequences; mayhem as the giantess, strung about with pots and pans, sword in hand, charges the mouth of Hell while her minions thwack and bind the devils to cushions in her wake. There is only one area of seeming calm in the painting – an almost unnoticeable island, right in the middle, where a pair of people sit, one with a raised hand, as if to say, 'This is what it's like; this is how it is.' 'It' could be 'life' or 'death'. Allegra and I chose 'life'. We chose to see Meg giving Hell a thumping. We thought it described something about us: we were women trying to make our presence felt in a hostile world. We were going to use cooking pots and cauldrons as our weapons. Stuff bloody men! Our father, we claimed, was an old-style left-wing misogynist with his white-goods women. We were new – our art and the way we showed it flew in the face of the Laurington's Siècle and what we thought of as its pretensions.

Mad Meg lasted a number of years as a cooperative showing young contemporaries; it caused a lot of controversy, was a lot of fun, but in the end, it imploded.

Dadda and Viva were together for fifteen years and Dadda was very famous by the time he died, suddenly, of a heart attack, without leaving a will.

Almost as soon as she'd dealt with his remains, Viva started pushing Checkie's claims on his estate with such ruthlessness that they would eliminate ours. But for the efforts of Harry Laurington, and another painter and friend of Dadda's, a man named Reg Sorby, who took over when Harry died, we wouldn't have inherited anything.

Dadda's death came to us as a terrible, unexpected wound. He was still quite young and Allegra and I still adored him even if we pretended we didn't. Afterwards, with Reg Sorby bellowing injustice in the background, the widowed Viva gravitated back to Siècle and the Trust, deposited Dadda's work there and began to push Checkie and promote her as the Australian expert on Henry Coretti, his life and work. Harry Laurington was dying and Checkie was poised to take over.

Nin had recently been born to Allegra and her husband, a crazy artist called David Silver. We all lived together in a large house without any furniture, except for Eli's bed – I got into breeding early and inopportunely on the rebound from Dadda's leaving us.

Eli chose to sleep under, rather than on, his bed – he liked to pretend we lived on a barge – without furniture, the possibilities are endless.

In our shared digs, we had our feminist meetings and decided what we were going to show at Mad Meg and what agenda we were going to follow. David mocked us mercilessly, saying we couldn't even speak English, let alone create art – he was possibly right about the English, as the politically correct do tend to destroy language as a means of communication, preferring to use it as a means of clan identification. But David was also jealous of what we did and the way we did it.

We'd just hung a show of mine when he got very drunk, picked a fight with another painter on the opening night in the gallery and proceeded to lay waste to everything. It was too much for Allegra, and to make matters worse we were completely broke. Allegra realised the world wasn't going to accommodate her dreams and marrying David had been a blunder committed because we were very fond of his two uncles – dear chaps called Bart and Miles Turner – who were in the gallery trade. Notwithstanding that she was the mother of a little child, she sank into a fatal depression and eventually took an overdose. Never in my life will I be able to reconcile my beautiful brave sister with the person who turned on her and took her life away, the person who killed the mother of Nin…

Her suicide drove Stella out of her mind. For a while I was convinced that Stella had Alzheimer's and would never again be her silly, funny old self. But I was wrong. We stayed out of Melbourne in Reg Sorby's retreat in New South Wales while he managed to cobble together enough written material to make a case for us to inherit the paintings done by Dadda between 1944 and 1961, which was the life of our family unit. Once we had a court ruling, it was safe to come home, but while we were away, Viva had tried to win David over to the Siècle Trust side of the argument. She tried to get him to stake his claim as Allegra's widower. But David doesn't do anything complicated like dealing with the legal system and in the end, although she persuaded him to come into her fold, she had to fall back on putting caveats on the work, which meant that we couldn't sell them or break up the collection without her say-so. She wasn't able to name everything we had, so a few items escaped notice and we did sell those in order to be able to afford to come home. Her caveats lapsed when she died five years ago.

Owning artworks carries some responsibilities, but these can be very hard to meet if you do not have any money to keep your collection in good nick. All I can afford for mine is insurance. I have always been custodian on Nin's behalf, she being too young when Allegra died to be a custodian herself: nowadays she says she's too busy to share the responsibility. I keep the paintings in storage, except when asked to provide work for exhibitions.

In the years since Allegra's death, David has become close with Checkie – not in a sexual way (Checkie is so precious it's said she is allergic to sperm except when it brings money with it) but in a business sense. Although David is chiefly an artist, he is also an archivist by default and keeps the Siècle archives. David and Checkie make a relentless pair – in addition to their claim of the

Siècle Trust's ownership of the paintings, they maintain Siècle is better able to care for them than I am and that they will deteriorate if left with me. The paintings, they aver, are of value to the nation and should be made available to the nation through the Siècle Trust. It has become a famous dispute with photos of the warring parties appearing from time to time in the papers when there's nothing else to write about. The most famous event in the history of the dispute is the hijacking of the paintings from the Trust in the 1980s by Reg. Reg was a very flamboyant man and his actions were somewhere between a publicity stunt and an act of righteous generosity. There's always footage of the rambunctious Reg whenever the matter comes up again – it makes for public entertainment and for refreshing the memories of the TV viewing public.

Marian pops her head around the door. 'You nearly ready?' she asks.
'Just a sec.'
'I'll tell them to wait.'
'I'll be there in a minute.' Even without Checkie on my back, I'm as nervous as hell about going public and being judged for my own work as I will be in the next few weeks. I try to tell myself that there's no reason to feel nervous; nervousness is just a neurotic symptom in a person who lives in a first-world country with the luxury of having a fine arts industry. Imagine, I say to myself, being transported to your situation direct from one of those countries where Eli goes to pen his reports. In those places women can be murdered simply for showing their faces or for walking out without a man to accompany them. Eli's always reminding me how well off I am and how nerves are a first-world luxury.

And yet, nerves I have and I can't seem to outwit them.

Today you can create a picture with the click of a button and all it will do is join the trillions of other images that people make unless you push it and prompt it and encourage it to belong to that set of images – millions of them rather than trillions – that might be worth looking at twice. Painting images often seems futile when you think of this. Futile and immoral in a world of suffering and out-of-control climate. Or then again, just an old habit that has hung on in spite of losing its value…

In a moment or two I will have to go before the cameras and I will have to create a positive impression – I will have to be the image myself, although I don't know for whom. I don't even know what a positive impression is any longer: over my lifetime the idea of making a positive impression has moved from being a person with compassion and tolerance for the displaced of the Second World War to the idea of refugees as invaders against whom we need to arm ourselves to impress in a world where it's winner takes all. How on earth does someone like me behave like a winner? And winner of what?

In my case, it seems to be a precarious art collection without a wall.

I only agreed to talk to the television if they conducted the interview at my launch and gave me a brief opportunity to explain my work. So here we are.

The eyelashes are black, not that they weren't already, and the lips are on, but not so garishly that they'll go bounding around TV screens in advance of my face. Here's Eli now, beaming at me round the door and holding out his hand for me. You wouldn't know it was the bogan of fifteen minutes ago – against the current sartorial trend for the open-necked shirt that makes it look as if you've been working hard, Eli is wearing his shirt with the collar done up and the splendid yellow tie he wore to his wedding. Thank God he shaved his beard off after he came home this time. To my proud eye, he looks great. He kisses my cheek and says, 'Get in there and sock it to 'em, Mum.'

Actually, I feel the presenter is on my side, but you never really can tell with the press. And on side today does not mean on side tomorrow. Thankfully we are not being recorded live. I don't think I could maintain my composure live.

But here we go: need for money, Stella still with us in an old folks' home, Allegra dead and Nin having been brought up by me. Nin's rights because half the paintings are hers. The settlement. The challenge. What Nin and I would lose if we acceded to the Siècle Trust.

So far so good.

Nin has refused to appear on TV. She has asked for privacy, but blasted David is trying to manipulate her into joining the Siècle Trust. So…next comes his statement that I have influenced Nin away from asserting her own best interests. To that, I reply, truthfully, that I do not believe in standing between young folk and their futures and that it is for Nin to decide what she wants to do, not for David and Cecilia. It is pointed out that as things stand the settlement gives Nin and me equal shares in an unequal number of works. We have between us at least seven major works which would enhance the Trust collection greatly. I agree that they would enhance the collection, but if the Trust really wants them, the Trust should buy them, and buy them at an open auction with Nin's assent. That way, we would be compensated and retain on-selling rights if the Trust should change its mind and sell them.

Although I do not say this, tonight's exhibition speaks for all my savings and if I sell no work, then I will have to sell the house and my studio and, as soon as I am eligible, apply for the pension. What I will do between selling the house and qualifying for the pension, I do not know because the rules of Social Security state that one cannot apply for the pension within five years of selling one's place of abode. Thinking of that makes me ask for a drink-of-water break with a you're-doing-great-Mum from Eli. 'No, I'm off track,' I whisper to him. 'I need to sell some of my own work.'

Anyway, I avoid the destitution and devastation line to say that the paintings under dispute were painted when Dadda was living with Stella and Allegra and me. *Where the Nice Girls Live* is a series of paintings of our teenage milieu. We were a pair of brats who drank Kahlúa with boys behind the cricket pavilion and thought we were being splendid and having a good time. We also played on children's equipment in a park over the road from where Allegra's boyfriend lived and the pictures show two lascivious teen-agers with beehive hairdos draped over the kangaroo and elephant rockers. Everybody smiles at this point.

Our upbringing was very different to Cecilia's. She was a pri-vate schoolie with the lot. For all intents and purposes, her assumed father was the rich and entrepreneurial Harry Laurington. When she was growing up, she was Cecilia Laurington. She had a name that carried clout, while the name Coretti barely passed the lips of the rich. Allegra and I were Corettis.

Your own paintings, now, what are they all about? At last! Well, they are quite relevant to what we are talking about tonight and I think they would please my father, although I paint to please myself. My father's theme was often commodities and how they fill up our lives, dominate our thinking and even end up, through landfill, being the very ground upon which we build the houses in which to put them. To him, it was as if commodities were alive and we were their servants. I've tried to take this idea further through an interest in advertising and how it has turned us into commodities.

Some years ago I was in Milan to acquaint myself with the city where my father grew up. Reflected in the dark windows of Galtrucco in the Piazza del Duomo were the bits and pieces of the bodies from a giant hoarding advertising the United Colors of Benetton. It was the family advertisement, the black, dreadlocked father, the Asian baby and the European mother, who was the image of Madonna, the rock star. Madonna's lips rode dimly in a fanlight above a narrow doorway and just underneath it in a panel of glass, the baby's fist, bright against her cleavage, seemed to be punching its way out. In the next window, a column obliterated the baby's body so that one fist shot out towards the father and the other from under the mother's chin. I could see, reflected from the opposite direction, the ghost of the golden Madonnina riding her pinnacle on the top of the Duomo and I thought *Madonna Madonnina*, two icons. What has the Madonna come to symbolise in this shopping-mall world? In Milan, the capital of fashion, she rides around in all those shop windows, feasting her eyes…so I gave her a shopping trolley.

Stuck in the middle of the Piazza del Duomo is the statue of King Victor Emmanuel, his horse's tail caught forever in a Garibaldian gust – is he sheathing or unscabbarding his sword at the feet of the Mother of God? Should he honour and worship her or run her through? How ambivalent he looks at the feet of the tiny lady with a golden shopping trolley, who is not looking at him, but craning her neck, searching for merchandise – or then again, being searched for by merchandise. I sling a Louis Vuitton handbag over her arm, some Prada shoes on her golden feet – the entire historical piazza now is glazed in the shopping moment.

I'm glad the interviewer likes the immediacy of painting reflections but they do take a long time to do. Victor Emmanuel was especially hard because I wanted him to be both monumental and fluid simultaneously. I've been realising this project for years, keeping myself going with less ambitious ones. In the meantime I've become older and the gallery where I used to show has closed and my dealer has retired. Since then, I've shown here and there until, unable to get support for my work, I rented this space for a fortnight to coincide with the Italian Cultural Festival going on just now in Melbourne. Yes, they were to include me in their program and the show was going to run for a month but somehow or other it didn't happen. And what I don't say is that the city council cancelled my booking for a public space without telling me, in order to put on an impromptu literary festival featuring the overflow of foreign writers from a big Sydney gabfest. But for the existence of this place and the kindliness of Marian, I wouldn't be having an exhibition at all.

Go on, smile, Isobel, smile. Sell, Isobel, sell. And for God's sake, don't complain.

I smile. I've done my best. And when I come out of the interview room, it's clear that the gathering has suddenly realised that the artist is actually me, the short person in her best black frock who was briefly serving out the drinks. And they're showing a bit more interest in the work – arms are pointing upwards and over and wrists are performing circuits.

Marian has sold a picture. That is something, even though it is the smallest picture in the exhibition. Mick is as pleased as punch.

Dear Mick, he doesn't know that selling a single picture on the opening night of an exhibition one has been working up for years counts for zilch. He thinks it's great. He thinks that during the exhibition, which will be up for two whole weeks, all these paintings will sell; I'll clean up and get ready for the next famous occasion.

It's de rigueur to send critics invitations, but that doesn't mean they'll come and even if they do, it doesn't follow that they'll write the exhibition up, let alone write it up before it's finished. They're always much too busy to attend launches, of course. There are the young and promising and the old big-name exhibitors to deal with. There are the blockbusters and the big events. There are the faculty in-crowds to please. A sixty-three-year-old female descendant of a prominent dead white male just isn't sexy. Nevertheless she will keep at it. The cow will jump over the moon from the middle of the Slough of Despond. It's in her. It always has been.

So now the night is over and we go home. Because it has been an occasion, we take a cab for which we have to wait until ten in the evening because of the weather alert. Louise-who-wants also wanted to share our cab but, blessedly, the beautiful Marian walked out into the road and hailed her another one. Eli is to leave for Afghanistan early in the morning from a mate's flat in town, so there were hugs and kisses at the door. Nin did not come tonight but there was a big bunch of flowers on my doorstep and a card with love and kisses.

The weather alert that was tipped to sweep us away, and was probably phoned in to the bureau by Checkie to blight the occasion, has done little harm, beyond slowing everything down. I have sold one painting and there is a reservation on another, thankfully a large one. Mick is jubilant.

2

✿✿✿

I had a phone call from Louise-who-wants this morning, asking me to tell her sister, if she rang me, that she'd stayed the night but gone out early. 'I stayed in a hotel in town overnight in the end,' she said, as if she was explaining something to me.

'Did you? Oh. Well, actually I'm just on my way out, Louise. I have to go and visit my mother in the old people's home. There's some kind of party on there. So if your sister rings, I won't be here.'

'Oh. Oh well, I gave her your number. I told her I was staying over with you so I wouldn't have to stay over with her.'

'I see.'

'Well, it's just a family thing. You understand, don't you?'

'Um…'

'I was so frightened that storm was going to happen.'

'Yes, it was all a bit of an anti-climax, wasn't it?'

'You looked *fab*ulous!'

'Did I? Well thank you.'

'When's it going to air?'

'Not sure.'

'Oh it'll probably be tonight, do you think?'

'Well, I guess it'll be soon, since it's topical.'

'Did you realise they were out filming the guests while you were getting your make-up done?'

'Were they?'

'Yes, I spoke to the interviewer myself, dear! Me! I told her you were the best painter I knew.'

'Well, thank you, but how many painters do you know, Louise?'

'Oh God you're funny. I actually know lots of painters, my dear. Even some men. I even came close to getting off with your brother-in-law once; did you realise that?'

'With David?'

'With David. We were at an opening at Siècle...can't remember whose...whose was it? Anyway, your sister Cecilia introduced us...'

'Um, Louise?'

'Yes, my pet?'

'I really have to go. My partner's at the front door in the car waiting for me.'

'Where did you find *him*?'

'Under a bridge, Louise, with his bottle wrapped discreetly in a brown paper bag.'

'God you're a scream! Anyway, darling, see you at the next class.'

'Yes,' and I put the phone down and swore that I will never again hold a workshop in my living life.

Mick was still in the shower – but it was true that we were off to my mother's old folks' home for a party.

The silhouette of my mother's head before she has seen me, a tattered old cat on a cushion of whatever she happens to be wearing, always evinces a primal love and joy in me – which is quickly shown the wings by a grand chorus of conflicting emotions. When Mick and I walked down the path of Broadlea this morning, the tattered old cat was sitting there just above the first-floor window-sill, facing away from the window into the breezeway. My heart leapt, as it always, always leaps – my mother.

She was having morning tea, a dip in the row of her companions' backs because she is as short as a sparrow. If I come earlier than this and she's only just taking her chair, she'll invariably catch sight of me with that mother's knack for sensing the presence of a child, and she'll start pulling faces and waggling her hands about: but once in her seat, her head no longer swivels on its neck. Dadda used to say, long ago in the days when he still loved her, that he'd clap her in irons if she didn't stop fidgeting.

Nobody's neck swivelled this morning: I suspect it's because their cervical vertebrae have fused, or then again, perhaps that's the way you're expected to sit in a Protestant hostel.

You can tell why the breezeway is called the breezeway because it is a long, double-storey corridor, flanked by windows, linking the bedroom wings to the circular hub of the home. On the ground floor of the hub, a dining room, kitchen and offices subtend the lift up to the next floor. On this floor, where my mother lives, there is an activities centre, a library and gym in the same kind of arrangement. I suppose a young architect thought the breezeway would be a nice idea, old folk sitting up comfortably, taking the breeze – and then thought, 'I'll put heaters under the windows for the winter time.' Actually, I like the plan, but it's quite evident that people either no longer know how to use a convivial space or they have never known, or then again, they just do not see this space as convivial at all. Or the age of conviviality has moved on, like one of the lands at the top of the Faraway Tree. Seems that Enid Blyton was onto something there, because that's what history does, gets sick of standing in one place and moves on, bringing a changed set of circumstances with it: in the twenty-first century at Broadlea, the heaters never seem to be off and the windows are permanently shut, as if adaptability were foreign to the Protestant mind. And perhaps that's a shortcoming of Protestants, really, they've always had to neaten things up in accordance with their own cast of mind. Old people fall over when they move, therefore keep them still; people who are still don't generate much body heat, therefore keep as warm as you think they ought to be. Stella, though she's ninety-seven, still suffers from hot flushes. She has been here over a year now – one day, when it was blazing hot, I made the mistake of opening a window at morning tea time to let in some air. It was one of the few times I drew signs of life from the assembled company. 'Some people are selfish,' said one prim old lady. 'Some people don't mind catching a chill,' barked another.

'Oh, so they're alive,' said Stella to me as an assistant nurse leaned over and slid the window shut again, saying to no one in particular, 'They feel the cold.'

'But I'm roasting,' said my mother. And she was – she was bright red.

Everyone ignored her and resumed their separate silences. They rearranged the pleats in their tartan skirts and slacks and folded their hands in their laps. One of them had an ironed hankie tucked neatly into her belt. It's a long time since my mother was able to wear a belt and in the days of hankies, she would shove them up her sleeve in a bundle – her legs, short as they are, were crossed over her stick and she jabbed the stick up and down in a temper so they kicked up in the air, '*Broad*lea!' she scoffed. 'Huh! *Narrow*lea, they mean.' I was the only one who laughed and she went into paroxysms, too. Then the pair of us practically rolled off our chairs when old John, a retired mercer, wandered into the gathering, undid his fly and peed on the floor next to the table. No one else even cracked a smile and that made us laugh all the more.

This morning, although she'd smoothed down the bashed old cat on her shoulders with a wet comb so that it looked like a flattened chinchilla just waiting to go wiry again, she was still very much the odd old lady out in the row of mass-produced Elizabeth II hairdos. She would have liked to have her hair done, but she couldn't because she couldn't risk water getting in her ears. She has grommets – or it might be more accurate to say she had grommets, because she's deaf all over again.

The ears are problematic and costly in more ways than money. Periodically she goes deaf. Is it wax; is it inner ear trouble; has she got her hearing aids in; are they suitable aids; have they been tuned;

does she wear them enough? She says she doesn't want to hear and then complains that she can't. She says that we only go to see the audiometrist because he's a nice-looking Indian and he sweet-talked me into believing she was deaf so I'd buy the most expensive aids for her. She isn't deaf; it's just that he plays tricks with her with that silly beeping machine of his.

Before we came down to the dining room for the party lunch we went to Stella's room, where her hearing was going through the 'I'm not deaf' part of her cycle – she was very crabby and could hear the 'spy' in her clock radio again. The one who's part of the surveillance. 'You don't believe me, do you?'

'No, Mater, I don't.' She's lived so long now I call her any variety of names that date back to Latin lessons in high school and beyond that to the cradle.

'Well just you go and sit on the end of that bed and take a close look at the clock. It keeps on going "bip". Go on,' she said, 'look at it.'

I tried, through look and gesture, remembering that Mick is a phlegmatic Yorkshireman, to send him a message to humour her. Meanwhile, I gestured that I would look, with problem-solving mien, at the clock while she went into a tizzy about her astronomical phone bill with its five pages of time calls. Mick, alas, misinter-preted my cues and when he tried to explain to her that the two instruments – clock and phone – were unrelated, she got short with him. Then, on reflection, she modified her story into a not-only-but-also tale of woe. Boys, apparently, come into her room on their way home from school and dial the time number every day. She's spied upon and sick of being spied upon. It's because Broadlea is in cahoots with a funeral home and when business is slack, they put them in the way of a few corpses. All one organisation. The food's terrible, they don't cook it on site as they say they do, they bring it in in big trucks, trucks that thunder past her windows in the middle of the night. In with the food, out with the corpses.

In spite of my efforts to tempt Mick to an efficacious channel, he persisted with his explanations. He said, yes, the building was under surveillance, but not in the bedrooms, only on the main doors to stop the Alzheimer residents getting out and to stop unwanted people getting in. No, she insisted, the rooms were under surveillance, too, and she wielded her stick towards a tiny Christmas decoration we haven't yet been able to get down from her pelmet. Somehow or other it's become tangled in the curtaining and we can't seem to remove it without hacking into the fixtures with scissors: it's like a miniature disco ball and sometimes it glints in the light. No use saying, 'It's a Christmas decoration, you silly old moo,' because she's seen that sign over the front door when we've brought her back from an outing: '24 hour surveillance', it says.

'What do you think they do with the information they gather on you, Mum?' My tone was induced by helpless irritation with Mick for not being able to anticipate the wily paranoia under the chinchilla hairdo.

'Hand it to the funeral people. What do you *think*?' she snapped.

'Have they shown you any designs for caskets yet?' When I'm irritable, I can't stop myself from testing the waters of logic's stockpot.

She gave me a fierce, tooth-grinding look. She only has one tooth to grind now and that's in danger of going, which will be interesting because the entire denture is slung around it.

'Well, if they're really serious about it, they'd be up here badgering you about caskets and asking you for a deposit from the moment you walked into the place. And, Mater, if you really were under surveillance in your bedroom you wouldn't have had to wait an hour for help to come that night your furniture went berserk and decked you. The night the Motte family vase rose up and hit you over the head and they found you stretched out on the flooring with the bookcase on top of you.'

'They lost the key to my clock. It's a proper case clock, that.'

'Well, never mind, we got you another key and the furniture's been behaving itself quite well since Mick made you a bookcase that actually fits in here.'

'Yes. I'm going to see that that's handed down with my bridge chairs when I go.'

'Oh good,' I said, and then to Mick, 'well, there's a point in your favour, my darling.'

'Darling, huh!' Stella snorted.

Stella has always pretended to be British and well bred, so the name Mater suits her. Here she is, ancient, her job of providing the Mottes with some badly needed heirs done – except that it was I who provided a male heir in the long run and that heir goes by the name of Coretti and, because I didn't marry his father, isn't, I think, the type the family was after. As if to fill the terrible gaps in her family tree, she's been seeking out relatives, real and imagined, for six decades. She has found hundreds of them to beguile with the old tale she spun us when we were children, that her mother was descended from a lord. It's cock and bull: her worthless descendants researched the family tree just in case they were entitled to a fortune but found only fraudsters and people escaping the bailiffs after shonky businesses went tits up.

To handle her, you have to be able to visualise the track she's on and steer for it, or another, more useful one, close by. You might spend your time sitting down during visits, but they're still as strenuous psychologically as a half marathon. She'll never approve of Mick and she's determined always to be more important to me than he is. That's another side to her character – one I dislike intensely, one that makes me wish against my kindlier instincts that she would bloody well die.

Sometimes our lives descend to a game of who resents whom with the greater justification. What I least like about her is her need to assert herself over the men in my life. She does it all the time and will even do herself damage when she fears that she will lose me to a man. Once, when I was on the verge of going away for a lost weekend, she stuck her hand in a blender and got it mildly chopped and very bloody to reclaim my loyalty. I was scandalised, but at the same time full of pity for an act of such desperation. She is so afraid, and in the midst of all her relatives, sees me as the only one she can rely on. I've tried to steer her towards psychiatry, but she won't condescend to it and she's probably right in this instance: psychiatry would only open the doors to more self-depletion than she's capable of bearing.

Poor old thing.

Poor old me, being stuck with such a poor old thing.

As we made our way slowly out of her room, down the corridor and through the breezeway to the lift, she hung back. 'What is it now?' I asked. 'Do you want to go to the toilet?'

'No. It's that Henderson woman, dreary minx. I don't want to go in the lift with her.'

'Oh, I thought Mrs Henderson was quite nice. Isn't she the one who reads the paper to you all?'

'She's only here because her husband is.'

'What's that meant to mean?'

'Well, we *pay*. The rest of us pay for it. You can't tell me she pays for it.' And she looked up at me with her fierce expression, as if I should somehow know these things.

'I'm sure she's had to pay the same as everyone else.'

'She still owns a house.'

'How do you know?'

'They told me.'

'Who's they?'

'Everyone.'

'Maybe it's just gossip, Mum. And anyway, there are some exemptions made to selling your house, like if other relatives live in it.'

I wished I hadn't said that because Mick started reciting the Social Security regulations, thinking he was giving me loyal support, and she ground her dentures even more and barrelled doggedly into the furniture with her walker. The lift doors closed on Mrs Henderson. 'Anyway!' shrieked Stella. 'I'd rather stay in my room watching television than listen to the minx. She doesn't know anything. She says "mis*cheevi*ous". If anyone said "mis*cheevi*ous" in our home, they weren't invited back. My mother insisted that our friends had correct pronunciation. People never got "*num*-onya" they got "*new*-monia". That minx says "*num*-onya".'

This was a dig at Mick, who's inclined to say 'n'monia'.

We have been invited, along with all the other relatives and carers, to celebrate Broadlea's thirty-seventh birthday. It seems odd that we should be celebrating this birthday. There wasn't a thirty-sixth one last year or a thirty-fifth the year before when Stella went into care.

She went in under duress. Although she had had one bout of prolonged dementia after Allegra's suicide when we lived for a while at Reg Sorby's retreat, she recovered from that once we moved back to Melbourne: it could have been the proximity of shops, for nothing brightens her life more than a spendathon. Whatever the cause of her return to health, she was well enough to live alone in her own home until she became acutely ill with the pneumonia that Mick didn't pronounce properly. At the time, her doctor, who'd sent her home with a cough, had set off on a world tour. Mick and I called on her and found her still in bed – she who would thunder out of bed each dawn to defy another day to wipe her out. She was too ill to move. We called an ambulance. She went into intensive care at the local hospital, stayed there three weeks and then was assessed by an old-age team, who sent her to a rehab hospital for further assessment. She was there for a couple of months.

I did all the usual things you do when your aged parent goes into hospital – I'm quite used to it as Stella has fallen over and broken her leg up a back lane, dislocated her hip after she forgot her key and tried to get in the kitchen window, had two hip replacements, broken her collarbone when skittled from her buggy by neighbours backing out of their drive, had a ganglion removed from her hand, had both eyes dis-en-cataracted and has otherwise qualified for casualty by busting open various bits and pieces and being covered in blood. And if that sounds like a list, that's only some of it. I've learned that if you have an aged parent and they damage themselves occasioning outpourings of blood, by far the best thing to do is not to clean them up, because if you bathe wounds before presentation, the casualty staff will tell you that you are wasting their time with someone who ought to be in a nursing home, whereas an old person covered in blood arouses even the toughest casualty sister's sympathy. When the crisis is over, even if you're feeling faint yourself, what you do is ring everyone. If you don't ring there will be a round of scolding and disjointed nosiness which it is better to avert. So, on this last occasion, the occasion of the pneumonia, I rang Stella's friends and relations – and, by gosh, there are a lot of them. I rang Cousin Audra (not Audrey) – the cousin mentioned at my do the other night – and Audra-not-Audrey went thundering down to the rehab hospital on the tram (which, I was told, clicked and clacked particularly loudly, I gather because I didn't offer to drive her), found 'Cousin Stella' in a state, asking to be taken home to her cottage, dialled my number and told me she'd organise to bring Stella home at once.

Audra-not-Audrey had to be bodily prevented from putting Stella in a cab and returning her to the Rats' Nest – as Nin and I began to call Stella's house, when we discovered rat poo in a couple of neat piles at a companionable distance from the television. Fortunately, I did not have to do the bodily prevention; that was down to the nurses, who then rang me and suggested a family conference which Audra-not-Audrey might like to attend.

Dutifully, we had a family conference, which Audra left in a flap to seek legal advice to prevent me from removing my mother from the rehab into a home for the elderly. The point she missed was that the council helpers who had been helping Stella for years were beginning to experience what I experienced, too much frailty – in her mid-nineties – to be left on her own. Audra wouldn't hear of it, she was going to repeat an exercise she undertook once before when the home threatened. She was going to move in with Stella to protect her from the evil designs of her close relatives, notwith-standing the catastrophe of her previous trial of this remedy, when I received a frantic phone call from Stella within twenty-four hours of the moving-in to come and rescue her as Audra was planning to pare her toenails. A day that had begun with furious scissors brandishment in the name of paying phone bills rather than pedi-curists and ended in an inexpensive and kindly pedicure at a local nailery, brandy and banishment of Audra by phoning first and saying we weren't coming home until she'd gone – but it was a banishment that didn't work, as Cousin Audra, whose cousinhood is at a third or fourth remove, has no one else in her life who can stand her ministrations except Stella and Stella kept inviting Audra back for more.

Stella is incapable of saying no.

Cousin Audra wasn't the only one against the hostelisation. I dropped in on the GP when she came back from her travels to let her know that Stella was soon to be placed in Broadlea hostel nearby and she said, 'What!' grabbed her phone and started dial-ling. 'We'll see about that!' she cried and showed me the door. The GP, a seventies feminist, thought Stella was a marvellous old woman, a bit untidy, brave as Buffalo Bill and sane as a doormat. Stella thought the GP gave the worst flu shots on the planet, handed out cholesterol remedies you wouldn't feed a dog and had misread the fabulous 'lymphoma' she had in her hand as a ganglion. I'd had to help her change GPs a number of times, but there were certain advantages in sticking with this one – this one made home visits, and, most important as far as Stella was concerned, this one stuck up for her against her relatives.

When she was unable to reverse the hostelisation, the GP was down at Broadlea the moment Stella moved in, registering herself as the visiting doctor – so our communication difficulties not only continue but have proliferated to include Broadlea's manager. The manager looks at me with a jaundiced eye. I have to find out for myself what's happening about Stella's hearing. Is it that the GP won't try to persuade Stella that she'd be better placed if she could hear? I know that Stella says, 'I'd rather be deaf than listen to the twaddle people go on with here,' but hardly anyone speaks around here except the staff and the visitors; the old folk keep almost completely to themselves. It's a shame, because Stella generally perks up when she can hear and participate and that makes others join in, too. The GP doesn't take my phone queries, never phones back and won't say whether or not she's managed to clear any wax from Stella's ears. I have to ask the manager if I can see the notes. The notes say things like 'chirpy'. But are the grommets we had put in last year still in place? Not a word about grommets. Drops? She can't have drops if she has grommets. It took an eternity to get a referral to the Ear, Nose and Throat Hospital to get the grommets in and it will be months more before they can see us just to check what ought to be checkable by a GP with an ear light. Meanwhile I'll go mad from having to say things over and over and over again at top throat. The audiometrist thinks her inner ears are quite okay but can't speak for the grommets because he's not an ear, nose and throat specialist.

People should be taken out and shot. En masse. Shot.

Well, here we are at Broadlea's thirty-seventh birthday party, four or five to a little round table in the dining room where, according to Stella, they have put her in charge of Evelyn. Evelyn used to be a pharmacist and now can't remember anything: she is chicken-shouldered, withered and thin and today, her pleasant, rubicund son is sitting up beside her adjusting her cardigan as we sit down. 'God your mother's funny,' he says to me. 'She calls this place "Narrowlea".'

'I know. That's not all she calls it.'

'She's really on the ball.'

'Well, yes and no.'

Relatives and carers are yelling to make themselves heard all over the dining room. 'Eh?' say the old people to right and left. 'Eh?' 'Whawozza?' Amanda, who is here for reasons that have more to do with not being able to find hostel care for people with intellectual disabilities than with her age, says, 'Eh?' and 'Whazzat?' for herself and the four others at her table whose relatives haven't been able to come to the gathering. They're all deaf. When I grow up I'm going to vote for regular ear inspection, a regime for wax removal and auditory testing among the aged and jail for anyone who overcharges on hearing aids.

There seemed some sort of urgency in this birthday invitation and suggestions of a special announcement. The usually quite spacious dining room is full up to the double doorways that flank the lift vestibule. There's not enough room for Stella to display her characteristic bossiness. Poor old Evelyn usually gets herded up to the table at meal times and others are shunted aside without ceremony, along with their wheelie frames, but there isn't enough room today. Stella isn't the only strong personality here – Rhoda, who shares the table under normal circumstances, is not behindhand in calling attention to Stella's push-me-pull-you antics. 'You're a bully!' she'll hiss, causing Stella to stand on her dignity and deliver a list of responsibilities she has around the home. Even now, a small distance away, Rhoda is pointing Stella out to her carer and whispering maledictions. An old Lithuanian chap at another table thinks this dining room battle is hilarious: there he goes, left, right and centre, arms shooting, lurching with laughter on his seat, like a hot-air man outside a sale at a tyre shop.

The administrators are here as well as the carers and all of us are wearing jolly crepe-paper party hats. The festive streamers are up and the physios are suspiciously merry. A lady none of us knows in a navy-blue suit is pulling the microphone towards her – people never smiled as heartily as this in the days before tooth veneer.

'Happy birthday everybody!'

Everyone shuts up. Knitting Neridda in her customary chair beside the entrance, where she counts the guests as they come in to lunch, goes on making covers for coathangers, her mouth poised to go one way or the other – it might fly open with glee, then again, it might clamp shut, making the whisker bristles stand out on her double chin. Either way, she'll keep right on knitting.

'Today is the thirty-seventh birthday party of our wonderful home, Broadlea. It's hard to believe that it's thirty-seven years ago today that the foundation stone was laid for this wonderful facility that has taken care of so many people.'

No shouts of joy.

'We have some great news for you that I'm sure you'll all be delighted to hear.' The navy-blue lady seems to be having trouble with the static in her skirt. More tooth veneer, widely displayed. 'Broadlea is about to add to its community.'

That's interesting. An amalgamation, perhaps?

'We're not only going to be a hostel, but we have received a special grant from the government to upgrade and add a hospital facility, as I'm sure you're all delighted to hear.'

Well, that is good news. They'll continue on seeing their residents through to the end, only now they'll have proper nursing hospital facilities to do it. Neridda's mouth fails to come open with glee; perhaps she hasn't understood. She pulls her lips into a gusset around her teeth under which her tongue does a circuit.

'Of course, it's going to mean some changes,' says the navy-blue lady. 'As I'm sure you'll appreciate, the alterations can't be carried out with the current residents still living here.'

Oh. Actually I don't appreciate that…

'But don't worry, there'll be plenty of time to relocate every-body and settle them comfortably elsewhere.'

Neridda's mouth gapes. 'Eh?' she says.

There is a lot of leaning forward, eyes agoggle and, 'Eh?' and 'Wosshee say?' and 'Oi can't hear.'

'We're not gunna 'ave to shift, are we?' says Marj, the hankie lady, solid in her views. 'We doen wanna 'ave to shift. Oi'm not shiftin.' On weekends Marj puts on a little pair of gumboots and weeds the courtyard garden. You hear the scrape…scrape…scrape of her weed pail along the concrete when you go to sit under the trees. She's got a nifty little weeder, brought down from the country for her by her daughter, Sharon, who's married to a farmer. Sharon and I have chatted a few times. I haven't told Stella, but I arranged with Sharon to take Marj's emergency calls from Broadlea – so far there haven't been any. Marj didn't learn her stoicism at Sunday School – she learned it in a grocer's at Yallourn, but that didn't stop 'them' from moving her family on when it came to knocking the town down to flood it for a power station. 'Oi've 'ad enough of movin',' she says.

'Just think,' says the navy lady, 'our own hospital. That'll mean residents will be able to stay on even when they become too infirm to live in the hostel!'

'Eh?' 'What?' Woshesay?'

And I find my mouth saying, loudly, atop my standing, if rather short, body, 'What you're saying is we have to relocate our relatives pronto.'

'Well, we've got a couple of homes with places, Isobel,' pipes up the manager from her seat behind the navy lady. The manager regards me as a pest to be put up with. 'There *are* places available.'

'And everyone will have to be reassessed by Social Security to see if they still qualify for hostel care…'

'Well, there are some people here, Isobel who are…'

'I know what you're going to say – too frail. And what it means is that into the too frail basket, the "too old" will also fall.'

'I didn't say that.'

'No. You wouldn't. But I'm saying it.'

'Sit down, lovey.' Mick paws my arm, I'm embarrassing him. So I do sink into my chair.

'Good on you,' says Evelyn's son. 'They'll just hive a lot of these guys off into nursing homes because they haven't got hostel places.'

'Oi'm not goin',' says Marj again. Stella is a good fifteen years older than Marj and looks down on her for her Ya-lawn origins. I like Marj because she plays life with a straight bat and has been known to laugh once or twice. I had fond thoughts of taking her out sometimes with Stella, but they don't socialise and Marj says she likes to keep herself to herself. But suddenly Stella says, 'Nor am Oi.'

I wish it was as comradely a statement as it sounds, but Stella is fond of distributing graces and favours among uncomplicated souls. She adheres to the mores of her mother, Euphrosyne Motte, who was born in the eighteen-sixties and classified people by shibboleth, as in 'new-monia'.

I feel for all the people in this room. They're just people who had the luck, or lack of it, to stumble upon this place. Some, like Amanda, have been here for years. There's Mrs Henderson, the minx, who opted in to keep her husband company; June, whose feet are like a mermaid's tail, flapping after her walker – she wanted to live out the last few months of her cancer here; and there's the pair of old ladies who weren't related, but wanted to be together in the one room and no other home would accommodate them – they've only been here a few weeks. It's hell looking for a hostel.

I feel like mounting a campaign. There's a hardening in my chest at the thought.

I feel like bringing down a government. I feel like shit.

I feel like the woman on the front of the French currency. I feel weak.

The days when people drank and smoked themselves to death have moved on – now it's 'Here's your hat, what's your hurry?' even if you're one hundred and ten and as good as dead already.

Nobody does protests anymore. They tell us it's because we're so much more prosperous now that there's nothing to protest about.

But there is; there is. All that's happened is the rhetoric's moved on. The weak aren't dead; they're just not part of the stock exchange. When Allegra and I were young we mounted the barricades, we shrieked against injustice. We were heard. Those in charge met us halfway. Freeways ended up not as wide as the traffic visionaries had predicted. When we opened Mad Meg, painters, like me, had wall space to call our own and critics to write us up, first in feminist magazines and later, by degrees, alongside the boys in the circulating art mags.

I'm going to fight this, but I don't know how.

In fact I know I won't be able to fight this because these days a new ethos rules. Nobody fights for the poor and oppressed anymore because there aren't supposed to be any. Standards are on the rise – like me. To my feet. I'm on the rise and I'm furious, but Mick is pulling me down by the sleeve and hissing, 'Don't.' And he's right, standing up and haranguing the meeting isn't going to help. I'm going to have to count to ten before I say another word. I've spent years having my personality changed by psychiatry as a person on a low income, learning not to sound off at the first salvo. Once Margaret Thatcher had declared 'There's no such thing as society', society was off and those of us who would change it had nothing to change. We had to do something else, just as I'm going to have to do something else now.

It's called Assertiveness.

The assertive are polite and get their way. They use techniques, like 'broken record', which is saying the same thing over and over again until you get your way. They say, 'You have your opinion and I respect you for it, but this is mine' and they say what their opinion is. They return broken purchases to shops and insist, politely and firmly, on repairs being done – and, if not repairs, then replacement – and if not replacement, then compensation. Checkie wants to replace the world with my absence from it.

I'm going to have to push in and bully a place in a hostel for Stella so that she won't be thrown into the last ditch of nursing home before her mind is total porridge. There's grit in the rolled oats yet.

Two women, who are going to supervise the relocations, calling themselves Safe and Sound Seniors, take their turns, one after the other, at the mike. They are called Janelle and Tahlia and they've obviously had the same Assertiveness Training as I have. They've dealt before with people like me. At least, Janelle has. She puts me to one side very nicely by saying that some people are determined to make things difficult, but they needn't be difficult.

Alas, I find I've sprung to my feet after all. 'Have you ever tried to find appropriate accommodation for your mother?'

'I find appropriate accommodation for older people every day.'

'Lovey…' hisses Mick.

So I sit down, shaking with rage.

'Everyone here is affected,' continues Janelle. 'But we have time on our hands and everyone will be found a place.'

I'm on my feet again, 'Equivalent to this place?'

'Yes. If you'll only be patient.'

'And live long enough!'

'Lovey!'

I pass my eye over the staff and I realise they all have their heads bowed. There's no escape from this room, every passage between the tables is blocked by walking frames and there's no open back door to slip through. Mick tugs me down again. But I've already had to do this once – phoning around, assessments (is she nuts or competent?), set-tos with undertrained assessors and children given jobs that are beyond their capabilities. I don't want Stella to end up mumbling into her bosom beside a bed from which she hardly ever moves at a place so far away from the city that it takes hours to reach.

Janelle and Tahlia are not setting up to relocate until next week. I shall get busy on the phone at once. I shall have her ridiculous doctor come and assess her as fit for hostel accommodation. I shall book an appointment at the other nearby Uniting Church home and I shall get her through the door first so she will still be up and bullying beautifully in no time at all.

But one of her bright hazel eyes is blind and the ophthalmologist doesn't know if it's going to right itself. She's almost stone deaf in spite of all the trouble, time and expense. It will all count against her when it comes to requalifying for hostel care.

I hate what lies ahead.

Poor Mick! I'm in such a tizzy when we get home that I'm practically ready to beat him up with frustration.

I call my house *Defenestration*, the cramped quarters you end up in once the window of opportunity has slammed shut. I hate myself clopping down its skinny hallway with big Mick squishing after me in his elephantine sneakers.

'Now, now,' he says when we reach the narrow sitting room with its Ikea couch and ambushed by relics from other lives. He's a gentle character, Mick. 'Calm down. You'll be able to get her in somewhere.'

And of course we will.

Australia isn't a place where there aren't any elderly and consequently no homes for them.

So!

If I wanted to take out my frustrations, I couldn't do better than set about getting rid of the scentless carnations mouldering disgustingly in their glass vase on the mantelpiece. I will. I will do that.

'Supposing,' I say to Mick as he follows me into the kitchen and I ream out the slime and concertina the flowers on their stems into the compost bin, 'that she'd actually had the good sense to go into assisted living before this? I guess there are people in that hostel who went there via the assisted living process, and what's their reward for having chosen bloody Narrowlea? They get chucked out because the standards for hostel accreditation have been raised so high it's impossible for anything more than thirty years old to meet them. We bloody well had to spend three solid months resurrecting her house from the rubbish heap it had become and sell it to get her into the place, now we have to go through the business of whether or not the bond rolls over for the next place, which might be a good deal more swank than Narrowlea and might cost a lot more. Or then again, it might be a dump. And it might be in Timbuktu. What's going to happen in the future? Every Narrowlea person is going to be put through the same almighty disruption. What'll happen to Amanda? What'll happen to Neridda? They've lived there for years – it's their home. It's always the poor who get relocated. The bureaucracy of the time thinks they look untidy and don't reflect well on the community and out the poor buggers go at the mercy of whosoever should deign to pick them up.'

'Aren't you exaggerating a bit?'

'No, I'm not. It's not as if they have reasonable temporary accommodation in Melbourne to tide people over while changes are made.'

'It wouldn't be feasible.'

'I dare say it wouldn't. And it would fill up and become permanent in no time. But we're in the situation where it would be damned useful if there were a place these people could go until the job's done, like a serviced hotel with a garden to sit in. Instead, it devolves back on those who've done the horrible deed already to do it all over again. I feel utterly trapped. Not to mention used. There's no compensation for this kind of thing, no onus on the closing home to do more than put us in the hands of an agency. And there's nothing to say that we won't be in exactly Stella's position ourselves when our turn comes.'

'Not many people reach her age.'

'Well, speak for yourself. Those members of her family who don't die in battle are very long-lived. I might be, too. I'm not just going to sit back and let it all happen. I could opt to be knocked off, I suppose, but while I'm fit enough and well enough, I want to have my go at life. So far, I've barely had a look in for looking after other people.'

'I know,' says Mick, 'my mother was a single parent who looked after her mother.' We've talked about this many times. Mick understands and I'm very grateful for it. His mother was like me, the family member who's been singled out one way or another to bear responsibilities that others, if they'd been here, might have shared.

No wonder people drink and take drugs – you'll find among the drinkers and the drug takers the folk who didn't warrant a place in a society that then turns around and says that they're the problem – or that there is no society.

But there's no point in saying any of this. It's obvious. Politicians who say things such as 'no child shall live in poverty' are just creating an opportunity to make themselves weep on camera. The people who urge them to say it are deluded and the people who listen and let their hearts be softened by it are deluded. If you abolish poverty, you abolish the poor. Sweep them off the streets into the dustbin of history so that middle-class jackanapes won't have to look at them.

Mick is doing four days' worth of washing up while I stand around cursing and fretting. He shops, he cooks and looks after my house and his, which is miles away in a country town. He drives up and down to the country to teach around my timetable. He spends his weekends with me. He thinks we ought to get married but what have I got to offer Mick? An old mother who seems set to live forever; Nin, a pioneer of lesbian parenting whose father, David, is a lunatic who'd like to have my blood in a cup; and Eli, my unorthodox, danger-addicted son. Mick has sons but they are not like Eli; in Mick's mind, there is an idea of a son that bears no resemblance to Eli.

Oh, where is my beautiful little rosy-cheeked boy, my little companion, my joy and steadfast friend? On a day like today we'd go fishing. We wouldn't catch anything, because our version of fishing was following bubbles on the top of the brown Yarra as we rambled the bank with the dog. If a romantic disaster beset me, as it often did, there was my blue-eyed boy. Once, when a lover failed to turn up at a train to see me off on a holiday, it was 'Don't cry, Mum. He's not worth it.' He was six. Then he said, as the train clattered out of Spencer Street, 'Come on Mum, dinner in the diner, nothing would be finer!' For a few magic years you think you know who you're looking at as young life unfolds so gorgeously before your eyes.

3

Eli's visit home has been very worrying. He'd rented a flat somewhere and wouldn't tell me where. Nin hardly saw him and he put in once-a-week appearances at my home where he'd either play a few games with Nin's son, Daniel, or lounge about dispiritedly, sighing and beginning to put questions that he couldn't adequately frame.

Was it just the way he saw it or were people in general completely without conscience? I'd try a few answers such as I didn't think the world was conducive to having consciences, that I was a person who had once had a conscience, but that it became heavier and heavier as I grew older and somewhere in middle age I had to put it down to rest or die under the weight. In my life the world had shifted from the morality of extended care that prevailed after the war to the morality of an insistence on peace during Vietnam and on again, in an utterly bewildering way, to the radical and widespread notion that greed is good after Vietnam. The last shift seemed to happen when Eli was a teenager and he told me that I was blowing my car horn at all the wrong places during football matches and cricket games. There was I, cabling cricket jumpers on the sidelines in the old bomb and remembering 'play up, play up and play the game – win or lose, the end's the same!' from high school and thinking he'd just done something brilliant and he'd say afterwards, 'You just don't understand. It only matters if you win.' I certainly didn't understand, the old philosophy felt right, it felt very right, even though – on reflection – it came from England and was an injunction to youth to obey the rules of the game and die for king and country. And after all was said and done, England had won, so it wrote the history and the songs. Those rules, I suppose, were altered when the US gained its ascendancy over old England and colluded with it to become 'winner takes all'. Subsequently we've all been caught in the greed-is-never-good dilemma, gazing at our own bejewelled belly buttons for want of other places to hang the bling that everyone has and talks about incessantly because fairness is unfashionable: 'Now, couldn't you tell us where you're living, dear?'

'You wouldn't want to know.'

And away he'd go, brows knit and full of the sort of lassitude that sends every mothering type in search of tonics. I'd want to commiserate with him, recommend some good books, suggest we take in a show or two, or teach Dan some new tricks, but there was no enthusiasm in him for anything.

Eli first went travelling when he'd finished his journalism course at university. He was going to 'get rounded' he told me. He was going to put the lessons of his childhood to the test. He was going to visit the third world on the money he'd made as a night stacker at Coles (i.e. I was going to fork out when he got into difficulties) and see for himself why it was that other people continued to be poor while we were swimming in glut.

He saw things that most men of his age had not yet imagined: the tunnels in Vietnam where the Viet Cong hid, playing tricks on the Americans with false trapdoors covering spiked pits and circular tunnels that led nowhere and were inescapable in the pitch darkness; the torture chambers of Phnom Penh, lined with numbered photographs of the slain – there he found children playing among graves and swinging from the very scaffolds their forebears had swung from by their necks. In Calcutta, he saw women and children delving through refuse like rats, and was so dispirited he became ill with amoebic dysentery from drinking unclean water.

He went to Pakistan through India, crossing the border at Lahore and then going south through the Punjab and Sindh to Karachi. His original plan had been to go from Karachi to Cairo and then into Africa and on to England, but what happened on the way to Karachi made him change his mind. He'd taken buses and local transport because he wanted to see how ordinary people travelled and anyway, he was on a budget, a very low budget. On the last leg of the trip, the bus broke down and he got on the back of an extremely overcrowded Toyota ute that came to the rescue. As he was climbing on board, an overburdened young woman handed him up a bundle; in her other hand she had a chicken in a sack and there was no way she was going to be able to hang on carrying both loads. Eli was pushed forward and lost sight of her, but found himself with room for his backside on the side of the ute's tray. He soon realised he had a wet lap and when he looked into the bundle, a little face was looking back at him. He'd been given a baby to mind – so he tickled it and played with its cheeks and hands. It took some hours to reach Karachi: the baby was very good but Eli's arms were aching. Although he kept his eye out for the woman, he couldn't see her for the crush. As the numbers thinned he imagined he must have forgotten what she looked like, and his growing fear was that the baby had been dumped on him. People started giggling at him, so he played the clown and got the baby laughing as though it was his. It was wet and he unswaddled it as far as room allowed. To his horror, he saw that its legs were malformed. It was a baby girl who would never walk. The mother, of course, had disappeared.

Eventually he was set down in the Bolton Market area in central Karachi, his arms still full. On what he thought was the way to a police station he crossed the path of a policeman and explained his predicament. The man waggled his head the way Pakistanis and Indians do. 'She's probably older than she looks,' said the policeman and he took Eli to make his acquaintance with the cradles around Karachi put out to take unwanted children. It was a large, deep, solid cradle, covered by a roof on poles so that in wet weather, a child placed inside wouldn't get wet.

'What, we just leave her there and walk away?'

'Yes,' said the policeman, 'you just leave her there and walk away. Don't look back.'

'The mother can't be found?'

'No. If she wants to find her baby, she will come here to find it, but she knows that by leaving it here, it will be taken care of. She can't look after it.'

'But I saw her, I can tell you where she got on and what she looked like…'

'The woman you saw might not even be the child's mother. This little one has had polio, who knows what's happened to her family?'

So Eli, who had done his best to fix up the sodden nappy, placed his baby in the cradle and walked off, but couldn't bear to go far. How was a little girl going to get by in that condition in Pakistan? The baby started to scream when she was parted from him, tearing his heart.

He took a room in a backpackers' hostel from where he could keep watch. Half an hour or so after he'd put her down, a woman in anonymous workaday shalwar kameez came along and picked her up. Eli decided to follow and see what happened. He wrote that he felt like a stupid Westerner, full of ideas of rescue and rehabilitation, while all the time knowing that although he could visit a foreign land, feed himself and be fed and sheltered as a visitor, he was in reality a helpless bystander. He was dogged by the feeling of being alone and unable to be present in the reality around him.

He'd never heard of the abandoned child system of Pakistan. What he learned made him want to write about it and the foundation that, since the nineteen-fifties, has run the biggest private ambulance system in the world and developed clinics, adoption agencies, hospitals and shelters for people in need. For the first time in his travels, something was in line with what he had learned as a middle-class youth in a prosperous country. He had learned more than 'winner takes all'; he'd learned to care and that caring is the beginning of belonging. He hunted down the founder of the foundation and organised to meet him. He was a very famous man in Pakistan, a Muslim of a minor sect who had no interest in pushing his religion, only in obeying the Quran by being a good person. Eli was flattered that such a person would make time to meet a naive young would-be journalist from Australia and wrote home to say he'd had his visa extended and was going to stay a while in Pakistan and find out more about it.

Eli has always loved children, although he has none himself. He loved his childhood. Notwithstanding that his father dumped us, he was a happy and imaginative child, but lackadaisical to the point where he'd turn up at his primary school in one set of clothes and come home dressed completely differently.

By the time David Silver came into our lives, he'd been smartened up a bit by a change of schools but he was still happy-go-lucky. The new environment – all male to compensate for an oversupply of women in his home life – gave him esprit de corps; there was a uniform to wear and it took a couple of years for his old habit of costume swapping to reassert itself. By the time he was fourteen and star of the school cricket team, his alarming propensity for losing expensive pieces of kit devolved into his being put in charge of the lost property box and from then on, he had an article for every occasion. He also had a side business, betting lost property fines on the football pool. I took news of the football pool in my stride, but, with hindsight, I can see that for the first time a rascal was beginning to reveal himself as being on board with my blue-eyed boy. This rascal was too laid-back to remove things like detention notes from the pockets of his borrowed trousers before they went in the washing machine: *Coretti missing periods one and two. Four hours picking up papers in the school grounds and organising the rubbish*, when Coretti had started out on his bicycle at crack of dawn. As for the punishment of rubbish removal, Eli wasn't Henry Coretti's grandson for nothing: Dadda used to haunt the dump for material. They were doing their work, that school, bringing out the inner boy.

Confronted with the evidence of tardiness at class, a look of deep pain would come over his face. He'd say things like, 'They made a mistake.' But it was a mistake 'they' often made and a couple of undercover trips on the tram showed me why he wasn't reaching school before ten o'clock. She was a pretty little thing who played the violin at the neighbouring girls' school and she was spending a lot of time on detention for lateness, too. They'd sit around snogging up the back of cafes in Glenferrie Road. David thought it was funny and told me to lay off him, but then, David would get stuck into him for being on the phone half the night sorting out the romantic problems of the sister school's orchestra.

David had a double attitude towards Eli – on the one hand, he couldn't allow him any literary or artistic success and he would say he was unintelligent; on the other, he couldn't deny Eli's sporting prowess, so he praised it in that backhanded way that men do when the most they can say is that a kid's performance was okay but it could have been better. Eli was actually a sporting star and David, a wisp of a man, had no talent for it at all.

Both David and Eli loved sporting statistics and among the feminist literature of the household were cricketing, footballing, tennis and Olympic books of records that were sometimes pored over for whole afternoons while balls were biffed around television screens during finals.

Eli was in sympathy with a companion male in a predominantly female household. The relationship would come unstuck, however, when we knew that David had lost his temper and attacked Allegra. Then Eli had a battle within his growing body, a desire to wallop David once and for all, offset by his knowledge of David's demoralising background. David was the illegitimate son of an insecure young woman who left him with her parents after her lover died and then went in search of another man and when she found him, he decided that he didn't want to take on David. As Eli grew, the conflict in him transformed itself into a realisation that he had power in the household. There were Nin and Allegra to protect in front of me. There was David to stand over, to tacitly threaten and cajole. There was an adult personality to formulate in a situation of intermittent family crisis. David was violent. He'd beaten up Allegra. He was sometimes aggressive towards me and he might harm Nin. This situation called up resources in Eli that hadn't before been realised.

Eli adored Nin, who was, indeed, an adorable baby. He liked to mind her and to play with her and it made a beautiful spectacle for Allegra and me. But not for David, who was jealous. Eli and Nin happily romping around confronted David with his own sad childhood circumstances – a household in which he made fleeting appearances between terms at boarding school and grandparents who would sometimes leave him at school, the only kid in the boarding house, during the holidays. He'd been lonely, demoralised and frightened.

To offset the deficiencies of love in his young life, David became a hard and conscientious worker; he was very self-disciplined and productive and here, he had the advantage over Eli – Eli was by nature haphazard.

During the break-up of David and Allegra after David wrecked my show at Mad Meg, Eli disgusted Allegra by acting as go-between instead of showing outright contempt for a vicious, violent person. She tried to account for David with feminist rhetoric, but for Eli, that is not where David fitted: his viciousness was learned . Viciousness, according to Eli, was an emotional tangle that could be unknotted. Eli was going to spend his adult life trying to unknot it. That way, he would save the world from itself. Eli, like Allegra and me, was full of reforming zeal.

While he was in Karachi, President Zia's plane fell out of the sky in a world-puzzling way. With the American ambassador and the US head of the aid mission to Pakistan on board, it took off from a display of military hardware that the trio and some top Pakistani military brass had been to witness. Almost immediately it began bucking up and down, then it lunged forward suddenly and ploughed into the ground. There was hardly anything salvageable of Zia's person but he left behind him a dictatorship of eleven years. He had ousted Zulfikar Ali Bhutto and seven months after the ouster, had hanged him and relegated his 'socialist democracy' to a rump, the Al-Zulfikar Movement, where Bhutto's children figured prominently and from where the eldest, Benazir, between bouts of imprisonment and house arrest, emerged to lead the Movement for the Restoration of Democracy and to take over the chairmanship of what remained of her father's party when her mother became too ill to continue.

Zia's dictatorship had moved the legal system of Pakistan towards Sharia Law of the Sunni variety. His ouster of Bhutto coincided with that of the Shah of Iran by the Ayatollah Khomeini, who had set about establishing Sharia Law in a Shi'ite Muslim state. The two states, Sunni and Shia, coexisted quite happily despite their religious differences, with Zia providing arms for Khomeini during his war against Iraq. This coexistence would have affirmed the view that the schism in Islam was of little importance at that time in the affairs of the Middle East. For the West, the schism was insignificant when compared to the Cold War, in which Zia was an ally. Zia's Hudood Ordinances were simply seen as high-handed and unpopular, rather than hard-line and fundamentalist.

Punishments under the ordinances were harsh: for instance, the amputation of hands or feet for theft and robbery, flogging for adultery or rape out of marriage and stoning to death for adultery or rape within marriage. In cases of rape and adultery, both victims and perpetrators were liable to be punished. A charge of rape brought by a woman required four adult male witnesses to stand up in court and say they saw it happen – if she couldn't find them, she would be deemed as guilty as her assailant, or more guilty, and the assailant would be let off the charge and she, punished. There were also personal taxes instituted, which had the Ayatollah involving himself, asking to have Shi'ites exempted as an article of Shia faith, which says personal tax is to be given directly to the poor and not to governments.

Many people in Karachi – ordinary folk encountered by Eli in boarding houses or tea shops – were keen to elect Benazir, who was expected to rescind the hated laws, but when he moved north, to Peshawar, he found an atmosphere that seemed only tenuously connected to Karachi, an atmosphere where Benazir Bhutto seemed far less likely to succeed.

Eli was learning fast. He had found Karachi quite vibrant and with-it in spite of the ban on alcohol. A victim of alcohol-induced headaches, he only ever drank beer, anyway. Peshawar, by comparison, was ancient and conservatively Sunni, its women invisible and kept so, even on the street, by their voluminous head-to-toe garments. *I wondered why,* he wrote. *It looked uncomfortable and hot and it must have been difficult to see where you were going, but the only time I came across women with their faces showing was when I saw a group of Kalash people being photographed for the* National Geographic *outside the Museum. Their dress was enchanting. The women's hair was plaited from the centre part and hung around them in coils. They wore massive beaded and embroidered headdresses that must have weighed kilograms and, around their necks, they had string upon string of orange beads. They also had big collars, almost like embroidered yokes – they couldn't possibly have done work in clothes like that. The brown-toothed, withered museum guards, swaddled in their drab garb, stood about, hands behind their backs, ogling. Brilliant, Mum, like a gash in the dun-coloured universe that is this part of the world.*

I had a few meals with the National Geographic *people later, made a contact or two and they said they'd have a look at my work – but to be honest, I'm not a patch on some of their photographers and I feel that what I want to say isn't for light reading.*

My boy was blossoming, discovering, putting his adolescence behind him.

We're right next to the Tribal Areas here. I'd go in there, but it isn't safe for Westerners. The hippies hire armed escorts and go in to buy their hash, but who's to say that the escorts can be trusted? They swear the hash is the best in the world and they're prepared to risk their lives for it, or do they realise they're risking their lives? The Tribal Areas have their own police force and Westerners are sometimes kidnapped and ransomed with nobody able to do anything about it. In Peshawar itself, the drugs culture is so pervasive that the rickshaw drivers have a thing going with the police whereby they spot a Western bloke and offer to sell him good brown hash in full view of the police and if they succeed, then the police come over and arrest the bloke, who then pays for his release without charges being laid and the cops split the take with the drivers.

Hash is smoked everywhere. Blokes sit around on these woven bed things in parks and drink tea and puff. I only drink the tea, but, although it tastes all right, I sometimes wonder what's in it that makes the taps corrode!

The Russians are pulling out of Afghanistan and you see these great, lumbering trucks full of refugees arriving on the outskirts from places like the Khyber Pass and the more southern, high-altitude areas like Quetta, where the Afghan-Pak border is just some dotted line an English chappie drew in a school atlas. Divide and conquer, I don't think! The Pashtuns are a pretty passionate lot who make their own rules. They're obliged by their religion to be very hospitable, but they're also obliged to murder you if you give one of their women the eye, which would be hard, given that they keep their women hidden in the depths of their homes. Their lands stretch halfway up Afghanistan and overlap Pakistan in a big, biting swathe.

There's a refugee camp called Kacha Garhi where I went to have a look. It's only a couple of kilometres from the university area near where I've been staying; it's on a kind of heath (where nothing grows), virtually the city's edge, but packed with tents and some of the Afghan people have been there for years and have even built mudbrick houses.

I wondered why they'd been there that long: I was told by a UN worker out there delivering food that they were driven out by fighting during the Russian invasion and now, they're too poor to return. No one wants them and the UNHCR can't move them on, so they make what life they can for themselves here. A brickie nearby employs some of them and I guess that's where they get their bricks. They're always in danger of being sanitised out of existence by official bulldozers, of course, but more and more and more of them keep arriving and there are lots of camps like this one. I'm going to try and write something about them, because everywhere I've been I've seen this – displaced people who can't get out of their situations.

You see kids out scavenging, like in Calcutta. They go right into the shit and the rubbish looking for food and things to sell. And you see them in the bazaars, looking for anything that hasn't yet made it to the rubbish trucks. And over all the distant cry of 'Allah-u Akbar; Allah-u Akbar' at prayer times through the megaphones on the towers of the mosques. Seems God's too great to bother with refugees.

I sent the articles he wrote to Australian newspapers, where editors would direct them to the travel sections! Most of them were rejected as being too unappetising, but a visit to a tenement inhabited by Afghan refugee musicians made the cut. Even so, the editor wanted more colour and less speculation on who these people were.

They flee for fear of being drafted into the Russian Army and sent to serve outside Afghanistan. They never wanted Sovietisation: it wasn't compatible with their way of life. The local mujahedeen kept the Russians out of their areas, confining them to the geographic girdle of Afghanistan's cities, but fighting destroyed their villages, their irrigation channels had been cut off and their animals had been killed.

This wasn't the type of stuff for travel sections, but the news editors didn't want anything on Pakistan or Afghanistan that hadn't come from the major agencies, so Eli found himself stuck for outlets. Funds were getting low, so he tried tutoring in English and, that way, made a number of contacts that allowed him to keep on with his journalism and gave him a few clues about being published in newspapers elsewhere.

Another guest in Eli's cheap hotel was an irritating American of about forty. *He follows me around all the time and wants to see all my photos. First of all I just thought he was lonely, but he wouldn't leave me alone. Every day, there he'd be telling me, 'Don't go here,' 'Don't go there,' 'You'll be robbed,' 'Don't give to beggars and be on the watch for distracting tactics – you'll be looking one way and someone will be robbing your back.' It was like being a piece of flypaper doomed to catch the same fly every day and listen to it buzzing in your ear all day long. Whenever I tried to give him the slip, there he'd be again, playing hide and seek in the dust kicked up by the rickshaws and the mule carts. Eventually, I got what I could of myself on a bus that was stuffed to the ceiling and carrying more people on top, got off a few stops later, went to a market and bought the full Dick Whittington kit and caboodle – and now you'd be looking at Eli Jan Coretti with a beret and waistcoat, baggy pants and a sack over my back. I've shifted digs, as you'll notice. And I've been out, unaccompanied, to the biggest of the refugee camps, Jalozai, which is out along the road towards Rawalpindi.*

I was tramping down the roadway when I came across a bunch of Dutchies trying to change a tyre on a four-wheel drive ute. You would have been proud of me! 'Gidday,' I said, and they nearly jumped out of their skins. They'd never been spoken to by a Paki street ruffian before, let alone one who spoke an odd brand of English and was a top tyre changer. I was pretty chuffed to be taken for a local, given that I'm a Coretti-Russell blue/blue cross in the eye department. Not even they, northerners though they were, were as blue as your boy. I asked them what they were doing and they said they were making a film on the refugee crisis for Dutch television.

The bloke with the camera was called Jager and I've made friends with him, particularly as he can get photos developed quickly so that I can stop sending you so many reels. I feel a bit less like a rookie now, because I know a bit more about getting into places than Jager does.

He's very conspicuous with his big movie camera. That said, there's a girl in his crew called Lotte who can speak Arabic, Dari and Pashto and she's only twenty-four. She's a blue-eyed blonde who's dyed her hair black, but that doesn't make her Pakistani. You know the sort, Mum, worn-out, body-moulded Levis, cotton blouse open down to the cleavage with those little dingle-dangle cotton things on the end of the string around the neck. She thought that wearing a headscarf was enough. Jane Fonda on safari. I may be a dope at languages, but I'll bet that if I keep my mouth shut I'll get further with these people than she does.

Eli had had the common sense to go to the camp with a flat-packed, low resolution camera that he wore around his neck under his shalwar kameez. He was out to take photos on the sly in case he wasn't allowed to photograph. He wondered if the crew would be permitted to film and, in the event, while he cowered low in the tray of the ute, lying on his cap and waistcoat so he wouldn't be noticed, a gun-toting, turbaned tough at the camp gate turned Jager and the big camera away, disregarding all the papers and permits he was carrying.

So we went and filmed among the poor unregistered bastards wait-ing outside the camp fences. When they saw Jager's camera, they started tugging at him, desperately wanting him to film them and take their plight to the outside world. Crouching Afghan women clambered over each other to speak into Lotte's recorder. None of them were wearing the burqa – they were working women from farms – but they all had head-scarfs and shouted over each other to make themselves heard. They'd been waiting to be processed for months. They were too poor to be able to afford the bribes you need to get into the camp. The better-off get in while the poor have to stoop to selling their daughters in exchange for drinking water. It happens all over the world. I've seen it in Thailand, in Cambodia and in Vietnam – girls for cash. Some of the poor bloody Thai women I met didn't even go by their names; they went by their brothel and a number.

He wrote of the Afghan refugee mothers' hands, clutching desperately for invisible cups, their mouths open with fear and thirst, and he couldn't imagine what such wretchedness would be like to live out.

To him, it seemed like Dostoyevsky's Russia – the used girls would come back to the camp dishonoured and have to hide away, sometimes injured, inside the roasting, putrid tents. Some of them were as young as ten and forced to act as leverage to get food and water for their families. Their pathetic eyes glowered out at the strangers from dark, foetid places.

The camp stinks. There are holes dug somewhere for latrines but the stench of human waste among the habitations made my head swim. That buffalo I saw drop dead in the Calcutta car park seemed bad enough, but there are rats here and I'm not a big rap for rats, especially rats near little kids. They tell me that little kids have starved to death in these tents but the caravan of arrivals is relentless. When you're fleeing annihilation, maybe starvation is better. Some start to unpack, but become so discouraged that they just pack up again and move off – probably to another camp just as wretched.

We saw a UN truck drive up and pass through the gates only to be mobbed on the other side. It crawled to the distribution point, blasting its horn. The women told us that inside the camp girls are swapped for sacks of rice. They scavenge with the mothers on the streets and in the rubbish heaps. Boys from inside the camp get work as paper pickers under a permit system, but it isn't especially enviable. They have to fill sacks the size of themselves and take them to a shredder, then they have to bundle them in a great clumsy bundler for men in Afghan berets who are designated to hand out the rupees. These men are sometimes Afghan, but often not. They've graduated through a rough system controlled by the camp mullahs, who are government agents.

Seasons came and went over the camps, bringing with them misery or relief. When flowers were in bloom, the outsider women were left behind to gather rags and fragments of wire, while the insiders were away picking for the perfume trade. Spring was the best time of year, but even in spring, day piled up upon day, children were listless and hungry and adolescent girls were hidden away, anxious and depressed. The women were dirty and felt it. Their men, also down, looked on, squatting about in the camp rubble, smoking weed that might have been their reward from an occasional job, like sheep or goat herding.

A man called Daoud spoke onto Lotte's recorder. *He was wandering round and round the crew, crying out that he'd lost his head. Lotte called him over to the mike. He said he couldn't think any longer. He'd been a farmer in Afghanistan where the ground, at least, was fertile. Here, in this hot and dusty place, even if you had seed, it wouldn't grow. He was ashamed to have left his home and brought his family to this. In Afghanistan he'd owned his own house, he grew melons, grapes, figs, onions, tomatoes and green vegetables. He wanted to go back – even if the land was devastated – but he had no money, his tent was falling to bits, there was no oil for cooking. The big camp supplied the outsiders with water only and then it often came at a hideous price and you had to tote it back to your camp site in a pot that might or might not have holes in it.*

While Daoud was talking, Eli saw some boys playing cricket with sticks in the dirt inside the compound. The Pakistanis were mad on cricket and it had taken off with the Afghans, too. Everywhere they could, people listened to the cricket on the radio, even outside the compound. Eli knew heaps about cricket. He had an idea that might get him inside. He'd come back later with a bat and ball. Meanwhile he asked me to send some photos from his school magazine.

While he was hatching his plan, Jager was offering to pay for the unhappy Daoud to go back to Afghanistan and to provision him if he could film the return. He would buy equipment and the needed tents back in Peshawar and help to arrange a small exodus. But Daoud fidgeted and dissembled then and Eli couldn't understand why. He wrote that given such an opportunity he'd jump at the chance, but Daoud wouldn't go unless a certain other man would go with him. *It's like… 'Oh no, not unless my brother's mother's aunty can come, too.' I mean, Jager couldn't take everyone. It was exhausting trying to get this bloke to see what was on offer. He wanted another bloke who was the local landowner to come with his family. He was one of these people who needed someone else to be in charge.* Eventually, Jager promised to look for the man Habibullah and his family. He'd try to stretch the budget to include them. *It'll be an opportunity, anyway,* wrote Eli – so I took it that he was going, too. Wouldn't his place have been room for another Afghan? I wrote back. He didn't answer that one.

The expedition to Afghanistan would take a while to organise. Meanwhile, Eli would go sightseeing with Lotte and buy a bat and ball for his attempt to get into the camp. He could pretend to be a local come back, hunting for relatives after an upbringing abroad.

I was wandering across the old city when I came across a shabby group of kids sitting on the ground reading a blackboard. It was where a number of laneways intersected, making an outdoor schoolroom on an extended corner. At the board was a middle-aged teacher in white shalwar kameez. He was a neat-looking chap with little round wire glasses and he had the nicest smile, so I raised my hand and called out, 'Salaam Alaykum.' 'And peace be with you, God willing,' he answered in English. 'What!' I thought my Dick Whittington outfit made me look just like everyone else. 'Ponytail,' said the bloke.

    'Oh, I thought if you had a ponytail, Allah would pull you up to heaven by it.'

    'No, no, no, brother. He does that by the beard. A good Muslim keeps his hair cut and clean. Ponytails are for Westerners. Come and sit down with us if you have the time.'

    So I put off going to the camp and decided to have a haircut first. I had a bat and ball and the photos with me and I had to sit on them so the kids wouldn't be distracted from their lessons.

    The bloke said to call him Afsar San. He's a moderate Pashtun from Kabul and was educated first in England and then in Russia, but now he chooses to live in Pakistan. 'I felt pressured to become a communist,' he said. 'But I'm a Sunni, brother.'

'Do you teach any of the camp children?'

'I teach street kids wherever they come from, boys and girls. There are a lot of orphans in Peshawar these days and a lot of them are Afghans. I've been teaching here a long time. I used to have a lot more kids coming, but these days, there are madrassas in the camps being set up for the boys. They're run by those crazy camp mullahs. They take boys from poor families, dress them up in smart uniforms and pay the families money for them. Then they sit them down in a group like this, only with no girls – they don't take girls – they keep their wives and daughters under lock and key. They sit them down and teach them – you know what they teach them? They teach them the Persian of the Quran. These kids don't know Persian! The mullahs tell them "what it means!"' he doubled up, laughing. 'Then those kids sit there in those camps in their black uniforms and sway back and forth all day long, reciting the Quran until they're mad with heat, but they know the verses by heart. Then they're taken away, given guns, which they like, having seen them in the camp, and they're taught that they are fighting a war for Islam and Allah. Imagine, a boy of ten or twelve, who's never had a toy and never played a game – he's given a gun. He's taught that death is glorious and if he dies in the service of Allah's just war, he'll go straight to Paradise where he can play whatever he likes all the time. So he wants to be a martyr; he wants to go to Paradise and for his body to lie in the martyrs' graveyard and be garlanded with flowers. He dies with a smile on his face, having asked his father's permission – or, if he has no father, then the permission of his beloved mullah. But he hasn't read the part of the Quran that forbids suicide, or the part of the Quran that forbids assassination. If he blows himself up, brother, no one will touch him, no one will claim him; he'll be left to rot, while the corpses of the people he has killed will be ritually washed and given a decent burial. The people who taught him to blow himself to kingdom come for the jihad aren't going to reveal who they are by going and scraping up the pieces – they're going to say prayers with the other boys

they're teaching. They're going to say, 'Think of little Mohammed in Paradise. Inshallah, you will join him as a martyr also. And so I run my school here and what I teach is Self Defence. To save these kids from a martyr's death.

'I tell you brother, there are billionaire Saudis in Peshawar who feed the camp mullahs money – they want to cleanse the world of infidels – like you, brother... You'd better start pretending to be a long-lost son of the soil come back to his homeland without being able to speak the tongue. How about it, brother?'

'I thought I was already doing that.'

'Learn a few things, brother. Watch me, I will show you what to do. I will show you how to crap, for instance. I bet you don't know how to crap in a Muslim country.'

'Well, I've had some practice...'

Afsar lives in Peshawar with his wife and sons. He has a daughter who went to Karachi to be educated as a teacher because in Peshawar, in the mixed high schools where she had had most of her education since coming from Afghanistan, women were invisible. The education of girls in these schools is 'insipid' – to quote Afsar – and uninspiring, so she lives in Karachi now and uses her talents there rather than wasting them in a backward system. Afsar runs his madrassa as a teacher on a small government stipend. 'Oh yes, it's possible to do that under Pakistani auspices,' he says. 'You can set up as a trained teacher. But you know... people, tourists like you and aid organisations, come and promise me money to build a school. But they never come back. They ask for money in the name of my school and never a rupee finds its way to me. I don't care, that's life – I'm a government employee on a teacher's stipend. I am one man and I have one hundred students. Not all of them are here today, as you can see. They come when they can. The rest of the time they try to make a living. They work in a shoe bazaar and can't even afford sandals. One day they will. I teach them Self Defence: the Self Defence of the written word and numbers they can add up to make a credible sum. I teach them to bargain and to wash their hands before they eat. We'll see who's alive in twenty years' time, eh?'

Through his friendship with Afsar, Eli began to understand some of the complexities of life in this border region, crisscrossed over the centuries by traders of different ethnicities. He learned about drug and gun smuggling and the smuggler's bazaar in Peshawar where you were taken by taxi, introduced to a warlord, who would then show you his cache of AK-47s, heroin and opium – you could be a local operative, a Western hippie, even CIA, it didn't matter, the smugglers had eyes and ears and muscle everywhere.

He sent me a reel of film to have developed and there he was with his mate Afsar sitting up smoking a hookah in a den. I wrote back smartly all I knew about the evils of drugs. He was too sports mad to be into drugs when he was growing up, so there was never a problem; now, he wrote that it was only weed. *But you said the best hash in the world comes from there*, I wrote straight back. *And marijuana can give you schizophrenia if you're susceptible.* I wasn't terribly impressed when he wrote back asking whether I was still drinking several glasses of wine every evening – *One thing is, Mother, they don't drink here.*

Afsar's lessons in Muslim etiquette were timely when Eli finally returned to Jalozai Camp with bat and ball. He was greeted at the camp gate by the same armed mullah they'd seen the first time. 'As-Salamu Alaykum,' he said, formally, remembering to tap his heart with his right hand. He indicated that he couldn't speak the language, but that he was a cricketer from Australia – descended from Afghan cameleers. Could he come in? And he flourished the bundle of photos I'd sent. They were pretty impressive: Eli leaping to catch a ball, Eli, bat in hand, at the crease, Eli au Don Bradman after hitting a boundary. It struck a chord. The mullah called another mullah and soon he had a circle of admirers looking at his photos.

Not much English was spoken in this territory, but enough to inform him that within the tent at the gate there was a registration tea party going on if he'd like to partake – a family was getting its ration books and permits. Inside, men sat on the bedsteads drinking tea, eating mints and being cooled by a rotating electric fan. The women were hiding their faces in a hot truck at the entrance where the children stood around, staring at the newcomer who was exciting so much interest.

Eli was invited into the camp and one of the guards, gun and all, accompanied him on a tour. People lived better here than they did beyond the walls, but *That wouldn't be hard,* Eli wrote. *The women on the outside told me that these blokes with guns had no idea what it was like to live as they did. They drove cars and lived in upmarket houses in Peshawar's new districts, while the women were trying to make money out of selling donkey bones! Donkey bones, Mum!*

The cricketing gear was a success. Boys poured out of the tents for a chance to play. *They were rapt. Poor little beggars have to make do with next to nothing and play in the dirt and the poor girls don't get to play at all.*

Could I send some money for cricket equipment? He thought if he bought them cricket equipment and gave them lessons it would be a way of finding out about their families – also, he wrote, a way of distracting them from the recruiting that was going on. He could quietly spread the word that there was other education on offer that didn't involve selling your sons into soldiery. *Oh, and by the way,* he finished, *I forgot to tell you that the pack with my European clothes in it was stolen out of my sack on my visit to the outside camp. I was able to buy everything back the next day from one of the bazaars in Peshawar. Part of the reason that I need more money.*

So I sent money for cricket equipment and Afsar helped him pick up more of the local language and he began to catch the drift of what people were saying. Lotte also helped. She didn't need him to accompany her now because she'd made a friend from the UNHCR who was part of the Good Offices mission to Afghanistan and Pakistan. He was in Peshawar overseeing the keeping of the Geneva Accords during the Soviet withdrawal. There was a group of people doing various things for his office; a couple of them were Australian.

Eli was more interested in Peshawar and what was happening there than in meeting up with countrymen, even if they were with the UN. He felt he could discover more by being his own agent. Inside Jalozai he learned that some people had been there so long their teenaged children were born there, *same as in Kacha Garhi,* he wrote. *They get work in the bazaars, these children, and develop a taste for Indian films and want to look like film stars. They forget all about being from Afghanistan and if there's talk of returning, they don't want to go. They run away rather than get onto the amazingly decorated Bedford trucks that go like a stately parade of caparisoned behemoths, jingling and jangling and tooting, laden with families and equipment, back to Afghanistan.*

The Bedfords were decorated in factories in the region where the smugglers' bazaars were. Photos came back of these towering ersatz temples, their intricately embellished ladders leading up from the ground to caverns within the luggage where the families would sit, to the outward eye, like maharajas. *These contraptions depart along the great A1 highway to the Khyber Pass and over into the border regions of Afghanistan that have been cleared of landmines and where, for the time being, the war has stopped raging.*

It was in one such convoy of Bedfords that Eli went into Afghanistan with Jager and the documentary crew. They were bound for Nangarhar Province just over the Khyber Pass and an area called Shinwar. Eli rode high up in the elaborate canopy of a Bedford, playing cards with some other young men for part of the way, but he found it was just too stifling and, once he had arrived undetected over the border, he swapped with someone in the crew's ute. Jager had managed to dig out Habibullah, the land holder, who spoke English fluently and well. He was the son of a rural landlord in the feudal style of Afghanistan. He was well respected by the people whose lives and welfare he'd been responsible for before the war drove them out: in exchange for a third of the take, he'd organise the selling on of their produce and keep their houses and equipment in order. Eli imagined that the system would work well so long as the ground was rich and productive as it was in the Shinwar region, but he wondered if things would go as smoothly in less forgiving terrain. The farmers had an education, but it was minimal. They were literate and could use figures, but Habibullah had been educated in Karachi and was several levels of sophistication above them. He obviously had great power and if he had it, no doubt others in his position with less intelligence or fewer scruples could misuse their power.

Habibullah and Daoud were enthusiastic about what they would do the moment they arrived. There was talk of mending the walls of the irrigation canals and of setting up cooking facilities inside any of the houses that remained. But the reality precluded this. When they arrived after a fraught journey of hours from the highway over potholed and torn-up land, people just dropped down from the sides of the trucks, raised their tents, handed round uncooked food and slept.

You could see it had been a nice place, Eli wrote. It was green, there were lots of trees. They'd had a good life once, growing cereals and keeping cows, but now the fields were full of tares, the main well of the settlement was staved in and they had to get water from the irrigation canals, which were also busted up and muddied. *There was enough rice, but cooking it was hard yards and it tasted like the mud slurry it was. The women set about making a kind of dough – like damper dough, out of coarse flour, and they made bread, but it wasn't very appetising. They had grain with them and they took it to the next village to see if they could get it ground, but the miller had cleared out and his mill was broken. There was another mill working, but it was a long way away and the machinery kept breaking down – a) because it was primitive and b) because it was so much in demand that the miller couldn't cope. They only managed to get one bag ground. It had to be enough for the time being, but it was pretty clear they'd have to get the neighbouring mill back into working order or be making the trips every other day.*

Even though the land around Shinwar was supposed to have been secured, there were still landmines there that hadn't been cleared, so it was very slow going, with someone out the front of the Toyota clearing the way with a stick.

When the women began winnowing, the mood picked up. They were glad to have their faces back and to be occupied with productive work. It was soon clear, however, that there was no prospect of schooling for the children – the school had been shelled and the teacher had fled – and if they became ill, then they would have to be taken back all the way to Nasir Bagh, so far over the border it was practically in Peshawar. They all had experience of Nasir Bagh – it might or might not have the medications they needed and the medical staff might or might not be able to help.

Once there had been civil servants whose jobs were to oversee the water supply in the area, but they hadn't been available for a long time and the water had by and large dried up. Pictures came home of Eli dangling from a long rope down a manmade chasm or Kareez, a hole leading to a system of water canals some thirty to fifty feet down. These Kareezes are the ancient water supply of Afghanistan that once fed fabulous pleasure gardens. After the age of the Moghuls, fruit was grown here for an excellent dried-fruit market. Figs were a specialty. Eli, who has always been a keen climber and tunneller, went down with some of the men to clean the Kareez. They would go down the narrow shaft one at a time to lift out sand and silt by the bucketload. I hated to see him in such a narrow underground place, but he said he loved it and could keep on doing more of it. The Kareezes run down slopes from a water source and are perhaps half a kilometre apart, guiding the water to where it is needed. It was gratifying when clean water came shooting out the end of the tunnel into the concrete canals, called jubs, which then fed the irrigation system.

This is right up my alley, Mum. I love doing this kind of thing – sure beats Lego!

I was glad he was having fun, but it didn't last long.

All this effort came to nought when they heard shelling and gunfire nearby within a week of their return. Shinwar was all but surrounded by troops and mujahedeen doing battle. There was nothing to do but load up the Bedfords again and go back to Peshawar.

He'd learned now why Daoud was so reluctant to return without Habibullah. If there is a context in which to make a return, then it is much more easily made: without Habibullah, the 'knowledge man', Daoud would have been defeated by circumstances in an even shorter time than it took the war to swing back into Nangarhar. A tent, some cooking oil and some money might mean mayhem, or nothing, without a community to put them to use.

Eli was very disappointed by the failure of Jager's mission and badly in need of a beer. Lotte knew where he could find some. Phoebe Häken-Green, the Australian girl in the office, was hiding a stash for the Australians in the mission. There were very few pot plants of the common or garden variety in Peshawar, but Phoebe had them. There was rubble enough to make crock for thousands of pots in Peshawar's streets, but Phoebe didn't resort to that. In place of crock in the pot bottoms, Phoebe used cans of Victoria Bitter; although they looked real, they were *like me*, wrote Eli, *fakes*.

4

When Eli met Phoebe, I was still living up in New South Wales at Reg Sorby's retreat with Stella and Nin. Nin was around nine and attending a little local school. Stella had come out of her grief over Allegra enough to be aware that her surroundings weren't what she was accustomed to and we were making frequent visits to Canberra for retail therapy. Home we would come, up the winding, mountainous roads behind a truck from David Jones containing a Fleur lounge suite that would suit a genteel woman living in retirement with a daughter who did nothing but paint all the time. Into the local township we'd go, after the installing of the suite, for coffee with *people!* Don't you know any *people?!* And I'd be bored to tears, talking to country drunks and liars while Stella tried to find out if she was related to any of them. When they found out we were living at Reg's, they all wanted to come and enjoy famous, rarefied surroundings, surroundings where Reg had gone naked with nymphs and been seen cavorting. Telephone numbers were exchanged. Stella has never been able to live without a phone of her own. The one we had for her at Reg's was just a disconnected handpiece in the days of her madness, but once she started to improve, I had it connected so she could spend her days dialling wrong numbers and receiving calls from people who thought they were privy to Reg's private number, which they were not. All kinds

of hoboes and fakes started to knock at the amazing front doors
that Reg had brought back from his days as an ancient hippie on
the Silk Road. They were carved wood, studded with metal bolts
and hung with chains and they creaked mightily on their hinges
when you opened them. For a girl who'd been raised in the country,
Stella was lax about opening them – I think it was fear of the doors
more than anything – and I was quite a fierce person to meet on the
threshold. We never knew if and when David Silver would find
us and press, indignantly, for his paternal rights. I began to miss
Melbourne and the old escape hatches I knew there.

We were being supplied with money by Reg.

Reg had coveted the home where Allegra and I grew up with
our parents in inner Melbourne.

'You don't need that place,' he'd say to me.

'But it's my mother's home.'

'She doesn't know where she's living.'

'She'll probably want to go back to her home, Reg.'

'Look, you'll need to stay up in the retreat for quite a while
until I can get the lawyers to see things my way and have the paintings legally restored to you and your family. How about I go and
live in your mother's house and rent it from you...tell you what,
I'll *buy* it from you. You haven't got any money, you need money.
I'll buy that house.'

'It's not mine to sell. It's my mother's.'

'Well, it's no use to you sitting empty like that plum in the
middle of Melbourne where plenty of people are wanting to live.'

'Including you.'

'Look, I could live anywhere I chose. I just happen to like that
house...and, if I bought it, it would still, sort of, be in the family.'

He was a manipulative old bugger but it was true we'd have
been better off selling Stella's house. In fact, it seemed the only way
we were going to get by was by selling her house. Or my house,
which Eli had been sharing with friends while he was a student.
There was still a mortgage on my house and students lived on there

when Eli took off on his trip. They'd be late with their rent and the garden was a wreck and I tried not to think about it, but it represented such a lot of work and effort with the bank and it was my one security. 'Come on, Isobel, realise your capital and sell up,' Reg would say. And I would have bad dreams that my beaut little house was falling to bits catastrophically and it would happen while dependable friends were visiting me. It was a two-storey, timber house, renovated on the cheap. In my dreams Eli would be living in it with me. I'd be sitting in the flat in the roof apologising to my dependable friends for the sudden collapse of walls around us, while acquaintances of Eli's, who were far from dependable, moved in en masse, making the whole building shake and begin to topple. My dependable friends and I would become a little insignificant enclave of oldies; the more dependable among them, to whom such things would never happen, would say, in firm voices, 'Isobel, you can't allow Eli and his friends to do this to you.' And then they'd consult with each other and shake their heads until they had to run for their cars that were parked nearby and save them from being destroyed in the total collapse. One of them would give me a lift, saying, 'This used to be such a promising part of town. We were all so happy when you bought here.' And she would drop me off under a big railway bridge where tramps were living in sleeping bags and where the only way out was up an escalator onto a station from which you needed a ticket to exit. Not only would I not have a ticket, I hadn't even the money to buy one. I was doomed to ride trains all my life, avoiding inspectors, trying not to be raped by other tramps and feeding myself through theft or beggary.

I was really fretting for my house and Stella was slowly coming to herself, so I put it to her that to save her place, we really ought to let Reg rent it from us so it would be generating some income. As things stood, we couldn't afford to be buying furniture and papering over the mudbricks so that Stella could have a salon in retirement…Senile she might have been, but at the mention of someone whose penis she'd seen depicted swinging in the breeze on the wall of a gallery putting himself up as a prospective tenant, she broke into a string of invective so fierce I had to crouch behind her new couch in case she hit me. She was roaring. What was I doing with her life? I was a tyrant, just like His Craziness, who had killed her daughter! (His Craziness? I don't know whether she meant David or Dadda and I don't think she knew, either.) If she, Stella Motte, wanted to live in salubrious surroundings, then she, Stella Motte, would live in salubrious surroundings and I could go drown myself 'in a vat of piddle!' Stella Motte wasn't going to agree to renting anything to anyone. It was beneath her. When I put it to her in top G from behind the couch that we couldn't afford her spending sprees unless we either rented out her house or sold it, she did one of her emotional swan dives, laid waste to the new furniture and ripped into the wallpaper, yelling, 'Sell it then!' Her father was supposed to have slaughtered all the pigs in his sty when the bank foreclosed on the mortgage on his property and she wasn't his daughter for nothing. She broke the side off a brand new armchair and buckled the fittings on her new lamp stands so they couldn't be used. These days, she'd be called 'bipolar', but back then, it was par for the course, only occasional and witheringly exhausting.

I was so angry I sold her house for cash to Reg. He put the money in a bank account in my mother's name, to which I had access. Stella saw the sum and believed she'd suddenly become rich. There were more trips to Canberra for hairstyles and clothes, replacement furniture, good crystal and an eighteen carat gold watch. She, who had been sitting around for a couple of years humbly and quietly knitting things at random and only requiring more wool, now began to resurrect her glory days. Except there weren't really any glory days and she made it all up as she went along.

Reg's retreat began to feel overpopulated with crazy people who could still drive but couldn't afford their own grog, and especially not the sort of grog Stella was buying and drinking out of Stuart crystal. Minor royalty emerged from an isolated farm – Lady Stephanie Plum was actually an old maid who'd been dumped by her family in a cottage they owned in an apple orchard. There was a religious Bulgarian of about seventy with a white crew cut who belonged to a doomsday cult and would come on Wednesdays to help Stella prepare for the Day of Reckoning. The Day came and went and he died and was replaced by a man who lived in the local town in a renovated Victorian cottage he rented from a local estate agent. He couldn't open any windows in the cottage because the windows had been renovated and the keys lost. He had to keep his front and back doors open all the time to let fresh air in. He owned the fattest bulldog I've ever seen. I'd promised Reg that we wouldn't have any pets at the retreat because of the wildlife, but the immense animal would come in spite of the injunction and poo in Reg's wildflower reserve. 'No!' I said. 'No, it can't go on. We should think about moving back to Melbourne.'

The wildflower reserve was Reg's idea of a sacred place. In there, there were rare orchids that he painstakingly pollinated by hand the moment they appeared. I'd met Reg through orchids and orchids had been the mainstay of Eli's upbringing because I could never earn enough money through art alone. I afforded my house because of orchids. When Eli was little I got a job in a public garden, potting orchids. The woman who hired me was a marvellous old dame called Beryl Blake. Well, I say old, but I'm more ancient now than she was then; she just seemed ancient. People who didn't know her feared her. She was short, squat, fat and red-faced: her hair was thin and grey and fell its short length in greasy straps. She had a mouth like a trout's and her eyelids everted around washed-out irises. She always had a bib of sweat on her copious bosom that made her dresses cling to her, emphasising her bulges and falling into pitiful flaps around her thighs. In summer she wore rubber thongs and in winter, lace-up black school shoes and ankle socks. And she had a deep, frog-croaking voice that came burping up from a heart of gold. She employed students in the holidays to do whatever job she could rake up the money for them to do. 'You never run out of chores in a garden,' she'd say. A public servant called 'Stewy' would find sundry funds for her and she was often in his office begging balefully for a bit more so she could take on another person with problems.

One year, when she ran out of money, she introduced me to Reg, whom I already knew, anyway, because he was a friend of Dadda's. Reg was illustrating a book on orchids and she recommended me as a person who could help him. So I helped Reg do the book and tried to prevent Reg from helping himself to me, and when the book was finished, Beryl found me more work. She was collaborating with a scientist at the University of Melbourne on the propagation of rare Australian orchids.

When Eli wrote home from Peshawar declaring himself a fake, I was doing battle with dog poo in the wildflower reserve and thinking to myself that I'd sooner be back in Melbourne working at a distance from Stella on those great fakes of the plant world, orchids, in a smelly university laboratory where Stella wouldn't deign to set a foot.

Oh Eli, I wrote to him in Peshawar, *I know a lot about fakes; not only have I met a great number of them, I've even studied their genetics. Artist I may be, but how do you think I came by our house and sent you off to school? And not only you, but Nin as well?*

Science is a refuge for me: it can be both intellectually challenging and aesthetically pleasing. I have a number of friends who are scientists and their mindsets are quite distinct from those of my artist friends.

Science is a bridge built in the present to link the facts of the past to concepts it anticipates in the future. Just now, instead of picking Stella up to go in search of a new hostel room – something I will have to do in the next hour or so – I'm considering Charles Darwin. What a bridge he built! He was fascinated by orchids, those great imposters. Through some mind-blowing coincidence, be it convergent evolution, exchange of genetic material between animal and plant or the constraints of natural laws on DNA, they grow to look like the mates of the insects that pollinate them – quite a lot of them even produce the mating pheromone of the female insect to attract males. The fooled male attempts to mate with a gaggle of pseudo females lolling about on their stalks like blow-up sex dolls and pretending to be the real thing without even providing the poor chap with a blob of nectar in exchange for his efforts. What's happening here?

It's an object lesson in chicanery.

It doesn't seem to matter that the pollinators bumble off course to do free work for orchids, useless species that they are, but you'd think the path of least resistance would be for nature not to have come up with the orchid at all. Orchids are freeloaders and occupy a realm well beyond artistic Surrealism – a realm that is entire, hooked up, workable and ongoing. Just like us.

What a delectable artwork I could make of Darwin's engravings on the pollination of orchids – it would be every bit as fascinating as the visible poems of Max Ernst. A graphic work that attracted my interest early is Ernst's *Une Semaine de Bonté*. It is a set of turn-of-the-century (nineteenth) collages, lizards' heads on women's torsos, that kind of thing, done very intricately and great to look at, but Ernst's fusions are those of the mind. Nature's fusions result in fabulous forms such as you find in the orchid's reproductive system – you could create a glamorous, incredibly sexy pastiche from them.

It would be all about allure.

That word 'allure' trots off the tongue with such a promising sound.

If you chop allure out of the equation, you can't expect sex to be exciting and fulfilling at all. I can't imagine good sex without allure.

In these early days of women taking on full participation in the running of world affairs it's hard to dissociate good straightforward sex-with-foreplay from the exploitative proclivities of misogynistic men: however, looking at a woman's body and making the assumption that she's out of her natural context because she's applying for work or doing work where attractive women are a rarity is not the same thing as looking at a woman in a ripe context and wanting to fuck her – or if you're a woman, knowing what you look like and wanting to be fucked. Gauging the situation is all-important and at this time in history we're only just working out what situations are acceptable.

Once upon a time, the tribe probably had to conceal the sexual emanations given off by women, or they would have been killed in scrum rape – sometimes they were killed, it seems; sometimes they still are, by men who can't discriminate between situations. In the normal run of life, nonetheless, forfeiting sexual highs for wet blanket public approval would be paying a price too high for wellbeing.

I know a lot about sex. I've had a terrific sex life – sporadically terrific, I have to say, because there's routine sex and sex, on the other hand, that explodes every cell in your body. You couldn't live with crescendo all the time, but it's there for special occasions. Especially for hoodwinking yourself. I have to admit that some of the best sex I've had has been deluded. I think it's the thrill of transgression that fires up orgasm – just as the feeling you'd like to eat a baby is assuaged by a sloppy smooch.

Even among the pious and politically correct you can't get past that element of secret liberty-taking. I've seen plenty of feminists absolve themselves from the rules when on fire with lust – they just sort of disappear and come back, glowing with the guilt of original sin. Nobody cares to remember that actually, underneath it all, we're animals and animals are lured into sex: think of the upside down waggling about of the bird of paradise or the head-thwacking of giraffes – they don't do it to get giddy or break their necks.

When I was younger all my sexual highs were achieved subversively; they had to be because Stella had been taught that sex was dirty. My loves were furtive and illicit. I had to hide my sexuality from Stella, who used to do me up to look like a hibiscus in a bed of weeds and then panic in case I lost my virginity. I lost it right under her nose with a man whose image was constructed for me by her – a medical man, jocular, smooth, sensual, flirty. Fifty feet tall and ten feet broad, blond, blue-eyed, a Chesty Bond in a white lab coat or laundered hospital gown, the coat of whichever one of his fabulous suits he happened to be wearing hung cavalierly on the hatstand of his consulting rooms where Stella was the practice nurse. He was Eli's father, Arnie Russell, ophthalmologist, a man of straw with feet of clay. Everyone wanted to lay Arnie – women primped their hair and wiggled their hips at a hundred paces. Feminine dew pearled in the trumpet of every orchid for miles. He hummed snatches of Cole Porter and fell into these mating niches evolved for the trapping thereof with the alacrity of a male insect who knew what he was up to. Young Isobel Coretti was too green even to put on palpitations when he fell into hers. The sex was entire, every cell in the 'armoury' discharged.

Too bad he was a prestidigitator who passed for an expensive version of the cheap Charlie he really was. In my imagination, he was a dramatic saver of sight who would take his skills to distant lands and cure ailing tribes of their blindness the world over while I brought up the rear with the mosquito swatter – in truth, he ditched me, took his legal tribe off to California and became even richer than he already was by opening a chain of laser clinics and entering into a string of laser-swift marriage turnovers. They say he's been married four times.

Since Arnie, I've loved men too young for me and men too old for me, daredevils and egoists with no parenting potential whatsoever. My imagination has set each one of them up with splendid qualities that would see Eli and Nin brought up sane and secure and see me into an admirable, rich old age.

They were gods and heroes all to me but no doubt they imagined they were living lives altogether different from the ones I invented for them: lives in which I was a peccadillo, significant only insofar as their other women were curious to find out who I was.

Or are women orchids in our way, trying to divert the pollinators from their predestined course? Such a huge amount of energetic signalling, competition and jealousy is involved you'd have to wonder why nature came up with sexual reproduction at all. I blame snails: they shoot each other at close quarters with mating shafts and remained locked together for ages – like jealousy and possessiveness all in one (and all along, they're hermaphrodites).

I've caused jealousy and felt it in equal measure. Because it's so overwhelming, I've had to give away transgressive sex as too extravagant and increasingly impossible with age, compensating myself with function, affection and reliability. And, of course, need.

All this makes you wonder why living things didn't just remain single-celled and go on eating each other and dividing for eternity. Why, given the choice of such simplicity, would living things modify the multifarious and coincidental worlds around them to keep themselves anticipating sex? Single-celled organisms didn't produce offspring except as a means of getting rid of their avoirdupois. The trouble is the subunits of DNA: it's every multiplicand for itself! Think of the thrust of DNA, that self-serving substance against the entire inanimate universe – that inherent will to transgress against the current order and subsume it into complicated life! Think of the imaginative leaps involved in a chemical deciding that complex makes for a better life than simple. How? Why? Is it just an experiment in compost?

Allure. I have to say that Phoebe Häken-Green was gorgeous. There's no two ways about it. She was a class apart, like Allegra. Pale blonde hair in drifts of silk around a sweet, naughty face that men fell for immediately. Just the sort of woman you wouldn't come across in Peshawar, Pakistan, not even as a visiting film star. Which made her all the more alluring. The UN owed her presence there to her antecedents. She was the love child of an Australian diplomat, George Green, and a simultaneous translator, a Swedish American, Fridlinda Häken, who became his second wife. All was cast aside for Phoebe Häken-Green, it seems – a first wife and a tribe of sons forsaken for the blonde nymph of the north.

The tribe of sons was Canberra Grammar'd, Sydney and Melbourne University'd, Public Servant'd and spread around the globe on missions to everywhere. They were spoken of highly and idolised by their sister of the combination name, who was a catch phrase in Canberra whenever the Greens were home there for a spell. Phoebe Häken-Green had her brothers' hostage negotiations to match, arms and drug caches, negotiations on trade deals and quellings of riots among wild Pacific Islanders. She had lots to prove and four abandoned boys to justify for her existence. Hard, when you're one little blonde girl. Becoming a film star or a model was too easy. She followed her glamorous blonde mother, studied in the US, became a linguist, and, to get her into the kinds of places her brothers had gone before her, she had degrees from American universities in sociology and psychology. And now here she was, equipped to work among Pashto- and Dari-speaking refugees, to find out where they came from and whether they could go back there.

When I heard of Phoebe Häken-Green of the green eyes, I knew this was it – number one, unlikely to be easily unseated by a rival. And what were Phoebe's hopes for Eli? She was obviously highly intelligent. She had lived a life of glamour and danger and she might have paired up with any major diplomat or politician, probably had paired up with one such or two or three such already; she was five years older than Eli. No doubt whatever that she'd flirted and had affairs in several places. She'd been recommended to the UN as a brilliant translator of a highly desirable language set. How much of it was the blind recommendation of the awestruck and how much the recommendation of solid promise?

Eli's credentials: he had the world's bluest eyes. So has anyone else who is the product of a blue/blue cross. Apart from that – he was a charmer, he was cock-a-hoop and daring. He had a good turn of phrase. Nor had he been used up and discarded on any of the social circuits through which Phoebe might have been whirling.

He found bunches of flowers for her in a desert.

There's a place called Flower Street where a bloke there puts by a nice bunch for me every day…mind you, it's sometimes Dried Flower Street because the market gardens around here are being affected by the influx of people and it's terribly dry right now. Yes, he was in love. Maybe she was out of his league, but nothing like *putting my credentials in her vases in hope.*

What was this I was feeling when I picked up her photograph and stared at it? Not jealously, surely? Not at my age? Jealous of my son's beloved? I couldn't help hoping she'd do something wrong, but if she broke my Eli's heart, I'd be over there in a shot…would I? To shoot her? Probably not. She was hugging a dog in the photograph, a St Bernard, obviously not in Pakistan. She must've wrinkled up a little bit by this? Surely? Laughing. Perfect teeth. Erk.

I have to say I felt relief when his visa ran out and he had to continue his journey. He did, after all, go down into Africa, to Uganda and Botswana and Kenya and I was there at Heathrow to meet him when he got off the plane from Nairobi. I couldn't see him in the crowd around the carousel, but then a dark, dirty arm reached down to take up a filthy backpack and the arm was attached to someone with knockout blues. My baby.

They nearly refused him entrance at my hotel. He looked much better when he'd showered but we obviously had to buy him new clothes as a priority.

I was on my way to Milan. I had a couple of weeks in England while Eli hunted up work. At least in London there were papers eager to take his articles and want more of them. So I went on to Italy and Eli stayed in London with enough work to keep him there for some months. I was back in Australia – and living in

Melbourne – by the time he caught up with Phoebe once again. She'd been head-hunted by the American Department of Defence and, before she started work in Washington, went to London to see if Eli still wanted to marry her.

Yes, he wanted to marry her. It would mean going to Washington to live.

I didn't quite know how to feel.

The unknown quantity. The possibility that it's just a huge crush.

To be allured is to be in a state of want. I made him promise that if he was going to get married, he'd marry here, in Australia, with me looking on. Thank God he interpreted it as my pride in him and not as my need for reassurance.

Without allure, we'd be bored to death and yet it can take us in so completely we forget who we are and where we live and what we are striving for. The allure of the mythical good life makes dupes of us all. The orchid blooms and we're seduced.

Which brings me to Stella. Not that I want to go to Stella, but I must. Stella has been frightened of allure all her life. If she's had unfettered sex she's buried it deep in the bottomless pit of misdeeds. A strict mother told her that if ever she became pregnant out of marriage, she would take her to a high place and, together, they would jump into the sea. Stella told me about it when I arrived home with Eli after an inadequately explained absence, but we didn't do any tramping off to cliff tops. She rather liked Eli. Indeed, she could have devoured Eli. Here at last was a male heir and his eyes were the exact right colour. Having been warned off men by her mother, she fell under the spell of a baby boy.

Euphrosyne – as her mother was called – also put her under an injunction never to say no. She had to agree to every request in the name of being demure. Women were to be beautiful martyrs and their compensation was to be in the hereafter at the side of the man with the halo and the holes in his hands and feet. Stella was bidden to make sense of this mishmash at all costs. Beauty was stained glass and Anglicanism. She had to subvert the natural beauty of things into the worship of a mangled god in a well-mannered way. No wonder she has resisted sanity. Sanity would disabuse her of the reasons she's concocted for being alive. But alive she is and these fripperies have nested in her framework, an infestation of battiness, for nearly a hundred years.

Earlier in the week, I investigated the Anglicans on her behalf, in case something good turned up in her old ethnic niche but I wouldn't put my dog in the Anglican home I saw. Cold, dark rooms and a converted garage of a dining room: it was a home for hoboes and unlucky ones at that.

This morning there's the Protestant home to go and look at. I put Stella's name on top of the list for consideration by the other Protestant home that has vacancies at hostel level and we are going out today to see if we can't clinch it.

I've tried to tell Stella as gently as I can that she should wear nice clothes and try to relax. I warned them beforehand at Broadlea that today was the day, but when I arrived, it was 'Oh *today!*' and I found her in her ordinary, somewhat dribbled-on clothes, booked in for lunch here. I had to get the manager to ring up and check that I had the date right – yes, I had the date right – then I had to take Stella back to her room: not something accomplished in a flash, particularly when the 'stroke lady' is hovering backwards and forwards without making any progress on the threshold of the lift. I had to find help to move her on into the lift, then get Stella and her frame in, then get both folk (the stroke lady is tragically young, perhaps in her fifties) out at the other end, walk the slow and rather long distance to Stella's room and find reasonable clothes that were clean. I had to take the shoes off – always a massive operation because the feet are clawed and crippled and no longer fit easily into a shoe – I've had to put new trousers on… 'I don't like those ones.' 'Well, I'm sorry Mum, but you're going to have to wear them today.' 'But I want the ones with the stripes down the side.' 'I'm sorry Mum, they're dirty.' 'No they're not, look in the cupboard.' 'Mum, I'm sorry, but we're running late and it's important that you look good and behave yourself so we can get you into the other hostel. It's much newer than this one – I believe it's very nice.'

Clothes on, then down to my jalopy, minute after long, slow fucking minute, ticking away.

The drive is the easiest part, through pleasant, leafy streets, but 'It's quite a long way away, isn't it?' observes Stella.

'Not too far.'

'But all that petrol money.'

'Don't worry about that.'

She fusses for change to give me and drops the contents of her bag all over the car floor.

'It doesn't matter,' I say. 'Don't worry.' And I think of Baudelaire and how he got away with hateful comments about his mother in poetry that people rave about. Voices at my ear tell me constantly to be like that myself and leave the silly old cow to her fate. The new, strong Isobel would, if she…if she…what? Was a shit like Baudelaire, probably.

We park, we progress slowly to the doorway. Its red eye blinks alarmingly at me as I punch in the security code. Silently the doors open. We crawl inside. Silently the doors close us in, guillotining off the day.

There's no one to greet us. There ought to be someone to greet us.

The sitting room to our right is like a demonstration room in a suburban developer's brochure. There are some smartly dressed old people sitting in easy chairs around one of those silent, fake fires. It looks fake comfortable. Somebody must actually hand-wash woollen cardigans around here – either that, or the oldies are kept in a constant supply of new ones – the pink, the red, the blue – and none of them shrunken from being flung in a machine, like Stella's.

Stella is tottering dangerously on her Wheelathon, as she calls it. 'I need to go to the toilet. Oh, I need to go quickly.'

So I hassle her forwards…um…where?

Oh, yes, there we are, a loo off the dining room.

We just make it. She sits on the seat and squirts for all she's worth. And it stinks. And it's a shame, but never mind, we've got here, now all we have to do is take it easy, calm down, wash the bits that need washing. Wash everything carefully, use the hand soap, lots of it… 'Oooh, it's cold.'

'Yes, I'm sorry it's cold, Mum, but we just have to get you comfy again and then we'll go into the dining room and I'll see if I can find the lady who was supposed to meet us.'

If there was a lady who was supposed to meet us…

I think there was.

I change her emergency pants and tuck her in, find the bin for the debris. Make sure every visible trace of poo is removed.

And eventually we negotiate the Wheelathon to make enough room at the sink, fix the toilet, get all four of our hands properly washed and dried on the paper towels – thank God for paper towels. The old don't seem to manage the air drier.

And we're set…but she starts to breathe funnily. And I recognise this breathing from one of the times Cousin Audra came to stay. 'She's having a fit!' said Cousin Audra. I said, 'She's having a panic attack.' 'What'll we do?' 'Dial an ambulance, please, while I try to calm her down.'

I sit her on the seat of the Wheelathon.

'There, there, Stella, quietly now, in through your nose, one, two, three…and out gently through your mouth, one, two, three, four. Just a little more out than in, Mumma, there we are.'

Five minutes of breathing normally and we are set to go into the dining room. Most of the guests have finished lunch and have left, but I take Stella up and sit her at a table. She is incapable of choosing what she wants to eat, so I choose it for her. I tell the lady on the food race that we'll both have chicken and I explain that we've come over from Broadlea at the invitation of the manager here to see if Mum likes the room that's available. The food lady intercoms the manager and, at last, we sit down.

Dutifully and obediently, like a little child, Mum munches her lunch, but nerves are making it hard for her to swallow, so I have to stroke her wounded old hand and tell her gently to relax. 'How can I,' she cries, 'when you're doing that to me all the time?'

So I snatch away my hand…and then try to cover up for having snatched it.

Stella munches for a while, ever so carefully. And then, just as the manager heaves unsmilingly into view, Stella shrieks and brings everything up on the tablecloth.

Well, all I can do is cry, really. But you don't cry, do you, Isobel – you keep a straight face when the manager burls up close and tells the whole building in a firm voice, 'Oh, she needs high care. She definitely needs high care!'

Sadly we trail our way out. Back into the car, back to Narrowlea. 'I'm sorry Bel.' 'No need to be sorry. The question is, did you like that place?'

'Oh it seemed all right. It was quite bright.'

'Yes it was, wasn't it? Very clean. The sitting room looked comfortable. Shame we didn't see the room, but perhaps if I explain what happened to the Broadlea people they'll explain to the manager here and we'll have another look when you're feeling better.'

So I explain to the manager at Narrowlea, who looks aghast at my tale and says, 'But Stella's much too bright for nursing-home care. I'll ring them up and explain.'

She rang up, she explained. They said my mother was too old.

When I'm dying I want to be as incidental as a cushion and as easy as an old pet cat. I don't want to be wasted time for someone else, but as things stand, I may have no control over my fate.

Whatever happens, I do want to die having achieved something: I don't really want to die under a bridge with the tramps and no railway ticket out to a better place.

5

☻☻☻

Sometimes you can feel as though you've achieved something, even if it's through the efforts of someone else. History is always in a rush to remember things, but in her charging forward, like Mad Meg through Hell, she will trample much and misinterpret plenty. She will run innocence through with her sword and drop truth from her bundle without stopping to look for it and gather it up again. Lately, History has been turning her gaze on the seventies art world in Melbourne and I have just been book buying at a launch in a friend's bookshop. The book has a feature chapter on the feminist art movement and on Mad Meg's namesake, our gallery. The author interviewed me at length about our methods and lack of them and our aims and superfluity of them.

I was given the section to read before the book went to press. The author used the information I gave her to chart Mad Meg's all-too-famous demise, David's wrecking of my show when he picked a fight with another painter, our going broke and Allegra's suicide. I was dubious about telling the story to someone who was going to publish it, but then I thought David epitomised the reason for Mad Meg's existence and telling the story added to what Allegra was trying to say about women and their art by running the gallery.

Another contributor to the chapter, a painter called Jan Laird, has had great success in life, going on from Mad Meg to big commissions and a name that competes alongside the men's. Recently she was commissioned by a public gallery in Paris to create the Australian Aboriginal component of a new building. It's a building that might have been created here – the concept being that Aboriginal art, being the oldest continuous art practice in the world, would form the outside and base of a building housing the art of the Pacific. I suppose there's more money for such a project in Paris and Paris is much more visited than, say, Brisbane or Darwin, but such a gallery would really have been at home in either of those places. Anyway, Jan says that without Mad Meg women artists in Melbourne would have been passed over no matter how good they were because that was the culture of the time: Mad Meg offered a place to go where there was support and exhibition space and enough noise made to attract attention. Jan admired Allegra for throwing down the gauntlet politically and taking it up to the men as far as she possibly could. Allegra exhibited Jan often in her early career when she began making statements as an urban Aboriginal with prints memorialising the fate of her mother's people, whose sacred sites lie buried under Melbourne. She joined the excavation of urban Aboriginal sites and went on to do some terrific prints of the unearthed past. Now she does glass and mosaic constructions as well as her prints.

Jan Laird is sixty-two. Without the Paris commission and the publication of this book, her name wouldn't be on everyone's lips. She's had to work under time constraints that are easily as tough as mine. She has three children and her output, like mine, has been delayed by commitments.

While the book-launching speeches were being delivered, I found myself standing behind an old Mad Meggian, one I never liked. She has a thin neck and a small head and, in profile, a nose that twitches at the end that, when stuck in a shelf of seriously new literature, looked as though it was going to reach right in and grasp something off the shelves without help from the hands. Elspeth, appropriately surnamed Roach, was once a politically correct Marxist Feminist who belonged to the group within our collective that Allegra and I used call 'the Troika' because they couldn't come to a decision independent of each other. Every opinion was prefaced with 'We think…' Elspeth is an art critic who likes the words 'banal and trivial', the clichés almost always used by art critics in lieu of that reverse cliché, 'stunning'.

Ah, stunning! A word that reels around the streets of Melbourne, whacking itself over the head with a dead mullet whenever the critics can't think of anything better to say. So popular is 'stunning' that it's been taken up by estate agents – 'stunning views' means you can see out two windows; 'stunning kitchen' means silver fridge, a silver wall oven and a hot plate that looks like a photograph.

The twenty or so stacker chairs near the stage were being occupied by ancient folk of the kind who give out opinions and university degrees. Very important gent at the microphone, too distracted with himself to do more than drop the names of his luncheon companions and those who send him emails from Cambridge; Jeremy, the old friend who owns the shop, beside the counter, smiling with arms crossed and…David Silver, standing next to him also with arms crossed and his mouth written across his chin, terse as a line of minimalist poetry. I nearly didn't recognise him – he's had one of those ridiculous number one haircuts. I hate them. David's emphasises his huge head. Now why would he swap a decent head of wavy black hair – no bald patches – for a Tim Burton skull? He mustered a filthy look to give me – although he scowls a lot, his face doesn't really suit it; he has a sharp jaw and the corners of his mouth came down so close to the bottom of his chin I imagined it detaching and falling off on the floor. He can be pretty good-looking when he smiles but he rarely does. Who invited him, I wonder? I expect he's on the bookshop's list but he wouldn't be on the author's, surely?

Surely?

Though maybe…

Other people smiled at me vaguely, as if they might have known me at some time. I put their non-remembrance down to failing vision and the decrepitude that is assailing us all at our age, however, I began to feel intensely nervy and guilty about having brought an old wound back into the public eye. I hope David isn't coming to the dinner. Maybe I shouldn't have been so free with the information.

I have bought the book, had it signed and now the author and her guests are entering in pairs from the street into the clattery, crowded restaurant. Once through the crush I can see Jeremy, who left the selling to his assistants so he could come to the dinner. No sign of David. I made sure I was among the later comers so I could keep an eye on where he went but I lost sight of him on the way here.

Jeremy is at the long, over-chaired wooden table that hasn't shifted in the thirty years people have been coming here for this sort of occasion. There's a vacant place beside him. He beckons me over and I'm glad to fall on his neck.

He has risen greatly in wealth and respectability since the little literary booth he used to rent near Mad Meg. 'Hello! Too long, too long!' he cries, as I sit down, noticing, alas, that bloody Elspeth Roach has settled in a little further up the table on the other side. She smirks at me, but there's an involuntary kinking of the neck, I notice, as if she's been pricked in the carotid by the sight of a friendship she doesn't want me to have.

Jeremy, who has read the new book, is keen to reminisce about times when we were struggling to hold on to Mad Meg and the book booth against developers with megabucks to spend 'renovating' our precinct. Jeremy's once-black hair is white. He's much more distinguished and much less dishevelled than he used to be. He's given up smoking, doesn't drink and his kids are Nin's age – thirty-odd. He looks as though he's just out of a rejuvenating bath, his mucous membranes quite pink with glee as he hugs me to his chest.

'How are you anyway, Isobel?'

I give him a sloppy smooch but, as it would be a lie to say I'm fine, I say, 'Could be better.'

'Oh?'

'Well, my mother's been booted out of her nursing home and I have to find her another.'

'M-hm.'

'And…' I tap the table edge. 'I'm being sued. Maybe you know.'

'Oh that?' He holds me back and sits down, hiding his gleaming membranes with his lips. 'She's serious then?'

'Checkie loves a good sue.'

'M-hm.'

No cackles?

Uh-oh…

Don't tell me he thinks the Siècle Trust has a point?

I hate to say it, but I think I'm off on the wrong track here. I'm such an impulsive person. I wrench a fingernail off with my teeth. It's like being in a skid: you know you're in it, you know you have brakes, but you can't seem to apply them effectively to come to a graceful halt…

Jeremy glances over at Elspeth, but she's busy receiving her entrée. 'You know,' he says, sounding irritable all of a sudden, 'you shouldn't have dusted off that old fight at Mad Meg for this book. It's all water under the bridge.'

'It's not water under the bridge for me,' I say, my belly hardening.

'But it was just somebody in his cups slugging someone else in the wrong place.'

'Yeah, like my brother-in-law at the launch of my exhibition at the gallery coordinated by my sister, who happened to be his wife.'

Jeremy sighs. 'Time to bury the hatchet?'

'Where? In his great hairless head?'

'You're still upset? After all this time? It's thirty years, for Christ's sake!'

But there was the damage David did, the gashed and holed work, the slung red wine. It was an act of complete shithood. The Mad Meg collective decided, with one abstention, me, to leave the show on the walls and invite commentary. I, I wanted to take it down, go away, hide, mourn my paintings, rid myself of human-kind, but instead, the wrecked exhibition was photographed, written up, featured. People said, 'Sue!' and 'Get even!' but I was demoralised and the idea of suing was alien to me. I wouldn't have known where to start and it was quite clear where it would end – David hadn't any means of making restitution.

'I don't want to be known as a feminist test case,' I say, 'the exemplary victim – not then and not now. I want to be known for what I do. That's not too much to ask for a lifetime of trying.'

Jeremy says, 'So why bring it up again?'

'Mad Meg existed because of attitudes like David's, Jeremy. It existed so that people like me could make a name for ourselves as artists.'

'And Mad Meg got a lot of mileage out of it. It was written up everywhere. You couldn't talk about anything else for a long time.'

'I suffered because of it. My work suffered because of it.'

'And David suffered because of it.'

'And he shouldn't have?'

It's no wonder I stay home. I used to get on terrifically well with Jeremy. I can feel my eyeballs lumping up over my half-specs at him.

'Isobel, those were the days of happenings. You've got to get over things like that.'

'Mad Meg failed directly afterwards.'

'Because you guys didn't keep proper books, you were too idealistic.'

'You mean you've suffered similar setbacks to that brawl, Jeremy?'

'Sure, we all have them. You laugh them off.'

'Do you?'

'Remember when those bastards who wanted to redevelop us out of existence backed their fucking truck into my shop? I didn't run away and cry about it. I went to the papers. I got compo.'

'I didn't,' I say. And I wonder how Jeremy thinks you can compensate the destruction of an artist's inspiration. I was appalled by the thuggery, desolate – you can't compensate for that. It felt like murder to me.

'But you didn't even try to, Isobel. There was a lot of sympathy for you. You have to grab the moment.'

'Who from? Your sister's husband? David didn't have a crumb to his name. Allegra and I kept him in food, shelter and funds. And anyway, what if you don't want to be a celebrity because someone's made a victim of you?'

'But the whole town was talking about your work…'

'For the wrong reasons!'

'…and hunting you out for your opinion and you were nowhere to be seen. You left it all to the others.'

'My sister was suicidal…'

'Tons of people get suicidal.'

'But Allegra was dying inside. She died.'

'We all die.'

Well, what do you know? I'm in tears. Doesn't take much to get me into tears, does it, world?

He takes no notice and starts talking to the people opposite. 'There was an old drunk who used to wander around Mad Meg filching cask wine and blowing raspberries. What was his name, Isobel?'

I could get up and go home now and swear off Jeremy forever, but I have to be tougher than that and they have to see that I'm tougher. 'Tom Courtney,' I say, blowing my nose and feeling the wad of goo come down warm into my palm.

'Tom Courtney, that's right.' And he leans over to the ageing couple sitting opposite while I come off the sizzle. 'We used to call him Courtly Tom because he was a parole officer at Pentridge and used to go out there in his tux on the tram and teach the crims the trombone. Isobel's sister Allegra put up an installation at Mad Meg where you had to walk through a gigantic vagina dentata to watch a video of a cunt being masturbated at the end of it and old Tom goes marching through with his bottle in a brown paper bag and says, "What's wrong with that person's ear?"...'

And they laugh now just as we laughed then...

So...have I always been too twee? Too timid? Could I have stood my ground? I wonder where I'd be now if I'd stood my ground. Maybe I could have been a hearty relic on TV! A smiling bag of pulp.

'God, those developers,' says Jeremy. 'In every day, they were, trying to buy us out left, right and centre and that bloody step-mother of yours, Isobel, she developed Courtly Tom out of his derelict's home when she opened that monster up on the hill.'

I'm just going to tell the others about the fight we had on our hands to relocate the detoxifying pensioners out of the building that Viva bought to develop for Siècle – when 'I think Siècle's a lovely gallery, actually,' fires off Elspeth from where her ears have been pricking. 'One of the best things that ever happened to the art scene in Melbourne.'

'But I was just going to say to Jeremy...'

'I think some wonderful work's being done there. It's beauti-fully managed. David Silver runs their archive brilliantly.'

'Well, yes, Elspeth, I'm sure that's so. David is a born archivist.'

'A born artist, too.'

'He was here tonight,' says Jeremy, 'looking not too bad, I thought.'

So I say, 'What's with that bloody silly haircut, though?' Trying to sound like a woman with a good thick hide. 'Don't tell me he's taken a dislike to his own hair! He had a good head of hair, the silly bastard, all thick and dark and wavy…next, he'll be getting rid of his hands and feet just to spite himself. His hands and feet are the best parts of him…'

Across the table, Elspeth says, loudly, 'Well, Isobel, I haven't seen you for a long time. What have you been doing lately?'

As if she doesn't know.

'I've just had a show in town.'

'Really, whereabouts?'

'Didn't you receive an invitation? I'm sure I asked them to send you an invitation.'

'Oh, there might be one lying around somewhere.'

'It was a beaut show. I went and saw it,' says Jeremy. 'I would have been at the opening night, Bel, but there was that crazy alert for a freak storm.'

'Yeah,' I try to quash the psychic dust storm in my head so I can hear properly. The only way forward now is straight. 'I've never heard one of those before and I've lived in Melbourne most of my life. I've never heard of a cyclone this far south. But it didn't seem to make much difference to the attendance. There were lots of people.'

'I know,' says Jeremy, 'I saw it on the telly.'

'Telly yet?' goes Elspeth. 'Oh yes, I remember. I remember the gallery now. You have to pay to exhibit there, don't you? But I didn't think that the bit on telly was about your show. Wasn't it something about Siècle? Everyone was so preoccupied with what was happening to poor David, I didn't take it in.'

'What's happened to David?'

'Oh, you didn't know? He had to have half his lung out. He's got cancer.' As she says it, I can feel the blood lining up to get out of the capillaries in my cheeks. Why are people like this? Why can't they just be civil and quietly give you a piece of information you might not have? She's actually gloating as she primly slices through her rare beef entrée. I turn to look at Jeremy.

'Oh! Oh, that comes as quite a shock, actually…I didn't know.'

'You didn't?' he says.

I feel like saying well, why didn't you tell me, but I say, 'No, I didn't. Cancer – how long has he known?'

'Ten, twelve weeks,' says Jeremy. 'I don't know.'

'Did it start in the lung?'

'What difference does it make?' Elspeth snaps.

'Well, he used to smoke heavily,' I say, and I think of David inhaling cigarette smoke as if it were as vital to his being as mother's milk. He would draw it in until you knew his toes must be tingling with the hit of nicotine. I was always told I was too cocksure for words when I advised against it – David ate apple pips, apple pips had a substance he called 'laetrile' in them, 'laetrile' prevented cancer. I got my ear clipped for saying that the people around him weren't protecting themselves with apple pips, but they were breathing in the smoke from his cigarettes. 'We were always trying to make him cut down or give up. And then, if it's localised in the lung…'

'Oh he gave up ages ago,' says Elspeth, licking her lips.

It sends me off on the wrong track immediately because I hate it that people are so stubbornly ignorant about cigarettes. 'That doesn't mean he didn't get it from smoking. He smoked twenty to forty filterless a day for years.' What I say might be true, but you can bet your boots that the words are just bouts in a knockout comp.

'Lots of people who don't smoke die of lung cancer,' Elspeth lowers her lids to half mast and pulls her chin in disdainfully.

I'm about to say it's possibly because other people around them smoke, but I don't. Instead, I ask, 'And you say he's had the op?'

'He had half a lung out five weeks ago. I'm surprised you didn't know. He'd have told his daughter, surely.'

That leaves me teetering. The inference being that Nin would immediately have told me.

Jeremy says, 'It's marvellous how quickly people get back on their feet after surgery.'

A sigh heaves itself up clumsily out of my lungs and tumbles, unnoticed, into my lap. When David and his sparring partner destroyed my show, the commentary even reached the major papers, but David and his rival recovered – the rival, a bloke called Barry Bull, is hung all over the country and he has an AO. David's work is respected rather than celebrated, but he also writes and has developed a name for himself for that, as well. People talk about him as if he were some kind of genius – all I can say is that I've never met such a contradictory person – at his wedding to Allegra, he kissed me, ran his hand down my forearm and said in the gentlest of all possible voices, 'You have ugly arms.' It was meant to be an endearment. Ugly arms, for fuck's sake!

'Oh I expect he'll pull through,' goes Elspeth. 'They can do marvellous things these days. When I spoke to him tonight, he said he only had a few hot spots in the bone.'

'A few hot spots in the bone!' Unintentionally, I hit the end of my waiting fork and it somersaults onto the floorboards. 'So the malignancy has spread?'

'That doesn't mean he'll die.'

'You mean it doesn't mean he'll live, Elspeth.'

'Oh, rubbish!'

But it's not rubbish. I bend down and scrabble around for my fork on the floor. She's stupider than I remember. I find it overwhelmingly extraordinary that everyone at the table – they all have good educations – thinks he'll pull through. They're all going at it now, hammer and tongs. Mind over matter: this one knowing that one who drank his own piss and lived. And look at so-and-so…it's all just the story of cure in the nick of time to them.

'He says he's going to fight it,' says Elspeth, smugly. 'So you can eat your meal in peace, can't you, Isobel? Or can you? Anyway,' she continues, 'we're celebrating Bronwyn's book launch. Here's to the author!' and Elspeth wields her wine glass on high. 'To Bronwyn.'

'Bitch!' hurdles my lips but in such strangled tones she doesn't hear and Jeremy shoots me a behind-the-glass query. 'He'll die from it,' I say.

And he asks under the hubbub how I know that.

'It's not a question of how I know it, Jeremy. It's a question of how I feel about it. And if you want to know, I feel bloody awful.'

I don't know whether anyone's chosen to tell Nin about David. Or she'd have told me, surely?

Surely?

Still, she may not have…

'So you don't hate him, after all?' asks Jeremy.

'It's not a question of love or hate. It's a question of being and non-being. He's tested extreme feelings in me for years and years.'

'So at least you know you have extreme feelings?'

'Something like that. Everyone's contradictory but I never met somebody as against himself as David. He's a bastard and yet he's managed to produce some charming art.'

'Sure…' Jeremy pats my shoulder and gets up to go to the loo, leaving me sitting in a painful place.

I'd just bought my house when David went berserk. I'd scrimped and saved for a deposit while under fire from the collective whose slogan was 'property is theft'. Stella found the house, actually – in her interminable befriending she'd come across an estate agent who took to her and worked a bargain for me. Eli and I moved into a little weatherboard on a huge piece of land in the staid Eastern Suburbs. After the show wreck, Allegra fled the digs we'd shared with David and came to me with Nin.

Finding himself alone in premises rented by someone else, David didn't know what to do. All he could think of was making himself indispensible to Viva and Checkie, keeping the door and helping with the hangs at Siècle. Checkie became his ally against me during Allegra's troubles and her death.

He's been Checkie's archivist now for years. He's good at it. He used to be a good painter, too, but he's always been fastidious, as if he hated getting paint on his fingers and clothes and he stopped using real paint long ago. Now he creates artists' books and I certainly don't begrudge him those.

Dear little books, they are, almost gamine, like Nin. Books with word nests in them, dainty, gorgeous words, roosting in the corners of pages – not a whacking great vagina dentata and a video of masturbation – you can't accuse David of sledgehammering in his art. And through the pages are neatly cut little passages that play new roles each time the page is turned. In a book he made for Nin that was inspired by the night Stella's furniture ran amok in her room and knocked her cold, the contents of a house ran through the pages to empty itself into a night party on a back lawn. Chairs and tables cavort and spring. Sheets and almond blossom fly away together to some life where the essence of good sheets is distilled in the senses. I was very taken with it when she showed me. I don't begrudge him his talent. It reminds me of *Une Semaine de Bonté*. He was the first person to draw my attention to Ernst and I'm glad he did. It's just that you wouldn't think the man who created such lovely things and had such delightful thoughts was capable of brutality and filthy rages, and David is.

Everyone is eating around me and my meal is slow in coming. Forks click, knives screech and lips are smacked – a game of who can devour their food with the greatest self-satisfaction.

I hated David for a long time for his sabotage; my emotions had me by the throat – here comes my pasta and once again I find that my emotions have me by the throat. He and his quarry thumped each other in the small space of Mad Meg, doing far more harm to my work than to each other – that's the way it is with brutes; brutes are so cowardly they even rampage with caution. They broke glass, threw wine and put holes through things – not neatly cut, sweet little holes, but jags and clout holes – yet they didn't need medical attention for their own wounds. I should hate him still. One moment he'll utter his favourite saying, 'we are what we do' and the next he'll be so over-brimming with jealousy – or is it genuine loathing for what makes my art – that he can't control his rage and wrecks what I do.

But he's just another person – I always tell myself that, just another person – and plenty of people are as two-faced as he is. Every day people do nastier things than destroy an exhibition. They rape, murder, pillage and silence. Eli sees it all the time.

Jeremy has told Elspeth that a rich bloke bought a painting of mine (actually, he bought the triptych, which is a cause for joy) and she's saying how she hates rich people and how the world is full of suffering children 'and they'll all be dead before tea time'.

I can't help myself from interjecting, 'Well, that's the trouble, isn't it, Elspeth? They won't be and you'll have to deal with them all over again at breakfast.' She looks me up and down, surprised. Yes, people do worse things than destroy exhibitions. They destroy souls; they rip up reputations…or worse again, children.

David was a ripped-up, abused child who turned into a vandal, but Nin doesn't need me to hate him – she's the only family he has left. There's already enough enmity between David and my mother – and because of that, I shall control myself. And I shall not say that if David has lung cancer, it's because he's been setting himself up for it for years…

'What's the matter with your dinner, Isobel?' goes Elspeth. 'Eat up, it'll get cold.'

I was just raising my fork to my lips to bite off a clump of spaghetti, but when she says that, I slop in some wine instead. My mouth is very dry. God I make myself laugh sometimes, I'm just like a dear old mate of mine who, not knowing what it was, took a chunk out of a red hot chilli in front of Checkie at an opening and when Checkie threw up her hands in horror, proceeded to quaff down the lot, saying, 'Delicious, eat 'em all the time. You should try one, Checkie.' Her mouth and oesophagus were numb for days and everything went numb for days at the other end too once the chilli worked its way through.

'What's funny?' asks Elspeth.

'Private joke,' I say, wishing that my dear old pal were with me now; she modelled for the show David wrecked. It was called

The Crushing. I had her with her flaxen hair and pink, vulnerable skin push up against panes of glass as if she were being crushed to death in a stampede. My fingers still remember the drawings. They were almost the best I ever did.

'I hate it when people won't share jokes.'

'Well, you'll just have to hate it, then.' But Elspeth has started jabbing her fork at someone else while I ferret in my bag for a saliva-inducing tablet – fancy being reliant on pills for your saliva! Can't even work up a good spit!

Pathetically, David bought me a new easel and a box of paints by way of reparation, came knocking at my door to deliver them but I told him straight and plain to go away. I didn't even yell 'Fuck off!' although Allegra did and threw a pot plant at him.

In a tight corner, I could forgive Allegra for suspending her ideology to come and live with me in my bourgeois setting, but I was angry about the pot plant; it was an orchid I was trying to propagate as part of Beryl Blake's project. Allegra wouldn't have known what the orchid was – she was in a rage and it was a missile. I picked up the bits and started to cry and she said she was sorry and would buy me another; she'd thought it was dying anyway. She had no clue. I'd been working with that plant for weeks, coaxing it along and finding out how it worked. To her, it looked just like the clump of spaghetti that sits in my oesophagus now, straining to make it down into my stomach. My chest is tight.

Well, it was all a long time ago, I tell myself. And even if the episode did contribute to Allegra's death, there were plenty of other things that made her want to die – like she wanted the world to change. She wanted women to be as free and powerful as men. Bitches like Elspeth hijacked her thoughts and turned them back on her, used her ladders to install themselves in power coteries and set themselves up for the money vamp when it rode into town with its blankets, beads and knives, while in the background, only just audible, Allegra's ghost was saying that you couldn't be bought if you weren't for sale.

I'll have to wait for the bolus of spaghetti to move on.

She died not long after she pitched my pot plant and that's when I learned something I hadn't anticipated. I don't anticipate much, but I should have known that David would badmouth us carelessly enough to have Viva and Checkie making us out to have been a pair of fools with our doings at Mad Meg, a drag on our father's career.

David took up their chant, adopted their self-righteous posture.

But I'm pretty certain Dadda loved us no matter that we were no good at arithmetic. I'm pretty certain he was quite proud of us, even if we weren't going to make any money. We were emotional. We made him cry, he made us cry – the tears were a measure of the love. When he died, Allegra and Eli and I – there was no Nin back then – barricaded ourselves into his hospital room and wouldn't let Viva in. She thought our behaviour was 'Risible! Risible!' Allegra went round for weeks then, calling me Isible.

Viva could have put us out of our ignorant misery about her role in Dadda's life when that happened but she didn't. She waited until Allegra was dead before telling me. It was hard not to feel despised during that long night – all night long, the bay water at the Laurington beach house where Viva told her story sloshed in and out of the history I'd been excluded from. Harry Laurington sent me down there. I wasn't expecting Viva – I just wanted to be in the place where she'd scattered Dadda's ashes. I wasn't allowed to know where she'd done it for a long time. All night long I had that low, bruised voice of hers telling me the story of my Coretti grandparents – how the name Allegra came from my grandmother and she couldn't describe the devastation she felt that my mother had been allowed to use it, while she, out of deference, had restrained herself and only bestowed the second name, Cecilia, on Checkie. She made it sound as if Checkie were Dadda's only genuine child.

It was so humiliating that she knew so much more about my father than I did and so very much more about him than poor Stella did.

I need some cold water.

Viva used to say that Allegra and I were directionless but we had direction all right. We were passionate; we used our passion to fight for women's stake in the world. First and foremost we fought for recognition of women's work. Mad Meg might have gone broke and been superseded by the reassertion of capitalist values but there were achievements. Feminism isn't dead – perceptions, expectations and conditions were changed in women's favour, the momentum goes on. A number of our painters are still working away, even if we've been subsumed by a world that doesn't continue the fight for our status.

'Please, may I have some cold water?' I ask the waiter's retreating back. He catches my request, turns and asks, 'Perrier or Mountain Springs? Sparkling or flat?'

'Tap,' I say, making a stand. God, I'm pathetic – but I will keep on fighting, bugger it, I will, I will!

The waiter nips into the nearby gents' with some ice in a glass, returns and clunks the water down in front of me, hard, not even looking. My chest's been splashed, but at least it's cold. I clink the cubes in the glass and sip. I can feel my chest opening up a bit. 'To Isobel,' I think. 'Honest water and cool ice to Isobel.'

And to Allegra: young, beautiful, famous and dead, people have been dropping her name for decades. To Allegra, the glorious harpy!

But if I was Allegra's daughter rather than her sister, I'd want to hate her for leaving me behind. Allegra used to say she was a lousy mother and she probably was, but that's no excuse. There are lots of lousy mothers who stick around – I know one intimately. Or is that unfair? Other people love her. She's helped a lot of people, been hospitable, kind…

Now Elspeth's talking about Jan Laird's Paris project and decrying it. 'Have you seen it yet?' she snaps at me – as if I go to Paris as a matter of course every year or so. 'It's ludicrous,' she continues – oh, I forgot about that word 'ludicrous': another of the critics' favourites – it's got nothing to do with Ludo, but a lot to do with game playing. 'Oh, but you like her work, don't you? You like pretty things.'

'Pretty things!'

'Glass and mosaics and crafts like that…'

I pick up the glass and hurl what remains of the water at her. Time to go.

Coming home in this condition – having to drink to stay sane — makes you think twice about being sociable. Does Nin know about David? I haven't had time to see her, although I left a message on her phone to contact me when she can.

6

I've decided that I hate artists and artists' coteries. They are all so full of themselves they can't talk straight about anything. It's always got to be one-upmanship: I'm smarter than you, I'm better than you, you're a talentless bore. Scientists aren't quite as bad as that. You can't get past the fact that a good scientist talks sense. A good scientist is logical and logic is Ariadne's thread – it brings us from the dark into the light of day.

I've made an appointment at the university with my good friend and former colleague in the orchid work, Vance. He's a retired professor these days. He'll be able to set me straight about the gravity of David's cancer. I really don't think there's any chance he'll pull through and I want to be standing on firm ground when Nin finally contacts me.

The first foxgloves of the year are out in the university gardens. There's a honey bee buzzing up a trumpet of one outside the library. How busy it is. If it was a European bumblebee, it wouldn't have to buzz to dislodge the pollen from where it is neatly stowed in batons above its wings, because it would fit exactly, but the Australian bee, being littler, has to work hard for its reward. There it goes now, its proboscis full of nectar to dehydrate into food for the hive and its leg baskets full of pollen for the next flower.

Vance made sure I have access to a library card for having been a research collaborator here and I've just been to the library to stock up. If I'm ever down a mine, may it be lined with books and I will bring to the surface every kind of wealth you can imagine. This place feeds me and makes me want to live. It is full of untouched plunder. I love coming here and it's thanks to my freaky employment history that I can.

I'm thinking of Beryl in Vance's anteroom and how we used to work together in the labs in this building in the height of the summer heat when the students were on holidays. It was on this side of the building, taking the full force of the sun. A puddle used to develop around Beryl's feet. It's all air-conditioned now. Vance's secretary buzzes him. She's shaped like a very large bee and happens to be wearing a striped yellow blazer. Vance has become important; he speaks here, there and everywhere about modern methods in cancer detection and so you have to make appointments to see him. His door whooshes open in milliseconds after the buzz; there he stands, chocolate-eyed and smiling. 'Isobel!' Deep velvety voice. I love old Vance. Enormous hands conduct me into his professorial lair.

Comrades.

His lair commands quite a sweep of campus. It's in the ginkgo and lemon-scented gum precinct, presently barricaded off with striped plastic no-go zones and wire grid compounds as the buildings grow bigger and better, higher and newer. To walk here makes me realise that the irreplaceable me of yesteryear has been replaced. These days we are told it is healthy to live in the present, but the older you get the more there is in the present to resent the loss of.

From inside Vance's room — which smells of medical handwash and warm vinyl — you'd think this building was really rather swish, when in actual fact it's a timeworn, concrete bunker with a slow lift and so many chips out of its fire escapes they're practically ramps. It used to be two floors shorter and, on the occasions when I worked here, the crush inside meant that we had to breathe in to get past each other and we'd bump elbows working at the same bench. In those days, when people had just learned to cut and splice genes, work went on in any space. There was equipment in corridors. The esprit de corps was high. Information was freely exchanged, shouted between labs — it isn't these days; now that gene sequences and sequencing methods are top secret, everyone's specialising and all the labs have security doors. It could be so hot over summer here that the molten agar we used to pour plates to grow our specimens on would fail to set in the Petri dishes.

It was before people knew about genetic markers and how to isolate them. Beryl and Vance were collaborating on methods for propagating the rarely seen and vulnerable Australian orchids that only flourish after bushfires. Vance was interested in the genetic aspects and Beryl was the propagation expert. The orchids are parasitic on certain types of fungus which they exploit for their value as delving, ramifying, moisture-supplying root systems and you have to inoculate sterile media with the appropriate fungus first up and then seed that with orchid seeds that are so tiny they don't carry enough nutrients to mature without input from some-where else – hence their parasitism. It was my job to isolate the appropriate fungus from the soil of orchids found in the wild and to get it going in purified form so Vance and Beryl could seed it. Later, they employed me to help them find out how the orchid got itself penetrated by the fungus so it could sprout – another bit of ingenious allure – God, orchids are lazy. (Or maybe fungi aren't choosy.)

My mother and sister thought that working with genes was shady. They deplored the conditions in both the gardens and the labs. The garden shacks were primitive and it was beneath my mother's dignity to have a daughter who 'worked in a shed'. My sister said it was exploitation to make people work in such conditions.

Whatever my relatives thought, I've never been grand or ideological in my tastes. At the time, nutting out obscure problems was an ideal escape from having been dumped by Arnie. Beryl, who, having personal problems of her own, took mine for granted, used to say that even if everyone in the country worked hell for leather on Australian botanical species, they'd never get the job of classification done before extinction caught up with them. In those days we imagined we were saving Australian flora for posterity.

One discovery Vance and I made in the 1980s, after extinction leapt up out of the bottle and claimed Beryl, was that rare Australian orchids don't pay their way. Brilliant tricksters they might be, but in the scheme of things, they're useless: they're too small, you can't sell them in flower shops, they have no export value, nobody needs to be cured of them and there were more profitable ways for Vance to spend his time. Nowadays the orchids occupy land that has the potential to be developed and thus to keep people in much-needed jobs and to create wealth. It's no longer a question of saving Australian flora for posterity but of exterminating them for posterity – for who will thank us for tiny orchids if they have no McMansions to test their mortgage-paying propensities in and no takeaway food to feed their children when they're at work all day, saving their splendid kitchens from being cooked in and their dishwashers from giving up the ghost in case they have to sell up in a hurry?

Vance is lanky and very tall, his pants are always an inch or two too short, so he has a nice selection of socks – navy blue with a small red paisley design today I see as he puts his feet up on his smart new desk. Long, thin, soft-soled shoes of the sort my mother deplores; shoes that gape at the top and whose laces pull the leather into scallops over the arch. He bids me sit down in one of the low front-row-of-the-auditorium padded chairs scientists prefer, particularly the long-legged ones like Vance who can flex their quads and glutes and give their ankles a work-out while sitting back, relaxed and ominous, and terrifying to novice seminar-givers. Never having been a front-row girl, sinking into the chair makes me feel like a mere pleat in the vinyl; I used to like to sit up tall on something hard, unthreatening and further back, among the ignorati.

'Hot spots in the bone,' he says. 'Doesn't sound good, Isobel. Lost half a lung, you say?' Soft glance over the top of the specs. 'Under most circumstances that would mean he was healthy enough to undergo the surgery and his oncologist thought it could cure him. But "hot spots in the bone"…' Sorrowful head shaking. 'The removal of the lung is probably palliative because the lung's rotten.' He swings his legs down to the carpet, stands, hands in pockets, stretches his back and strolls to the window. 'I agree with you, it doesn't look good.' Turns to face me, one elbow on the window ledge, the other weighing up a ball of air. 'Mean survival rate about eighteen months?' He flicks his thick brows at me.

'I thought as much.' Maybe Vance is expecting me to burst into expressions of grief, but it isn't grief I want, I want facts. I must look ungrieving, because he continues, matter-of-factly now sauntering back to his desk, scientist to scientist, 'Metastases in the bone means advanced disease, as you no doubt know. Maybe one person in fifty might last five years…You say he smoked?'

'Yes. But he gave up some years ago.'

He stands pondering the ceiling's soundproofing, hands back in pockets, 'Yes, well, cancer can take years to become a tumour – even as long as forty years. People are stupid about it.'

'I was stupid. I smoked.'

He laughs, and says over his shoulder, 'I know. I used to smoke yours, don't you remember?'

That's true. It was at that time that scientists started giving up cigarettes and Vance was half-hearted about it, being a bit too young to be absolutely serious. He's only six years older than I am – but heaps more qualified. Lots of the middle-aged senior staff here had pipes and made out that pipes did less harm to the lungs – but the puritans, who were also top-of-the-heap experimenters, weren't fooled: all sorts of people were dying early deaths from lung cancer and academic distinction didn't save them.

'I smoked with a baby on board.'

'But you were only a baby yourself. And how is Eli?'

'I'm not sure I know, but he's bound to be fixing the world wherever he is right now. Mothers are the last to hear.'

'Oh, I fixed the world once,' Vance laughs, 'only it broke again.' He pats down his fine, dark baby hair onto the balding head underneath.

'Yes, I remember your turn at fixing,' I say. 'You had a lot of fun at it, but I suppose the world can only be fixed so many times before it's so stuffed it has to be chucked out.'

'Well, we had a jolly good go at chucking it out, Bel, but it was too big to fit in the bin!'

'So you reckon it's going to chuck us out instead?'

'Seriously,' he picks up the pin tray from his desk and turns it round and round slowly in the very wide span of his fingertips – I used to draw Vance's hands when he wasn't looking, their hugeness makes their fluid and able articulation stand out, 'I think we've got a while yet. We make progress. We learn a lot. We might be much more powerful wreckers than ever before, but we're also much more powerful thinkers. I'm sanguine about the future. The young are adaptable. The ones I've met have good ideas. I don't like all this doom and gloom crap.'

He puts down the pin tray and sits down, tenting his fingertips under his chin.

I'd forgotten how pro-science Vance is. It's his religion and he's trying to cheer me up with it. 'Some of the young are very good communicators,' he says.

'And some of them not so good. My lot never answer their phones. I'm trying to find out if Nin knows about David without upsetting the apple cart. Sometimes she makes it bloody impossible not to.'

'Oh yes, Nin. Gee, have we been talking about her father here – that louse who vandalised your show…and your poor sister, I seem to remember?'

'Yeah.'

'You've been too good to him. Did he ever get round to helping you bring up Nin?'

'What do you reckon? He was a great nuisance. He's never been capable of bringing up a kid. I was never able to get proper custody of Nin because he'd make it so difficult, threatening to counter-sue then withdrawing the threat then tormenting us with phone calls at every fluctuation of his mood. When we moved away after Allegra died I had my phone number privately listed and he didn't have the nous to find out how to contact us. Apparently – after having resisted learning to drive for years – he went out and got his licence, drove up to the area where we were, drove around like a maniac for a while, couldn't find us, ran out of money and drove back to Melbourne. By the time he got back, the car was undrivable. Anyway, he only ever had an intermittent income, we were better off not being tormented by him and he didn't have the living skills to persevere with a custody case.'

'Does it matter that he's going to die?'

'Well, no doubt it does to him!'

'But to you?'

'I'm not sure. I really don't know how I feel about David – all I can think of is the word "dreadful", and that refers to my state of mind. We tried to have a relationship with him when we came back to live in Melbourne again, but it was pretty soul-destroying. By the most rotten of coincidences, my mother and David have birthdays within a week of each other: we tried, with disastrous consequences, having a joint celebration, but the tensions would start the moment the arrangements were made – David would be coming, then he wouldn't be coming, then he'd swear off coming, but the moment we were all seated in the restaurant, he'd turn up with a bottle of plonk and sit down beside "my daughter" and Mum would primp up her lips and start to snipe. They'd squabble – a couple of times we were thrown out of restaurants and then taxi drivers would see a fight in progress and wouldn't pick us up.'

'What? Real physical fighting?'

'Yeah. She'd slam into him with her handbag and he'd start kicking her in the shins. It was dreadful. Poor Nin would spend the month of May in tears and I'd spend it trying to comfort her while David either behaved like a pint-sized Rottweiler or, to make things up to her, bought books or carefully chosen artwork. By the time Nin's birthday rolled around in October, there'd be competing invitations, disjointed noses and more weeping. Nin and I would do mutual strengthening exercises and sometimes we'd plan to leave them to it. "Let them tear each other apart," we'd say, "then we won't have to put up with them anymore." And we'd fantasise a restaurant scene in which Stella and David created mayhem and were carted off by the police and flung into jail for a long time while we went to Paris. "Would we visit them?" we'd ask each other and say, "Nah!" and curl our lips and shake our heads.

'A couple of Christmases ago, Nin's partner's mother, who's a climate-change activist, bought David a barometer and he said, "What do I want one of those for? I don't care about the bloody weather." The partner's mother yelled out, "Well, you ought to!" And he yelled back, "Don't tell me what to think, you stupid twerp!" And the Christmas lunch that Nin had prepared was wrecked. He's just a walking antagonism.'

'You've been much too tolerant, Bel. It's ridiculous.'

He's right, so I change the subject and we talk for a while about his family. Suzanne and Vance couldn't have children, so they adopted two of them. I don't really know the younger one, but the elder is a daughter called Lexie. She's now over forty and runs a vineyard in the hills above the Yarra Valley with her husband. After the drought had been going for five years, Lexie and her husband thought about a second income stream and built a storage facility into the hillside under their crop and I store with them. I was up there recently putting away the remnant of pictures from my show and I had lunch with Lexie at her cellar-door restaurant.

'It's not common knowledge that I store with Lexie,' I say to Vance. 'I'm under attack again for the ownership of my father's paintings and they'd pounce on me if they knew I stored them in a fire-prone area.'

'But they're bloody good storage facilities, Bel. I'm not just saying that because of Lexie. You know, they've been very thorough: they've got climate control, security cameras and you couldn't beat their rack system, it's terrific. It's state of the art.'

'Oh yes, I know that, Vance, but just for now, it would be better not to reveal that my father's pictures are up there.'

'Well, you'd go a long way to find storage as good as Lexie's. It's full of safety features. The family are planning to sit out a fire there if they get caught. Truly, it's that safe.'

'Do you still have your bush patch up there, Vance?'

'Sure. Although it's pretty weedy these days. I haven't seen the profusion of orchids we used to get for a long while.'

'No rain.'

'No fire. That's what makes them germinate.'

'Yeah. Well, there's bound to be a fire. You can't go this long without water and not have a major fire.'

'Twenty-four years since the last one.'

'Gosh yes. Remember that dust storm? I was here that day, the sun was just a little red patch in a dirt-coloured sky and it was raining flaming gum trees all over the city.'

'We can expect more like that.'

'Climate change?'

'Yes. They're predicting much fiercer weather events. The statistics have changed.'

'It's not because we're better at measuring than we used to be?'

'No,' he says. 'The core samples and the data coincide. The weather's changed.'

'Everything's changing. The world at the top of the Faraway Tree keeps moving on. It used to be really free here in our day, didn't it? I mean in this building. You didn't have to pussyfoot about with secret numbers to punch into doors. We shared. We were optimistic, open. Now science has become a business. How do you feel about that?'

He pulls meditatively on his earlobe and says, 'Inevitable.'

'I don't think that's how you used to feel. I thought you were pretty passionately for an open environment in science.' He was, I know, because he used to lead debates about it.

'We lost that argument. And anyway, people who've got talent in making science pay made it pay. We were so strapped for funds before that happened we couldn't have done anything like what we've managed after setting up the new system. It's not as if discoveries are kept secret indefinitely; there's a time limit on withholding information.' His calm voice has developed a crack in it. 'Look, Isobel,' he continues, tapping the tented fingertips together again – so stiffly, he never had stiff fingers in the past – and leaning towards me earnestly, 'Selling stuff is one thing; science is another…'

I leap in…why do I always leap in? But my mouth is saying before I can stop it, 'I know they're different species, Vance, but one has compromised the other. Marketing is the orchid and science the delving fungus on which it feeds. The fungus doesn't need the orchid.'

The new crack in Vance's voice is a hard, sad, crack, like a neat, smacked, one-run cricket ball. He used to hit sixes and make hundreds at every innings. 'I'm sorry Vance, but I feel we've been robbed of something.'

'But Bel, research takes investment, and investment needs money, heaps of money. We can't just doodle along and say, "Oh, look, this is a good doodle"…'

'Like I do.'

'No Bel, you're an artist.'

'It's not a job you get paid for. And I often wonder what it is I *do*, Vance. In terms of world enterprise and contribution to the great "going forward" of humankind?'

'Paint pictures. I can't paint pictures for nuts. And you're a clever person, Bel, the world needs clever people.'

'Not clever artists.'

'Your work has more meaning than you think. Remember all those ideas we had way back when? They've borne fruit. Who'd have thought you could go from looking at the interaction between a plant seed and a fungus to mapping cell-surface markers on breast cancers? We learned a lot about nature's tricks with our little model.'

'But you could have done all that without me.'

'That's just what I couldn't have done. The point is that I did it *with* you. We did it together. And now you're doing what you alone can do. Look at it this way – ideas are parasites on people. You can be a person without having any ideas but you're a person with them. Think of orchids as marvellous experiments in life forms. They are, you know. They're authentic beings.'

7

✿✿✿

I used to enjoy spending my life in the company of clever people like Vance. Clever pursuits take your mind off grief. Making discoveries is joyful. The sap rises and splashes through your brain when experiments reveal good thinking and Ariadne's thread leads you on to do it again. It doesn't work like that in art. The will to create comes in spurts and unless you can live with your art obsessively and all the time, it comes out in spurts and not as a considered, long-term pursuit. To be a good artist you have to work at it constantly; the best art grows continually and smoothly and not in spurts. You come to a point where the dialogue has to be continuous or it is damaged. My life's not right for the continuous dialogue. Living around Stella is like flying a plane with felt propellers. I have to pretend a different reality to find my concentration.

There were no places vacant with the Protestants except the one that refused us.

I've tried the Anglicans twice. After all, she's an Anglican. I still can't get out of my mind the place that looked like a converted garage; it makes you wonder about the accreditation laws that Narrowlea is closing down rather than this place. I'd hesitate to put a human being in there for any reason. I realise this about the Anglicans: they care for the very poor and the very rich – people like my mother they leave to the Protestants. The second Anglican hostel I saw was far too expensive.

So that left us with the Baptists, the Jews and the Catholics. The Baptists weren't taking and if they were, they'd want an arm and a leg by way of deposit. The Jewish home was frenetic: an old business woman with dementia was joy-riding the lift and circulating through the lounge rooms, checking 'the staff'. 'The staff' were, by and large, holocaust survivors. There's a place at the Jewish home but I have to admit that this is not my mother's cultural milieu.

There are a hundred people to rehouse from Narrowlea. I've scouted the entire neighbourhood within a twenty kilometre radius of home for vacant places and found four. There are two places with the Catholics. First, I rushed to the Catholic home near Narrowlea and practically collided with another woman doing the same thing. This was a nice home and I would willingly have taken the place, but I felt I ought to defer to the other seeker because she has a father to place and her mother is in the nursing home over the road from this hostel, so I ended up ringing the second Catholic home, Holy Redeemer.

Holy Redeemer is further away but has 'full facilities for ageing in place' and has a vacancy. So here we are at their activities day.

I've developed a need for a view, or a taste, anyway, since the need can't be met. When we lived at Reg Sorby's retreat, we could see the Great Dividing Range spreading in all directions, north-westerly to distant plains and south-easterly, plunging and rising, a vast dolphin pod, to the invisible coast. Eagles and swifts would soar above the dark clustered canopy and in my heart I would soar with them, so sure was I that flying creatures love to fly.

Yet sometimes it was too grand for me, that view, the cumulus rising up and up until it seemed crowned by an empurpled sun-shaft-hurling Queen Victoria whose chariot wheels seemed apt to grind the mountains down under her dominion.

It's easy to feel like that when you're Australian, especially an Australian of polyglot origins – half of them British – as most Australians are. God alone knows how the Aboriginals feel and have felt through two hundred years of it. Imagine Queen Victoria living the life of an Aboriginal…well, you can't, she didn't and that's the point.

Funny that Queen Victoria was only five feet tall and yet threw such a shadow across the empire on which the sun never set. Ridiculous really, one of the ludicrous facts of history. A fact that warped the grand vista – painters like David and Gros are to blame in their apotheosis of that other short person who threw a long shadow, Napoleon, back in the days when it could be said that what painters did spoke for the way people carried the great world in their heads.

For me, a simple view from a window into a garden can be enough, like looking out from Mick's sitting room in the country to catch sight of a ginger-brown butterfly in liquid sunlight delighting in moving air over new-mown lawn. Looking out makes me forget myself and want to enter the view, have it in my pores, *be* it – perhaps that's why I think this aged care place is such a good one. It's on a high knoll above a green park down in the dell beneath. Here and there are stands of white-trunked eucalypts, the sort that lose their bark in spring, exposing a delicate green tracery, like the lees of broken bubbles. You can see remnants of a Federation garden; old palm trees up the drive to the house are yanked up like schoolgirls' ponytails in intricate braids with teased-out tips.

But I stand alone at windowsills; Stella isn't interested in views. She'd rather look at the appointments and the furniture. We are in the manager's office. 'Nice old desk,' she says, blowing her ever-dribbling nose and raising the drape rosettes that used to be her eyebrows.

'Did you like da room, Stella?' booms the manager, an explosive Dutchman called Kees.

'Oh it was right enough. But I'm not a Catholic,' and she fidgets with a Kleenex in as Anglican a fashion as she can.

'Nor am I,' he booms again, a man with no control on his volume knob. 'I'm an atheist. Da sisters say prayers for me but it makes no difference. You don't have to be Catholic to be in here. Da point is, did you like da room?'

'Oh it's nice, yes. But there's a man's clothes in it.'

'Oh, well we'll have to rustle him up to come and keep you company,' he cackles.

Not to be outshouted, Stella erupts angrily, 'THERE WAS A MAN'S SUIT IN IT, you oaf.'

'All right, all right. We just hadn't removed dat suit. We ought to have, but people don't always get around to what dey ought to do.'

'I ought to pull your nose!' She would, too, if she were steadier on her feet: she pulled the nose of her GP-before-last when he said she was passive-aggressive.

'Mumma,' I say, 'it's a nice room. It has a little garden you can look out onto. And, really Mumma, it's the nicest room I've seen.'

'BUT IT WAS A MAN'S ROOM.'

I bend closer to her, bringing her eyes in line with mine, 'Well, how about we just try it for a start, eh? There was a dear little sitting room nearby where we can make tea and there's a television, a radio and a piano in there. I think the people here know how to live in groups, not like Narrowlea…'

'But they're all nuns and priests!'

'Only some of them. There are lots of folk in here like you too.'

She has mutilated the Kleenex and her eyes are glistening.

'But what about the petrol?' The bottom lip quivers, like the lip of a child who is going to wet its pants with fear.

'Never mind the petrol.'

'What about the poor car?'

'You needn't feel sorry for the car, Mumma. The point is if you don't like the room, we'll have trouble finding another one as nice. Look, you'll have your own little bathroom and they can supply you with a very comfy chair and you'll be able to watch whatever telly programs you like, or look at some of your books or look out onto the garden…'

'Onto the garden! Huh!'

'Well then, I've heard they've got a walking group and we saw on the way that the gardens and houses round here are very pretty.'

'But it's hilly,' she whimpers.

God turn me into an amiable old cat when I'm senile…with a humane, non-autistic vet nearby. My dentist's autistic; I wouldn't want to be dispatched by him.

Kees yells, 'Well, let's come along den and join de others. Dey're having deir afternoon tea; Sister Angela is playing the piano and someone's come in to sing.'

Stella knows it's just about her last chance, so she puts the Walkathon down purposefully on the carpeted floor and rickets along in its wake. The dining room is broad and long and light, the main room of the old house in its park-like surrounds. The old people are sitting in groups of about eight around tables neatly set with white cloths and light blue china tea things and up on a raised stage by the furthest windows, little Sister Angela in a cardie, skirt and flatties that only just reach the pedals is playing incidental tunes crisply and well while she waits for the singer who's probably the old bloke we saw having a gargle near the tropical fish tank in the hallway. A number of the religious here are obviously retired teachers and so they are articulate and have some skills. That's surely a plus? Whatever Stella thinks. I've actually seen talking in groups in this place.

Oh please, Stella, please, just like it for my sake. I know it's you who has to live here, but everything else I've seen is so drear or inappropriate, so waiting-for-death. Why does it have to be my decision? I suppose you would say, 'Well, it was you who decided to sell my house!' And you'd be right. I sold it sooner than sell my own, but when we moved back to Melbourne, because the Siècle Trust put caveats on Dadda's paintings and we were unable to sell them, I was forced to sell mine, too. If I was cruel and high-handed with you, I had to do the same thing to myself – we were forced to rethink. It sometimes happens. Sometimes there just isn't the money in the kitty to provide the things you need. Sometimes you have to change the things you need to fit the kitty and we did change them, Stella. You bought your cottage and I bought mine. And now yours is gone because you are too old to live in it and we needed the money for your care and because the care failed you, here we are…

The woman in charge of the leisure program, Rosa, comes up to us, looking to me like the real version of what Hollywood idealised in Sophia Loren – curvily and lustily Italian, the hooped earrings, the dark hair bronzed to hide the grey, the lips full and riding her face like a boat on a pleasure trip. She has the accent of first generation. She says, 'Wailcome, Stella,' and sashays on ahead of us to the table where we are to sit. Some of the people I met on my preliminary visit last week are sitting here: a teaching sister from country Victoria called Sister Colleen who can't be much older than I am, a little old Babushka doll of a Russian woman and an ample woman of about eighty with a moon-shaped face, called Mary, who seems especially pleased to see us and sympathetic about our dilemma with the Protestants. 'It's cruel,' says Mary, 'downright cruel. It won't happen here, Stella, just you come and live with us.' The Babushka nods smilingly in agreement and Mary adds, 'We've got Sister Colleen to protect us, haven't we Sister?'

Sister Colleen says, 'Welcome Stella,' in the accent of eighth generation, and holds out her hand to squeeze Stella's. Stella winces in pain because her arthritic nodes are tender, but Sister Colleen just runs her tongue up under her top lip, chasing a crumb, and says, 'God helps those who help themselves, Mary.'

'Oh he mightn't notice us if you didn't speak up, Sister,' titters Mary as Stella sits down clumsily, put off balance by the handshake.

'We were taught to speak up in my order,' goes Sister Colleen above the clack and bumble of cups and cake.

'Well, you've got a good example to follow.'

Sister Colleen nods. 'She means Mary MacKillop,' she explains to me. 'She's going to be our first saint.'

Perhaps this remark isn't met with universal approval, because across the table from Sister Colleen is a severe, thin, blue-rinsed person who shoots her an under-brow look from the rim of a dainty cup that doesn't match the rest, all colourless irises and drawstring mouth. 'That's all still in the hands of God, Sister,' she chides.

'Just a formality now, Mother Oldmeadow.' Sister Colleen sits back, crosses her bare legs with the comfy sandals on the extremities, looks at my mother and says of Mother Oldmeadow, 'This is Mother Oldmeadow, Stella, formerly headmistress of a big city convent.'

'Ew,' says my mother, overcome with hierarchy. 'How do you do, Mother Oldmeadow?' To which Mother Oldmeadow nods in superior fashion, willing her mouth to loosen into the primmest of smiles.

Sister Colleen rides on over the top of the introduction, 'Out in the country if you don't ask, you don't get.'

'Shhh,' goes the Reverend Mother, mouth back in a pucker, as *'I will take you home again, Kathleen...'* rises mellifluously from the breast of the old Irish gargler. *'Across the waters wild and wide...'* and we could be on a ship, having drawn a mixed bunch at our table. A newcomer to the table, an observant old lady with thin, hairdressed hair, lounging cheeks and bright blue eyes up under a theatrical drapery of skin reaches across, takes Stella's diseased hand and soothes, because a tear is trickling down the bridge of Stella's nose and lands, ker-plop, in her cup of tea.

God knows...is it the sentimental old song – one of her martyred brothers was a tenor – or is it the unAnglicanness of the place? There's a plaster Mary wreathed in white lilies in the foyer. Or is it sheer exhaustion? I can never keep track of Stella, an ancient child, still obedient to her long-dead mother who must have been one of the great moral tyrants of the universe. Where on earth did Stella hope to end her days? She made no plans, named no preferences, just let it all happen and complained at every turn.

Or didn't I listen? I drew the line at recruiting an Anglican vicar for her while she was still at large: her local parish was famously against the ordination of women. She might be, too, for all I know. Anyway, I couldn't stomach the hypocrisy of her having lived for years within cooee of the Anglicans and never going to them. Well, I suppose it was hypocrisy or maybe it's just convenient now for me to sit here thinking 'hypocrite'. She never had the nerve to go, that was the problem. She would have liked me to go for her.

Rosa-Sophia sashays by with scones and cream; Stella leaves off looking balefully at the blue-eyed lady, removes her hand, grabs and scoffs a whole scone so gluttonously she gets cream up her nostrils. That makes her laugh, trying to stop herself from exploding, grabbing for serviettes, rocking back and forth. The blue-eyed lady is laughing too as the song comes to an end and people applaud. 'You'll fit in,' she goes. 'Bring her back here, lovey, she'll be at home.'

'But I'm not a Catholic,' goes my mother.

'It doesn't matter,' says the lady, 'Edna over there's not a Catholic.'

My mother, face dripping scone, cranes her head around to look at Edna. Edna is very drab on the eye, as if she were the only virtuous person at a Bacchanalian knees-up. The sight of her brings on a laughing fit. 'Hey Bel.' Stella turns to me. 'Edna could be one of Aunt Nina's deputies out collecting for the Maimed and Limbless. Ha, ha, ha, ha, ha, ha!' Then, with a rising voice, she announces to the company, 'My sister Nina was a so-sigh-etty woman, y'know. Spent her life raising money for good causes.' Another set of companions in different surroundings would have asked, 'Oh?' and given her the opportunity of raving on while they drank her wine or pitted their origins against hers, but here, the drawstring lips on Mother Oldmeadow pucker to a nipple of disapproval, she rises to her feet, rests on her stick, turns and makes her way out, leaving Stella disconcerted.

'Oh don't worry,' goes her new blue-eyed friend – who's called Loreto – flicking an indicative glance at Mother Oldmeadow. 'Some people are against Sister Angela's playing.'

'Oh?' say I, thinking it more likely that Mother Oldmeadow is against Stella. 'Sister Angela seems to play very well.' And I think of Ray back at Narrowlea, whose racket on the pianola once sent a visiting dog running for cover.

'Some prefer not to hear the old tunes. A bit too lowly for them. Mother Oldmeadow was the superior at a swank ladies' college,' says Loreto, repeating what we've already heard.

This sets Stella off at a gallop. 'I'm an old boy of Scunthorpe Boys' Grammar,' she goes, 'I was brought up on a prop-er-ty out Scunthorpe way. They took the sisters of the boys. We had a head-master whose brother liked to tipple. He taught us English, his name was William Wentworth Tees and he used to say a poem about himself, "Here lie the bones of W.W., Never more to trouble you, trouble you." We had a kleptomaniac in our class. Her name was Jill Hitchen – the Hitchens were prominent Anglicans. Jill had bad breath and dandruff flakes the size of autumn leaves. People she was visiting were warned to put small, tempting objects out of her reach…'

'Really?' says Loreto. 'I went to the parish school in Croydon. I'm only named after a posh convent.'

Her voice varying in intensity as she tests her listener for the level of interest, Stella continues with the Hitchens, people of social standing in Scunthorpe, but not people who stood as high as the Mottes. She has had ninety-eight years of life to beat into submission and it is still recalcitrant; it still doesn't obey her rules. If it did, she would be drinking pink gin in Clarence House, which would have been left to her by her 'first cousin four times removed', the late Elizabeth Windsor, née Bowes-Lyons. If life obeyed Stella's rules, the Queen Mother would have written by this, claiming her as the lost branch of the family – the branch that the current lords of Glamis Castle were just waiting to be dispossessed by, the branch from the son of the tenth earl whose parents were married when he was nine, the day before the earl's death. So there!

Loreto laughs and laughs, but it may be at Stella's face rather than her stories as not only is it spotted with cream but every expression in a very big pantheon is traipsing across it. Stella will defend her patch until her last breath. What we are witnessing is the penultimate utterances of a daughter whose mother sought to exclude the lower classes from her life by the repetition ad nauseum of acceptable words and pronunciations, at their worst when bundled into verses such as *We have a mulberry tree, We have a persimmon tree, but we do not have a laver tree* – sayings that shrinkwrap her world to a suffocating core of prohibitions in the midst of which she sits, fighting for breath as she spits out the long, loopy mantra. Surely someone, some day, will understand: surely she will be rescued before, as W. W. taught her '... *the curfew tolls the knell of parting day*...'

Old pathways in the mind have been brushed off: quotations and verses I have not heard for years come tremulously out – even some that I haven't heard before emerge from where they've been stuck in the molasses of her childhood...until the afternoon-tea takers are tottering off and I am marshalling her, still reciting, but desperate now that the audience has dispersed, to the car.

With a final flourish on our way back to Narrowlea and bitterly because she seems to have been overrun by history, she recites: '*Out flew the web and floated wide/ The mirror crack'd from side to side/ 'The curse is come upon me,' cried/ The Lady of Shallot.*' For, whatever her views on Catholicism, Heaven, Hell and the class structure of Australian society, she has signed the paper that will very soon make her a resident of Holy Redeemer.

8

An email from Nin. Nothing about David in it, but could I have Daniel to stay tonight? Could I come over and fetch him? Doesn't say why and, when I ring, doesn't answer the phone. Damn the young! I stick myself in the car, fuming, but that doesn't clarify anything. Nin's usually quite good with letting me know in advance when she's going to lumber me with the child. I'll have to get straight with her and tell her that explanations ease the psychological burden. It's not that I don't love Dan. He's a great little boy. Generally three-year-olds are as their imaginations expand and they make their wonderful grasps at language. I'm keen on the company of a three-year-old for half a day; I can go even longer before resentment starts to show its ugly head, but there are times when I've had Dan for twelve hours at a stretch when only three or four were requested and I feel I'm back in the baby glug of Eli's childhood when laundry detergent in refillable plastic containers threatened to crown the mountains of my wonder. Nin is a ditherer; she has no timetable and when she gets stuck into something, she forgets what time it is – like, just as valuable to me as it is to her.

It's some time now since Nin tried for a second child and miscarried. She was depressed by it and decided to put off going back to her work as a coordinator with a firm of arts consultants and stay home with Dan for a while. I don't know that it was the best decision she could have made, but she was finding she didn't get along with her boss, one of those women who make it difficult for the young mothers on their staff by giving them more work than they can complete in the flexible hours they're supposed to work. So Nin has been at home testing the employment regulations to their limits. To help out, I had Daniel one day a week up until the week before my exhibition, but since then, my schedule has been thrown out by Stella's relocation and I've had to renege temporarily. Maybe the briefest of all possible emails is part of my punishment for being human.

Nin and Wendy live in a northern suburb where you don't often see men pushing the prams and on the rare occasions you do see them, there'll be two men pushing one child. The children are children: sucking dummies, screeching in supermarkets, dropping their school projects into the gutter as they climb out of the car or marching into the playground full of pride with a colourful board under their arms. Parents drop them off in the mornings, also full of pride and watching them go, pressing lunch boxes on them and hats and slapping sunscreen on their faces. In the afternoons, it's often grannies who wait on the footpath with littler folk in strollers and the avalanche takes to the streets and parks to play the games that children have always played – climbing, pirating from upper decks, slipping down slides or corralling the old folks on the seats with, 'I'm hungry', or 'Can we buy some lollies?' or, on the times when I've been among them with Daniel, 'Will you be the prisoner?' This is a demographic where the children who aren't first generation refugees are conceived by turkey baster or by the biological clock on agreement that there will be a partner in evidence to support the mother in the arduous task of child-rearing. The breeding set rent houses with two, preferably three, bedrooms from absent speculators who bought in the eighties boom, renovated and leased to mature-age students: this clientele has since graduated but been unable to afford to buy because the stock is depleted and the price of housing within striking range of the city has soared. The speculators are now millionaires, often offshore millionaires, and the breeding set are at their mercy. The back of Nin and Wendy's house, although it looks swank, is actually parting company with the front because the extension (out into the postmodern backyard with what used to be symmetrical high hedges of pittosporum, symmetrical paving stones and interstitial grass over which nature has reasserted her predominance in a gloomy, spiky and untidy kind of way) is on a separate concrete slab underneath which the drought has played havoc with the soil. Nature has caused ostensibly unmendable, handspan wide gaps to open up between the rooms on the slab and the sitting room.

It is into the sitting room that I have walked with six bottles of brined olives to smooth my passage, it being November, when the pickling is finished after six months of sitting in a dark place and sometimes being turned along with the chillis and lemon slices that all came from Mick's garden. Yes, I do paint, but I also pickle.

I know that the olives are there to avoid the issue of Nin's secretiveness versus my curiosity, but I'd rather advert to gardening than to pain to begin my descent to the nitty-gritty. I have summoned up my garden karma from my suburban cupboardful of karmas and I have a picture of my olive tree in the corner of Mick's country garden firmly in my mind. Gardening is almost as satisfactory a diversion from what ought to be happening as science used to be, but it tastes nice as opposed to bringing in money. You can experiment in a garden and you can learn. Daniel's mothers are all for organically grown foodstuffs, so I'm doing my best to stay on side by being politically correct and working at insects and blight with tea-leaves, soap, organic pest oil, lemon juice and garlic spray. I am trying to fit in. Wendy's mother, though a climate change enthusiast, is an insect exterminator and tells Daniel to stamp on snails. But Daniel rather likes a snail and at my place we have snail races across the lid of a compost bin and we look for snail neonates under bricks and once we saw a giant slug laying her pearly eggs from under her mantle into a pile of flower pots. We loved it; we watched week by week as the baby slugs developed and, when they reached seedling-devouring size, we popped them over the back fence into the next door neighbour's derelict backyard.

I have rescued Mick's garden from the aftermath of the Battle of Marital Breakdown and, with visions of a healthy family, I've planted trees and reared crops as pesticide freely as I can, given that I first chose to grow apples and reared instead codling moths in exportable quantities.

Nin is looking a bit shamefaced. Apparently Daniel packed his bag this morning, spat the dummy and said he was tired of his mothers and was off to stay with me. She is hooking her flexible be-socked toes around the edge of a just-visible coffee table where newspapers, crayons and jagged bits of paper that Daniel has been cutting out to make puppets are struggling against the laws of nature to stay on board. It's as though a willy-willy has just been through and transposed three lifestyles. A boy's shoe in the fruit bowl, a line of drying bras and pants on the back of the couch where Nin is sitting, a broom athwart the floorboards, many heaps of flattish things toppling because they are not all of the same flatness – like ring binders and slippery video covers, a child's plastic art smock, camera lenses, padded post bags, three or four magnifying glasses, industrial earphones, teaspoons united by yoghurt to the sides of cups and a camera or two.

In spite of his packed bags, Daniel isn't here. He and Wendy are at a shopping mall somewhere awaiting the RACV with a flat battery. I resist the urge to think that Nin is taking after Stella in the chaos department – because, of course, I also take after Stella. Our family is not Ikean – clutter we have, but categorise it we do not. 'Let sleeping dust mites lie,' I say to myself, as I have always said, being a person who sneezes when dust is aroused, but maybe there aren't any dust mites here because Nin and Wendy hire someone to come in and dust, vacuum and mop around the heaps.

Nin, under a brisk little haircut that flies out in tassels when she shakes her head, is not finding the conversation on gardens any easier than I am.

Our hovering problems are not limited to David. There is also Wendy. I hardly see Wendy. It must be six months since she came one evening to pick up Daniel at my place. Dan was dawdling in his bath and Wendy just took a magazine, sat down and read it, never meeting my eye. No formative news was forthcoming about anything. No friendly greeting. Sometimes it seems to me that news transmission from this household is left almost entirely to Daniel.

'Any news of "Rampa"?' I ask Nin at last. 'Rampa' is what Dan calls David.

Nin is quick to answer, 'Nup.'

Daniel has told me that Rampa comes calling on him. 'Chickie' also figures in conversation. 'Chickie not likes me in office,' Daniel will say from time to time. 'Chickie not play wiv me.' Apparently 'Chickie' has one very upmarket toy, a kind of waterfall or ball rolling device – I can't work out which – kept on the large back balcony of her apartment where Daniel is allowed to play. The apartment adjoins the gallery. If it is raining – which it almost never is – Daniel is allowed to play inside alone in a room with Checkie's other toy. He has to knock on the door to be allowed out.

So I ask Nin now about this second toy.

'Oh,' she says, 'it's an inflatable thing with a weighted led light in the bottom. When you knock it over, it shoots a pair of feelers in the air and kind of…shitters.'

'Shitters?'

'Well, shimmers and glitters at the same time. You know… shitters!'

And I try to think of a thing shittering, 'What? A kind of Shitter Bug?'

'Yeah, that's it, a Shitter Bug!'

'The only shitter bug I know of is the dung beetle.'

'This one shitters in the dark. Checkie brought it back from Paris. I don't think she bought it for Daniel specifically. All kids who visit Siècle get the same treatment. She sticks them out on the balcony or shuts them up in the room with the Shitter Bug. If you eat there, the poor kid still has to go on the balcony or get shut up in the room.'

'Eat there?'

'Well, me and Dad. Me and Dan. Me and Dan and Wendy. You know. Sometimes you get asked.'

I fail to refer to our being sued by Checkie – for it seems to me strange that you would dine with a person who is suing you. Perhaps I'm paranoid, but in almost the same breath as the discussion about Checkie's winning ways with children, Nin has let it slip that she might not need to place Daniel in child care. She thinks she can work and look after him at the same time. Has she had an offer, I ask. Well, she's considering something. A friend who owns a gallery says she could organise some events there. She could do that from home. Ideal, I say. Yes, she says, but avoids my eye. Do I know the person who offered her the work?

'I don't know,' she says, 'probably not.' But she is biting her lip and she isn't a good liar. What does she mean? That I've got Checkie's character wrong? That she's afraid I'll burst a boiler when I find out she's thinking of working at Siècle? I must not burst a boiler if she is thinking of working at Siècle. She grabs hold of one knee in both hands, one of her fingers capped by a hollow Bob the Builder that she's deftly hooked up from the floor. Flippetty-flip goes Bob the Builder.

Poor Nin, she'll learn one of these days that to tell a good lie you need to disentangle it from the context of your guilt. She ought to know by now: she has my example, I've been lying to Stella for years, making out that her clothes are 100% cotton because she's 'allergic to synthetics'. All I have to do is put black felt pen stripes over the rest of the information on the clothes labels and make it look like the kind of thing a manufacturer put there. But when Nin buys Stella clothes, she doesn't bother to doctor the labels and then she wonders why Stella doesn't wear anything she's spent time and money on selecting. Bloody Nin, she's so stubborn. Sometimes it seems she'd rather end up weeping over lost time and effort than confess to herself that the allergic Stella spends her life wearing synthetics to which her skin shows no adverse reaction at all, but the moment you mention the presence of synthetics in something, she gets itchy and forlorn. Either Nin's plain bloody lazy or she wants to think that what Stella says is credible. Or then again, she could be forgetful or cross herself because Stella doesn't have enough reality on board to accept gifts without reciting her list of preordained tastes and allergies.

Or maybe she's just assertive, in the modern way, but about the wrong things.

The phone goes. 'That'll be Wendy,' she says to me and shoots a hand out, thumb poised to chop off our conversation.

'Yep,' she says, gets up, strolls nonchalantly across the chaotic room, knees hyperextending, 'Yep,' again. Gleeful laughter, back turned to me, Bob-holding hand ruffling the cute haircut, toes of the bare feet flexing. 'Yep, yep! You betcha. Yep, she's here. Okay, how long? Twenty minutes,' she says to me. 'Can you wait that long?'

'Sure.'

She says, 'Yep, bye,' into the phone and then, 'I thought you might be painting or something. We could bring him round to you.'

'I'll wait.'

'Bloody battery's always going flat – we don't use the car enough. Price you pay for being green.'

'Mine's got a hole in the radiator. I have to fill it before I start the car up every time. I haven't managed to improve yet on the Maserati.' The Maserati was the first car I owned, a Datsun Thousand wagon with dicky front suspension. I drove it for more than a decade.

'Yeah, the classy Maserati, eh?' says Nin. Having relaxed a little bit on the furry pelt of Wendy's words, she has a fit of the giggles. 'Remember when the Chinese kid from over the road got hold of his dad's pile of porn magazines and you let us have a look at them "with adult supervision", and then stuck us all in the car and drove us out to that great big dam to put them in a garbage bin in the picnic ground.'

'You were supposed to forget that. I was meant to have scrubbed all the filth and exploitation from your naughty little minds. Particularly as we went for a picnic afterwards.'

'Enough to make a kid want to go and grab another pile of porn!'

'Shut up! We've always been innovative with rubbish, our family. It's in the blood. We furnished our house from the council chuck-outs. Eli got our kitchen table and chairs off a skip when he was about eight. He always had an eye for useful rubbish. It's a skill handed down from Henry Coretti, who used to paint rubbish assemblies and have a special relationship with the person who ran the dump.'

'I remember her! She had a big box of plastic nose guards and gave us all one so our noses wouldn't get burnt,' says Nin, remembering the marvellous Bridget Kelly, dump caretaker and supplier of hubcaps and objets d'art to Henry Coretti.

'Yes, she had several gross of those. Very practical woman, Bridget Kelly.'

'I don't think they have people who superintend dumps anymore,' says Nin.

'More's the pity. Bridget was a good old stick, just that it wasn't the acme of suburban life to be seen associating with her. But they rose, the Kellys – we used to call them "the upwardly mobile misbehaving poor" because some stuck-up sociology bitch used to talk on the TV about "the downwardly mobile genteel poor" back in the eighties when Bridget was had up for vandalising plastic bird netting to rescue fruit bats.' I've made her laugh at long last. Generally we get along pretty well, Nin and I. We're similar in temperament…innovative, but a bit lackadaisical.

She says, 'Dan likes a rubbish heap. He's made you a windmill out of paper cups, you'll be pleased to know. It's for your garden to scare off the birds.' She plunks down a bowl of pecans in front of me. 'You can have a vodka if you want…'

'P'raps not, babe. If I'm driving. Can I ask you something?'

'What?' she says, quickly.

'About David? I know he's ill.'

She perches on the couch, Bob-flicking, head down. Then she hoists her head up to look me in the face.

'You know he's going to die?' I ask.

'Well, he doesn't think so,' pouting, 'I don't reckon he will.'

'What makes you think he'll survive?'

'Oh…' she beats the toy up and down on her palm, 'I don't know, really. It's what he says.'

'What does he say?'

'That he'll lick it.'

'Do you love him?'

She shrugs, beating the toy on her fingers now and looking away from me, then, freshly, 'Daniel kind of loves him.'

'In what way?'

'They play footy. Outside, of course, you wouldn't catch them playing footy in Checkie's precious premises.'

'He's living there then?'

'Yeah, since he had the op.'

'Why didn't you tell me about that?'

'Dunno,' she says, looking down, a dollop of light sliding back and forth across her pout. 'Sorry.' Tears shoot out of her eyes sideways and she squashes them off with hyper-flexed fingers. 'He didn't want me to,' big sniff, 'just the way he is, I s'pose.'

'Do you think he thought I'd cheer, or something?'

'Maybe,' she turns round to face me, nodding her head earnestly as she says, 'but I know you wouldn't. I know you wouldn't Bel.' And I wouldn't; she's right about that – you can sneer too long and too hard. 'Guess there's no point in telling Gran?'

'No love, you must realise by now that there's no room in Gran's repertoire to be reasonable in any way about David.'

'He might even die before she does. I *did* think, Bel, that maybe he didn't tell you because he really believes he's going to get better and there'd be no point in burdening you.'

'Oh darling, you do have such a good opinion of people. David's an eternal little boy, in need of good opinion and gentle love, like yours, but he's determined that I'm his enemy.'

'Well, aren't you?' Very tunefully aggressive and leaning forward now, bottom lip far out.

'Look, however you feel about your father, he will never ever stand in a woman's place and sympathise with women's views. He really does think women are lesser beings, there to be toyed with and enjoyed on some levels, but not to be taken seriously. His own mother abandoned him, don't forget.'

'Yeah. Well, my mother abandoned *me*,' tapping Bob the Builder frantically on her fingertips.

'Allegra ditched us all, darling. No one could have foreseen that.'

'She didn't love him.'

'She didn't really know him. She was very attracted to him. When we met him he was really happy and funny. I think it was the excitement of being in Melbourne. He'd been living in Sydney up until then, sort of shacking up with his Uncle Bart.' Bart Turner ran a wonderful art gallery, called Turner, in Sydney: I met him when I ran away from home, pregnant with Eli. 'He used to sleep in the picture store of the gallery whenever he ran out of money for a place of his own – which was practically all the time. When he wasn't with Bart, he used to live in flophouses. Things had gone stale for him up there.' Here, in Melbourne, Bart's brother, Miles, had a gallery called Figments. 'They were hopping down here. And then, he was bowled over by Allegra. He loved the way she looked – she was both classically and unconventionally beautiful, just so herself. He loved how she looked and he loved the fact that Bart and Miles thought highly of her. They loved Mad Meg and they helped us to set it up. Bart and Miles were a great pair of blokes and up until he met us, they were David's only port of call. Those two, Allegra, David and I were all in love with each other in the beginning and it suited us all around. David had somewhere to be among his own contemporaries at last. It looked as though it was going to go really well. We were art world adventurers – all of us – out to upset the status quo, and by God, it needed upsetting!'

'Uncle Bart was gay, wasn't he?'

'Yes.'

'Maybe that's where it comes from.'

'Your lesbianism? I don't think gay comes from anywhere in particular, baby. It just is.'

'I remember that gallery in Sydney. It was all concrete. I used to hate going there.'

'Brutalist architecture. All the rage. It wasn't meant to be kid friendly; it was dreamt up by big kids – a thousand and ten things to do with concrete.'

'But Bart was nice even if his floor was bloody cold and hard. Eli used to say he had asterisk eyes.'

'He was lovely. He was our main inspiration when we set up Mad Meg. He was right behind feminism.'

'But Dad wasn't?'

'Your father was a great fan of Pop art. The women's movement had only just taken off when he came to Melbourne. I think he resented it because it was Bart's new enthusiasm.'

'And he wanted to be Bart's enthusiasm?'

'Something like that. But David has never trusted women.'

'He seems to trust Checkie well enough.'

'I don't think that's because she's a woman. I think it's because she's a lever. But I'm not going to go there; it's something you'll have to work out for yourself. No, I think David can't trust women because he loved his own mother and she ditched him. After that and his upbringing in a household with misogynistic man at its head, he just couldn't believe that women had as much right to full lives as men.'

'His mum had other kids down the track, didn't she?'

'Yes. As you know, David grew up with his grandparents and she married someone who didn't want him tagging along.'

'What happened to Dad's father? Why wasn't he around?'

'I thought you knew that, too. God knows I've tried to keep you in the picture.'

'Yeah, but it's hard to build up pictures from little bits and pieces.'

'You can say that again. My whole life is bits and pieces.'

'I keep trying to put it all together, but it's hard. I don't even know what Dad's father looked like.'

'I don't think David does, either, but he was Dorothy's lover. He was married to someone else and had a family. She worked for him. He set her up in a flat in Bondi, she got pregnant, David was born while she was living there and he was about one or two when his father dropped dead suddenly and Dorothy had to go back to her family. Her father, old Cec Turner, was a real bastard by all accounts and he gave Dorothy a very hard time. She was the only girl in a family of five kids. There was a suggestion that Cec interfered with her when she was a kid...'

'Erk!'

'Yes. It was pretty erk. It was her mother who looked after David, but when Dorothy got married and her bloke didn't want him, Cec insisted that he was sent off to boarding school – he was only seven. Sometimes he was in there for his whole school holidays because his grandfather wouldn't let him come home. He had a hell of a life.'

'Why did Dad's gran put up with Cec?'

'Life's not neat, Nin, billions of mistakes happen and people just go on, trying to make the best of their circumstances. Therese Turner was very young when she married Cec – only in her teens and she pretty soon had five kids – Dorothy was in the middle of a whole swag of sons. It's quite possible Therese didn't realise what was happening. Imagine what it must be like to find out something like that. It'd just about kill you, I reckon. And your instinct would be to protect your kids. You'd have to be there to stand between your kids and the other parent. If you left, then you couldn't prevent what happened between them. You might be so poor you had to leave your kids behind. On the other hand, the court might order shared custody and you had no power over what happened when you weren't there.

'Just think, Nin, it'd be an awful thing to have to tell a kid that their father was despicable...In the nineteen-fifties, you had to sue for a divorce. You had to prove irretrievable breakdown of marriage – a lot of people just cleared out and hid for at least two years until the other party could sue for divorce on the grounds of desertion...And supposing they didn't sue? Supposing they were angry and vindictive? There was a lot of vindictiveness under that system. There's still a lot of vindictiveness, but at least the problems related to protecting yourself from a violent or hideously transgressive partner are out in the open now. At least people admit that it happens and admit that it's a big problem – we're just a pack of monkeys, really, but at least there are places to go. Domestic violence is a frightful situation.'

'Crikey. What did the old fucker do for a living?'

'He was a night watchman...used to pinch stuff from the places he was supposed to be minding and flog them off. He stole dozens of dressed chickens from the Trocadero Ballroom when his kids were small and sent the whole five out taking orders to get rid of them. He also stole the family cutlery from there – all monogrammed with T, for Turner, of course.'

'It must have been horrible to grow up gay in that family.'

'Bart was a pretty good boxer. He decked his father and pissed off in the end.'

'Was Miles gay?'

'No darling. Miles has a wife and a son. He's retired now and lives down on the coast. David used to show with him when he first came down to Melbourne to be near Allegra. He doesn't have anything to do with David these days because of the debacle at Mad Meg. Bart kept up with David for a while, but even he was disgusted and only did it because without him, David had no other family.'

'And now I'm his only family?'

'Yes love. I suppose there are other members of his family around somewhere, but David's never looked for them and they've never looked for him.'

'Gosh, Figments is still famous, even though it's been shut for years.'

'Yes, Siècle is the only one from those days still in the area. Figments was great. It was just up the hill from Mad Meg in a warehouse. Bart brought his artists down from Sydney once to have a big double show there called Turner at Figments. That's when David met Allegra. Bart and Miles were very good at promoting the work of young Australian artists. They took it right up to the taste makers and the big name galleries. Turner would still be going if Bart were still alive and Miles only gave up Figments because he wanted to live out of Melbourne – I think the excitement had gone out of it by then – for Miles, at least.'

'Why's that?'

'Perhaps he was afraid of becoming what he despised. His painters went on to become big time. They were the best of that generation…'

'Except for Dad?'

'Look, David wrecked himself in mid-career, Nin. No one wanted to handle him for a while…'

'After what he did to you at Mad Meg?

'Mainly. But there were other things. He was feral, a terrible drunk.'

'Doesn't drink anymore.'

'Well, that doesn't surprise me. He probably can't with all the chemo he's receiving.'

'Oh, he could. He just doesn't,' she says as if she is sticking up for him…then, a little bit aggressively, 'Anyway, what happened to Mad Meg?'

'I thought you knew that, too.'

'Bits of it, but I want to know what you think.'

'Well, Mad Meg was great, but a bit of a failure – not in the feminist sense, but financially. We didn't have any business nous; we thought we were living through a revolution or something – well, Allegra did. Bart and Miles had nous. They definitely took after their mother; Therese trained as an accountant when she had David to look after. David takes after her in looks – she was a nice, compact little woman with thick, dramatic hair that clung to her head like David's before it all fell out.'

'What happened to her?'

'Died. She was old.'

'So he lived with Miles after he came to Melbourne?'

'Yes. Sort of "camped" with Miles when he decided to stay down here and I remember how jubilant Miles was when Allegra relieved him of the responsibility. David kind of went from minder to minder…' and it occurs to me that he is still going from minder to minder. People are very stuck in their ways when you look at it. It's very, very hard to break out of the mould. Maybe you can't.

'Are he and Checkie an item?' I suddenly think to ask in case history is going to repeat itself right down to the level of the bed.

'No.' Nin looks startled.

'Just wondered.'

'He has his own room. She likes having him around now he's stopped smoking and he's very neat. And he knows everything about art that interests her, Bel.' She brushes the back of her head with her toy-free hand and looks up at me at last with an expression verging on anger. 'And he's talented, you have to admit that…'

'But that's not…' My mouth again. I was going to say that's not the point; I've never said David didn't have talent or that his work wasn't interesting. Nor have I ever said that he didn't know what he was talking about. He can be quite convincing in what he says – but it doesn't take a genius to pick his prejudices. And it's very, very hard to tell a child that their father is despicable. 'It's not straightforward, Nin. I find him a burden.'

'Because of me?'

'Well, I need to be honest here. David was never capable of looking after you and he gave me bugger-all support, material or emotional, if you really want to know. Whenever he gave us anything it'd come in a large wad so it looked as though he was giving us a lot. I got into a rage once and worked out that he averaged about a thousand dollars a year towards your keep and that didn't nearly cover costs. He was never amenable to anything when you were a child – I couldn't ask him for anything – in fact, we spent most of our time hiding from him so he wouldn't aggravate us. I know he's been a better father to you since you grew up – but it's easier to be a father in absentia than the hands-on dad of a little kid. So, in that way, I've had to carry David. But he's a burden to me also because of what he did to my show and because of the appalling way he treated Allegra.'

'Do you think he was responsible for her death?'

'Well…I'm not going to ask you the silly question he always used to ask us whenever we found him baffling. He used to ask "What do you think I think?" As if we could make his own thoughts clear to him. You have to understand that David's childhood and adolescence were completely stuffed up. Bart and Miles did what they could for him, but he'd been ridiculed or assaulted by his grandfather for everything he did, every aptitude he showed… In the end, who killed Allegra? Maybe Cec Turner.'

Or then again, maybe Allegra herself. Love keeps me steering shy of blaming Allegra. If she'd known how many houses of cards she would bring down, how many hearts she would break – and whose – she wouldn't have had the callousness to do away with herself. Of that I'm sure.

'And then, there's depression. Depression puts you outside. You live like a shade in Hell. You daren't tell the people you love what you see and what you experience for fear that you will drag them into the whirlpool with you. I know this because I've been there. "Love" just becomes a cardboard coin to trade. You can say you love someone and they love you, but really, it's just a syllable in your mouth, you become an alien, un-human, your body functions like a check-out chick upfront…Oh, I'm sorry, darling, now I've made you cry.'

She flings herself on my neck, great globular tears budding from her lashes, splashing us both. 'You're good at tears, my baby.' I pat her back. 'But if it's Checkie who's made you the offer of work, be very careful. She might be my half-sister, but her mother was a crocodile and I think Checkie is, too. I fear she's using David to get to you to spite me.'

Nevertheless I can see that Siècle is one direction in which Nin could turn to her great advantage. She could become part of it and, as Checkie hasn't any children…But no, Checkie will leave Siècle and its story to the state – at best, Nin would end up as her minion. I set her back down on the couch so I can look at her with more composure. 'So what do they want you to do at Siècle?'

She wipes the tears off her cheek with a lavish twist of the hand and shrugs, looking down into the plastic face of Bob the Builder. Then, disingenuously, 'How do you know they want me to do anything?'

'Because I do.'

'Wish the art world wasn't so full of scheming. It's not my fault, is it?'

'No. And I suppose they could do with someone like you, someone who isn't a born bitch. You always sound so pleasant, like fresh air.'

'Yes, Checkie is a bit of a bitch, isn't she?' She laughs through her tears. 'She's such a smarm on the phone. Calls herself Che-chilia Coretti.'

'Of course… eyelids at half mast, UberMelburnian intonations, *Che-chilia Coretti speaking.*'

'You got it.'

It's sickening to think Checkie has as much right as Nin or I have to call herself Coretti – but go on, Isobel, accept, accept, what's in a name?

'I'm glad she's not your mother,' I say.

'So am I.'

'If you were her daughter, you know, you wouldn't be with Wendy.'

'Why's that?'

'Whatever your sexuality, you'd be married off to some rich bloke.'

'But Checkie's not married herself.'

'I'm sure Viva tried to make it happen. There was a terrible crumb in her life once who came from a rich family – his surname was on the lips of all the arterati; they were even going to announce the banns at a top notch church, would you believe? They became high church Anglicans with big black crosses around their necks for a while there after Dadda died. But it didn't happen.'

'Checkie might be a rebel against Viva?'

'Oh darling, don't be fooled. She's a clone: all she needed was Harry Laurington's money and gallery know-how to set herself up in her own way as a wealthy woman. I think Checkie hasn't married because she hasn't met anyone who would suit. If she had a daughter, she'd be on the lookout for royalty or a billionaire to add more rungs to her ladder. Checkie's all about hierarchy, position.'

'Why would she want to get hold of me, then? I'm a lesbian mother.'

'You've got cachet, babe. You're beautiful, you're personable, you know the family history and you're Allegra's daughter. She'd love to get hold of you.'

I don't add that she'd love to get hold of the paintings, too, because that could lead us to bedlam. Nin stands still now, tossing the toy limply and looking dazed. At length, she says, 'How do you work out that she'd use me socially?

'It hasn't occurred to you?'

'Only…kind of…hmm.' She puts a hand on her hip and looks to me for an answer.

'I don't know, Ninny. I might be quite wrong, but I'm not altogether wrong, am I?'

'But Checkie likes Wendy…And I have to say, Aunty Bel, that it's more than you do.'

Well, this puts a different complexion on things. A large, dry peanut butter sandwich-ful of news. Think of it. Wendy and Nin both under Siècle's wing.

No, I don't adore Wendy, it's true. She's branded me as a homophobe. But I'm not objectively a homophobe. I just don't think I share Wendy's values, whatever they are – I have a darned hard time working them out. I don't think the same way as Wendy.

'Are you worried about the paintings?' Nin asks.

'Of course.'

'Don't forget there'll be Grandma's money one of these days. That would keep you going for a bit.'

'Oh Nin!' Now I think it's my turn to cry. But you don't cry, Isobel, do you, because guess what? Right at the psychological moment – even though you wouldn't cry anyway, would you? – we can hear the latch clicking and Daniel running up the path. Nin gets up and walks really fast down to the door, with 'Guess who's come? Guess who's come?'

'Sibella!' shrieks Daniel and hurls himself into my arms – Sibella is the name my father called me and it came miraculously from Daniel's lips as he struggled to say 'Isobel'.

'Hello Danny-boy,' I try to say joyfully.

'I not Danny-boy. I'n Ironman.' Daniel has come up with 'I'n' as the opposite of 'I'm not'.

Wendy follows him in unsmilingly. Wendy would rather I was out of their lives. Wendy and I in the same room together make Nin nervous. Now that Wendy's here, Nin would like to shovel me out the door. She perches forward on her toes, 'Go on, Dan, get your gear.'

'Why Sibella not have a sleepover at our home?'

'You're going to have a sleepover at hers.'

'I want she have a sleepover here. She can sleep my bed.'

Wendy goes, 'Your Mummies need to relax, Dan. It's been a sorely trying day.'

'What means sorely trying?'

'Tiring. We're tired,' says Wendy.

'No, you not.'

'Daniel.' Nin is breathing heavily. 'GO and GET your GEAR!'

And I know where Nin is. I've been there – the child of your body and the mother of your mind are making life difficult for you and your lover.

No, you can't get out of the world, Isobel. You're in it for keeps and if you have to unravel Nin's cryptic silences, then Wendy is out to invent ulterior motives for what she thinks are your ulterior motives.

Daniel comes hurtling out with his paper-cup windmill, his red Spider-man cape and his Ben 10 trolley and wants me to carry him out to the car. 'Dillbone,' I say to him, 'I haven't got ten hands.'

9

A letter addressed to Eli came here this morning. I wish I knew where he was so I could send it on. I'm beginning to fret that he hasn't contacted me by now. I hate being anxious about Eli because it wrecks my concentration and my ability to handle my million and fifty commitments.

When he brought Phoebe back to marry her, they were full of plans. There was an apartment to buy in Washington, a Porsche...

'A *Porsche!*' went Nin. 'How can you afford a *Porsche?*'

I was still driving rattle traps and Nin was riding a bike to school.

'Mon-ney!' sang Phoebe; she had a marvellous voice, deep, rich and tuneful. 'We're rich folk now.'

'*You're* rich!' Nin twitted. 'Eli's not.'

They had booked a flash hotel in town and now we were sitting on the floor of the humble single-fronter corridor with bedrooms off that had served as our home since I had to sell up the beloved bungalow of my nightmares. Around us was a mound of tissue paper and London bags and we drank lemon and ginger tea and ate homemade plum cake with double cream. Phoebe was a glamorous angel descended into our midst, decked out in the latest and loveliest chic clothes.

'Oh, I went *mad* after Pakistan,' she sang. There were bags, too, full of things for Nin and me. 'Don't *worry!* The salary's *fantastic!*'

'Will you go back there?' I asked her.

'Oh, I have to all the time. It's part of the job. The US is heavily involved in Pakistan. I have to go to high level meetings with generals and do all the translating.'

'What do you wear then?' asked Nin. She was trying to picture Phoebe among the generals looking as she looked on our floor – 'like something out of *Harpers Bizarre*!' as Nin was fond of calling the *Bazaar*.

'Oh civvies, Nin.' She was smiling. There was no doubt about it. She was sweet and charming and warm and even my wayward, questioning Nin was awestruck.

'You mean pants suits?'

Eli butted in. 'You don't wear pants among the generals, Nin.'

'Cockhead.' Phoebe lay back in his arms. 'No Nin, you wear conservative stuff, you know, navy-blue suits and you put on a head-scarf if you're among strict Muslims. I wear a scarf because they don't come across many blondes over there and you get all sorts of reactions to blonde hair. If I hadn't spoken the languages better than the other candidates, I wouldn't have got the job because of my hair.'

'You could always dye it,' said Nin.

'Well, I do sometimes, Nin, but I'm so fair that the dyes can look weirder than the natural thing, so I have to compromise. I do hair chalk, but if it's really hot, it gets messy and runs everywhere.'

'Nothing worse than being the same colour as your hair!'

'Well, you'd look funny, Nin,' said Eli.

'Bel would look funnier. Sort of striped.'

'Well thank you, Nin. So, how often do you go?' I asked Phoebe.

'It depends what's happening. It's quite interesting at the moment. Benazir's in trouble.'

'Do you know her or something?' went Nin.

'Shut up, Ninnie.' I said. 'Everyone calls her Benazir to distinguish her from her father, who used to be the prime minister. We seem to like her over here, Phoebe. What's her problem?'

'Well, she hasn't been able to change anything. The Hudood Ordinances are still in place and a lot of people hate them. And she's only young. She's a woman. She's got a hostile president and army chief – it was the army who did her father in. Anyone who's prime minister of Pakistan has a network of obligations replete with nepotism and paybacks for favours. There are no democratic institutions strong enough to override local and tribal interests. That's just how it is there. Nothing like here. Eli was telling me about Italy and his grandfather's story. In Italy the fascists killed off the liberal democrats and socialists with the result that the strongest anti-fascist force there during the war was the Mafia and the Mafia got their funding from outside and it was impossible to get rid of them afterwards. You think of it – peasant Italians couldn't read and write; they were in the hands of local fixers. It's the same in Afghanistan and Pakistan and now there are pan-Islamic groups emerging, like this Al Qaeda mob. Al Qaeda means "the base" and I guess it's their intention to spread their message from "the base" of fundamentalist Islam. The fundamentalists want to re-establish Islam as it was in the days of the prophet, but Islam's never been as it was in the days of the prophet in Afghanistan and Pakistan, where you've always had to buy your way into your social position and the weak seek protection from the local strong man. And if you want to buy anything in Afghanistan, you buy it with drugs.'

'Really?' I began to think about Eli and the photo he'd sent home of himself with the hookah in the hash den.

'Well, they have to keep themselves somehow, Mum,' said Eli, reading my mind.

'Yes,' said Phoebe. 'They don't have other things. So, in a place where you can't get pharmaceuticals but there's an abundance of opium and hash, that's going to be your source of income. Opium's everywhere. Newborn babies are anointed with rubs made out of it to send them to sleep. Mothers blow opium smoke into the kids' mouths or spit the juices from their chewing wads of raw opium into them. And then imagine sitting on your haunches day in and day out weaving carpets as some of them do. It's slow going. They have to compare every new bit of pattern with a piece already done, because they can't count, so there are no patterns or anything, so they relieve the tedium with a ball of opium gum in their cheeks or some smoke from a hookah. They use opium and hash like we use aspirin. When I was in my old job, I used to see Afghan women going out from the camps during the sowing season to put in the poppy crops for opium dealers. They used to go out over the mountains, on foot – sometimes the journeys would take days to these hidden valleys…and they knew what they were doing when they got there because they'd been croppers in Afghanistan. They'd sow them and then, at harvest time, back they'd go with their little knives to scrape the seed pods and set them oozing milk. They leave the milk to set into gum overnight on the sides of the poppy heads and then they'd come back and scrape it off. They went and did this all willingly – it's part of an old, old trade that's been going on for centuries. Any efforts to stamp it out fail because they just set up black markets in the camps. They grow hash, too. They mature it in sheep or goat skins and you can tell where it's for sale when they hang the tails up outside their tents.'

Eli was looking anything but a junkie. He was spruce, shaved, over-the-moon in love. Eyes closed, he locked his knees around Phoebe and rocked her from side to side while she talked. 'In the West we've only seen citified Afghans and Pakistanis, the small educated elite and the chaps who drive buses in England. There are huge numbers of people – I mean millions – living rural or nomadic lives. They've never held a pen…'

'Although,' Eli interrupted, opening his eyes to beam at her, 'they have seen television.'

'Yeah. TV's like opium there. They watch the soapies and the cricket. If you turn on the news, all you hear about's the cricket.'

'And beating the Indians.'

'Oh yes, I forgot. Beating the Indians, that's a national sport. On the radio in Peshawar you can get Voice of Afghanistan, Radio

Free Afghanistan and Voice of Unity. The Voice of Unity is the station of the Afghan mujahedeen; the Pakis think it's sponsored by the CIA and maybe India. Won't go down well in Pakistan if the warlords take over and the Indians are backing them. They'll hate that more than they hated the communists. They're so scared of being encircled by the Indians.'

And Eli did a war cry. Phoebe said, 'Cockhead!' and they rolled over on the floor like a pair of children.

Eli wanted the wedding to happen at Bowradale on the east coast, where I used to take him on holidays when he was a child. I'd also take Nin there from the New South Wales side of the border when we were living at Reg's. It's just north of Victoria, beside the sea – a place where a wide blue river meets the ocean, a place of colour, light and soothing sounds, a heart-lifting, soul-immersing place that takes you in its arms and adores you. Or at least, that's how I always think of it.

After much deliberation and with guilty consciences, we left Stella to sit out the wedding under the watchful eye of Cousin Audra. She might have come with us, but, feeling upstaged by a bride, she was on her most button-pushing dignity when we took Phoebe around to the Rats' Nest to introduce her. The remainder of the Motte crockery was out in unmatching array and tea dribbled down the Doulton spout alarmingly. Stella never liked a female to be better looking than the women in our family and said so at length to Phoebe in as roundabout and aristocrat-including way as she possibly could. Phoebe listened respectfully with head bent and hands devotionally clasped while Allegra's wonderful, curling, light-trapping mane was alluded to, as were her eyes of miraculous turquoise. On examination, Phoebe's hair was found to be straight and her eyes of a 'fairly common blue'. 'Like Eli's,' teased Nin.

Nin and I had bought Eli a beautiful suit and two gold wedding rings, he having sent the sizes on before arrival. Shoes were a thing he decided he could do without, possibly following my father in his contempt for highly polished feet and their fascist connotations. Phoebe wore no shoes, either, although I learned later that she had a pair of Manolo Blahnik's in her luggage. Quite why I'd had to buy the rings rather than their buying them on the spot in London was a mystery – until Nin showed me a book on wedding etiquette that Cousin Audra had given her against the day – it seems that the groom's family pays for the rings. They also, the book suggested, pay for the honeymoon. These things were news to me.

After Pakistan and then winter in London, Eli and Phoebe wanted to walk on fine sand, to paddle in froth, feel the sun's rays on their skin. They were married on the beach under a marquee with champagne and strawberries (I understand that was the bit Phoebe's parents paid for as it was the only bit of the bill, apart from the drinks, that I never saw). They played music they weren't allowed to play in Pakistan and danced. The honey-coloured Phoebe – in defiance of the Princess Diana, full regalia times – wore a short yellow dress and carried a bunch of bright daffodils (extraordinarily cheap for a wedding bouquet, I discovered when I paid the florist).

Under Phoebe's influence, I'd splashed out on a Dead Sea mud pack and fingernail brightening apparatus pressed on me by some Israeli backpackers who'd set up a stall in our local mall and were ripping off passers-by by buffing one fingernail on a customer's hand to a blinding shine. 'Oh,' Phoebe had cried, 'brilliant! Must have!' At ninety dollars for two packs. On the day of the wedding, I had shiny fingernails that were all different lengths when I compared them with the individually illustrated, long white talons of Phoebe's mother, Fridlinda, who obviously hadn't pulled a garden weed in her life.

It was the first time I'd met Phoebe's parents – I hadn't even spoken to them on the phone. Eli had been sprung on them out of the blue. 'Always thought she'd marry a diplomat or an exiled princeling of some sort,' George Green said. He was sixty-ish, stocky, affable, champagne-pouring; he wore punter's pants, had a big double chin and it wasn't hard to envisage binoculars slung around his neck.

Whatever he thought of Eli, he spared no shekels on Phoebe's wedding present – a large drop pendant of high quality Brazilian citrine on a handsome gold chain, 'Here you are, darling,' he said, clasping it around her neck, 'not pregnant, are we?'

Phoebe sprayed him with daughterly contempt.

'Oh good,' he said, 'didn't like to think you threw yourself into wedlock for that kind of reason.'

'Don't be silly, Dad!' but he just gave a smiling hmph and turned his attentions to Fridlinda, under whose belt Phoebe had been sitting for eight months on the day of their nuptials.

Fridlinda slid her highly manicured hand under Phoebe's jewel and said, 'You know, Daddy went all the way to the Iguaçú Falls for that citrine. We were going to have it cut into a pendant for me, but anyway, it suits you so much better, darling. Citrines ward off the evil eye, did you know?' Two of Phoebe's four brothers were at the wedding and the one who'd arrived on time, Charles Green (a replica of his father), reeled away from the cluster around Phoebe in good-natured contempt.

'Charles?' his father chided.

And Charles said quietly, 'Well, what a thing to say to a bride. I think I remember you giving Fridlinda diamonds when you married her.' He was looking at me, or rather through me – I just happened to be where his gaze landed – and pinched his bottom lip to stop his head from going its own way and shaking its disapproval.

'Gawd,' said Nin at my side. And then, in a whisper, 'I hope Phoebe doesn't turn out to be like *her!*'

'More likely wants to get away from her, darling,' I whispered back: reason told me Phoebe had already done that by working abroad.

Eli hadn't met Fridlinda before either. He kept winking at us and clasping Phoebe's hands as if at any moment she'd vanish. I would have liked him to be surer of himself, but, although he was nervous and his hands trembled every now and again, he was glowing with happiness. Phoebe also seemed in a state of bliss, although I thought I detected a slight hesitancy beneath the glow – perhaps her victory in bagging Eli hadn't been a victory in the place where she'd most intended it to be.

The second brother, Ned, slimmer and younger than Charles and nifty in a smart suit, arrived in his Porsche at the lunch in the old pub over the road, having missed the ceremony because he'd been held up at a business conference in Sydney. Eli's grasp on Phoebe became noticeably tighter in the sharpening atmosphere. He'd cover her arms with his as if warning off other males. Ned was clearly contemptuous and started to support Fridlinda in mocking the menu, while Charles again threw his constrained exasperation around in his seat, coming out at last with, 'Just because you were late for the wedding, Ned, doesn't mean you can cover up by criticising the occasion.'

'More champagne, anyone?' George wafted around like a stallion showing off the goods to a group of horse traders. 'Jolly nice champers, this Bollinger. Do you have enough there, Isobel? Coretti…Coretti…you any relation to that painter chap?'

'Aunty Bel's his daughter,' piped up Nin. 'And she's a painter, too. A better painter than he was in my opinion.'

George chuckled somewhere around the tonsil level. 'The young today are all tremendously opinionated,' he said. 'Suppose it's a good thing, really. Can't have faint hearts in this world. Now tell me, Eli, old chap, where did you come by a name like that – Eli? Biblical, isn't it?'

Eli looked queryingly at me. 'Well actually it was my father's choice,' I said. 'He found some scrabble letters on the street on his way to see me after Eli was born and he pulled them out of his sock where he'd put them and they spelt Eli.'

'You're kidding!' George smiled thinly.

'Not at all. It's what he did. My father had a sense of humour.'

'You can see that in his paintings.'

'You know them then?'

'Oh, I've seen them in auctions.'

'You go to auctions, then? Are you a collector?'

'We've got one or two pieces, yes. But this name, Eli. It's biblical, isn't it?'

'I haven't much acquaintance with the bible, but I suppose it's biblical,' I said.

'Old Testament?'

'Old Testament.'

Fridlinda broke in here. 'Jewish,' she said swiftly.

'Must be difficult, Eli,' chuckled George, 'travelling round a place like Pakistan with a Jewish name.'

Eli looked blank, holding his head enquiringly.

'You didn't have any trouble then?'

'Sorry, have I missed something? Is my name Jewish? I never knew. They called me Elias in Pakistan.'

Intense chuckling from George. 'Quite right, too. I never thought Jews were any different from Christians. Everyone was equal at my old school in Edled.'

'*Edled!* Do you mean Adelaide?' Nin exploded.

'What a funny little family you've married into, Phoebe!' George chuckled on, then turning back to me, 'But Henry Coretti's a name. Do his works bring much?'

'I don't know.'

'You should. Art market's firming.' And so it was, back then. 'Prices are rocketing for his generation. Wasn't he married to that woman who runs Siècle Gallery. Fine gallery, that…Now, wait a minute…Isn't it her daughter who runs that place? She'd be your sister, then?'

'My father had two families.'

'What, both at the same time?'

'Complicated. Artists' lives are often complicated. You've got two families, too, George. So I guess complications aren't restricted to artists.'

'But I had mine in sequence. My first wife was Enid…'

Phoebe got up, leading Eli away from the table as Fridlinda put in her dollar's worth. 'Enid said I had cruel lips.'

'She was right,' said my forthright Nin.

Fridlinda looked at me. 'Oh, I always thought my lips were rather mysterious. Artists have difficulty with them when they paint my portrait.'

George cackled like a man who pays to have his wife's portrait painted every year or so.

'Coming swimming, Nin?' called Eli from where he and Phoebe were about to mount the hotel staircase to change for swimming. Nin pushed back her chair noisily and rushed, rudely eager, away.

'I don't like this place,' rejoined Fridlinda as Nin was fleeing. 'And I don't like talking about families. People's business is people's business.'

'I couldn't agree more,' said I. 'As for the place. I used to bring the children here when they were young. They loved it and Eli chose it as the place for his wedding.'

'Have you paid for it in advance?' asked Fridlinda.

'Yes, it's all paid for,' I said.

'Pity. I was going to offer to send them up to Sydney for a week; I don't think they'll have much fun here.'

'Eli wanted to show Phoebe all his old haunts. We used to love coming here. Well, I'm going to take a walk and then have a swim myself,' I said.

'Oh, well, if you come back via the hotel, I'll come swimming with you,' Fridlinda said, 'now we're friends,' and she smiled at me sideways, coyly. I didn't think she had much of a mouth at all.

I haven't spoken to Fridlinda since. I think the young enjoyed the wedding, if she didn't. Charles Green thought Bowradale was a great place. The rocks there are Indian red, laced with purple and white sea wrack. I took Charles exploring and we collected spiralling cats' eyes to take home with us. He and I swam together while

Fridlinda sat in the hotel and sulked and George drank. Charles and I have remained occasional friends and I liaise with the rest of the family through him when I have to.

I feared that with those two people as parents, Phoebe didn't stand much of a chance of turning out as lovely, intelligent and good-natured as she seemed. I hoped that she had in her what Charles Green had in him, a psychic spirit level that had a penchant for righting itself.

When we arrived home Cousin Audra was not in evidence and Stella was sitting up in the dark watching telly. She and Audra had fought and Stella had lost her temper and broken the light bulb in the sitting room with a broom handle because Audra said one of the shades was full of moths.

What is it with Stella and light fittings that she breaks them when she's angry? Perhaps it is that along with not liking to hear what goes on in the world, she doesn't want to see it, either. It's not as if she watched news and current affairs on that telly of hers. She watched quiz shows and would have rung in whenever the contestants got things wrong because she knew better, but she was never fast enough to catch the numbers on the screen and sometimes they weren't on the screen at all, so she just rang me to check with me that she was right and the people on telly were wrong.

Mick and I – with uppityness and no sign of volunteer help – have started to move her out of Narrowlea, not without impressing upon Janelle, Tahlia and the management that we have found *hostel* level accommodation for Stella in spite of her age.

So there.

Stick that in your pipe and smoke it.

When we turned up at Redeemer with some of her things, Kees had actually come up with a better room. Someone had died. I think it was the dried-flower lady I met on my first visit. She was quite perky when I met her. 'Dead now,' said Kees merrily as I plunked a load of Stella-alia in the base of the built-in cupboard.

As I sorted and stacked, I recounted the dried flower lady telling me how she did all the arrangements we could see in the vases in the sitting rooms and the plastic glads, zinnias, lupins, tulips and roses garlanding Mary in the vestibule. She lived in such a forest of figurines and devotional objects it no doubt attracted the eye of God to the room, so he took her to make way for an Anglican in need.

Stripped of the ornamentation, the room is of a cheery pinkish colour with a comfy bed and a proper recliner chair courtesy of Redeemer. There is a pressure mat on the floor to warn the staff when the frail aged rises in the night to perform his or her offices in the en suite. The wardrobe is adequate for Stella's supply of clothing, but not for her books and writing things; there is space, however, to add a piece of furniture to accommodate those needs. Alas, none of the furniture from Narrowlea can be transported because it's all the wrong shape, designed to make her comfortable in a long, narrow room whose writing table used to straddle the water heater. I bought her the writing table in the dim hope that it would accommodate her prolific card-sending, stamp-losing, yellow pages balancing, homemade gift receiving and endless arithmetical additions of the items on her phone bill. The table was chock-a-block in no time, the drawer was jammed shut and she was constantly losing her dentures on it in a tooth glass full of putrid water. I had wanted to buy her a pretty desk with nooks, shelves and drawers for her to keep her bits and pieces in, but it was too high for Narrowlea's window and anyway, who knows what she would have kept festering in there – quite possibly friendly vermin. Now I'm glad that I didn't buy that – it wouldn't have fitted at Redeemer, either.

So...now Mick and I are in the Outer Circles of Ikea looking for a suitable piece of furniture and I am feeling less than capable of making the terrifying journey through and down to the cashiers.

He doesn't realise this but I'm getting frantic: Eli has been gone for weeks and I still haven't heard from him. We've tried to work out a system over the years whereby we keep in regular contact but it's always breaking down. Phoebe used to fill me in sometimes when he was off somewhere on a hair-raising adventure but now I just have to guess. I've no idea what he's up to and that is a bad frame of mind for me to be in when I enter Ikea. I can only ever make it through Ikea when I'm perfectly sane and reconciled with the flat-packed, ready-made concept of life.

Mick, unaware of my phobia, whoomps along ten paces ahead, swinging the instore bag like a slingshot champion off to slay a titan. Virgil to my Dante, he is not. We pass Billy and Lack. And the stackable, rockable, transportable Gullhomen chair made from leftover banana leaves. And now Biom and Ektorp and Wilma; Kvart, Klubbo and Blad. Mick shows no signs of being out of his depth – whoomp, whoomp, whoomp! go his size-fourteen Reeboks on the unforgiving floor past enough tea light holders to fill every opportunity shop within a hundred-kilometre radius for decades. I must remember what we are looking for. We saw it together in the catalogue, the Leksvik workstation with its pulldown desk, ample book hutch and space for my mother's treasures. I must stop thinking of the cruel clergyman in *Fanny and Alexander* and children being whipped in cold weather with birch rods. I must think instead of Greta Garbo, who, if she'd set foot in Ikea, would have worn large dark glasses and a fabulous long woolly coat pulled up to the cheekbones. She would have come on her own, bravely, on a foray, as a product of Sweden that could not be sat upon, switched on and off, converted, handily stored, crammed into a small space, or accommodated in a metre-square bathroom on the Vitaminer Bil rug in the shape of a Volkswagen, pampering her face in the Grundhall mirror hanging over the Godmorgen double sink solution.

I will live, I will live, I think I will live.

'Hurry up, lovey,' goes Mick in an unfriendly way that hurts my feelings and when I catch up with him, he shoves a wire arrangement for saucepan lids intended for the back of a kitchen cupboard into my arms when what I need is a reassuring full body hug and it's too much, I just start crying. He pretends he hasn't noticed and plunges on to the home office section, so I just drop this saucepan lid rack noisily and sob on the spot.

'Where am I going to paint?' I moan, when he comes back to hassle me onward.

'Lov-ey!' He picks up the wire arrangement and shoves it back into my arms. I want to drop it again.

'I'm sick of the sight of your back!' I sob. 'At least have the decency to walk beside me.'

'Why don't you just keep up?'

'You think I'm putting it on, don't you? You think I really can stand being in here, don't you? I'm not Greta Garbo, you know. I haven't got a great big coat up to my cheekbones and dark glasses.'

'*What* are you on about?'

'Fuck! What am I going to do with that corner bookshelf of hers, with the bridge chair and the hall table from Narrowlea? Where will they go? There's nowhere for them to go!'

'Forget them! We're buying a workstation. We'll worry about the other stuff later.'

'This *is* later! Oh, it's all later. All these people trying to make homes inside jam jars! Where am I going to paint?'

He doesn't answer. He's found the workstation set up and he's looking for someone to write out the docket for him. But they're all turning the other way, going on tea break, answering phones or not there at all.

I slump to the floor.

'Lov-ey, lov-ey???'

I haven't really fainted. Do you know how it is when you haven't really fainted? You just can't quite stand up because your legs won't do it and your head won't let you.

'Sorry,' I mutter and sit up while people walk around me, staring.

The floor of Hell will be hard as this and covered in arrows that only show the way to more of the same. I slobber over the bottom chromium rail of the information station, reminding myself of similar slobbers as a child on the chromium rails on the backs of bus seats. I'm the sort of child who spoils everything for the others. I'm too much, even for myself. Some school headmistress inside me hauls me upwards to stare myself in the face and tell me what a naughty girl I've been and that I'll never get on. But where will I paint? And what? Jumble? Junk? The Jamsjö table lamp?

I pat Mick's upper arm. 'Don't worry,' I mumble, 'I can't go on, I'll go on.' And now there's someone at the desk, writing and ignoring my tantrum. What would be cheaper – rent storage space or rent a studio? I can't afford to do either. I'm utterly sick of having no room to stand back and survey what I'm doing, of having no means of transporting a large canvas from A to B without having to dismantle a room and set it up again.

I'm utterly sick.

'Sorry,' I say as Mick whoomps off crankily through the Circles of Sloth, Lust, Gluttony, Greed, Anger and Heresy, the outer, middle and inner rings of Violence, through the eight Evil Pockets of Fraud, the four rounds of Treachery to the basement to where Satan's minions are checking the sinners out onto the dock from which the large items come sliding out on unslobbered-on chromium trolleys preparatory to loading them onto roof racks of cars that then roll down the concrete ramps and out into the starry, starry night. Well, less than starry, starry night, glowering and granular as it is with pollution and summer drought.

I've behaved very badly.

I visit a shrink occasionally to cope with feelings like these. I promised him that I'd up the dose of antidepressant when I felt like spitting the dummy, so, apologising to Mick for my break-out of rottenness, I crack another half tablet, forge my way into my studio, burrow for a sketchbook and spend the evening recording Hell from memory. But Mick doesn't get it and it doesn't put Hell out of my system and I've been instructed, again by my shrink, to avoid going to Hell. My obsession with Hell is ruining my life. 'There is no Hell,' says the shrink as I sit in his Hellish consulting rooms in a Hellish chair, gazing upon a Hellish sofa and wondering if anyone of his patients is gauche enough to lie in that cold, dark, leather-studded place and put aside the ignominy of using a fellow creature's flesh to make it – indeed countless fellow creatures' flesh to mass-produce it – and imagine instead that they are in the exalted presence of Freud. (Whose presence was just a bearded old shortsighted bloke with an Eastern rug over his lumpy-looking sofa, anyway.)

Oh, *Lasciata ogni speranza voi ch'entrate*. Oh, *Abandon all hope ye who enter 'Here'!*

'Here' is where the past gets put in its place. Here, the past was yesterday. Here, today is the beginning of the rest of your life. Here, nothing was made before today.

There is no history anymore.

'Here' used to be 'now' and 'with me', but now nothing is more immediate than 'Here', because 'Here' is today. It throbs with news, is pregnant with tomorrow, but never quite gives birth to it. Today exists in contradistinction to everything that is past. Even shop windows are past. Ikea doesn't have them; it just puts you straight in with the muck.

No, Isobel, no, it doesn't matter. Smile. It wasn't meant to be like that. It's never meant to be like that. Every action has unintended consequences. Life is full of ironies that nobody anticipates. And that's the point of an irony, isn't it? There's Ariadne's thread to take you through Ikea and you're an idiot for letting go of it.

But I've made Mick cross and now he has driven off to the country in a temper and I don't blame him. He isn't usually temperamental. He's generally patient and stands by me in all the tedious things I have to do. I don't know where I'd be without Mick.

10

It is Saturday today. I'm wishing for Mick to return. I'm nervous about it because on Thursday something very unnerving happened. A man came knocking at my door; at first I didn't know what he wanted but he was clearly furious. I thought maybe, in my absent-mindedness, I'd parked him in or a branch had fallen off the over-large tree in my front yard and dented his car, or his kid, or his wife, or, or...

He was waving a paper around in my face. 'What is it?' I asked. He was Chinese-looking and his English wasn't very good.

'Look! Look!' Banging the paper with the back of his stiff open hand. I'm always wary when lone men come knocking, thinking they can see that there isn't a man around to defend me bodily. I've always had to defend myself from predators, and there've been plenty of them right from the time I was a very young mother with a little child. Whatever neighbourhood I've lived in, posh or poor, there have always been predators and I've always been their object – small, female, defenceless, even though in my heart I'm brave and fearless and perfectly able to defend myself.

On the other hand, if that's how I've seemed to men, to women I must have seemed strong and protective because I've sheltered frightened girls from fathers and frightened wives from husbands while abuse lurked on the far side of my door – remembering this, I took hold of the paper, the man still grasping one side of it as if he feared I'd rush off and destroy it.

'Bastard not pay,' he said. 'I find this address.'

'Oh.' I could see Eli's name written on the page. 'A residential agreement?' I asked.

'Rent. Rent. Two months. Bastard not pay.'

'Oh dear, you'd better come in.' So I changed my defensive face for my sympathetic one and ushered him into the house. I followed his sweating body and nervous stench down my narrow hallway and into my slightly less narrow living room. He perched on a chair at my table, shuddering with tension.

'It's okay,' I said, laying a hand on his arm. 'That's the name of my son.' And I pointed to Eli's name. 'I take it that you were the person who rented him his unit?'

'You got it, lady.'

'Well, don't worry. I'll put on the jug and make some tea. How do you like your tea?'

'Not like tea. Water, just water.'

So I filled a glass of water for him and one for me, carried them in from the kitchen and sat down next to him.

'Now, could you please give me a close look at the paper and we'll see what we can do?' said I, imagining it was just a matter of money and Eli's forgetfulness.

So he handed me the paper. It was a rental agreement for $300 a week with a $5000 bond, signed by Eli (who, as a schoolboy, made a very good fist of my signature, but never mastered his own).

'He not pay last two month rent. Meant to pay every two week. Unit in bad condition, very bad condition.'

'Oh.'

'I go to see it. Terrible, terrible.'

'I don't quite understand, you know. Eli went overseas weeks ago now. His lease ought to have finished in late September or early October. I don't think he was even living at the unit before he left.'

'He there all right!'

'Gosh. Well. I can see you're upset. But I promise you he did go. He flew out the morning after he came to an art exhibition. He was there with me. The date was…'

'Bastard here, he not pay! Lot of damage!'

'Oh dear. Maybe I should see the unit…although I never saw it in the first place to gauge what damage has been done.'

'A disgrace! Smashed mirror in bathroom, stain all over floor! Terrible! Terrible!'

'Oh!'

'In bathroom, on floor. Big stain – bleach from blood. Someone fighting.'

'Oh dear, Mr…?'

'Liu, my name Liu.'

'Have you called the police?'

'No. You muss come. Come!'

He was parked out the front and I hoisted myself into the passenger seat of his Toyota van. It was one of those vans that has plenty of room in the back for toting things around, clothes or furniture. It wasn't new and the dashboard was sun-cracked, but, unlike the jalopy Eli had been driving around during his stay, it was tidy.

'What do you do for a living?' I asked him, trying to be sociable – I, who seem to do nothing much for my living, except breathe.

'I own two house,' he said.

'How long have you been in Australia?'

'Lady, bleach on my floor to get rid of blood!'

'To get rid of blood you think?'

'That why people use bleach. Believe me, I know this.'

'Blood? It might have been something else, surely – my son can be very untidy. He could have dropped a bottle when he was cleaning…?'

'All over wall and floor. Terrible.'

'And you think it was a fight?'

'Muss be a fight. Bleach everywhere.'

'But my son's not a violent man.'

'Violent, violent!'

'But I've never known Eli to be violent and I've known him all my life.'

'Sometime mother not know son.'

The place was in Collingwood, only ten or twelve minutes from me. Mr Liu owns two of four townhouses built where a couple of cottages once stood on the edge of a laneway. They are nondescript, the dirtied cream of 1980s or '90s fling-em-up and plaster-em-over boxes with undercover parking. Eli was supposedly living in a back one with a shiny black front door and a straggle of ivy sprouting weakly from where the downpipe made an imperfect connection with the ground.

Mr Liu put the key into the door with a shabby rattle of the other keys on his ring and we stepped straight into the front room, a depressing cream box, smelling of Glen 20 underwritten by stale-ness and grimy around the edges but not startlingly awful. It was empty of furniture. I noticed the venetians on the long front windows at about foot height, carelessly let down as only Eli can let down a blind. There was a door on the right-hand side behind where the stairs went up to the next floor directly inside the front door. We went through to the kitchen. 'See, see! Tiles, tiles! They wrecked with the bleach!' And it was true that some terracotta tiles on the floor had taken on a cloudy look, but I wouldn't have called them wrecked. I began to tot up the cost and wonder why you'd put down real terracotta in a rented unit until I realised the tiles were seconds, with chips out of them well before the grout was laid.

On the second floor, there was a bedroom and there things took a turn for the worse. Bleach had been scrubbed across the wall beside the en suite and there was a large colour-drained stain in the doorway, half on the floor tiles – once again terracotta – and half on the beige carpet. It looked as though it had been there for some time, it was dry and the carpet was shrunken and powdery-looking and it did look rather as if there was a blood stain underneath. 'Terrible, terrible,' said Mr Liu.

I had to agree. The mirror in the en suite had been violently smashed and the sink in the vanity was cracked through. I thought I could detect old meat hidden somewhere.

It's very scary in civilised Melbourne to walk in on a scene like that in a dwelling place that has bottom-of-the-heap written all over it. Little swarms of panic started running all over me, tightening my guts and clenching my gorge.

'We'd better ring the police,' I said, swallowing, and I took out my phone and dialled. For once the person who answered did so straight away and wasn't in Mumbai. In a panicky voice I asked for the police to come. 'There might have been a crime committed here,' I said when I was put through. 'I can't tell, but I think you'd better come.'

Then we stood about in the crummy place where neither of us wanted to be – me, because it baffled me to sickness and Mr Liu because he hadn't wanted anything like this to happen, his dreams to be smirched.

And to think that I'd thought that Mr Liu had wanted to molest *me*!

The police were there fairly soon and I found myself explaining that my son had left two months ago for Afghanistan...

'Is he a soldier, then?'

'NNNNo. No. No.' I was already being turned upside down by an avalanche of wrong directions that could be taken here. It was a constable in a tight blue jumper who interviewed me. He stood with his legs apart and his arms crossed over his chest. His shoes were old but shiny and he flexed one knee continually and watched the toe of the shoe on that leg as he did so. Now and then he looked up into my face, his bottom lip stuck out and one eye slightly off centre as if he were trying to nut something out. 'Just a minute.' I fought for my story, for what I knew of my story – aghast at the same time that I knew so little. 'He's a freelance journalist. He goes over there to report on what's happening with the reconstruction of Afghanistan. He started going over there years ago not long before the Taliban took control…'

'Taliban!' His mouth came open.

'NNNNo, not like that. No, he never went anywhere with the Taliban. Eli was largely in Pakistan where he was trying to help the Afghans establish an open press by setting up radio and TV links. He's not a terrorist, definitely not a terrorist. Whatever's happened here…Well, I don't know what's happened here.'

'Bit of a hero, then, is he?'

'I suppose he is. Yes. He is.'

'What, does he come home to visit his family sometimes, does he?' His voice sounded as if he might just be able to piece things together if there was a wife and kids involved…marital trouble, that kind of thing…

'No, there's no wife and kids here. He was married, but…All I can tell you is he came home for a rest after one of the women journalists he was working with was killed in February in Afghanistan. He took time out.'

'He's not still married, then?'

'No.'

'What, strong silent type is he?'

'I wouldn't say that. Just that his life's very complicated and he doesn't tell me very much. He has to be secretive because of what he does.'

'Or he keeps things from his mother. Wouldn't be the first time…'

How I hated the all-knowing look on that man's face! 'Oh, I don't think that's it. Not at all. He's a bona fide journalist.'

'Not still in contact with the wife?'

'No. It's well in the past now.'

'So no point in trying to contact her?'

'No.'

Then he started talking about soldiers and the Australian commitment.

'Well, it wasn't the war,' I interrupted. 'There have been three prominent women journalists killed in the past two years. Not by firepower in war. They've been murdered by people, their own people, who don't want women to be reporting on the news. The murderers are very conservative. They don't like seeing women in Western dress, let alone delivering news bulletins.'

'Muslims, eh?'

'Well, yes, of course, I'm talking about Afghanistan. It's very much a Muslim country. There are conservative and radical Muslims the same way there are conservative and radical Christians.'

'And your son's over there writing about it, is he?'

'Yes. That's what I've been saying.'

'Does he get depressed?'

'Yes, probably.'

'Is he on medication?'

'More than likely.'

'What, he suffers uppers and downers, does he?'

'Yes. Yes, he does,' said I to a cop in a suit too small for him.

'Down when he was home this time, was he?"

'I suppose so. He's been down for such a long time it's hard to know.'

'Was he ever violent?'

'No. Never. But all that might be completely unrelated to what's happened here...completely unrelated. It's just that he's been going to Afghanistan now for years...'

The policeman decided he was dealing with something that needed higher input, so he had his companion take copious photographs of the damage and told Mr Liu to leave things as they were until they'd been over the dwelling with a fine toothcomb. Then he took me back to the station. As I was leaving, I promised Mr Liu that I'd cover the damage to his house and wondered in the police car afterwards how I was going to do that...

a new bathroom, a new carpet! I can't even afford those things for myself.

At the police station I waited, with my arms folded and sighing at almost every breath, for about twenty minutes on a vinyl bench for the senior inspector. While I was there, a madman reeled in off the street, covered in blood, and announced that there'd been a stabbing down the street. Right in the middle of gentrifying Melbourne, five or ten minutes from my home. In Melbourne, home of snobby galleries run by the never-let-them-see-the-blood-on-your-hands likes of Che-chilia Coretti.

I phoned Mick. I didn't quite know what to say, except that there was a kerfuffle over Eli's accommodation and I'd try to sort it out, but it might cost me some money. Mick went on about rent and bonds and how landlords are obliged to take the money for repairs out of the bond. I didn't tell him the full story; it wouldn't have fitted into a phone call and he wouldn't have been able to grasp it, anyway. Mick and Eli have hardly met and when they crossed paths during this visit, Eli was distant and a bit surly. When I explained what I knew of the situation with Phoebe to Mick, he thought he understood, yes, such a thing might well account for a man's moodiness, but surely going back to Afghanistan afterwards hadn't been a great idea?

Mick was born in the blitz in London. He recounted how an uncle of his had suffered shell shock after the war. He'd been parachuted into France, been snagged in a tree in a mist and spent the night not knowing that his feet were only six inches from the ground. He was taken prisoner and carted off to Germany. He never talked about the war afterwards.

I sat waiting, juggling my mobile phone, sighing, thinking of this response of Mick's to Eli and how we ended up talking about both my parents also being war casualties: my mother bereaved, my father a refugee. I sat thinking how I never wanted war to touch my son. How I brought him up without guns, sent him to a school without cadets, but failed in the meantime to curb his social conscience. So he goes back and back to Afghanistan.

After their wedding, Phoebe went back to her new job with the Department of Defence in the States. She was working on the Afghanistan desk because of her network on the Afghan-Pakistani border. It complemented what Eli was doing, scouting for stories to write in the area. Someone Phoebe had known was a fighting Pashtun whom everyone called Bollywood. Bollywood had been supplied with stinger missiles by President Reagan to shoot down Soviet helicopters, which he'd done with great success, except that he lost a foot during the operations and had to ride into battle on a pony. Eli went off to Peshawar to write up his story.

Bollywood was a businessman who went to Peshawar during the Soviet era and built himself a white marble mansion in nearby Hayatabad. Phoebe had spent quite a bit of time there with him and his family; she was friendly with his wife. He was a minor warlord in Nangarhar Province over the Khyber Pass from Peshawar, very near the area that Eli first visited with the Dutch television crew.

After the Soviets' long and bloody leave-taking was over, any accord that had existed between the warlords who'd been fighting them fell apart and they started to squabble very fiercely among themselves. It was out of hand, but Bollywood, being a Pashtun whose connections with the non-Pashtun commanders were strong, remained a very useful contact for the CIA and the US Department of Defence.

Eli wrote that Bollywood's mansion was unlike anything he'd seen in Peshawar and stood out in what was then a choppy sea of mud dwellings. Bollywood had an older brother who was a big time tribal leader of Nangarhar. He grew opium poppies on his land and lived off the trade that was now many decades old. How would a good time with Bollywood not involve taking drugs, I wanted to know. Oh, no, no, no! Eli told me – no, observant Muslims don't take narcotics; their trade is with the decadent West. Besides, the poppy growing was only a temporary phenomenon to hold on to the land until better days would allow it to be used as it formerly had been, to feed and supply the people.

That was bullshit. I already knew that drug addiction was rife among Afghans and always had been. Phoebe herself told me that even babes in arms were drug-addicted. I felt I was catching an insincere vibe behind 'Observant Muslims don't take narcotics'. It stung me in the same way as the policeman's implying at the scene of a crime that my son could have been keeping things from me. During the Bollywood years, I began to distrust much of what Eli said, but if I wrote that I didn't like the sound of Bollywood, I realised that I just wouldn't hear about that part of Eli's life. When I made the first motherly protest, I was told that Bollywood was worth several score of the men I'd had in my life and that if I wanted to look to an example of virtue and courage, I need look no further. Bollywood was a patriot. He was fighting for peace and democratisation: he was an ally of Ahmad Shah Massoud, the Tajik warlord of the Panjshir Valley. Massoud was a great hero, the hope of Afghanistan, didn't I realise?

Firmly in this belief, Eli went freelancing alongside Bollywood's foot soldiers, who were going into Afghanistan to help Massoud take control of Kabul. I have photos that he sold to the *National Geographic* of Bollywood and his men, a raggedy group of illiterate farmers and villagers, trudging through valleys and over mountain passes, hauling equipment over torrents of water with the kind of nylon ropes we use to keep our purchases from Ikea on the roof rack. When the fighting was bad and they had to tough it out, they hid in caves in the Hindu Kush and were fed by a network of sympathisers. Some of these caves, I learned , were hung with carpets and lined with Kalashnikovs. Photos were put up of tanks with roses spewing out of their muzzles and they painted portraits of Massoud on their shields. It made me think that behind every army lurks a tribal confederation just waiting to supplant whatever civilian system it represents.

I tried to imagine what was happening, but I only ever received intermittent news from Eli, and the Australian papers were scant in their coverage. An attempt by the UN to broker an Islamic State of Afghanistan came to nothing. When Massoud actually did get to Kabul, the other warlords wouldn't sit down and govern with him. The grizzly Pashtun, Gulbuddin Hekmatyr, who'd spent his youth flinging acid in the faces of female students at Kabul University, wanted to be the leader of the government and when Massoud withdrew from Kabul to let him in, he only lasted one day before there was an attempt on his life. Such was the animosity towards Hekmatyr that he decided to take the city by force of arms. He laid siege, shelling from the peripheries and killing scores of people daily.

I just wished Eli would leave and leave for good. I was relieved when a call from him came through from Washington to tell me he was fine. 'Practise not worrying,' he said. The statement felt like hubris, but I took control of my feelings so that after I heard his voice, I could walk through a supermarket without having a nervous breakdown – for a day or two – then once again I was as besieged as Kabul. Grotesque imaginings had me reporting weekly to the shrink. 'Ring them,' the shrink would advise. 'Just to say hello. Ring them up and see.' But every time I rang, I'd be put through to voice mail and neither Eli nor Phoebe would get back to me. Where were they, what were they doing and why couldn't they let me know? The shrink suggested possibilities – high-powered jobs – he had no doubts that they were good people, after all I'd painted such a glowing picture of Eli, he couldn't possibly be a wrong 'un, could he?

The detective's office was all done up in the blue and white checks of the Victoria Police. I was given a recorded interview that lasted about an hour. I sighed the whole way through, guilty that I knew so little of what Eli did while he was in Melbourne, but it had been that way for years. He wouldn't *let* me know. What would the detective think if I said that Eli was adamant that he wanted to be by himself when he was here? I didn't say it. I burbled on about his coming to my exhibition launch, about the suit he'd given me to mind, how he wore it to the exhibition opening and how he'd seemed all right, almost his old self. How I didn't know what plane he'd taken except that he told me it was an early plane and he was going back to Afghanistan and he had said goodbye after the exhibition, saying he was going to stay over in town with a friend. I didn't know who the friend was.

All the while I was trying to prevent the demons from battering down the doors of my sanity. What, oh what could he have been involved in to leave a place in such a state? Or was it such a state? I reconstructed, I deconstructed. I looked for clues. Did Nin know anything? I felt certain that she didn't – Eli stayed away from her as well. I didn't mention Nin to the detective, who was kind enough to drive me home when it was over because suddenly I was shaking from head to foot.

Did I have someone to look after me? Well, I had a friend, but he was away for a few days and there was a doctor, I could go and spill the beans to him if I needed to. I told the detective not to worry about me. I was sensible enough, depression under control for several years, I'd never had to be hospitalised for it; I knew what to do. He said he'd ring again the following day to check that I was all right. Meanwhile, they'd try to contact Eli and find out what had gone wrong at the unit.

And so I am jolted out of my little middle-class suburban world into the great, reeling chaotic sphere of my son's life. I feel like the Black Knight in Monty Python's Holy Grail, armless, legless, headless and calling for a stretcher to carry me off. 'Come on there, pick up the bits!' 'Show some spunk!' 'What do you mean you can't fit everything onto the stretcher?' 'Here, then, *I'll* do it!'

11

He can't have been involved in violence, surely? And yet, he seemed like a stranger in my son's body when he was here, he was distant…the communication gap was too wide to cross…well, if I'm honest, it's grown that way. I can't understand him – this man who left behind a vandalised living space. If it was his home, his dwelling, and he was the vandal, then he's offended against him-self. Maybe he has been turned into a brute, a shit, and I just can't see it! Maybe he's mad…

Eli has never known his father – indeed, I only knew him for eighteen months. Perhaps there's something in Eli that I never calculated on being there. His father was a volatile, passionate man who said to me that it was all or nothing and – was it of course? – it was nothing, because all was going to cost him too much. And I was a child.

I've never said this to Nin because she has the task ahead of her, but in my opinion boys who grow up without fathering do it hard. No one to impress, nothing to live up to, just a woman to protect and guard, trying to make her cleave only to him so that he'll survive. It can warp a boy. He doesn't like competition, doesn't tolerate men in his mother's life.

There've been lots of men in mine and I've never stuck with any of them.

Of course, it could be me.

Maybe it's me.

Plenty would say I'm to blame, but really, it's just one of those insoluble messes that you have to live out – my compartment in this great thing called life, which offers up messes wherever I look.

After I came home from the police station, I had a stiff whisky and sat down to watch telly, but my head was full of depressive buzz and I couldn't hear what was going on, so I went to bed, telling myself there was nothing I could do except cover Eli's expenses and wait until there was an explanation.

Even from this panic-prohibited sleep, I reasoned, I could get back to a feeling of sanity. I've returned from depression as often as I've been able, there are ways, but after Allegra died, I lived in the white-noise high-tidal zone for years and years and, but for chance moments of clarity, I would not have known there *was* a way back. Now I've made the journey, I know the way. Ariadne's thread is in my hand and I'll never again let those towering waves of atoms pull me from this anchorage.

But how to sleep, given my present woes? Because you don't sleep, Isobel, do you? In sleep you can be reduced to helpless decrepitude: your long dead Aunt Nina can come smiling in with a fresh young face, beautifully made up in the colours that suited her so well, freshly dressed, lovely and young and she's come to visit another person at the old person's home and she sees you there and says, cheerily, 'Hello darling.' Not 'What are you doing here?' or 'Let me get you out of here.' But 'Hello darling,' on her way through to see someone else before she goes out shopping in that wonderful, bourgeois, confident way she used to shop – as if shops were palaces where you played the role of a princess whose patronage was craved.

Unlike the shops of today, where you're the prey and they're the predators.

When I ask my psychiatrist how he copes with other people's misery day in, day out, he says he has a knack of never taking his work home with him. He has a glass or two of good wine with dinner and becomes a creature of his home. I'll bet he doesn't cut himself off completely, but even if he's partially successful, it's something to learn.

Objectivity should be able to carry you over the chasms that exist in the mind; it's those bombarding tides of noisy atoms you have to beat. Nature. And nature has its way. You have to live with your emotions, ride with them when the going is rough, rein them in when and if you can. Become the Layne Beachley of neurosis.

I can tell myself this, but I can't quite do it.

My mother has a way. Her way is to slip into situations that she believes, on the instant, are so happy and salubrious that all life's problems are solved and happiness will reign forever from the golden moment onwards. Over and over again, there's that sacred moment where the horses hold themselves in single line before crashing through the barrier and, in an instant, it's gone – the silk sash with which Stella ties up her perfect world turns into a noose in her hands. She sulks, she stamps, she misbehaves and throws away her mind right up until the next moment arrives. And she will go on doing that until she dies.

It's a widespread trait, really: moments of perfection inter-spersed with chaos. There are just those who ride the bucking tumult and those who refuse to: the crazy and the smug old sane.

It isn't true that people change. As a child, I thought that when told a story of righteous behaviour, people would immediately see the error of their ways and adopt the ways of the righteous. I was taught this by the occasional Sunday school Anglican on my way to what they imagined would be confirmation and safety within the confines of Anglicanism. The never-having-to-look-sideways-ness of the communion. But it didn't work. I could see that they had all the characteristics they professed to despise – they were uncharitable, blind, materialistic…clannish. In clannishness was rescue from ever having to think or do for themselves or find a path in spite of their religion.

What am I to do about Mick? If I let loose my galloping fears about Eli, I can't expect him to mount the horse of reason and round up the galloping fears – he's neither athletic nor heroic. Common sense ought to tell him that I'd be best left to my complicated life, but he doesn't seem to have much sense where I'm concerned. He isn't exactly an optimist, but keeping me company seems to do him as much good as it does me. He spent his youth dealing with a divorced mother and a crabby old grandma, so for him my family situation is familiar territory.

He's someone I met on the off-chance when I was trying to learn about imaging on a computer. He was taking the class, a friendly, helpful, affable big bear. We went to the pictures together. He told me he could be stubborn when I asked him what his faults were – and he can be stubborn. His star quality is that he's a peace bringer – Nin loves him. He's reliable, steady. He's a wonderful 'grandparent' for Daniel, with whom he gets stuck into boys' stuff. He has grown-up sons who keep in touch all the time and that's a very good sign to me. But gold upon gold, he's not put off by my mother and her helplessness. It's just part of life to him – his life, while it doesn't have brutes and murderers, has old people in it as well as kids and babies.

Mick would be a loss.

I don't know what the real situation is with Eli. I certainly don't know how to describe it to Mick. So should I even try? Or should I leave it to fate? Would that be fair?

Perhaps it's time to up my antidepressant dose again, or maybe it's just that I'm overwrought. Those who've never walked down Suicide Road can't know what it's like. I'm not recommending it. The mud of the River Styx never seems to wash off. My sister was a deliberate suicide, whereas if I die before my time, it'll be suicide by default. I trip myself up, I have accidents like the accidents my mother has when the world does something she doesn't approve of – like gashing herself in a blender once, so I'd come to her aid and wouldn't go on a lost weekend.

But I'm not as bad as she is. Not nearly.

I don't consciously wreck my life. No – I panic, I have little car crashes which I know these days to avoid – I give up driving the car when I'm in this state.

I go and pound a treadmill at the gym because not only have I been told, but I also know it to be true, that exercise is good for depressed people.

There's nobody else in the gym at the moment. The gym is in a hospital and I ended up coming here when I had an angiogram that revealed plaque in my arteries and that explained my angina. (The plaque is explained by years of smoking and feeling under-rated – true, just the feeling that no one appreciates your sterling qualities can change the insides of your arteries through the action of negative hormones.) It's a little gym, used by the staff and patients. If nobody else is here, then the noise is at the level of clunking machinery accompanied by slight movements in adjacent rooms where people work on fundraising programs. If I close my eyes and walk very fast, then I make a harmonious rhythm inside myself, I think of where to go with the paintings, of how I'd like to resurrect in one vast piece the drawings ruined by David. Perhaps I could stitch over the wounds he made. The best drawing in that series was of my dear old friend, Bridget-Kelly-of-the-dump's daughter Maggie, shoved up against the glass in front of the picture, her cheek, hand and bare breast flattened against the pane, her red-blonde hair crushed into waving shapes. Oh it was a good picture. It was called *The Crushing*.

In my mind, it adverted to the calamitous noises that used to go on when David and Allegra lived over my head in our share house. He used to beat her up. It was surreptitious, done when he thought we weren't there. She would never talk about it although we had evidence; we'd heard them yelling at each other upstairs, and thumping and crashing and her emerging behind prodigious hedges of hair, saying as quickly as she could that she was just going out, she'd be a while…we knew. He'd stay up there brooding for hours and then appear and ask surlily, 'Did she say where she was going?' And we'd say, 'No.' And he'd go out and come back with flowers and ask if he could borrow the vacuum and he'd be cheerful with Eli, try to get him on side by talking about football. And he'd chop wood for our heater and walk the dogs. And be all smiles when she returned. And she'd go to bed and he'd dance attendance on her...

Until the next time.

The spite and cruelty worked on him by his circumstances had entered him and came thrashing out onto Allegra. And then she was pregnant and something irreversible had begun. In my heart of hearts I felt I could do nothing for her, so I painted *The Crushing*. David more or less recognised what I was painting and why. He was hopping round my studio like a cross little frog, bobbing up and down with his fist cupping his chin. It made me terribly nervous. Something violent was going to happen. You always knew it was going to happen. Maybe the fight he picked in Mad Meg was vengeance: he was affronted, not just affronted, but confronted as it became obvious to him what I'd done. I'd drawn the psychology of victimhood – a psychology I know firsthand. Victimhood is not what the self-help gurus call the 'Poor Me' syndrome; victimhood is a state of deep and anguished confusion, of deracinated sense. It is being crushed up against the window glass and unable to break through.

Oh Eli, where are you and what have you done?

Oh dear, and where is it writ that even when you're in a state of despair you have to tolerate idiots? I have enough to cope with without bloody Audra ringing up to harangue me about Mum being in a Catholic home. Didn't I know my mother and she were confirmed as Anglicans together? Didn't I know that there was a bishop in the family and that he sent my mother a postcard of the Scunthorpe Anglican Church after her confirmation and wrote on it 'To Bunny with love from "The Bish"'? *Bunny!* And when exactly was I proposing to go and visit my mother on the next occasion, for Audra was going to come with me now that she is unable to take public transport due to a cat-scratch allergy.

'Aren't you a pensioner, Audra?'

'What's that got to do with anything?'

'Well, you're entitled to cab charge. You can take a cab up to see Stella whenever you like.'

'What! Oh…cab charge is only for shopping.'

'Well, I'm not a taxi, Audra.' And I put the phone down in her ear. Twenty minutes later, the phone rang again. It was from Redeemer telling me that they'd had a call from one of Stella's relatives demanding that she have Anglican communion.

I said, 'Fine. If Audra's prepared to organise it and Stella wants it, I have no objections.'

'You wouldn't be prepared to organise it, then?'

'It's not high on my list of priorities. Stella has had nine-tenths of a century to organise her faith; if she hasn't done it yet, perhaps it's a measure of how sincere she is.' I was glad when the girl at the other end laughed. 'Your mother's so funny,' she said. 'She's wheeling the house cat around in her basket now.'

So I rang Audra back and said, 'Audra, you'll be alarmed to know that Stella now keeps a cat in the basket of her wheelie frame. If you're allergic to cats you'd better ring up the home first and have them take it away from her before you come.' That little speech was the only piece of satisfaction I've had since seeing that abominable unit.

Right now, nothing is being done about finding Eli because Christmas is upon us, which means it is the season of maximum family crime, relapses into alcoholism and outbreaks of eating disorders. Only rookie cops are minding the police stations at Christmas (and international criminal hunters are having a break).

How do I know? It's the delight of Christmases past, of the year when we experimented with having David actually inside our home for the lunch. It was twelve years ago, Eli in Washington and Nin still living at home. No Daniel yet. Why did I allow it to happen? Perhaps it is I who am the idiot and I shouldn't put up with myself. Stella invited Audra. Nin was having her first trial with a girlfriend, a very droll person called Portia who parried her cutlasses of wit on a Christmas galleon across whose deck the cannon kept shifting. Stella was trying to scare Portia off, but she wasn't scaring, all the cannon were firing inwards. I was at the helm as usual. As usual I'd struggled to make an edible meal. I'm quite good at Christmas trees but lousy at turkeys. Fortunately, Nin has culinary skills and is able to relight ovens that go out mid-turk and rescue sauces mid-clump. So the early comers were assembled: Audra flopped in, red-faced, at ten a.m., saying, 'The heat, the heat, I've had to drive all the way and I've got a sprained wrist and a broken toe – don't ask me how I broke the toe.' And Stella asked her.

They were drunk and roaring by eleven.

Idiot Portia didn't stay in the kitchen helping us but entered the fray. I'm glad Nin dropped Portia; Portia loved to tell everybody that they were ignorant and that the Motte cutlery, put out for the festivities, was only silver plate. 'Silver dipped,' went Stella and Audra concurred, adding that the Mottes from whom she too was descended had a solid silver service. You never saw such a thrust and parry of common-or-garden old Grosvenor Plate in all your life.

Then David arrived. He was quite nice to everyone to begin with. He had a lovely present for Nin, a whimsical miniature doll's house.

Could it possibly, possibly…?

No, of course not. It never does, you idiot, Isobel, does it? It never does. It's just that the doll's house was so intriguing it took Stella a good hour under the influence to work out a nasty thing to say about it.

'What's it made of? Oh…paper…But it's only a sort of a…a sort of a card…'

'You could make money with those!' piped up Audra.

Did anyone care that Nin and I had created a table in the presence of enemies? Did the lamb lie down with the lion? The answer is no. A dead turkey flew. A man went mad, armed with a blunt bread and butter knife – Grosvenor Plate, of course – in a house full of women. The man would not calm down and had Stella bailed up, at top throat, in the bathroom.

I rang the police.

Two eighteen-year-olds in uniforms too big for them turned up and that's how I know who minds the police station on Christmas Day. Audra would have pressed charges had it been in her power to do so, but she was not the one assaulted. Stella did not press charges, nor did I. Some people think that the way to solve domestic violence is to press charges, but you need to be incredibly brave to do that and it's you who needs to be locked up afterwards, not the perpetrator because the perpetrator will be released one day and come looking for you. The violent believe that violence is the answer to their problems like others believe in prayer. I just told myself that I would never invite David into my home again.

David left and drove off in a backfiring car.

Portia sat around, hysterical and panting out things like 'Oh Nin! Your family is hilarious! Hilarious!'

Audra took Stella away with her and neither of them was seen again…just like in a children's story. Not. But I had a peaceful January. And in February Stella got another friend of hers to ring and say, 'Don't you think it's time you made up?'

And now it is Christmas Day 2007 at Redeemer and Mick is here (I haven't dared to tell him the story of Eli yet) and we have taken Stella to the mass in the chapel and Stella looks like a toad whose head has been stepped on, her eyes rolling in ripe fury. People are 'body of Christ'-ing all around us and Stella is saying, 'Huh!'

Well, I think, with the mad, the answer is to take them one at a time. More than one at a time leads to the kind of debacle we had those twelve Christmases ago. My logic then was throw them all in together and then you won't have to protect yourself because each of them will act as a foil or distraction for another. For instance, I thought that David would act as a foil for Nin and her first foray into same-sex love. I knew that Stella wouldn't be able to cope with two women making a go of it together, but David, because he hates the bourgeoisie, would. I thought they would cancel each other out. I thought we could build them into their own little concrete cocoon and repair for drinks to the back veranda. I didn't count on Audra seconding Stella in a family stoush. Nor did I imagine that Portia would be another maddie. The problem, eventually, was Nin and me – we wanted a normal Christmas with trees and presents and things – the sort of Christmas Nin has told me she is giving Daniel at this very moment as Stella is grumbling up the hall to the dining room, grinding that pulverised tooth of hers and mentioning the word 'cat', that creature not being, at the moment, in her wheelie basket (after all, it is Christmas and the cat has been put outside). Daniel, I was told, would be having a tree and presents at Gorgon's (Gorgon being what Daniel calls Wendy's mother) in the embrace of Wendy's three siblings and their children. There would be Christmas bonbons, running in the park and picnic blankets in the thinning shade of the drought-stricken trees. There would be champagne and nobody like George Green pouring it or Fridlinda Häken-Green complaining about the venue.

So now we are sitting at the table, Mick on one side of Stella and I on the other, and Mick mentions how sensible it is of the home to have electric candles in lieu of real ones. Festive and not danger-ous. The chicken is being served. Quite pleasant chicken by the look of it, with a modicum of festive trimmings. Mother Oldmeadow is at a table over the other side of the room and we have Father O'Brian and Brother Donald, both of them teachers in their day.

Brother Donald was a Christian Brother. Taped Christmas carols quietly in the background.

'Where's the cat?' goes Stella.

'They've put him outside Mum. During lunch.'

'Why isn't the cat being given Christmas lunch?'

'Well, I dare say it'll be getting the leftovers.'

'Leftovers, huh! I want to share my lunch with the cat… Here, Puddy, Puddy, Puddy, Puddy, Puddy…'

We can see the cat looking in from outside the window.

Father O'Brian stands to give the blessing.

'Puddy, Puddy, Puddy…'

'Hush, Mum.'

'I WANT THE CAT TO SHARE MY LUNCH.'

Lovely Liz from the nursing home rushes up to Stella and takes her hand. 'It's okay, Stella. The cat'll get the leftovers. You'll see.'

'…for these, Your gifts…'

'I WANT TO FEED THE CAT.'

The Babushka, unnerved in her senility, starts to sing 'Jingle bells, jingle bells, jingle all the way…'

Steam starts to come off the top of Stella's head. As we pass the condiments, she begins to stamp, first the left foot, THUMP, then the right, THUMP. 'Now, now, Mum…'

'Oh what fun it is to ride…' goes the Babushka, feebly, but it's not Santa's sleigh that's coming, it's Stella…She starts to sing – at first in a low and grinding way, 'Buggery, buggery, buggery, buggery,' and then the volume increases, 'BUGGERY, BUGGERY, BUG-GERY, BUGGERY!' and it's surprising how far an old woman's voice can carry, rising above the benediction at a table full of priests, like Tartarus's roar.

'I think I've had enough,' says Mick. 'I'll go and wait for you in the car.'

He made me a beautiful Christmas dinner in spite of everything. He wiped away my tears.

Mick. The food he cooks me is perfect, except for the turnips. I have to stop him from slinging turnips into everything. That's a problem with your Yorkshire man born during rationing. He's learned to live with turnips so well he's even developed a taste for them. Turnips he loves and me. Where would I be without him? He has carried, accompanied, driven, assembled, sorted and supported while Stella crumpled, wilted, thurped up breath between her teeth, tottered, staggered, collapsed and collided and introduced him to the staff at Redeemer as 'him'. She barely remembers his first name, let alone his second. More than once she's said, 'He's only after *her* for her money.' It makes me contemplate eldercide.

Mick tolerates Stella and is endlessly patient with her, not allowing her senile jibes to penetrate. The fact that she would have made them before she was senile doesn't perturb him. 'Windbag,' he calls her. When we settled her into Redeemer at last, it was as if we'd chucked a rock into a beanbag full of dust, such an airing of lost recriminations and unguided missiles came up with the impact.

I would not have been able to cope with Stella without Mick. I'd be a heap of chagrin and rotten temper and I'd have taken it out on everyone around me. This I Know.

12

Daniel didn't have such a hot Christmas either, because Gorgon made him go to bed with the light off. He wept in self-pity when he told me.

'But there might be good things in the dark,' I suggested.

'No they isn't. They's monsters.'

'Who told you that?'

'I don't know.'

'Well, they didn't tell you the right thing.'

'You let me have the light on.'

'Yes. But I'm an old softie.'

'What means softie, Sibella?'

'Well, walls are hard and beds are soft. I'm more of a bed than a wall and Gorgon's more of a wall than a bed.'

'Beds are best.'

'They don't keep the wind out.'

We're going to visit Great Gran, even though she doesn't deserve it after Christmas Day's performance. It is New Year's Eve, Daniel has a present for her and the mothers are worn out again. He's sleeping over with me tonight. We are driving past my psychiatrist's rooms above which there is a gigantic girl with the close-set eyes whispering into the hearing aid of a poor old crone who's been placed in a home. The girl is smiling, but those are not the muscles of sympathy she's exercising, they're the muscles of gloating exaltation. Some wag has scaled the shop awnings and blacked out one of her teeth.

'Three cheers!' I hate that ad.

'What you say that for?' goes Daniel in the back.

And my mouth starts a long, theoretical monologue about the blacked-out tooth, which Daniel interrupts to ask if I'm old yet?

'A bit,' I say.

'Gorgon's old,' he says.

'I'm nearly that old.'

'Why we get old?'

And my mouth goes off in a long-winded theoretical monologue about growing up and growing old and when I've reached the explanation of decrepitude, Daniel says, 'Gorgon's got stripes up and down. Like this,' And I watch him in the rear-vision mirror as he draws vertical stripes with his index finger over his lips. 'You not got stripes. You not old. What means die, Sibella?'

'Well…' I put the car into gear. Daniel and I take lots of trips to the museum… 'you know how in the museum you see the animals and they're not moving anymore…'

'Because they finished they turn?'

'Yes, that's right.' That's what I've been discussing with him lately, that life is 'having a turn' (what I don't tell him is that often enough, it's a turn for the worse). The explanation was partly expedience because Dan is learning to share his toys, but it also felt like a good way of explaining that life isn't forever. Gorgon's sister-in-law died recently and Gorgon cried and told him she was sad. So why was it sad that Sylvia died? Well, it was sad for Gorgon because she wouldn't see her anymore…

'Will Great Granma die?'

'Yes, she'll die.'

'Today?'

'No. I don't suppose so. We'll see her today.'

'When she finished she turn, will we see she in the museum?'

'Well, that's a good question. I hadn't thought of that. I suppose we could have her stuffed and put in the museum, but then again we might put her into a grave.'

'Like Sylvia?'

'Yes.'

'Why?'

What do you say? Because the wolves will get her? Or shut up. Or I don't know. Or because she'll go off if we don't either bury or burn her. You have to be careful what you say to children – who would have thought that Nin would remember those porn magazines? Maybe the soul is the best way out of the death dilemma at this stage, although the scientists seem to be saying it's best to be absolutely honest so that children won't fall into the God trap. But then again, is God a trap? When I told Daniel about how elephants are sad when other elephants die and they go back to grieve over them, Daniel drew me an elephant and then put a cage over it with a handle on top and so I asked, 'What's that for?' and he answered, 'A basket with a handle so God can carry the elephant to Heaven.' No, God isn't all that much of a trap... But he is a bastard, because that's just the kind of drawing David would do.

'Why Sibella?'

'Why what, darling?'

'Why we put Great Granma in the earf when she die?'

'Well, when you die, your body can't do living anymore, so you put it back in the earth to make more things for the plants and animals to eat.'

'And the germs?'

'Yes, the germs like to have a munch.'

'Are germs bad?'

'Well, they do work. They make the dirt for us. We wash our hands to get rid of them because we don't want them to munch us up while we're alive. Everyone's got germs, but their own, friendly germs.'

'In they tummy.'

'Yes.'

'And the bad germs in they poo?'

'Yes, the old ones that aren't doing good work anymore.'

'Why we do poo?'

And so it goes for several kilometres. No wonder the Mummies are tired.

It is going to be stinking hot today, an El Niño shocker. You'll soon be able to hear the asphalt ripping away from the road top as the wheels turn. Something that works in my car is the air-conditioning and I'm very glad of it.

I'll never be wealthy. Let's face it. I will never be wealthy.

I may never own another car. It is a toss-up as to whether it would be more expensive to buy a new car than a thirty-year-old replacement radiator for this one, but there is the air-conditioning – I can only hope that the heat dial doesn't go into the red before we reach Redeemer…

Stella likes to feast her eyes on Daniel, who is a very good-looking little boy with blue-green eyes and masses of dark curly hair, like Allegra's. Stella confuses Daniel with Eli. She remembers having Eli around as a little boy and having to think up how she came by this grandson from her nineteen-year-old daughter. When the dreaded Audra turned up wanting to be a long-lost cousin, Stella introduced me to her as Bel Gilchrist, borrowing her maternal grandparents' name, until it occurred to her mid-introduction that if Audra were indeed a cousin, she could well know WHO THE GILCHRISTS WERE. OMG. So she claimed that my husband, Arnold Gilchrist, who was 'away fighting the war in Vietnam', was descended from the very same Gilchrist family that presented the world with her mother, Euphrosyne Isabella, née Gilchrist…now wasn't that a mouthful! And would you look at the monogram on this spoon? Yes, that was right, G for Gilchrist…marvellous people, related to the Queen (like the Turners being related to the Trocadero). And so Arnie Russell, Eli's true and natural father, was passed over in the nimble acquisition of more than adequate social status for the daughter who'd been fucking an associate of the firm Stella worked for.

Well, we made it just before the needle on the air-conditioning went into the red. Stella is sitting up in her room with her air-conditioning on full blast plus swivel facility, shredding a Kleenex by sticking her ancient thumb through it in front of the telly. Her anxiety melts to love in her face as Daniel and I come in. 'My grandson,' she chirrups. I sit down on the bed beside her, 'Allegra's grandson, actually,' I chirrup back. She laughs as if that couldn't possibly be true and runs the non-Kleenex forefinger adoringly down Daniel's cheek.

No cat anywhere today, thank God.

'I thought we might go and check out your little sitting room today, Mum? It's nice and cool in there.'

'My little sitting room?'

'Yes, there's a sweet little room just down the corridor with things to make tea and a little courtyard garden outside, where you can watch the birds through the windows.'

'But I haven't got a sitting room.'

Away goes my mouth again, explaining how the world works and how, even though she's comfortable here in her chair, there's not really enough room to entertain a child who likes to do more than sit on a bed. I tell myself she needs the exercise and, that being new here, it's important that she finds companions. I suppose that her world has shrunk right down to the great efforts she has to make in getting herself from A to B; much of her mind is occupied by just putting one foot in front of the other and pushing the Wheelathon along.

But I might be wrong. Recent recitals of long-lost slabs of Tennyson and Scott hint at old pathways being opened up, of deep memory resurfacing, of enjoyment in losing herself in words, of savouring phrases and how one might say them. I've noticed Daniel learning like this, by turning the coinage of language over and over in his mind and in his mouth until sense and reason fall into place and are inculcated alongside commonplace understandings and the mind goes searching for more.

The little sitting room is just two doors away from Stella's. Slowly I take her through the doorway and towards a group of chairs around an occasional table. Two nuns are watching the news on television, and a third, the bush sister, Sister Colleen, is busy at a laptop by a window under a light well that adjoins the courtyard garden. I'm comfortable with this slightly scholarly scene but I wonder if Stella is. I catch Sister Colleen's eye and ask if it's okay for us to take some biscuits from the tin in the kitchenette and to make a cup of tea. She says it's there for everyone.

I know what Sister Colleen's doing. She's on a crusade. There is a considerable government contribution made to Redeemer over and beyond the contribution made by the church, but now the church's contribution has come in, not earmarked for anything in particular, and Sister Colleen has set up a strong, flat-vowelled lobby for air-conditioning in the nursing home part of the building. It's difficult to see why the whole building isn't air-conditioned in this day and age, but I understand that the nursing home wing is badly in need of improvements. Sister Colleen's letter is part of her campaign against the lobby that is for improvement of the group entertainment area rather than the nursing home. This second lobby wants new equipment for showing films. They want a giant flat-screen telly and video equipment so that they can watch films other than those that can be shown on a rickety pull-down screen with a projector. I think they're a bit sick of *Oklahoma!* and *Mary Poppins*.

Daniel shoots into the kitchen and grabs the biscuit tin. 'I think we're only meant to have one each, Dan. Then we leave the tin for the others. This is a sharing place. Here, pop them on a plate.' So he pops all the Monte Carlos on the plate, counting 'one, two, three' and delivering seven.

We are about to join Stella, when 'Ewwww,' comes a voice from above and I look up the length of an ebony stick into the prim smile of Reverend Mother Oldmeadow. 'I see,' she says and what she sees is probably the greed of a lapsed Anglican's great-grandchild. 'Yes, we do share our biscuits.' And she turns her back on us, leaving me to work out for myself whether or not there is a kitty – or was it just that she was coveting a Monte Carlo? So I ask 'Is there a kitty?' And she just waves her free hand dismissively and breathes in audibly through very distinguished, elegantly flaring, vermicularly veined nostrils, making me feel that there probably is a kitty but not for parvenus like me.

I load a tray with tea for Stella, tea for me and milk for Daniel, which occasions another lingering of the superior eye and a swan-like turning of the head with mild fluttering of the upper lip as if to say, 'Now you've used up all the milk.'

Well, I can't be bothered with her and make my way to our little cosy corner, a table away from new arrivals and two tables from Sister Colleen, who is now sitting down with the receptionist from the hostel's front desk, folding the letter she's been writing, tapping it on four sides and putting it into an envelope with a look of pending victory on her face. 'There, Ida,' she croaks, 'if that won't do it, I don't know what will.'

'D'ya want me ter put a stamp on it, or've you got some yourself?' asks Ida.

'Doesn't need a stamp. Put it in the internal courier bag. I'd like to see their faces when they open it.'

Ida laughs, throwing back her headful of spiked black hair. 'I'd like to, too.' She's a plump, pleasant girl from Trieste. I met her outside where she goes for a smoke with other staff members on her break. Most of the staff smoke around here; there's an offertory of butts to the God of easy-going sinners in a scantily shaded nook beside the back car park.

Daniel has found a silver pedalling thing to play with, a bit like a bike crank. He's curious to find the rest of the bike while Stella and I play guessing games as to what this piece of equipment might be.

'There,' I say to Stella, 'this isn't such a bad place.'

'Nope,' she says, having become jolly of a sudden. 'It's quite nice. Hey you...' she says, pointing at the secretary.

'Me?' goes Ida.

'Yes, you.'

'What've I done?'

'You turned up in my bedroom last night. How'd you know I was up? Were you spying on me?'

Sister Colleen goes, 'Oh, she's Redeemer's guardian angel, aren't you Ida? God told her you were up.'

'God? What was he doing in my bedroom?'

'He's everywhere, love,' goes Ida. Then to me, 'Your mother's a scream. It's the pressure mats we've got in their rooms. A light goes on in the office and we go in to have a look.'

'That man came in the night before!'

'She means Kees.'

'I asked him what he was doing in my room in the middle of the night and he said, "What do you think?" He wanted to come into the bathroom with me. Don't tell me God sent him!'

Sister Colleen roars with laughter and shoofties Ida out into the corridor ahead of her.

A little Mount of Piety is developing around Mother Oldmeadow. Young nuns apparently come in for instruction in the ways of Catholic decorum. Mother Oldmeadow is seated at the summit on a commode-like chair, the kind of chair you might have for the Pope if his bowels were a tad shaky, and the younger nuns, four of them are gathered at her knee on pouffes and footrests so that the whole tableau takes on the shape of Mary with Jesus' corpse athwart her knees, or then again, the leg of one of Picasso's gueridon tables without the top. I can visualise the painting Picasso would have made of the scene – he would have put a top on the table and on it, he would have placed religious paraphernalia so that the lowly nuns, in their subtending scrolls under the instruction of Herself at the leg bulge, would be trying to guess what was up there – just as Picasso's mistresses waited under their gueridons unable to guess that the tops were littered with secret allusions to women who weren't them.

'Where's the wheels, Sibella?' asks Daniel apropos of the pedal device.

'Oh, is that child touching my stepper? Tell him to stop. It's for my use only,' goes Mother Oldmeadow, ruining my trance.

'Sorry Dan, not ours I'm afraid.' I lean down and pull it away from him.

'Awww!' he says.

'Leave it! Leave it right there where it is! Don't you touch what isn't yours.'

The rebel is rising in me and I have to count to ten to stop myself rising to my full short height and hurling the bloody thing at her.

'Aww,' says Stella. 'Never mind darling, I'll buy you one for Christmas.'

'It's not a Christmas gift. It's an aid for strengthening my muscles!'

'Christmas is over,' says Dan.

'I'll just put it over here out of the road, Mother Oldmeadow,' I say and go to put it beside the wall.

'Don't. Touch. It. Leave it right where it is!'

'But we're sitting here.' And there's no Sister Colleen just now to defend us.

'It's where I sit to do my exercise. I like it left there, just where it was before that boy started fiddling.'

'Oh well, come on Dan, let's turn Great Gran's chair around so we can sit at the next table,' I say and stop myself from chucking the thing on the floor just any old how, because after all my mother has to live here and she doesn't need me to make enemies for her. I put it down carefully in the place where old blue-rinse wants it and she says, 'That's better,' grandly and turns her attention back to her flock.

Is it because I resort to explaining things that I get caught up with dictators like Mother Oldmeadow? Why is it that I immediately want to explain the situation to her so that she'll get it and calm down? So that she'll know who Daniel is, who my mother is and will make up her mind that they're inoffensive and that it won't do any harm if Daniel has a little fiddle with her muscle-strengthener? Why is she so aggressive and why am I so meek? It's certainly not because I'll inherit the earth. All I'll inherit is debt. Passive-aggressive, maybe that's it – I'm passive-aggressive, like Stella, who pulled her erstwhile GP's nose for saying so. There used to be this word 'sensitive' to cope with chaps like me – 'It's all right,' they'd say, 'she's just sensitive.' And it would be all right. I was allowed to be sensitive, like Allegra was allowed to have 'a Latin temper' along with her 'Byzantine face'.

I shove another Monte Carlo into my mother's mouth before she can get terse with Mother Oldmeadow only to be spoiled by Daniel, who asks, 'Why you teeth slippy Great Gran? My teeth are stuck. Are you teeth stuck, Sibella?'

'Yep, mine are stuck.'

'What means stuck, Sibella?' he asks, suddenly uncertain of the word.

'Opposite of slippy, Dan. Things that stay in one place are stuck, things that move around are slippy.'

'Why Great Gran's teeth are slippy?' Stella, insulted to the quick, taps him sharply over the head. 'One of these days yours will be slippy too, kiddo.'

'I not kiddo. I'n Daniel.'

He doesn't cry.

He's not a sook, thank God. Nevertheless, our little outing is turning sour. I suppose we could take a trot past the goldfish tank, or push past the tableau vivant over there to have a look at the books in the library, but the energy to do so has left me. My imagination has deserted me. My will has deserted me.

I can't be bloody bothered.

Benazir Bhutto was assassinated last week.

There's rioting in Pakistan.

Nobody knows if Eli's there or in Afghanistan or not.

They haven't been able to trace his departure and think he must have taken a connecting flight because they can't find his name on any passenger lists. I'm tired. Bereft. Almost frantic in my inner self. Perhaps it was his blood someone tried to expunge from that floor.

I can't go on. I'll go on. A little boy needs his great aunt to take him to visit his great-grandmother so he can deliver a little handmade gift to her: a boat made out of a matchbox with a piece of notepaper for a sail. He wanted to do it. He thought Great Gran would like to go sailing, that it would make her feel better. I'm the one who has to negotiate this exchange and make sure it brings about the desired result – a smiling Great Gran and a pleased Daniel.

Now we have to steer past an intemperately hard tap on Daniel's head by Great Gran.

Daniel rubs his head looking to me. I mime a kiss. He asks me if I think the sea is alive? He is sailing the boat across the tea tray. What a good kid he is! But 'What a silly question!' says Stella, still in a self-righteous grump.

'No,' I say. 'It's a good question. The sea moves around as if it's alive.'

'Is it?' asks Dan.

'Depends on how you look at it, Dan,' I answer, but Stella cuts in. 'It's made of water, how could it be alive?'

'I'll tell you later,' I say to Dan. And I will. It will be one of those long, loopy explanations about imagination and nature and different ways of thinking and we'll go in and out of all the little undersea coves and visit all the creatures there and we'll swim through reeds as stealthily as fish.

'Will the sea die?' he asks.

'Gee...we couldn't have it stuffed if it died, could we?' I answer. 'The stuffing stuff would get all wet...'

'That would be funny!' laughs Dan. 'What's stuffing stuff?'

'Like inside your teddy bear.'

'Kind of 'terially?'

'Yeah. Material.'

'There's sea in the aquarium.'

'So there is. And sharks.'

'And stingrays. Sibella, can we go to the aquarium...
Pleee-ase!'

My mother is bored. Dan is bored. We can't get to the garden
window because Mother Fucking Oldmeadow's contraption is in
the way. Dear God, how am I to make an ethical decision here? It
seems that we are to be the victims of Mother Oldmeadow's decisions. I could saw through the legs of her chair in revenge, but I
think we'll return to my mother's room if we can get enough air into
her lungs to get her there. It's just I can't be bothered to get up yet.

Why am I thinking of a rambling old mansion in the Blue
Mountains with a great veranda and a glorious view and several
generations living there and an old person dying day by day peace-
fully in a nice big comfy room inside with random visitors and
extemporaneous snacks and meals?

Mother Oldmeadow, in superior tones, is urging her flock of
followers to bear with *Difference* for God has ordained it. Mother
Oldmeadow hasn't said so in so many words, but it is clear she is not
in favour of the air-conditioning lobby. The *Difference* she is coyly
alluding to appears to be Sister Colleen. Only collective prayer will
lead the *Different* back to Christ's true course. When one sister, a visitor from outside, younger than the rest, is having especial difficulty
with the *Different*, she's told it's not a matter for individual action
but for group entreaty in the presence of the plaster intermediary
which represents the female parent of the divine in the chapel by the
front door. And there was I, impiously thinking that group prayer
was a very cunning way of shrugging off responsibility for a stoush.

'Thank you for your advice, Mother,' says the visiting sister,
sitting back on her heels.

'Take a little vice and add,' snorts Stella, loudly – the miracle
worker has obviously been at Stella's ears. Steel beams of sight
come boring our way from Mother Oldmeadow.

Sister Colleen re-enters the room, hands on hips. She bowls up to the laptop on the desk under the skylight, saying to no one in particular, 'My Mother House taught me to speak up. If you don't ask, you don't get. If it's good enough for the masculine hierarchy to have air-conditioning as well as all the creature comforts, then it's good enough for the old folk – four to a room – in the nursing home here.'

The tableau freezes. How is it to cope with the *Different*? The good old different! If only the undifferent would yield. Allegra and I were peaceniks when we were young: how naive we were! We certainly never predicted block-headedness on this stultifying scale. Socialism was going to create a whole new set of circumstances for us. The sitting rooms of old people's homes were going to be hives of industry: we were going to paint, sculpt, write, fly the occasional plane and take the children tenpin bowling. We didn't anticipate this mini Afghanistan here at Redeemer. Suppose the aid organisations managed to get buildings and air-conditioning up for the elderly of Kabul (supposing there ever were elderly), wouldn't they be just like this? Old women of one faith dividing along sectarian lines to fight for their brand – Sister Colleen declaiming, 'Progress!' Mother Oldmeadow strenuously enunciating, 'Obedience!' in the deathly museum of our hopes.

I get the old lady to her feet; she hunches under nearly a century of living, balances it on her skinny old shoulders, points the Wheelathon to…where? And takes a first, shaky step.

13

I can't imagine putting my affairs in the hands of Mother Oldmeadow and I feel deeply sad for anyone who has to. Yet, generations of women have done just that throughout the Christian world for centuries – for centuries we've been bidden to set some bloke on high and invest him with all the power we can imagine over our lives. I hope religion never stages a comeback as the great panacea for the sufferings of life, but I fear that it will come back, that we'll invent some new, elaborate hoax for ourselves that, if we don't look sideways or behind the smoke and mirrors, will hypnotise us away from being what we are: creatures in a universe, creatures able to act on our own behalf, and, if we put or minds to it, on behalf of those who are afraid of life.

I know a few people who stick to religion and they seem to do so more out of custom than out of the conviction that Christ rose again or that Moses split the sea in two. Checkie, I feel certain, does it to create an impression. She loves church music and rows for the side of choirs and pomp. Well…fine! I actually like to hear a soprano soar into the vaults myself – but let it be for joy and hope and the beauty of singing and the human voice: though we die, we are alive and when we are dead, we will have lived. Let it be. But don't go to your grave mean, covetous, full of jealous sentiment and spite.

I'm not a litigious person. The only time I've had need of a lawyer was when Reg Sorby lent me his to get Viva to pull her head in about my right – and Nin's – to a fair share in Dadda's estate.

Apart from that, which I'll admit was a debacle, I've steered clear. The first time I bought a house, I did my own conveyancing – I remember ringing up the lawyer of the woman whose house I was buying to get some needed particulars and being told I couldn't have them because I wasn't a lawyer, so I had to go to the woman herself. It worked out right enough, although the seller, a divorcee who'd been given the house in a settlement, thought I was strange, by which I suppose she meant that I wasn't what she'd been expecting – a man, or a man's representative. No. I was just me: one of the first unmarried women in the state of Victoria to be allowed to have my own mortgage. I owed my luck to a recommendation from Vance – a mere PhD at that time, a post-doctoral fellow no less, not even on the permanent payroll. I'd gone first to the bank with references from Beryl Blake and been turned down, because Beryl, though a distinguished Doctor of Science, had never had enough clout to have a mortgage of her own – wrong reproductive organs.

I've had much more need of GPs than I've had of lawyers. Although I go on about my mother's GP, I like and appreciate my own very much. Mine is a soft-spoken, middle-aged chap of Greek heritage. He's not ambitious; he's in practice with a friend in a dilapidated house several doors up from mine. You can have your pathology specimens taken on the spot, they bulk bill and there is a woman dentist in the practice, too. 'It's not ideal,' my GP tells me, resignedly. The Greek Church owns the land and won't update the premises, but 'I meet people I like and sometimes I go home happy with a job well done. If I had my time over, I'd do it again.' They speak Greek at the practice and most of their patients are Greek immigrants. Sometimes people have to stand in the waiting room with its array of mismatched chairs, and usually there are kids playing with donated toys on the floor, and there's trust. Where would we be without trust?

In a lawyer's office.

The lawyer is in town on the twenty-fifth floor. When you exit the lift, there's a wall in front of you with the names Raven and

Barrat in golden printing on it, so that you see your face distorted by the 'a's and 'r's as you glide to the right where an unpersoned shiny plank is attended by a bright red upholstered chair in a chrome cage that does for legs. Something slim and black lies on the desk beside a screen and you can see as you approach that it's a gadget – perhaps for rounding up lost sheep.

A person eventually teeters in stage left in a too-tight lime-green frock and black heels that throw her arch forward so far you can see the articulation between tendon and bone at the ankle joint. 'How may I help you?' she asks as if she's the fixture and you're the fluff and you ask for your lawyer and she takes you to an empty, glass-panelled room with another shiny plank on a cage, only this time, the plank has a glass jug of water on it and four clean glass tumblers...let's keep everything transparent. Kafka without the termites. And when you've been sitting there long enough to feel uncomfortable and are beginning to wonder if they remembered having put you into the room, in walks smiley with his polished dome that gives you back the glazed-over surroundings. 'What can I do for you?' he asks.

Rub some mud on your head, I feel like saying.

My lawyer received a demand from Checkie's lawyer before Christmas. I was to furnish reasons why I should not surrender the paintings. I was also to furnish details about where the paintings are stored and the adequacy of the storage.

I said I thought the demands were ridiculous and intrusive, since the paintings were awarded to me in a court settlement. This surely amounted to being sued twice for the same thing and was therefore a vexatious claim.

'Yes, yes,' he agreed. 'Vexatious. Some people stop at nothing.'

'That must be good for business,' I remarked.

'Well yes,' he laughed uneasily, 'that's what we're here for.' And he sent off my thoughts on the matter to Checkie's lawyers, saying, 'Sometimes it's enough to make them back down.'

But Checkie loves to sue. She's made quite a killing from it: insurance claims, defamation, use in publications of Siècle's images without consent; she's well known for it. Now, her lawyers have responded. Their client has a case. Their interpretation of the law says that I was granted custodianship of the paintings in the settlement; custodianship is not ownership (tell that to the Aboriginals).

I have to sort this state of affairs with Nin, as she is joint custodian. It would be sensible to divide the inheritance since Checkie is suing me but not suing Nin. So…here I am at Nin's house, jousting with delaying tactics again.

According to my lawyer, Checkie's lawyers can quibble about the settlement in this way. Under the terms of the Siècle Trust, to which Dadda was a signatory, they can assert rights and contest ownership.

I might as well consult the I Ching as decide which way to jump. Maybe I shouldn't jump at all, except that I'm obliged to say something in reply to defend my right to the paintings.

I've been sitting up here at Nin's for a good twenty minutes playing games of patience on my laptop, waiting for their ladyships to notice that I'm here and in need of input. I bought myself a suite of several different types of patience and I eliminate them as soothsayers by how easy they are to get out. I then take medium chance games and play against the likelihood of my getting them out. A run of wins means I'm on the right track – Eli is not dead or a thug and there are still numerous moves to be made in life before the game is up and I lose my son and my house. Three wins in a row of a one-in-five likelihood game means the week ahead has good auguries. Three losses in a row means the reverse. But if I go down the ill-favoured track, I reason to myself, I'm only going to enjoy life the less and waste it the more.

The psychiatrist told me when I first turned up for help with my depression that I was the one who had turned up, therefore I was the one who needed help. The old mother, the suffering son, the persecuting half-sister and brother-in-law and the unlucky niece had not turned up for help, therefore they didn't need it. Tell that to the asylum seekers: it's no more logical than setting your mood by the stars or the outcome of a series of games of patience.

The psychiatrist says there are no outside rules, only those we carry on board ourselves – so you may as well arrange your life just to please yourself. What if it is in your nature to be philanthropic, though? And to believe that a peaceful environment is the best place for life to prosper? Acting in accordance with your conscience might leave you in the position of someone who is loved and appreciated or it might leave you where you started – weighed down with too much responsibility. I'd like to be loved and appreciated, but these days it is fashionable to say deprecatingly of people like me that we are approval seekers and that it's all right not to be liked. Margaret Thatcher, after all, was not liked and she saved Britain. Didn't she?

Where I started was with God the Anglican and the all-pervading Anglican Jesus Christ. It didn't take much formal instruction for me to cotton on that this was the bit of religious instruction where I belonged. Aunt Nina was the great, all suffer-ing example (and Stella had received that postcard from the 'Bish'). Turn the other cheek, be kind, put yourself in another's shoes, be helpful. Yet, in the natural world where we are all destined to be car-bonised or to turn into nutritious dirt that will or will not be of any use to the planet that sustains us, there's nothing but motherhood to support Christ's teachings and Christ was a man with a mother.

No. To be good along Christian lines means believing in righteousness and righteousness is not something you can neces-sarily discern in yourself – you can only see it at a distance. It isn't embodied: it's occasional. Anyone who thinks they are righteous must lack certain sensitivities. They must be blind to squalor and not much moved by cruelty, ignorance and poverty. They must live in denial of their own faults. They must be complacent. They must never have had to make the decision to chop off the fingers of the hands clinging to the loaded and sinking lifeboat. They must never have faced the prospect of losing their own fingers and drowning themselves.

Putting yourself in the position where you are in danger of losing your life is but a breath away from suicide. To the suicide I suppose that everything stops mattering at the moment of death. Peace, then, to the suicide – but to we who survive…broken-heartedness, truncation, division, Janus-headed judgement and the requirement to reconstruct around this hideous wrong.

The assassin is on board the lifeboat and one's life is always surplus to need.

So where does that leave righteousness? It's something in the ether that is only sometimes available.

I've been sitting here so long, the battery in my laptop has grown hot on my knee.

I am sitting on one of Nin and Wendy's two sofas in an island, the width of my bottom, between multifarious piles of stuff. My folder containing some timeworn shots of our picture collection has fallen spine first down a crack in the seating and is castigating me with its fannyful of agenda. We've been drinking tea in Turkish glasses and avoiding getting to the point, hence my abstracted ravings and excursion into patience. Daniel has gone to see the Women's Circus with Gorgon.

I clap shut the laptop.

Nin hasn't received a Statement of Claim, nor has it been suggested that Nin will be sued. The claims are being made against me. Yet the paintings being sought are jointly owned. This is not something Nin wants to talk about and yet, talk about it we must. We have to decide which of the paintings we are to nominate as hers and which I will claim as mine.

Wendy has a mirror on her lap and is French plaiting her own hair as if nothing out of the ordinary is going on.

'I'm sorry guys,' I say, 'but the claim isn't going to go away and we really have to deal with it.'

Nin goes behind the chair Wendy is sitting on and holds up a strand of hair. 'You've left a bit out,' she says.

'Blast! It's really hard trying to French plait your own hair.'

'I'll do it for you if you like…'

'Nin!'

'It's all right, Bel, I can do it and listen at the same time. I'm a mother, don't forget.'

'Well, we've got to decide who owns which pictures…'

'I don't see what the problem is,' goes Wendy. 'You never look at them anyway. They're stuck up in a warehouse somewhere you haven't even got the decency to tell us…'

'Oh cut it out, Wendy. If you two wanted the paintings you could have had them. Instead, you leave everything up to me – storage, insurance…'

'Why don't you just go and get them and give them to Checkie? She can look after them for a change. After all, all that's happening now is you're shelling out to have them stored…'

'Shut up We-en,' goes Nin. 'That's not what it's about.'

'I'd like to know why not!' Wendy fixes her impenetrably dark irises on the ceiling and this brings a heaving sigh up out of me.

'Sometimes you're as sensitive as old goats' tits, Wendy,' I say. 'The pictures are all my father left that I can legally claim as mine. They are all I have of his. They are pictures of my adolescence and of Nin's mother's adolescence painted by our father. If I can't hang them on my walls it's because I haven't any walls to hang them on. I would have to sell them to be able to afford the walls.'

She yawks her mouth down at the side and rolls her eyes over the roof to settle on me. 'I've heard all that before. The fact is, they're just sitting in some shed somewhere.'

'Off track, Wendy! We have to decide who owns what paintings specifically. In the past I've had sole responsibility and sold work from time to time to keep the family going; we now have to separate out Nin's from mine.'

'Why can't we keep going in the way we have been?' goes Nin.

'Because we stand to lose my share to Checkie, Nin-compoop. She's suing me, in case you've forgotten. The case will have an outcome and she can't sue me for what I do not own – or at least, have in my custody. Now, let's get down to tacks. I've been thinking about it even if you haven't. The only painting I stake a claim to is *Where the Nice Girls Live No 2.*'

'Does that mean it's the most valuable?' goes Wendy.

'No, Wendy. It doesn't. It means that it's the one I want. Of all the paintings in the suite, that one has most significance for me. It was hanging on my wall when Allegra died. For me, she is in that picture. Nin, I thought you might like the one of Allegra sitting up on the kiddie kangaroo in the playground, looking like Eve Marie Saint in *On the Waterfront* but with different hair and smoking a cocktail Sobrani. She had so much make-up on you could have lifted it up in one piece and put it away in a bag for later.'

'What's that one worth?'

'Wendy, pull your head in.'

'Only asked.'

'Have I ever dudded you and Nin?'

'Not that I know of.'

'Well I'm not about to start. I've got no idea what it's worth. Or very little idea. Paintings can fetch extraordinary prices or be passed in at auction, way below the reserve. It's a long time since any major work by my father was sold. And you can bet your boots that if we put it up for auction, some smart-fart auctioneer will buy it through a third party and then sit on it until he can make a killing. That's how the market works these days. It's hard to know who to trust.'

'I don't understand why Nin can't give her share of the paintings to David to manage. After all, he's supposed to be the expert on Henry Coretti, isn't he? And they'd come back to Nin anyway, wouldn't they? Plus be looked after properly.'

'Wendy, are you just being devil's advocate or do you really not understand? We have to clear up ownership of these paintings. I need my share just as much as Nin needs hers. If Nin gave hers to David, where would he keep them, do you imagine? At the Siècle Trust. And the moment David died, which he will do soon, believe me, Checkie would just seize them. Nin couldn't mount a case to get them back. Have you any idea how much money, time and resources it takes to fight a court battle over ownership? I want to warn you that if David or Checkie or anyone else has suggested to Nin that she surrender her share of the work into David's care, it means that the work will end up in Checkie's hands and not in Nin's.'

'You're paranoid about Checkie and David, Isobel,' says Wendy.

'Am I? And what if their cordiality to you has nothing to do with affection and everything to do with Checkie wanting to rob you? Checkie has never taken no for an answer. She's covetous; she always has been. And she wants to be famous. She does not have ordinary human feelings for other people: her ego is built on being Henry Coretti's daughter. She and Viva have been spreading Viva's story of love requited for decades. She would like the rest of the story never to have existed. She wants to be written up in *Women's Weekly* as *Paintings Back Where They Belong* so she can show everybody how well preserved she is from never having gone out in the sun.'

'Well, at least she'd put the darned things on show.'

'The arrangement I've made might well mean they can go on show once the case is cleared up!'

Nin has plaited and pinned, and pinned and plaited so that Wendy has had about five hairdos in the time we've been talking. 'Checkie does send Daniel outside whenever we're there,' she says, lamely.

'He likes going outside,' Wendy is quick to answer.

'Oh, I can just imagine it!' I say. 'Daniel does what he's told with a smile on his face to keep the peace. He's going to turn into a peacekeeper, that little boy, and one day he's going to be wondering where his sense of himself has gone — because it'll disappear into the squabbling of the loudmouthed combatants. He'll have been robbed of it. He doesn't like it at Checkie's. He's told me often enough. Honestly, you two have entered untried ground in bringing up Daniel. Sometimes you have to think things out from the point of view of the kid, you know.'

'Homophobe!'

'So that's all you can say, Wendy! That's not the point I was making. If you'd listened you'd have heard me putting in a plea to allow Daniel space to create a personality for himself…'

'Space! Just look at the state of this house, Isobel! You can't move for Daniel's space!'

'No. Not the space I'm talking about. You still occupy centre stage even in the midst of Daniel's mess, Wendy. Anyway I didn't come over here to have an argument about your family situation…'

'Well, why did you bring it up?'

I'm almost at boiling point. Mustn't bubble over the top, Isobel, easy now… 'It's Nin's birth family situation that's relevant here. I brought her up, her father is dying and her "aunt", if you can call Checkie by so friendly a name, is a person who doesn't give a shit about Nin's child, or, very likely, Nin. All she wants to do is steal these paintings from us and look as though she's justly taken possession of them. If you think auctioneers are shysters, they're saints compared to Checkie fucking Laurington. But we're getting off track again. We really do have to decide now which of the paintings belong to Nin and which to me. Nin can do whatever she wants with hers, but if she gives them to David or the Siècle Trust, then she'll do so entirely against my advice and my wishes and she knows it.'

Nin is flipping that bloody Bob the Builder toy around on her finger top again. 'Put it down, Nin! And stop being so bloody pig-headed!'

'These plaits look like shit,' says Wendy and Nin bursts into big, fat tears. When does she not when faced with conflict? – and runs from the room.

'Nin, come back here!' I yell.

'No!' she yells back. And, 'Fuck you, Wendy! Your face is the wrong shape for French plaits, anyway!'

Slam!!!!!

I stand up. I say to Wendy, 'Just look at her, Wendy – all her life long other people usurping her space! Pretending they're more important than she is! She owns something in those paintings and if she lets them go, she's letting her future security fly out the window. Here's the list and some old photos of the work. Some of the photos are missing, but I'll go and do a complete inventory; I have to, anyway. But the choices need to be made NOW.

'I have to photograph my share of the paintings to show that they're in good condition; therefore I need to be clear which paintings are mine and which are Nin's.

'It's high time the pair of you started learning what these paintings are in all respects: emotionally, culturally and financially and where Henry Coretti stands among his fellow painters. Don't rely on David for information, even though his opinion is, in some respects, worth considering. Do the research, Wendy, and stop pretending you're the victim of circumstances and fate. After all, you're not a moron. You chose Nin and the pair of you have already taken serious steps into the middle of your lives. It's time to take some more now and GROW UP!'

Oh dear, I'm sitting at the wheel now and it's not good car-driving karma. I'll have to make my way through the burbs with great care and, when I reach home, do the job of sorting the work out myself, since I can't, on the face of things, trust them to do it for me. They're just as likely to come back at me in righteous rages. It'll all be my fault. I'm such a shit, I must be to blame.

If I assign what I think of as the pick of the crop to Nin, it looks as though I won't be safeguarding them and I'll be left with nothing much to fight for. Time to chop the fingers off the side of the overloaded lifeboat. Or that's what my conscience says. In this condition. When I'm feeling frustrated, humiliated and angry.

My foot is trembling on the clutch, preparing myself to start up, when Nin hurtles out of the house, slap-bang onto the street beside the car. She jumps in beside me, flings her arms around my neck. 'Oh, I'm so sorry Bel! So sorry! I love you very much! You're a patient, good and loving person! I'll choose. I promise. And I'll hold on to my share.'

Well…thank the good dirt into which we turn for that!

'I love you, too, darling.' And I do. 'Just please be brave for me. It's not that hard. We really do have to live as sensibly as we can and not let people who've treated us badly get away with what belongs to us.'

Mick has been testing and retesting floodlights and lenses in my hallway, although it's not as if we are going to enter these photos in a high art competition. He has bought little arc lamps – cheap ones – and extension cords; loves a gadget, does Mick.

Lexie's place is a forty-minute drive from Melbourne, on the edge of bushland that used to belong to Vance and Suzanne in the days when people were trying to get large areas of it protected by the Victorian Government. We used to busily plant trees out there as part of a community project called A Million Trees, now the few that survived the planting have probably been done for by the drought – so much for all our good intentions.

The floor-to-ceiling racks of the storage facility are about twenty feet high and I'm beginning to wonder how we'll get decent shots of everything for the court case. We need to be able to show once and for all that the paintings are in good condition and likely to stay that way. No doubt they'll have a decent stepladder – you don't go to all that trouble to create good storage without a decent stepladder…

14

My car doesn't have mod cons like a CD player but it does have a tape deck and air-conditioning, so, with Mick at the wheel, and the passenger seat in recliner, I slipped Fernando Sor's arrangements of Mozart for guitar onto the deck and listened to soothing music most of the way up to Lexie's place. My favourite piece, played deliciously by Turibio Santos, is *Grand Solo*, with its glorious conversational pauses, its nods and bows, its elegant dancing and conversing and graceful verve. Mozart's life was turbulent and yet these elegant fragments flowed. You can listen to *Grand Solo* on many levels, down to the notes being plucked, with confidence and discretion, on the guitar. It's music that knows where it's going and takes you there, albeit that the fields outside the window of my peace bubble were parched and the countryside was oppressed by drought all across the valley floor. Not only has there been no rain here for years, but there was a severe frost at the end of winter and many of the vintners are in trouble.

Soon we were meandering up into the hills, where Lexie's enterprise missed the frost and still sees enough highland moisture to keep her vines cropping. In spite of all, she's had good vintages for two years in a row, but this year doesn't look promising. Everything is friable, crumbly, ready for flames and it is hard to think of abundance. The sight of it made me feel hesitant, as if I'd made a silly mistake by using Lexie's storage, but it was reassuring to pull into her lower drive behind its high fire-deflecting mound.

Her upper drive forks off at road level and leads to her vine-yard and cellar door: tourist buses were grinding gears up the slope, kicking up a lot of dust. Lexie wants to have the drive surfaced to stop dust getting onto the vines but it's an expensive business and she thought she'd get the bunker done first – that way, the money she earns from storage can go towards the surfacing.

The bunker is nicely tucked in under Lexie's hill, sheltered from the prevailing north-westerlies. Lots of artists and artisans in the area store with her and a number of people who are afraid of bushfires in extreme summers like this one, and mindful of the horrendous ones that have torn through this area in the past, store their valuables here while they go to sit out the season in the city. It's essentially a big factory shed with insulation and climate control inside. There's a well-stocked office with an airlock and the art-works are stored in a cube within a cube of other storage, so there are two layers of fire retardation before they are reachable. The rates are good, the building is new and more than meets current bushfire specifications.

Feeling lulled by a liquid trip of the mind with Mozart, I let myself approach the photography in a pretty good mood. Eli, I tucked away for the time being in a gentle, forgiving fold of my grey matter. There was lighting to be fixed, a ladder to be scaled by a big man – Mick – and photos to be taken of largish works from close up. In the event, there were missed edges, refocusings and disagreements about the colour adjustments – how is it that Mick and I see colours so differently? I kept saying, 'No, sorry, you have to *match* what's in front of you to what's on the camera.' 'But I have.' 'No, no, no, no, give it here!' 'Well, you get up the ladder and do it then!' So I got up the ladder and did it and the difference between his photos and mine is very obvious to me, but not to him. He *prefers* his, but, I think to myself, *it's not preference we're after, it's verisimilitude.*

What I see is coloured by what I have been seeing since I was a teenager. I know these paintings; they are my memory trace, the subtle piece of graffiti on the wall of the toilet block, the sloughed-off boredom in a tossed bottle, the evil being born in the eyes of a boy as he watches the instinctual seductions of Allegra – and my own anxious and resentful expressions bobbing in the wake. I can't expect Mick to see what I see and when I try to point it out, he's less than enthralled. We squabbled on lightly and resignedly until lunchtime, when Lexie, a Gen X Amazon with a high blonde ponytail and a filly's gait, swung downhill from the restaurant to invite us up to her parents' table. Vance and Suzanne have joined the Australia Day throng: they're here to look at their patch of bushland and they want to join us for lunch. Mick said he was looking forward to meeting Vance at last.

It's a blessing that Mick is easily brought around to an even temper; we don't have to waste chunks of life in high dudgeon and sulks, but I do know that it depends on me to set the direction. If I plunge, he plunges too, so it's better not to plunge. Busloads of day-trippers, juggling bottles of wine and little platters of finger food, the women carrying their high heels, their feet aslant on Lexie's steep lawn, were sitting down in groups, tasting glasses slung around their necks on lanyards. This demographic, on the shadowy side of the property where the grass is still greenish around the duck pond, all shoulder strap and clavicle as we picked our way among them. Legs oozed like umber from skirt tubes onto the tartan-gridded picnic rugs. The men wore floppy shorts and cotton shirts with all the buttons undone, their big feet arching and flexing round the rubber toe-trees of their thongs. 'Geez,' said a pierced piece of girlery close at hand, 'these boob tubes sure squash ya tits.'

The national day out.

By the time we reached the restaurant on the hilltop, I had that duck pond-cum-dam on my mind and was considering its position relative to the storage bunker. Dadda's voice was saying in my ear, *A sensible person would have stored them in town,* but Lexie's voice was saying, 'It's okay, you know, downhill all the way, the water can build up quite a force. Besides, the bunker's flanked with water tanks that hug the walls.'

I told Dadda's voice off, I said, *Look, you, Lexie's got fabulous shins – see how long they are from the knee to the ankle! They're perfect, like her storage. You'd break your toe on those, so just get out of my ear.* But he was still there tickling my neurosis until I felt compelled to ask, 'Wouldn't the house be likely to go up, situated uphill where it is?'

'Yes. It would. That's why we put the bunker down the hill. House up for the view and bunker down for safety. It would be pointless defending the house; we'd defend the bunker. But, in the first place, the house is made of mudbricks and, although they're labour-intensive, they're fairly easily replaced, and in the second, it would only catch alight through ember attack because it's skirted by the vineyards; the bush doesn't come up to it. The wind would need to be very strong and very high to rain embers on the roof. Don't worry, Isobel, the set-up's quite special. I can give you a plan of the place and the fireproofing rationale if that'll help you make a defence with the lawyers.'

'Good idea. Yes, I can put it to them that the design means the paintings are pretty safe.' Dadda's presence was growling and grinding his thumbs against his fingers in the way he used to, but I told him, *Down, boy. Allow me to be alive and dealing and yourself to be dead and out of it.*

'I'd hate to lose you as a customer, Isobel – you're the celebrated example. I was going to ask you when the photos are ready if we could use them in our brochure? Accredited and low pixels, of course.'

'What, a sort of "guess whose work is stored out here" advertisement?'

'You don't think it's a good idea? It's just that you need to use every asset you can to get custom these days. No such thing as discretion anymore.' And, in the most open possible way, there's nothing discreet about Lexie – she is frankly and strappingly the new blonde Aussie, tanned, trained and savvy. She's a credit to adoption. Maybe she's the beginning of a new race sent to replace the vacant, blue-eyed staring blonde of yesteryear.

'Well, it's an idea I'll take on board,' I say, 'but I'd have to caution against advertising where Henry Coretti's work is kept until after the case is settled. And even if things go my way, I might still be bound by conditions of storage closer to town.'

'I hope not. As I've said before in another season we could show those paintings if you'd like that and then you'd get past the objection that they're important work that's never seen.'

'Well, of course. You've got great walls in the house. But I am a snob, you know. You would have to accompany it with pretty special stuff…'

'You and Nin could curate it. You could choose.'

'Well, yes, that would be fair. But it might entail more work than you'd imagine, because to show Henry Coretti, one would have to borrow from private owners. Checkie wouldn't be letting us have anything from Siècle, that's for sure…But yes, the possibility of a public show up here would be one argument that we could put on behalf of our claim.' But I could hear Checkie's voice in my head now, breathily mocking the thought of Henry Coretti and the hillbillies. Lexie shows local art and I'd have to admit that it's more of a community enterprise than a fostering of great works.

'Of course, you could,' she said, cheerfully. 'It might never happen, but then again, it might. Anyway, add it to your argument as a possibility and we could talk about it, couldn't we?'

'Yes, of course we could. And thank you for the offer.'

This talk made me realise how very, very proprietorial I am about these works. My responsibility for these paintings comes straight from my heart and the thought of even putting them on walls with lesser art fills me with anxiety. They need their own space. In my mind, they have their own space without which they would not be properly seen.

There are tables on a terrace with paved peninsulas into gardens of standard roses that are holding up well under a regime of almost no watering. Big, ruby-red Mr Lincolns nest in the branches in opening flushes behind little box hedges, some of which are browning. The sky is hazy overhead, dusty, but on the sunny side of the hill you can still see to a distant horizon beyond the rows of vines sweeping away in a long stretch to the road as it disappears into forest. Lexie is optimistic about getting another vintage. 'But it's been the toughest year yet,' she says. 'There's been quite a lot of burning and raisining. We might have to sell the crop as table grapes. We try to let the grapes speak for themselves in our vintages, and this lot could just be saying, "Eat me!"'

Lexie wasn't brought up on lollies. Decay hasn't touched her. Her only concessions to 'bling' are her wedding and engagement rings and a plain gold locket around her neck. She's Gen X dentally perfect. You could even call her teeth 'mighty', they're so strong and straight and white. She has a smile that wouldn't have been possible for girls of my generation; in my day, we used to pout with our mouths closed and our colossally Cleopatra'd eyes were the windows to our souls.

Mick is asking about vintages and Lexie rattles off names: 'Cab Merlot, Cab Sav, Merlot and Pinot Noir; even the pressings can be good.' And she continues about the benefits of growing grapes high up. 'It captures the dew and rains quite well just here, but fifteen kilometres back along that road you came up, they're in a rain shadow and fifteen kilometres in the other direction, you hit rainforest. It's all a question of the lie of the land.'

We take our seats but Mick suddenly starts bumping his great legs about, rattling the cutlery and looking under the table. 'Good God, what's that?' he asks and comes up laughing. It's a baby wombat being chased around the tables by Lexie's youngest girl.

'Oh, it's Gordon,' says Lexie. 'The mum was bowled over down the hill and there she was with her little head poking out between the back legs, so-yo-yo cute! So we brought her up here to raise her…The kids called her Gordon before we realised she was a girl.'

'How do you tell?'

She picks up the little creature with a swoop and points at its belly. 'You turn them over and you can see the little pouch beginning to form when they're still pretty young. It's a funny little concavity to begin with and it forms back-to-front when you compare it to other marsupials so the mum won't cover the baby with dirt when she digs. The first time I saw one, I thought it was a malformation and took it to the vet! We've had a few up here over the years. They're not at all road wise and get skittled.'

She hands me over the little brick of a thing and I stroke my finger around its velvet nose. It's the loveliest feeling – not a thing you can do without exercising your smile muscles. I put a fingertip up behind Gordon's claws into her cupped foot and feel the furred membranes between the walking pads and massage them as I used to when I owned dogs to make sure there aren't any pebbles or grass seeds caught in there. 'Oooh, she likes that.' Lexie smiles.

Vance and Suzanne have finally tamed the road up from their patch, Vance in the lead. He comes over to the table and pulls out two chairs. 'We should take a photo of that, Bel. Wombat cuddling on Australia Day.'

'Or even make it an annual Australia Day event,' says Lexie.

'Hi.' Vance leans down and kisses my cheek. I introduce him and Suzanne, who's just behind him, tiny, plump and puffed from the climb, to Mick, who's in the middle of asking Lexie how long the grapes have been in. While Lexie explains that the vines have been in for twenty years, it begins to seem an indecently long time since all this was virgin bush and I was a young woman in it, ten or more years younger than Lexie is now, kneeling down over my drawing pad alongside Reg Sorby, drawing orchids and fending off his lecherous advances. Allegra, certain that Reg would succeed in his attempts at seduction, used to quiz me mercilessly after these expeditions, but Reg had plenty of women to keep him occupied;

he didn't need me. He was fubsy, couldn't keep his hands to himself and didn't even try; it used to make me wonder how he saw the world – maybe as a great sex act with him as principal rooter. There'd be cries of 'rape!' from the puritans these days. Indeed half the painters of the sixties and seventies would be in jail for unrestrained lust.

'Watch it doesn't pee on you,' laughs Vance and I hand Gordon to Lexie's girl, who's ten, tall and blonde like her mother. There's definitely a new breed being born. 'Gosh, Suzanne,' I lean across the table to her, nodding towards her granddaughter, 'do you have the same difficulty I do? Coming up to people's kneecaps in the trams?'

Suzanne laughs. She's even shorter than I am. 'I can't even reach the passenger straps in the new trams,' she says.

'I think they've overlooked something. My niece Nin was downed by a flying pensioner a while ago when a trammie slammed on the brakes. It was right outside the Eye and Ear Hospital, which was just as well because she burst a blood vessel behind her eye, poor thing. Had to get off the tram there and then and seek medical attention.'

'Beware flying pensioners,' says Mick.

'Baby Boomers morph into Baby Bombers.' Vance takes up the wine list. 'What are we going to have to drink here, Lex?'

'I've got some of your favourite Sav Blanc on ice, Dad,' says Lexie, turning towards the shady, low-slung restaurant, her arm around her daughter. 'I'll send some out. I'd eat with you but we're flat tack today with all the visitors. Have a look at the menu. Anyway, here comes Alicia to take your order.'

Alicia is Lexie's sixteen-year-old – another tall blonde. She's wearing a long black apron over black pants and a white shirt. They all have waists, these women – long, slender and beautiful. It's hard to imagine how intestines fit in under them and how Lexie regained shape after giving birth three times – maybe human flesh is taking on a new property, kind of melding with elastane so that it snaps back. And vertebrae have to have been lengthening and strengthening: my rib cage isn't all that far above my hips. Maybe something's happening to bodies; the plot's getting better – more like Mozart's *Grand Solo*, where each note creates the next one as if you could pull a magic tassel in the universe and bring forth flowingly, any small, natural gestation you might care to and that natural gestation would go forth, eat fabulous food and flourish. What, I wonder, were Lexie's mother's circumstances that she had to give away such a sane and sturdy creature? Was she a sane and sturdy creature herself and if so, how did she end up giving away her baby?

I so envy Vance with his mind full of the minutiae of the genes – the foldings and unfoldings of the magic ladder of life, the comings and goings of shapely little molecules through thin and slippery and secret places to make the Gordons and the Lexies. And then there are the attack strategies of life's freeloaders and the defence strategies of cells that are just out for themselves. It's so poetic it should be in the grammar and experience of all of us; we should all be sitting at the edge of the exciting dark, dangling our increasingly gorgeous legs over the edge, ready to fish up another brilliant ruse of the universe – instead? What a jigsaw we live in – Vance in his vinyl-scented tower, me in my nonexistent studio and only the most happenstance of links between us.

Oh dear, Lexie has a bloke cooking dampers on a barbie by the cellar-room door. Australia – beer and singlets or imitation beer and singlets. Reg Sorby used to go way out to the sweat-soaked inland draggle towns to paint the real ones – flakes of men with the sunken eyes of lost Europe, the lees of failure. People who were born for something other than life handed out, who were chased, harried and worn away to the dryness of deciduous leaves in the desert. 'Look at me,' his paintings of them said. And you'd look and maybe you'd feel like a pervert and think 'poor brutes', but then again you might see it differently – you might take the view of the indifferent rationalist and think that there isn't room for every-one and that's life. In return for their portraits, Reg would paint for these benighted souls fat-bottomed nudes and rooting Bacchantes on the walls of their pubs – news of his exploits would filter out to the cities, the press would go out to have a look and the forgetful and forgotten and the never-thought-about would be exposed. And Reg would have a sell-out exhibition back in town.

'Penny for your thoughts, Isobel?' Vance says.

'Meandering as usual,' I laugh.

'Eli?'

'Well actually no – not immediately in my thoughts, but then again, yes, because he's always there. I haven't heard from him and he's left a mess behind. I don't know what to do – in fact, there isn't anything much I can do…'

And Mick explains how Eli's abandoned unit had a bloody patch on the floor which had been washed with bleach and how bleach destroys DNA and how the police haven't come up with any leads and how there isn't even any evidence that Eli left Australia after my exhibition.

Vance pats my shoulder. 'Sounds as if your plate is overfull, Bel.'

'A permanent condition with me, it seems.'

'Ours was, too, for a long while,' Suzanne commiserates. 'We've virtually had to give up on Timothy.' And she explains to Mick how they adopted another child besides Lexie, a boy. 'Things have just gone from bad to worse with him. The door's open if he wants to come back but there's a limit to what we can do. He came to me through my practice. I'm a GP. There was a homeless girl who came to see me. She'd already had to give up two children through drugs and alcohol. When Tim was born he wasn't noticeably on the foetal alcohol spectrum but she was using and she wanted me to take care of him while she detoxed. It wasn't a question of adoption at first and I persuaded Vance to take him under our wing until she was out of detox and could look after him. Lexie was already ten and doing really well. She was a great baby right from the start. She always wanted a smaller sibling and so we took on Tim. It was only a temporary arrangement at first and then it became permanent. I anticipated a number of problems with him, but you can't anticipate everything and I guess you learn that as you go.

'He was slow to grow, he cried a lot, he was slow in being able to focus his eyes…well, that's how it started. I took six months off to try and establish a routine but he was really a full-time child. His mother left detox and went onto benefit and the DSS found her a place to live – a flat in a high-rise, which wasn't ideal, because Tim screamed day and night when he first went back to her. And then, of course, she got back onto the drugs, started peddling them herself, was arrested and Tim came back to us after the DSS exhausted what they thought of as better alternatives. They said he was malnourished, but that could have been the foetal alcohol syndrome – he had some other markers, like the eye folds and a really low philtrum…'

'Philtrum?' I ask.

'You know, the two tracks between your nose and your top lip.'

'Oh, so that's what it's called. I never knew it had a name. But it's a funny thing, isn't it? You kind of wonder why it's there.'

'The snot gutter,' says Mick.

'Yeah,' Suzanne laughs. 'Well, Tim hasn't got much of a snot gutter. But he's actually very nice-looking, don't you think, Vance?'

'Sure. If you overlook the piercings.'

'Oh yes, the bloody piercings. Vance put his foot down when he came home with a tongue job…'

'Well, I couldn't bear him clacking the stud against his teeth the whole time. And then I couldn't bear the thought of him break-ing his front teeth on it, either – it cost a fortune for us to have his teeth fixed. Part of his problem was a high palate and not enough room for his top teeth to come down. And getting him to the den-tist was a chore in itself. He's so impulsive, if you managed to get beyond the waiting room without him doing a runner, you then had to stand guard on the tray of dental stuff to stop him grabbing it, just like a baby grabs everything. I'd have to bark at him all through the whole procedure.'

'Yes. He'd only do what Vance told him.'

'Not always…' Vance puts his hands up in surrender.

'Ah, the old baritone syndrome,' I say. 'I know that one. What is it about boys that they can't take anything seriously if it isn't said at several octaves below soprano? My grand-nephew started noticing that people's voices were pitched differently even before he could talk. He used to practise his baritone when he was still in his nappy.'

'Well, Tim was hell for female teachers in school – absolute hell,' says Suzanne. 'We tried everything we could think of – classroom assistance at an ordinary school, special schooling, private schooling. But I would have had to give up work to take care of all his needs. I wasn't willing to do that and he ran wild, went on sprees, started drinking himself. Meanwhile his mother died of an overdose.

'We were in and out of court with him. He'd get drunk, steal a car with a mate, drive like a maniac, get arrested, it just went on and on and on and on. Once he moved out of home, we started finding things missing. He was stealing from us. To add insult to injury, he'd trash the joint to make it look as if it was someone else. Then he took up with a homeless girl called Olive and next thing is Olive's pregnant and Tim's doing a stretch for dealing.

'Well, we saw to it that Olive got the proper medical care, but when we were offered up the baby by way of payment, we just had to say no.

'I mean, Isobel, we were well meaning. We did everything we could think of, but there are times when you just have to throw in the towel or wreck yourself. Thinking about Tim exhausts me and I can understand how thinking about Eli must exhaust you. I'd sooner cuddle Gordon. Come and sit beside me, Isobel, let's cuddle her together.' She hoists Gordon up onto her lap, 'She makes you feel good.'

So the okay, uncomplicated, flourishing life of Lexie is offset by Tim, and, like me, Suzanne has to divide up her time into unrelated chunks. The world looks around, sees someone capable and dumps its problem there, not for a moment considering that the dumped-upon are trying to create their lives, too.

'You know,' says Suzanne, 'I see all kinds of things in that surgery – drugs and drink are only the start of it. I see poor women coming in wanting genital reconstruction after being mutilated because it's their custom – and *then*, I see long-time Australian residents coming to me wanting cosmetic surgery on their genitalia! Honestly! Aren't they aware that vaginas come in several variations? What's happened to the Women's Movement? They're frightened that if their labia minora show, men will reject them. Almost all the young women I see have hairless pubic areas and when I ask why, they try to tell me it's more hygienic! Imagine having your pubes ripped off! I marvel at the ongoing stupidity. One of these days women will come to me wanting to have zippers put in to avoid vaginal birth.'

She hands me little Gordon and I hold her to my breast, where she feels warm and sacred. 'You have to wonder at people, don't you, Isobel? What could be more beautiful than an infant and more hideous than a brutalised adult? I hope your Eli turns up safe and sound. I'm sure he will. From what I hear, you've been a very supportive mum.'

'But I've been an easy mark for predators and that's been hard for him. People pose as one thing and all the time they're someone else. Some make a lifelong practice of posing, you fool yourself with others and yet another category crawls out from under an image that you thought belonged to them only to find it wasn't them at all. I feel as if I've been abandoned by myself. Half the time I'm kind of…AWOL. I have a damned hard time feeling authentic.'

'You have to come back into yourself, Isobel. I know it's hard, but you need to.'

'I make so many mistakes.'

'No, you're tempted to believe that you're the cause of other people's mistakes, and you're not…'

'But I do make mistakes, Suzanne. I make so many mistakes…'

'It's your confidence that's gone. Tempt it back; it'll come.'

'How I wish I was as centred as you are.'

'I've got Vance. He has his great works and I have my medicine. We've never had to envy each other – or not for long, anyway. There've been some very hard times. It was hard not to be able to have children. We lost three; one at term and two inside two weeks. It was hard. I felt incompetent. Lexie redeemed my motherhood instincts – we're very lucky to have her. Tim, however – Tim's had time in jail for GBH, for God's sake! I'm damned sure Vance never taught him to be violent. Vance is a pacifist, a gent. These days I can't even like Tim, and yet he was a little boy in my arms once. I can only put it down to brain damage.'

We give each other a reassuring hug, put Gordon down and watch her trundle off.

Vance pours wine for us all and I ask him how his patch is going.

'Hot and bothered. Ants principally.'

'Well, at least they'll be farming some fungus for the orchids,' I say. 'You have to marvel at life, don't you? How ingenious is that? Ants farming fungus and orchids seeding themselves in fungus to take a joy ride on an extended root system.'

'It's a while since we've seen any orchids there,' says Vance. 'There weren't any this spring. In the past I've had four or five little clumps that I've kept going with hand fertilisation, but it's a losing battle…' Vance gives me a wink and pats my wrist. 'If he's in trouble, Bel, I'm sure there'll be an explanation.'

'You must think I'm a fraud or a fool or something. It's just raining separate patches of shit all over my brain at the moment.'

'I'd never think you were a fool. It's the last thing that would cross my mind.'

So I feel my lips smile between mooning cheeks, warm tears sliding under lower lids. 'Thanks,' and once again I'm hesitating above a meal I ought to be enjoying.

It was a good meal and the wine was pleasant and the conversation had shifted onto cheerier ground with Lexie's successes and Daniel's sweet young ponderings, his curiosity, imagination and sense of fun. I was feeling restored when Lexie came out to share a drink with us, bringing a prospective client with her…Right in the middle of my good feelings – Elspeth Roach – never did a pair of nostrils hitch and shudder with such an unexpected bonus.

'Ew,' she said. 'Isobel. Yes, I know Isobel.' And she let out a breathy little laugh. 'So you keep *Where the Wild Things Are* out here, do you?' And of course, she meant Dadda's pictures, *Where the Nice Girls Live*.

Fuck!

Her head snaked around on top of her long neck as she took in the people at the table. Her breathy laugh came out sounding like Weet-Bix being shaken in a tin. 'Look,' she said, turning to Lexie, 'I don't think I'll be storing with you after all. It's all too out in the bush to be safe, really.' And away she went, on long, thin feet, like an emu's, towards the car park.

'God, who's *she?*' Lexie gawked.

'How rude!' went Suzanne.

'Never mind, Lex,' went Vance. 'You don't need clients like that…'

'She's a close chum of David and my stepsister, I'm afraid.'

'Oh, I'm sorry Isobel, she introduced herself to me just then. If I'd known…'

'Never mind. Never mind.'

And Mick says, 'She didn't look all that lethal to me, lovey…'

'I'm sorry, but that's just what she is. She will have rung them by now and told them where the pictures are. I was hoping for a little more time to prepare my case.'

'Aren't you exaggerating just a bit?'
'No.'

Oh dear, I feel so beaten, so mournful and peculiar I can hardly move. It is as if my authenticity is shut up in that shed, rendered in 2D by my darling bastard of a father and I am just a flake of paint, masquerading.

15

We drove home in silence, my reassurance smashed and Mick unable to believe that there are people in the world whose greatest happiness is dudding others.

We were barely home when the insults began to fly. David Silver was off his head with exaltation. 'We've got you, Isobel! We've got you!' he trumpeted down the phone.

'No you haven't,' I tried to say, feeling the wheel rims of my soul juddering over a bed of rocks.

He hooted. 'We've got you, we've got you!'

'You'll have to fight me.'

'We'll win.'

'You won't.'

'Hoo, hoo! We'll win! We'll win!'

I wouldn't have told Mick about such a stupid call, but the phone kept ringing every twenty or so minutes with the same taunting, vicious pleasure until at last Mick thought David might come and do me damage. He took the phone from me and roared, 'If you don't piss off, I'll set the police on you!'

Baritones! Thank God for baritones! But that didn't mean that Mick would be there to protect me during the week and it didn't mean that Nin would be safe from David's maniacal behaviour either.

If only Eli had been around, we could have asked him to look after Stella while we hid for a while. But Eli wasn't around. There'd been no developments over Christmas: the police hadn't managed to pick up a trace of him and the forensics came up with nothing either. It seemed the best thing to do was to warn Lexie that there might be a confrontation and hide out at Mick's till the drama died down. I rang Redeemer and explained the situation as best I could to Kees. 'Nin and I might have to take a bit of a break away,' I said. 'It might mean a fortnight or so without seeing her while we work out the best way to tackle the situation.' Then I had to front Nin and Wendy at their house, because – with the excuse of David this time – they were incommunicado and it was impossible to get through to them by phone (or even email for that matter). After a battle royal with Wendy over whether or not it was gutless to flee, it was Nin, surprisingly, who turned the tables on her. 'You're right, Bel! Checkie shouldn't have those pictures. And as for bloody David…He's a bastard! A total megalomaniacal bastard! He's gone too far. All he wants are those bloody pictures and he's not going to have them. I am. I know the ones I want. They're pictures of my mother painted by my grandfather and I want them. And I've got news for the lot of you…' Nin fished in the fruit bowl, pulled out a test kit and held it on high. 'Pink!' she cried. 'I was going to tell you but that bastard started ringing up. And then I thought maybe I shouldn't have it because it could turn out like him. I was going to have an abortion and go back to work. How dare he terrorise a pregnant woman! I'm going to have this kid. I've decided!'

'What!' shrieked Wendy. 'Are you pregnant, Nin?'

There are no Jane Austens quietly scribbling long observant sentences on doilies in this household.

'How dare he terrorise you, my darling!' Wendy threw her arms up and flung herself on Nin, full of joy. 'Another ba-by! Another ba-by!' she sang, dancing around like a cowboy with Nin in her arms. Two minutes' worth of passionate kissing later, she cried, 'Well, you can piss off now and have your morning sickness down there with them, then and I'll guard the house.'

'Like a chihuahua.'

'Like a piranha.'

There's no logic to life. A fertile egg had attached itself to Nin's insides and caused her to make a decision, just like the flying pensioner who broke a blood vessel behind her eye on the tram.

And something changed in me, too. I could see their complete joy in each other, their love of their kid and their kid-to-come and their topsy-turvy home and I felt love for them both. I even hugged Wendy hard and long, and kissed her.

Mick's house is a family home, so there is plenty of space for us not to trip over each other. It's a two-hour drive from Melbourne. On the way, the usually lush countryside looked scant and skewered by the sun as if for the most meagre of picnics, but we were high on Nin's news and the drought was a distant reality outside the car. Daniel was enjoying himself in the back in his kid seat, 'I'n having *two* babies,' he announced. 'They in my legs. This one's a girl,' and he patted one thigh, 'and this one's a boy.' And he patted the other.

'What are their names, Dan?' we asked him.

'Lightning and Princess.'

'That'll be good. The new baby will have two friends to play with.'

'Lightning's the boy and Princess is the girl.'

Here, at this time of year on the stubbly back lawn at Mick's, the spotted pardalote among the ripening nectarines says, like a primary-school teacher in a playground, 'In you go. In you go. In you go.' A pretty little bird, but I wish it would shut up. Sometimes I say, 'In you go,' right back to it and that does shut it up for a minute or two. Then it'll say, 'In you go,' again, with less certainty than before and it won't repeat itself. So I'll say, 'In you go,' and it'll fly away – possibly to seek instructions from a Higher Bird, or because suddenly the playground is empty and it's time to go in itself.

I can paint down here when I'm by myself but not with Mick in the house. I feel the presence of the past when Mick is here and I can't quite get on top of it. In the best space, the sitting room, the colour of the walls gets me down. The house was professionally painted and Mick's wife thought she had chosen the kind of mauve that roses sometimes provide, on the blue side of pink – that's not how the walls turned out. They turned out on the pink side of blue. Not restful, just insipid. The room ought to celebrate green because the garden comes right up to the windows. What is needed here is a Matissean palette to lift the spaces, to fill the length of the house with delight for the eye and the width with light. I can feel the colour scheme but there's no opportunity to put it down. Maybe I should make an opportunity while we're here. Perhaps we should go into one of the larger towns where you can buy decent house paint and nut out a scheme. I tried to ask Mick whether we could do it this morning but he wasn't interested. After all, Mick has history, too; maybe he isn't ready for a change. He and Nin are having a cookathon and, not being a cook, I'm twiddling my thumbs and playing with Dan. Yesterday we made a feeding loft for dinosaurs with clippings from the lawnmower. There are mini hay bales strung up and stuck to the side of the toolshed with sticky tape and we thunder up for a feed after a good dinosaur fight with the snapping plastic heads we bought at the museum. In another box in the garden we've made a dinosaur nest that's hatching out some Funny Putty eggs stuffed with dinosaur jelly babies.

Wendy rings up a few times a day. David still hasn't stopped pestering her.

'Call the cops,' said Nin last night, suddenly full of responsible direction as if she's been rammed by maturity amidships.

Dan and I have been for lots of walks. People grow good roses down here. We'll get some nectarines and there are a few plums on the Satsuma I put in last year. The passionfruit vine is absolutely covered in ripening fruit. But the pear blossoms had brown stuff oozing out of them in the spring and no fruit has set on them. I hope they're not blighted; blight means you have to cut pear trees out in this part of the world. Maybe they're barren, but then, I only put them in last year. Things will get better. They should. They will. I have a little system going on where I make soil in Mick's back garden. There's a worm farm for apple, pear, quince and plum waste and a snail bin for lily leaves. I have a little cellulose digester on the go, away from the rest on a piece of concrete – rotting wood will bring down the structure of leaves eventually. A good garden needs to feed on what it grows. I've told Dan that to stay alive, every single thing has to eat something else. 'And I mean everything, Dan. Big things eat little things and tinchy things eat up big things. Not all dinosaurs ate grass; some of them ate other dinosaurs. It happens all the time. It never stops.' I think that's a good way of thinking about the world rather than setting up the goodies and baddies model. In the world of the shops, however, goodies and baddies rule and Dan's life is studded with superheroes. He's brought down a boxful of them. Accommodating the universal eating paradigm is difficult when superheroes are imperishable, so I've taught Dan to say that his superheroes are not biodegradable. 'Can you say non-biodegradable, Dan?' 'Not yet. Maybe soon.' Now, he thinks that non-biodegradable is a good way to be. 'But how will the biodegradable things keep going if superheroes can't die? What if everything turns into a superhero? Then they won't be able to eat each other and the rubbish dumps will be full up with broken superheroes.'

'Is that good, Sibella?'

'Well, the worms eat the dead things and make good earth from them.'

'Poo erf?'

'Well, yes, poo earth. Good poo earth. The trees and flowers and veggies and animals eat that poo.'

'Trees and flowers not got mouvs.'

'Well, no. Trees and flowers sip up the worm poo with their roots. The worms can't eat plastic and superheroes are made of plastic. And if the worms can't eat plastic and there are only plastic things, they can't poo and the trees and the flowers and the veggies and the animals can't grow. How will Princess and Lightning manage if nothing can grow?'

'Turn into superheroes.'

'But if you're their dad, they'll be humans, like you. They'll have to eat something.'

'Will they do poo, too?'

'You bet.'

'Has poo got germs?'

'Not the worm poo, no – but our poo does. Our poo's got bad germs. That's why we don't touch it.'

So he turns his toy camera into a gun for shooting germs dead and I find myself lying behind a patch of arums having my germs shot off.

This morning I had my chest X-rayed with a plastic cash register while I was dozing on the couch and he wrapped me up in Mick's crepe bandages – there's a whole boxful left over from the football-playing youth of his sons. Once I was mummified, Dan sat on the couch arm and drove me off to hospital at top speed. 'A dinosaur bited you,' I was told.

I'm a bit sick of lying under the arums so I've suggested yet another walk. As we amble down to the nearby farm paddocks, the place is not exactly abuzz. Even the bees take it slowly down here and the starlings sit along the wires, observing rather than chatting. Ants in single file on tree trunks, dry garden tangle, scent of cow dung. A teenage dude on a skateboard, nonchalantly trundling across the T-junction, and behind him, coming up the footpath, a gaggle of long-haired girls in a conspiratorial, fast-moving, stiff-legged huddle which splits suddenly in two to pass us and continues on, scheming on how to pass the dude without seeming to notice he's there. Down into the dip we go and there, in the paddock, are Patrick and Manoly, the two steers who are agisting beside the town's creek. We stand at the wire fence until they come over for a nose rub. Patrick is large, fat, black and white and a bully and poor Manoly has a soulful brown look. This time last year, we had the Two Ronnies – Ronnie Barker was fat and had an over-the-counter moo, whereas Ronnie Corbett was a dark little squib who snuffled. While we're watching, Patrick casually mounts Manoly and pees on him. Dan stands there, holding out handfuls of long grass, amazed.

'He weeing on he.'

'Yes darling.'

'Why?'

'I don't know.'

'Is that good, Sibella?'

'I don't think it is, particularly. I think Patrick's a bit naughty.'

Patrick dismounts in favour of food and Manoly sets to, whacking his tail around to hit himself on the flanks like the masochist he is. 'They got sun-ting in they's ears,' says Daniel.

'Yes, number tags, can you tell me what colour they are, Dan?'

'Lellow. Why they got lellow in they's ears, Sibella?'

'It's their earrings, I suppose.'

'Aminals not wear earrings.'

'These ones do.'

'Why?'

What do you say? So they can send the tags back to the farmers when they're killed? 'They might be going out, Dan. What do you think?'

'To the shops?'

'They might be going to buy new dresses, or hats?'

He laughs. 'That would be funny.'

'They might be going to a party?'

'Can we have a party?'

And I think of having a party to take our minds off the boredom. 'We could put up a tent in the backyard,' I say.

There are some beautiful bulrushes in the creek, standing very, very still. Ibis pluck the ground in the trodden-up wake of the dairy herd. There's still quite a lot of moisture in the soil and it's green around the watercourses. If all else fails, could I live here?

There's a store (for sale), a pub and a milk bar in the shopping strip.

Two mechanics, one at either end.

There's a country butchery (for sale) and a tractor store.

There's a primary school. It's a pretty little school with a friendly playground.

There's an RSL, a bowls club, and Scouts.

And that's about it.

A post office that doesn't deliver.

Every now and then, you can hear the overhead creaking of a cockie.

I've done every walk I could take in a three-hundred-and-sixty-degree radius from the house. Most of the area is fenced paddocks for feeding cows. There's a gully. It's an hour's drive to the sea.

You know you're in an exciting place when one of the activities listed on the noticeboard of the store is 'read the noticeboard'.

Daniel says his legs are tired and he wants to go back to the house where Mick's sons have left behind toys that belonged to the seventies when they were growing up. Clip together knights and cowpersons, police and soldiers, horses and motorbikes. These toys were from the height of feminism when girls could do every-thing – perhaps they're meant to be unisex. There are plenty of baddies to round up with handcuffs, bows and arrows, guns and crossbows but nobody to do the housework.

The teenage girls are now flicking their fingernails on a far corner and laughing very loudly while the dude describes slow circles on the bitumen on his board. The ants are still filing up and down the tree. Occasionally, a starling will shift a wing and shuffle and somewhere, a block or so away, someone is starting up a muffler-less quad bike. Quad bike riding starts pretty young around here; you even see little girls roaring round the streets in pink helmets. Daniel tells me he'd like to slam me in jail again behind the kiddie fence we bought to stop him wandering when he was little. This game involves releasing me so he can catch me doing bad things again. Once in a rare while, he opts to be the baddie, but I'm not allowed to find him until I've looked everywhere else but where he is. I'd rather lie down and be bandaged up again. Maybe holding a newspaper, except that Dan can't resist thwacking open newspapers with pretending swords. I wonder if combat is as necessary to human beings as eating is? I suppose it is, really – after all, you've got to fight your way to the food in the wild.

We dawdle into the drive and I am just thinking that I should spray the roses with anti-aphid stuff, when Nin bursts out the front door, ashen. God! I hope Mick's okay!

'Gran's had an accident! She fell out of her bed last night and broke her elbow.'

'Oh fuck!'

I should have known she'd have an accident. What do you do when your daughter has a pressing need to be away? Break a bone. My immediate return is required. Mick and Nin have already packed the sandwiches and the thermos.

I get into the car, as so many desperadoes do in thrillers – only not this type of car, which is built like a sensible boot – and looks like one, on wheels. Dan comes tearing after me, calling out, 'No!' while Nin races to the front fence and says, 'Come on Dan, jump up here and wave goodbye to Sibella.'

'I'n not Jumpabere!' he wails. 'I'n Dan! No, Sibella!'

'Sorry, darling, but I have to go, you show Mum the germ camera.' Mick embraces me through the window and I bounce out of the drive, backwards. Bounce because, although Mick is doing his best to ride his marital breakdown with panache, that panache doesn't extend to his driveway, which has suffered concrete dislodgement over the years and has a crater with lifting edges just inside the gate.

I feel overly gallant going it alone to my mother's bedside yet again, but realistically, I have to. A break at this time of her life could signal the end.

It could. Apparently, it's quite bad.

So it's back through the paddocks, through the shreds of forest and the pine plantations that line the roads, past the three or four memorials to kids who've written themselves off joyriding for want of entertainment. Back through the petrol station towns, the spruced-up village with the craft shops and then the freeway. And the freeway. And the freeway. And the sculptural fences on the freeway edges. And whizzing by the suburbs, spreading like a plague of McMansion boils – and in and in and in like the zoom on a satellite map. To the hospital at last. And the skirmish for a car park.

It's a pretty bad break, they tell me at the hospital. She is in dreadful pain, crying out, 'Lord, Lord, take me, PLEASE.' They waited until I came to sign the 'Do Not Revive' form in case she succumbs under the anaesthetic, so I feel wretched that it took two hours to drive here. She is probably in as much pain as ever her fiancé was, lying on the battlefield outside Beirut. I can only reassure myself that she has had more life than he did; she is leaving descendants. They wheel her away to operate.

I try to comfort myself with the thought that there haven't been any extended bouts of agony in her life, or not that I remember. Just lots of short incidents. She broke a leg but she was younger then and physically more able to take it. The recuperation was long and needed the rehab hospital. There was boredom, ennui, aches, pains and trouble, but she was going home to her own house that time. There was her garden, the neighbours, the cat, the dogs. I was there to care for her, to take her back and forth once she was able to walk again. I was there for the animals. Then she dislocated her hip and had to have a replacement – it was the same story, but the hip kept on dislocating – there was minor agony, but once the paramedics had given her the morphine shot, 'Take me to the Waldorf Astoria', she'd cry – she liked the hip hospital; it was worth the private health insurance. This time, it's a compound fracture and there are nerves involved, so it is agony. I can't hope that her Lord takes her in pain. I want her to die in peace. There's the cat at the home to go back to and a soft toy replica of her favourite dog, although she's forgotten she ever had a dog.

I'm walking up and down, up and down in a waiting area, arms clamped across my chest beside the stuck-together plasticky chairs in their heartless rows on long-wearing, don't-show-the-dirt blue carpet. The place is shady, a bunker of concrete with a dirty plate-glass window high up, screening out what ought to be contact with the relentless sky. So much dust in the air and much of it landed on the bits you most want to see through. The only bright spot is a woman in a long purple shirt with a red hijab, leaning forward on one of the chairs. She has her hands open, prayer-book style and her eyes closed. I guess she is praying.

Up and down, up and down – waiting. It's probably what's meant by Purgatory. You're purged of your will to live, purged of happiness, of want, of decent, ordered, thematic thought. You live in the atmosphere of Unknowingness, where you can hear what might be the atoms knocking on your cochlea, where you breathe them up and they invade your nose and lungs, inspecting your interior for its breath-worthiness. You're just an accidental form in the scheme of things in a waiting-room Purgatory. The woman in the hijab is staring into space now, breathing heavily. I come face to face with a framed picture of a pink lotus and a green lily pad on a blue pond – is it supposed to be my compensation? I don't suppose it's meant to remind me of a job-lot interior designer buying up bulk crap for hospital interiors. Perhaps if I brought my sketchbook in here, I could sketch away while I waited and nobody would be adversely affected…the woman catches my eye; I smile at her; she crunches her mouth on one side in peremptory recognition. She has terrific hands, long-fingered and strong. She catches me staring at them and grimaces again.

I could talk to her, I suppose. Might be better for both of us if I talked to her.

'Hello,' I say. 'Where are you from?'

She frowns. 'Australia,' she says, crossly.

'Oh dear, sorry.'

'Why are you sorry? You're an Australian. You have nothing to be sorry about.'

'Didn't you just say you were an Australian, too?'

'I am an Australian citizen, same as you.'

'Same as me,' I say. 'But, although my mother won't admit it, some of my forebears came in chains. I'm guessing you or your family has resettled here from somewhere else.'

'I don't like it when people ask me where I'm from,' she says. 'I'm an Australian citizen.'

'But you came here from somewhere else. We all did. Except for the Aboriginal people.'

'That's true.'

'When I was a child – I was born just after the war – we were taught to ask people where they came from as a sign of friendship. We were the receiving culture and we were welcoming newcomers. That's just how it was.'

'I suppose…' she says, flaring her fingers and looking into her palms. Then she says, in dull resignation, 'In Asia they ask you how old you are.'

'That'd be considered rude here. In many parts of Asia, I believe they revere age.'

'Yes. They do. Old people are looked after by their families. Not like here.'

I don't feel like telling her that my mother lives in a home, so I sit down beside her and say, 'You have lovely hands.' And I hold out my hands for one of hers, which she gives me. 'Beautiful. So strong.'

'They have to do a lot of work,' she says, her eyes sad.

'Are you waiting on news of a relative?' I ask.

'My mother. She is very old. She has broken her wrist.'

'Mine's broken her elbow,' I say. 'She's about to turn ninety-nine.'

'Mine is ninety-four.'

'Well, there. We have more in common than our Australian-ness, whatever that is. Do you look after your mother at home?'

'Yes, I do. She is hard work. She is a very strong woman. It takes three people to hold her when she gets going.'

'Do you have anyone to help you?'

'Sometimes.' And I can tell by the way she says it that help is as enthusiastically given to her as it has been to me.

'Family?'

'Oh yes, I have family.'

'I suppose you have to look after them as well?'

'Yes. I am housekeeper and cook.'

'Do the Aged Services people come to help out?'

'I get four hours a week. It's not enough.'

'I know the story. My mother lived on her own until she was ninety-four. I lived close by.'

'It wouldn't work with my mother.'

'I see. You seem depressed.'

'I'm very depressed.'

'Because of your mother?'

'It's hard enough to look after her when she doesn't have a broken bone.'

'Will she be in hospital for a while?'

'I don't know. It's only her wrist. When I broke my wrist, they didn't keep me in at all; they discharged me straight after they set it. I just had to go home and keep on working.'

'I gather you'd prefer it if they kept her in for a while?'

'Maybe I can do some *work!* I have a husband and sons to look after. I need to go to the doctor myself. Something wrong inside from lifting. I need to get help.'

I've been holding her hand since she gave it to me and tears are beginning to well in her eyes. 'I know what it's like,' I say. 'I've been there. In fact, I am there, though not quite as badly as you at the moment. If my mother comes through the operation, she will be discharged to aged care. And she'll have convalescence first.'

'You think your mother will die?'

'She might. Anaesthetics can kill old people.'

'I don't want my mother to die.'

'No. I don't want mine to die, either. It's hard, isn't it?' We sit back, contemplating, still holding hands. 'My name's Isobel,' I say at length.

'Mahanoz,' she says.

'Ma-ha-noz,' I say. 'How do you spell that?'

'M, a, h, n, a, z.'

'What kind of name is that?'

'Doesn't matter.'

'Guess not, Mahnaz. Have you been in Australia long?'

'Twenty years. All my family here now. I have boys in high school. You?'

'Oh, I've been here all my life. I have a grown-up son and I brought up my sister's girl. My sister's girl has a little boy.'

'She's married then?'

'She has a partner.'

'Not married?'

'No.'

She lets go of my hand. 'It's different here in Australia to where I come from. Every woman married where I come from. Except one my sister. She not married, just work, work, work all the time.'

'What does she do?'

'University.'

'Oh?' But Mahnaz isn't inclined to elaborate, so I imagine her sister might be a cleaner or a secretary or a canteen worker.

She turns to me suddenly and says, 'You nice. You want to come and have some tea with me sometime?'

So I say, 'Yes, yes, I'd like that very much. We have something to share, don't we – old mothers.'

So we exchange addresses and phone numbers and I see that she lives out near Monash…

'Ms Coretti?' A nurse is calling me to go to Stella.

'Goodbye, Mahnaz. I'll give you a call to see how you get on and we'll make a date, okay?'

'Okay. Maybe we see each other, Isobel.'

Stella's operation was complicated and she was under the knife for more than an hour, but afterwards, she was well enough to go into a ward. Her bones are so weak they can't take screws and so everything has had to be set with great care and fingers crossed.

She shares her ward with a dreadful young bloke who stinks of cigarettes and is constantly nicking out for another. He's covered in tattoos and wearing shortie pyjamas that ride up to afford unwanted glimpses of his wherewithal. He is next to the window and Stella is next to the door. There's not much to look at outside; there are excavations going on that rattle the windows but blessedly don't penetrate any further into the space. Stella's eyes have opened a few times, her colour is good; she is a funny little heap in pale blue with an oxygen mask and a drip taped into her frail old arm. Once or twice her mouth has flickered into her dear old smile. She has the Motte family smile that glides out and shines with sweetness. I'm glad it has survived the crush of genes down through the centuries. Too few people can smile as she does.

Look at her.

Year before last, she was the tottering mistress of her indescribably cluttered Victorian terrace in Hawthorn. It was a strip of council-created cleanliness from front door to back becoming narrower and narrower, the piles of rubbish higher and higher, until she lived in a corridor of muck subtended by little islets of habitation budding off through the doors.

Nin and I used to clean things up a bit before the council help came. We'd have to spirit her rubbish away because if we put it in her garbage tin, she would retrieve it – even put it back in her fridge. She was certain we couldn't be trusted to throw anything out. We would choose the wrong things and we wouldn't do it according to the law. 'They', the mysterious 'they' who feature in so many people's lives, were always watching, always promulgating some arcane law that meant she had to wash up her tins, soak the labels off and throw the labels and the tins out separately, or what? Go to jail, go directly to jail, Stella Coretti née Motte, and forfeit your pension to your jailer. I could just picture her, rattling the bars of her cell, howling out, 'Injustice!' until one of her legal Motte relatives came calling and avenged her on television in the sight of the nation.

The drains could be clogged with fat and tea-leaves and old bits of tuna, but water had to be run into the sink for the label soaking. She would store the labels in the upper basket of a shopping trolley and we were not allowed to touch them until there were enough to fill a large cereal packet, but we were always waiting on the packet, because every time she went to the shops (which was every weekday) she'd buy two for the price of one and open both. She would leave them open on the benchtops in her kitchen because, she said, it was easier to find them that way – her kitchen was laid out how you wanted it and no one was going to interfere – after all, in the years of her madness, she had to do without a kitchen – she, the only decent cook in the country.

Nin and I would have to smuggle some of the packages into a garbage bag and divert her attention while Nin shoved in a pile of other stuff, to which I'd give her clues when we were coming in at the front door, tied up the neck and chucked it over the fence into the lane behind the house. Then, as Stella set about pushing me up ladders and testing fire alarms (she would ring me up in the middle of the night to tell me, admonishingly, that her fire alarms weren't working) or stood by criticising my ironing, or ordered me

240

to ring up and get proof that certain of her bills had been paid, I would adjust the blind of the kitchen window so that she couldn't see Nin diving over the back fence and racing down to the park to dump her rubbish in the nearest bin or skip. When she'd finished her tirade, she would say, 'Who keeps doing that to my kitchen blind?' and giving it a yank that sometimes brought it down into the horrendous sink.

I'm afraid that Nin and I fed her companionable, TV-watching rats with Ratsak in the end, but when we saw them sitting up, swaying side to side with illness and waiting to die in front of *The Price Is Right* with her, both of us shuddered like weaklings and phoned Eli, who happened to be home, so that he would come and dispatch them. So great an act of courage on his part was this that Nin and I forgave him for not doing one single other thing to help in her relocation to a home.

Oh Stella, you used to have flair! You had a feel for colour, shape and disposition. Periodically you would 'tart up' the house where Allegra and I lived as children. You would have it looking accommodating and full of welcome. We would feel we were going to have a good time just by crossing the threshold. If only I could reward you for that – but these days the sentiments behind cosy, loving appearances aren't cosy and loving, they're based on envy, competition and greed like that fake fireplace at the home that turned us down.

Will I miss you when you die, Stella? I miss you now. Aspects of you – your lovely, sauntering walk, your twinkling hazels, your deft little hands, unencumbered by arthritis – although nervousness made you clumsy, made you fail to get the tops off sauce bottles so that all our doorjambs were dented with crushed lid marks... God, you didn't know much, did you? How come you didn't know that you can wind a rubber band around a sauce bottle top and it will magnify the strength of your grip several fold; you can run a metal cap under hot water to loosen it; you can tap it all around smartly but gently with a knife handle to let air in and it will loosen quite soon – instead, you wrecked all the nice old lintels as you inserted your bottles, rapier-like, into the jambs, brought the door back smartly and crunched your way to misshapen lids and splintered necks. You silly old moo! You used to pour the sauce out through a tea strainer to make sure you weren't putting glass on our plates. Will I miss that? No, I won't miss that – that worry, that despair, is just part of your ingrained character, the barrier against a reasonable life.

So full of bitterness are you, so full of strife and anger. We didn't take your brothers from you, Mother. We didn't take your lover, and yet, you'd often treat us as if we were to blame for a war that happened before we were born. What kind of thinking is that? Do you imagine we carry the prehistory of ourselves? That we can consult it and agree with you that things were bad? New bad succeeds old, Old Lady. The uneven wheel rolls on. It takes you and me away and leaves the world to Eli and Nin. The weight is redistributed, made new by altered circumstances.

Nevertheless, I love you, old lady who bore me.

The remnant of your loving glance, the dearness of your crippled hand.

I love you even though you can be a high-pitched pain.

You poor old thing, living on and on and on because the past says you must.

If life were just and I were in charge, we'd do death differently. Once we felt replete, we'd be able to say, 'it's time to go'. We'd be able to go in style. It would be as significant an occasion as a birth. Nobody would be allowed to make that decision for us and only in exceptional circumstances, like crippling illness or pain, would we be able to decide to die before reaching, say, the age of eighty-six – because that's the age that women reach. Yeah, eighty-six would be the age of consent for death; we might lower it to eighty-four for men, since they don't live as long. Today it isn't rare to reach eighty-six and if you're already sixty, chances are you'll get to eighty-six. At sixty you're usually still quite savvy. If you were in good health and could look at twenty-six years with optimism, then eighty-six seems to me to be a good age to say you'd like to die if you feel replete with life.

By the time Dan's sixty, he might be looking at thirty to forty more years with optimism. There's a lot you can do in that time if you're sharp enough and well enough and live in an age-tolerant society – so much, in fact, that by the time you reached the age of consent, you might find yourself choosing to live on in good spirit. You might well be socially productive into the bargain.

I don't especially want you to die, old lady, but if it had been the norm for your age group to choose, then you might have gone easily at eighty-six. In comfort. Except you would have been afraid. Because you believe in that superhero, God, and his disapproving Anglican heaven where you'd be expected to sit still and look pretty, even though there's an exploding girl inside you, a fidgeter waiting to be set loose on she knows not what.

A doctor comes by. It's as I thought. She will be here for quite a long time, knitting.

We used to call her the Midnight Knitter when she lost her mind after Allegra's death. She would knit endlessly, not to any pattern, but part pattern – a cuff here, a heel-turn there, purl and plain, cable stitch, window stitch. We just supplied her with ball after ball of bright wool, and away she went, needles in, needles out, clickety clack, clickety clack, counting off the sorrow and the years.

16

I stayed most of the night at the hospital, just in case there was a turn for the worse. I went home about four a.m. and slept for an hour or two, showered, breakfasted and came back to sit beside her this morning. She's awake.

She tells me that the man outside on the building site who rides the load on the crane came swinging into her bedroom last night.

'What, like Errol Flynn?'

'Oh, he didn't look like Errol Flynn.'

'Was he nice?'

'No, he wasn't,' she says.

'Oh, I'm sorry.'

'No need to be sorry. It's not your fault.'

'How are you feeling?'

'I ain't got no feelin's, Dorty.' It's what my grandfather used to say to her – only he used to say, 'I ain't got no teef.'

Over in the other patient's territory, above which the crane rider would have had to go surfing for his tryst with Stella, one of the smoker's friends is visiting him.

'Didya fucken ring 'er?' the smoker begins.

'Why don't you ring 'er yer fucken self?' answers a scraggy man with tattoos joining the bottoms of his baggy shorts to the sock tops rolled down over boots.

'She'd put the fucken phone down in me ear.'

'Shoon't a fucken hit'er.'

'I never fucken 'it 'er.'

'Ya fucken did, man. It's why yer in 'ere.'

'I fucken never. She just rammed me with the fucken car…'

Stella whispers, 'Noice.' And she winks at me.

The smoker has had his shins scraped off. 'You fucken hit 'er first, ya fucker. Yer've gotta go to court fer grievous.'

'That's a fucken lie. Just because she's yer fucken sister ya believe every fucken thing she says.'

'Ya busted 'er nose, ya fucker.'

'Did ya fucken ring 'er?'

'No. I never. An I'm not fucken gunner, either. Ring 'er yer fucken self.'

'Aw. I just wanna know about me fucken kids! I want 'er to bring the fucken kids to see me. Get the wheelchair, will ya? I wanna go out for a smoke.' And he winks at me, but I've already been winked at by Stella and the conspiracy's against him.

I've asked if my conspirator could be moved to more salubrious company but the hospital is full to overflowing. They certainly didn't have room for poor Mahnaz's mum. It was as she predicted, a broken wrist didn't warrant an extended stay. Mahnaz and I agreed to meet at her home for tea this afternoon.

David has been prowling around my house – there is a heap of squished-out cigarette butts behind the street tree – so much for his giving up smoking. I've rung Lexie and, yes, he's been out to the storage place demanding to see the pictures. Lexie has been sensible enough to have her husband send him away. David is cowed by big men and baritones, but actually, being tall and plain-speaking, Lexie might have frightened him herself. My landline was ringing when I went home after seeing Stella. I could tell it was David by the angry tone it made. I'm doing my best on my mobile in the meantime so the others don't lose touch with me, but I'm not very competent with it and in this state of nerves, I can't seem to use it properly.

Mahnaz lives in unfamiliar territory and I took a few wrong turns, not being map-headed. Three U-turns later on the same stretch of road and I found the proper entrance to her street. At the number she'd given me, I found a driveway for about six cars in front of the grand portals to a McMansion.

I pushed the buzzer and, thinking that it didn't look like the sort of house where I'd expect to find someone like Mahnaz and maybe I'd read the address wrongly, I was delving in my bag when the door was flung open and there stood, not Mahnaz, but a woman as short as I am, with high cheekbones, avid light-brown eyes and a shock of grey frizz standing up on her handsome head. I felt sure I'd seen her somewhere before.

'Hello,' I said. 'I'm looking for…'

'Mahnaz,' she crooned in a ripe voice and started nodding. 'Come in.'

'I'm…'

'Your name is Isobel.' She had a knowingly quizzical expression on her face. 'I used to see you at the university.'

'Ah, that's where…'

'You worked with the genes and immunology people. We shared the same lift.'

'Oh yes, of course. I remember now. Your name's…'

'Meetra.'

'That's right, Meetra,' I said, thinking to myself that she'd do very well on a reaction time test. 'What a small world we live in! Are you visiting Mahnaz, too?'

'No, no,' she smiled. 'I live here. It's my house, too.'

'But aren't you…'

'Professor of Pharmacology. Yes.'

'That's right! Your department used to be above ours. We couldn't wait to get rid of you and when you moved over to the medical building, we took over your space in about half a day and we were still overcrowded. Gosh, that was a long time ago. But aren't you Polish? I thought from your accent you were Polish.'

'No. I'm not Polish. I come from Afghanistan.'

'*Re*-ally!'

'Somebody has to come from Afghanistan. I do.'

'Really? My God! And Mahnaz…'

'Afghan, like me. Mahni is my sister.'

'Well, Allah-u Akbar!' I said. 'She wouldn't tell me where she came from.'

She cackled in an electric kind of way and cocked her head. 'She don't like to say.'

'Why ever not?'

'Mahni like to be an Australian. You met her at the hospital?'

'I did. Our mothers broke bones at the same time.'

I've got a hide! I thought that Mahnaz's sister was bound to be a cleaner or a secretary or a canteen worker. I thought refugee? She probably had to take what she was given. I never imagined it would turn out to be someone like Meetra. And what a snob I am! I never realised I was such a snob. It shouldn't matter what work Mahnaz's sister does! It shouldn't make any difference to how I interact with Mahnaz. At least, not objectively. But subjectively it does – because if Mahnaz had an uneducated, hard-working sister, that would signify a different kind of family from this one. But here I am and I am the guest here and this is not my house and if it were a different type of house, my situation would be the same, I would still be searching for an appropriate way to react with Mahnaz in her day-to-day ambience. There, I've given myself a lecture in Sociology 1.

Meetra has ushered me into a large, light-filled sitting room, set with chairs and sofas enough for twenty people. It isn't the norm in Australia to have such rooms in middle-class homes. The sofas and chairs are arranged in a square around low tables, much more formal, and larger than the type of room I'm used to. It evokes the atmosphere of a respectful meeting – such as one might have when presenting a small, but not frivolous, petition to a politician. I wonder what the history is behind this style? Is it a buffer between the formal anonymity of the street and the intimacy of home life? Perhaps formal life intrudes further into Afghan homes than it does into Australian ones.

I guess the whole social arrangement is different. Afghanistan! I can hardly credit it. I thought Mahnaz was Middle Eastern, certainly, but Afghan didn't cross my mind. I thought maybe Egyptian or Lebanese...

For a moment or two I find myself doing battle with a giddy feeling of surprise, but after all, I have come here to see Mahnaz and I am not going to be put off or intimidated by something I simply hadn't anticipated. I guess that Anglo-Celtic-Italians are either inside (down halls in the womb) or outside their homes and that they reserve formal set-ups for offices and institutions.

I decide to sit down, bottom pushed well to the back of a stiff sofa well within the room and immediately I feel more in command for not having teetered at edges. Meetra sits down beside me. 'Mahni!' she calls and I can't understand what follows. I ask what language it is and she answers, 'Dari'.

'Oh. This may sound odd, but my son speaks Dari.'

'Really? What he's doing speaking Dari?'

'He's a journalist.'

'Oh la-la. He works for a paper, TV?'

'No, not exactly. He's a freelancer with Reporters Without Borders. He started his career in your part of the world, actually, in Pakistan. He became enthralled by the Edhi Foundation and its work providing ambulances and shelters. He...'

'But I know of this Edhi. He is a good man.'

'He certainly is.'

'And is your son still there?'

'Well, he's supposed to be in Afghanistan right now.'

'Afghanistan?' Her eyes widen in surprise. She pronounces it Off-gone-istan.

'Yes. But I haven't heard from him for a while. I don't know if he's still there or even if he got there. I'm actually terribly worried about him.'

'Oh, Off-gone-istan. It depends where he is. If he's in Helmand Province or Paktika or Paktia, or Khost or Ghazni or Kandahar, you are right to be worried. The Taliban are there.'

'Well, I know that he goes to some very dangerous places. He's just had a year back here but now he's gone again. For the last few years, he has been trying to help set up local television in country areas and he's been trying to protect women journalists from the terrible consequences that can come from showing their faces in public. There are women who've been attacked with acid or been murdered by their own family members – fathers and brothers. One poor woman was assassinated in front of her children. My son is trying to help change attitudes at the same time as keeping up an information flow about what is happening in the reconstruction. His reports have been on Tolo TV, that's a pretty big TV channel, isn't it?'

'It's the biggest. Everyone in Kabul watches Tolo.'

'Well, as I said, Eli speaks fluent Dari and looks the part. They call him Elias Jan, I believe.'

'I haven't heard of him. But I will look out for the name next time I am in Kabul.'

'Oh really? You go sometimes, do you?'

'Of course. I am Afghan. It is my home.'

'Really? Well, my son's real name is Eli. He's worried that when the NATO troops withdraw, there'll be a reactionary blood-bath and any of the progress made will be forfeited…'

'I know it!' says Meetra, nodding in earnest, her eyes flashing. 'I am working in an organisation. I go to Kabul twice a year to do the administration. We train teachers and we teach life skills. In fact, I'm going to Kabul in April.'

'Well, I must say that when I came to visit Mahnaz I never thought I'd find myself sitting up talking to someone who regularly visits Afghanistan.'

'Well, I can try to find your son if you want it. I have contacts in the Afghan Embassy. They don't issue visas to everyone. They will know if he has one for there, and if so, they'll have his itinerary…'

'Are you sure? To tell you the truth, the police are looking for him over an incident that happened at the place where he was living before he left. It's been months now and they haven't come up with anything. He wasn't on any of the passenger lists bound for Afghanistan…'

She nods appraisingly, then says, 'They are so lazy these people. Passenger lists are not the place to look. You have to go to the Embassy.'

'I believe they have the Department of Foreign Affairs looking into it.'

'Hoh! They probably give it to an official who wants to take his holidays…Leave it to me. I'll find out for you today! But first, here's Mahni with the coffee…'

'You'll be able to find out today!'

'Tea, Mitty,' says Mahnaz. 'She said she wanted tea and so tea I have made.' And Mahnaz, dressed in a beautiful green gown with a matching scarf pulled over her hair, puts down an immaculately prepared tray on the low table and in the blossoming fragrance of cardamom I am able to draw breath and realise who I am – an honoured guest – and where I am – in the heart of the house.

'You look lovely, Mahnaz. And what a lovely tray you've prepared.'

'Is nothing.'

'Is everything.'

Meetra flaps her hand. 'Muslims have to be sociable,' she says. 'It's our law.'

'Well, it's a good law.'

Mahnaz hands me a plate my mother would be proud to own – a proper piece of bone china. I put it on the table in front of me and look around the room. There is a large, no doubt Afghan, rug covering the floor. The hard, straight-backed sofas and chairs are upholstered in material that you would never find gracing the chairs of the middle-class Melbourne sitting/lounge room, it being way too declarative in brown and gold. No paintings on display but the curving wall that divides us from the rest of the house is only waist high. It displays such things as a tall brass teapot, lapis lazuli boxes, silver carrying baskets, which, when she sees me staring, Mahnaz starts to explain, 'You take your…'

'It's for when a girl visits her mother-in-law,' Meetra interrupts. 'She takes her soap and everything in one of those.' Mahnaz pours the tea and hands it to me, resignedly. Obviously, 'Mitty' is a force. 'Mitty' is someone to be reckoned with. Suddenly, 'Mitty' asks, 'And what have you done with Ursula, Mahni? She was here a minute ago.'

'She went to…oh, here she is, no need to tell you where she went.'

And a large-framed, red-faced Caucasian woman comes rolling into our midst from the inner sanctum, brushing big white hands down her stomach and saying in an Aussie accent, 'There, that's better.' She puts a hand out to me and says, 'Ursula O'Connor. I'm doing the biography.'

'Oh?'

'It's time someone did it. This woman is amazing.'

And it transpires that not only is Meetra a distinguished scientist, she has brought more than thirty Afghan families to Australia in as many years. She set up businesses for them to work in even before she qualified for citizenship herself. She was working in France when the Russians invaded Afghanistan and her brother was here on a training scholarship. 'Eventually I caught up with him,' Meetra says, 'and together we decided that Australia would be a good place to bring the whole family, even though it's very far from Afghanistan. So I came here. I got work and started to think of ways to bring out my family.'

'And you brought out thirty-four families,' says Ursula.

'Gosh,' say I, 'all immediate relatives?'

'Yes. Brothers, sisters, children, parents, cousins…thirty-four families.'

'Gosh. There are only four people in my immediate family; five, if you count the littlest one.'

'Afghans have lots of children. I have four sisters and six brothers. I am the second born, but the eldest girl.'

Mahnaz ruffles her brow and cocks her head slightly as our eyes meet over a tray of sweets.

'She's just been telling me she was born in a snow drift…' says Ursula.

'Really?'

Mahnaz's mouth is doing the thing it did when we had our first conversation, turning down at the corners and twitching resignedly as Meetra takes up where she must have left off when Ursula went to the toilet. 'The year I was born it was very cold in Afghanistan during the war. My mother, I don't know why, decided to go outside. I was born suddenly in the middle of the courtyard. Because it was cold the windows were closed and at ten o'clock, all Afghan families they were listening to BBC radio for the news. My father was very busy listening to the news, and nobody heard my mother was crying, calling them and I stayed more than, say, thirty minutes inside of the snow with my mother. So they said, suddenly, "Oh, where is…?" and they looked and they searched and they called and they found her in the courtyard. They took my mother and called a doctor. The doctor came and he said that okay, the mother should rest. He gave something. He said, "We are not sure if the daughter survives or not." Well, they wrapped me in a blanket and at four o'clock, five o'clock in the morning, my aunty turned the light on and said, "I'll go and see if this girl... She doesn't cry. Whether she survived or whether she died." So, when she's looking... apparently, I was sucking my thumb and I took it off and I smiled and my aunty, she was always telling me, she scared from me. "This girl has power," she used to say.'

'I was born in sunshine,' says Mahnaz to me. 'Sensible.'

But Meetra has swung the subject away suddenly to a place near Herat that I've never heard of –

'Churcher – ron,' Ursula repeats.

'No. Cheyrr-cheyrr-on. C. H. E. G. H. C. H. E. R. O. N. People would say because of the lack of water and the land situated at the skirt of the mountain that was the reason they were very poor...In nineteen-ninety the people had no money to eat. They were selling their children. But in two thousand five, I sent approximately thirty tonne in medical equipment because the French people, they built a hospital but without any furniture. So we sent a container of supplies to help them. And to an Afghan doctor that I met, I said, "I sent it to Cheghcheron," and he said, "Oh, don't need to send to Cheghcheron, because Cheghcheron got suddenly very rich." I said, "How?" He said, "Growing drugs." And they were all driving the four-wheel cars. I was surprised. I didn't go to Cheghcheron, but all I know is helicopters come directly on the field, get everything and then they go. Where they go, nobody knows. But landlords, they get their money.'

Ursula puts her cup down, knowingly. 'Dubai. They used to go to Dubai. And Dubai to Germany and sometimes to the USA...'

'Yes, maybe to Spain.' Meetra narrows her eyes and points a finger.

'I think there might have been a major pathway through Germany,' says Ursula. 'I know of some brothers who set up in Germany and Dubai in the "carpet business". No doubt they were selling carpets but they also owned extensive poppy fields. Supposedly they were harvesting the stuff for the pharmaceutical industry in Germany, but if so, it was enough to keep the world in morphine.' And she says to me, 'One of the Taliban's credos is to weaken the West by flooding the markets with Afghan drugs.'

'Hoh!' goes Meetra. 'Propaganda. Taliban don't like drugs.'

'They do…' says Ursula.

'No they don't, madame. Taliban are very religious. No stimulants. Nothing. It's the Haqqani network, Al Qaeda, and the Westerners themselves. Why do you think the people in Cheghcheron grow suddenly rich? Through people who pay them lots of money for leasing their land to grow poppies.'

So, what's going on here? Maybe Meetra would sooner be definite than right. Or is she truly unaware that these days opium is a major source of income for the Pakistani Taliban? I'm about to say that it was once true that the Taliban were very straitlaced about drugs and dealing, but not now, when Mahnaz pipes up, 'There's a big drugs problem in Afghanistan. The carpet weavers sit smoking pipes – even their kids who work with them smoke hash pipes.'

'For them it's like aspirin,' Meetra cuts in. 'It comes out through their milk to the children. Those women need rehabilitation. I want some money to build centres for this. A place where they can stay for however long it takes. Six months, eight months, a year and they can do vocational training while they are there. Not carpet making, something different. Food technology, maybe. The carpets are beautiful bu-ut,' she sings, 'the work hurts them…and low returns. Better to use aid money properly in sustainable projects.'

It's obvious that Meetra is in charge of all the information around here and she has the propensity to moderate every word that's said, but suddenly Mahnaz is laughing. 'She never stop! Nothing too much!'

Meetra pouts good-naturedly, flicks a hand and shrugs.

'These baklava are delicious, Mahnaz. Did you make them?' I ask with an eye to the sisterly relationship. Before she can answer, Meetra says, 'Mahni is a good cook. She doesn't cook sweets,' as if cooking sweets were the sign of a bad cook. I can't help liking Meetra for her eager, forthright ways but I'm beginning to remember what it was like being a younger sister. Everything you say gets qualified from above; you rarely have the right to be right.

'I've heard about all the different ethnic groups in Afghanistan,' I say to Mahnaz, 'which one do you belong to?'

And again, before she can answer, Meetra pipes up. 'Okay, we are a very interesting group of people. My mother is Pashtun, my father was Tajik.'

'Then presumably, Mahni's mother is a Pashtun and her father was a Tajik?' I taunt, but it goes nowhere.

'The warlord Massoud was a Tajik, was he not?' asks Ursula.

'Panjshir Tajik,' Meetra says.

'Is there a difference?' I ask.

'Tajiks identify themselves by the region they are from. They are not nomadic or tribal people. They are left over from a widespread settled community of former times.'

'That's not generally the case in Afghanistan, is it?' asks Ursula.

'Not among the Pashtuns. They are tribal people. The herders – the Kuchi – belong to the Pashtun; they are different again; they are nomadic. They supply most of Afghanistan's meat.'

'Lamb and goats?' Ursula asks.

'And chickens. Some of them are settled and breed chickens, but mostly they follow the pastures. No paddocks, like here. It's too high up.'

'Do the Sunnis and the Shias get along?' I ask.

'Yes. Before the wars, everyone in Afghanistan gets along. Why not?'

'I don't know. I'm just curious and I heard they have their differences. In Australia all we used to have was Catholics and Protestants. There was a very obvious social divide. It was a bit like Northern Ireland, wasn't it, Ursula?'

Ursula opens her mouth to answer but Meetra pre-empts her, too. 'You?' she asks me.

'I'm not religious. But I've always lived in a Christian atmosphere.' What I don't say is that it was a muddled Christian atmosphere. I spent my formative years with intolerance on one hand and hypocrisy on the other. What I've really lived is a Western democratic life, Australian style.

In what could be a tone of compensatory forgiveness for my having no God, she says, 'I think Australian people are very friendly.'

'What about you, Mahni?' I ask. 'How have you found it, living at home and looking after your mother?'

'Oh, okay.'

'But it's lonely,' I say.

'It's lonely.'

'It's a British culture,' I say. 'Inward looking. Over the fence is okay. Sharing recipes, but we keep to our own houses unless invited. And invitations are generally for special occasions. It's easier to be born into that culture than to come into it from else- where, especially if you're used to a more communal way of life.'

Meetra says, 'But new arrivals, ethnic groups, we come with problems.'

'Well, of course; if they had no problems, they wouldn't have to move. But don't think there aren't problems here, too,' I say.

'Everywhere humans are living there's a problem,' says Meetra.

'We have a big one,' I say. And I mention the lack of rapproche- ment between Europeans and Aboriginals and how Aboriginals were denied the vote and excluded from the census and written out of Australian history until the 1970s when the Land Rights movement began.

But Meetra isn't inclined to comment on that, she says, 'Sometimes you meet, say, a Sri Lankan: in their own country they have problems with Tamil Tigers and now, being in Australia, they did not forget that. And now they are trying to deflect it on others.'

Ursula comes in with a story she has brought back from Adelaide: Somali Muslims are complaining that the Lebanese who own their mosque are discriminating against them because they're black. 'They don't let the Somalis park their cars in the car park,' she says. 'When a Somali widow rang up after her husband's funeral at the mosque, to ask for his death certificate, the imam wouldn't hand it over until she'd coughed up for all the funeral expenses. Her husband had only been dead three days. In Australia, the place that holds the funeral is supposed to lodge the death certificate automatically.'

Meetra hoots with laughter. 'This is imam! No humanity!'

'I was brought up Catholic,' says Ursula, 'I lapsed years ago, but do you know, it wasn't until Vatican II that I was allowed to talk to my Protestant neighbours when I was wearing my school uniform. We were okay at the weekends, but at school…nuh. Different schools, different cultures. That was the first experience I had of this sort of division and the stupidity of clergy. When John XXIII became pope, my mother rushed in next door and hugged the neighbours, saying, "I always knew Protestants had souls!" And just look at the Catholic clergy now! Ducking for cover after it's revealed that paedophilia wasn't just an isolated occurrence but an entrenched observance! Even the Pope wears Dorothy's red shoes like some perverted Wizard of Oz.'

And so the conversation went for another hour. Trying not to spill the beans of my situation with Eli, I attempted to introduce the sort of things that he might have been involved in that would have accounted for the condition in which Mr Liu and I found his unit, but apart from Meetra vouching for the decency of ninety-nine point five per cent of Afghans living in Australia, I didn't get far. She'd forgotten her boast that she'd find out where Eli was right away while I was there. All I learned was that Mahnaz means 'Moon' and Meetra means 'Sun' despite their having been born at polar opposite times of the year. Inevitably the sun is mightier than the moon, if a lot less subtle. The moon must slide in and out as the clouds permit.

I shall ring Meetra tomorrow and take her up on her promise to find out about Eli. After visiting my mother, I am lying low in the darkness of my house. The message bank on my landline is full, but the phone keeps ringing, so I leave it off the hook for hours at a time and try to sleep with the doona pulled up over my head.

I took the luxury of a Yarra-side walk on my way home from the hospital tonight. I sat on a jetty by the river in the twilight at about seven o'clock, fearing that if I went home any earlier, I might be accosted by David. It's better to park the car some blocks away and sneak up the back alleys to avoid contingencies. As I sat there watching the reflection of a white tree trunk break up into a massive, energetic pattern that seemed to crackle over the surface, a piece of graffiti caught my eye. Someone had written in small letters on the edge of a step 'Ikarus + Ovid'. Ikarus, plus Ovid, I thought, who would write something like that today when no one studies Latin any longer? And, in any event, it isn't Ikarus about whom Ovid wrote, it's Icarus, with a c. It was one of the first poems I learned in Latin. It really moved me. When Icarus flew too close to the sun and the wax in his wings melted and he fell from the sky, his father, Daedalus, cried, 'Icare, Icare! Ubi es?' 'Icarus, Icarus, where are you?' and he saw the feathers in the water and had to bury his beautiful boy, cursed by his own invention. Now the tree trunk seemed to be shattering into the feathers of Icarus and my heart was breaking.

During the Taliban occupation of Kabul, Eli was back in Washington. We were in contact for a couple of years and I would hear of his efforts to write something comprehensive about what he knew. Then he went silent and I heard nothing from Phoebe either. I had no idea why and I was worried sick. They were out of contact for many months and then, out of the blue, Eli turned up on my doorstep. He was looking dishevelled and sick. I put him to bed. He started shaking all over. I called in my understanding GP. Eli was wrapped up on himself, shuddering and weeping. What had happened to cause such a breakdown?

Charles Green was the only relative of Phoebe's who treated me with any decency: he was on a post in Geneva and I'd rung him for a not very reassuring chat about Eli and Phoebe during their long silence. He'd told me not to worry, that there were some difficulties they were working through and that they would contact me sooner or later. He couldn't tell me what the problems were and when I asked if they were marital or related to work, he said he couldn't say, but he was sure they'd let me know eventually.

Eli was almost unable to communicate when Charles rang me. He was aware that Eli had come home and wasn't surprised to hear that he was in a bad way. He told me that Phoebe had recently turned up in Geneva. She'd been back and forth to Pakistan many times during the long silence. This time, she'd been on a short visit, having told everyone it was for work. She was supposed to be doing groundwork for a US-sponsored pipeline across Afghanistan. The Clinton administration had already rejected the proposal because of Afghanistan's instability and reluctance to recognise the Taliban as Afghanistan's legitimate government, nevertheless, things might change once Bush took over the presidency. Phoebe was in Pakistan, supposedly talking to her contacts about possible strategies in the lead-up to Bush taking over from Clinton. Eli was in Washington. Actually, Phoebe's department hadn't wanted her to go to Pakistan; they'd wanted to send someone else and it was nothing about pipe-lines, but rather to probe intelligence people about a rumour that Al Qaeda was planning major sabotage on US soil. The person they'd wanted to send was junior to Phoebe, was of Middle Eastern extraction, spoke Dari fluently and was male, but instead of her organising for him to go on the commission, Phoebe sent herself.

She did indeed end up speaking to the intelligence people who were supposed to be seeing the young man and did indeed get valuable information out of them but her superiors were furious that she'd broken ranks. They also found out that Phoebe and the young man were having an affair.

'In my day,' said Charles, 'it was the women who slept with the men to get promotions, but this guy was an ambitious, canny young piece of work and in my opinion, it was he who duped Phoebe. Anyway she turned up here in Geneva to see me on her way home in a mood that was both triumphant and surly. She knew she'd be in serious trouble for not sending the guy, but at the same time, she had the information the department wanted and she was going to upstage him. But that wasn't all. She'd been to see her friend Bollywood while she was in Pakistan and hadn't been able to resist a "little present" given to her by Bollywood's brother. It was a statuette of a rooster made of processed heroin in an opium and clay slurry, covered in plaster of Paris and then painted as only Afghans and Pakis can paint a rooster. She showed it to me – she's always got to one-up everyone, has Phoebe. She was going to go back to Washington, triumphant with her information and then party her brains out on "dud chook", as she called it.

'I asked her, "What about Eli?" and she just said, "What about Eli?" I said, "What, you've thrown him over for this new guy's charms, have you?" and she just invited me to have a bit of chook before she got on the plane.

'Well, I wasn't in a quandary about what to do. I'd been fore-warned. Phoebe often used to come back to the States via me; the CIA knew that. They'd tailed her. She reckoned she'd set up these meetings herself, or at least played some big part in setting them up and she was angry that they weren't going to send her. She was angry that they'd chosen junior lover-boy to go. She'd been out-manoeuvred and didn't want to admit it.

'I knew what was going to happen. I was going to put her on the plane, there'd be a CIA guy on board and she'd be arrested and charged with espionage or some such once they reached American air space.

'As things turned out, she was busted for drugs. Maybe Bollywood's brother was pulling strings with the CIA behind the scenes. She never got to tell her story. I rather think the drugs charges were a foil. If she'd been charged with espionage or some other crime related to what she'd done, it would have caused an unwanted sensation.

'Eli rang me and said he'd stand by her, but then I had to tell him about the circumstances. He was gallant. He'd still stand by her – but in the event, she rejected him. She said, "No! I'm going to do this all myself," and she didn't once look Eli in the face when he turned up at her trial.'

All the time they'd been off the radar, Phoebe had been behaving strangely. She was sniffing coke. She tried to hide her indulgences from Eli and when she wasn't really succeeding to do that, she diverted her own attention by succumbing to the flirting behaviour of her young colleague, upon whose brilliance everyone was commenting.

'I suppose she felt under pressure to bowl this young guy over,' said Charles. 'She's at that age where if you don't climb in your profession, you're going to get knocked off. Phoebe's tactics have always been to sprint out in front and dare everybody else to catch her. Well, she's been caught. Won over by the competition and then thrown over. That young guy is a major negotiator for the Americans now.'

Eli was crushed. He'd realised Phoebe was addicted to party drugs. He confessed to having had to go cold turkey himself to break a developing habit a couple of years after they were married. 'It was heroin then,' he told me, but he hadn't been so bad that he needed methadone. 'She did, but she wouldn't admit it.'

During her trial he kept his mouth shut about being betrayed. He only spoke about her addiction. He had to see her sentenced to eight years with parole in five.

So much for beautiful Phoebe of the yellow dress, silken hair and swirling allure. She was released in 2005, by which time the crashing of the Twin Towers was old news and she and Eli were divorced. These days I'm told she lives in upstate New York, teaching languages at a college.

Eli was a long time recovering. He adored Phoebe and I don't think he did recover fully, but he did continue with his work and he did continue to go back and forth to Washington. He'd just become a US citizen when Phoebe was arrested.

He said he was clean. I certainly hope he was clean. I pray that the trouble at his unit isn't about heroin.

17

Deep in the night there is hammering on my front door.

'Come out, Isobel. I know you're in there.'

It's so tiring!

And tiresome!

And what would he do if I opened the door? Other times he has come strutting into my life – everything's going to start all over again. He's planned it all out – he's going to do this and I'm told I'm going to do that. He won't go. Hours and hours and hours will be wasted, coffee drunk, mounting tension, explosive argument, violence on the brink – and, if it spilled over, I know this from Allegra, he would hit me with an open hand to the back of the head. And hit me and hit me and hit me. Back of the head because it doesn't show the bruises.

On and on goes the hammering.

No use trying to sneak out the back and down the alleyway to my car, because he has a car – at this time of night, he'd hear it starting up, know he'd flushed me out and give chase in his car. No, I tell myself. You have to stay put, Isobel.

A window down the street goes up and a voice yells, 'Shut up! Fucking shut up, will you? If you don't shut up, I'll call the police.'

Why should my days be so tainted and embarrassed?

I hear the front gate click and a minute later, an engine starts. The car turns and its lights shine full beam in my bedroom window. All he'll get is the glare from the blind, I tell myself. He sits there for a while until an ambulance comes along and he has to shift.

I am going to have to get out of here.

There are very few places you can turn when threatened with violence. My closest friends live out of Melbourne these days and even if they were here, David knows who they are and would target them. I could go and stay in a motel – but for that, you need money and I don't really have money to spare on motel rooms. And if he followed me…

I'll have to go to the police and seek an intervention order. I did it once before a long time ago, before Nin was eighteen. It took all day. Interviews, explanations. And then it was twenty-eight days before the magistrate would hear the case. The case was heard. David wasn't present. He didn't agree with the order; all he would agree to was counselling. I had no physical evidence of damage. Well, I wasn't going to waste any more of my time.

Why? Why sit in a room with the same obstinacy over and over and over again? The same kink in the same nature. The same blindness. So much so that in the end you think it's you who's the one with the screwed-up mind. I don't want to do it.

So I find myself out on the road driving: cross one minute, resigned the next. Fearful. Bored. So bloody bored with recalcitrance! I don't know where I'm going, except that I seem to be following the route I took yesterday. Maybe I am going to Mahnaz's house. I seem to be. Well…I still have to ask if Meetra can find Eli for me…

The suburbs pass and they pass and they pass until I am making the mistakes I made yesterday, turning back on myself, turning into Mahnaz's street and…here I am, crunching over the gravel in the big driveway once again, reaching the mat, ringing at the door. I wait. I can't hear anything. I look at my car. Should I go back there rather than ring again? Should I find a magistrate and start to file an order? I ring again. This time, a voice. 'Salaam!' it says. It sounds like Mahni, but she doesn't open the door. 'Is that you, Mahni?' No answer. 'It's Isobel. Could I talk to you, please?'

And the great door opens a little bit and Mahni's face peeps out. She sees me and says, 'Come in, come in.'

And I follow her in. And she opens the door from the foyer into the great room, which swims before my eyes as if asleep in filtered light. Yes, it swims because I am crying. 'Mahni,' I say, 'I'm sorry. I've been attacked, I…well, not attacked, but intruded upon and I need to hide and pull myself together.'

We perch, side by side on one of the sofas. 'I'm so sorry,' I say, and I start to shake and weep in spite of myself. She sits there, her fist on her mouth, staring.

'Oh, I hope I haven't frightened you,' I say, now managing a laugh. 'It's my brother-in-law; he's harassing me over some possessions. You see, I brought up his daughter when my sister died…It's complicated. But he won't leave me alone.'

She takes her fist away from her mouth. 'He has hurt you?'

'No. No. Not physically. Just mentally. But he frightens me and I want him to go away…'

'Mah-ni!' calls an old voice from the depths of the house and it's followed by a stream of what is clearly invective in Dari.

'My mother,' she says. 'You sit there. I go to her. I come back.'

So I sit among chairs and sofas which seem like an extension of Meetra's personality, upright even when dozing. And blow my nose and my breath comes back in a more tractable rhythm. I feel the hectic velvet of the upholstery under my palm and I am as glad of the firm uprightness as I would be with my hand on a sturdy horse's flank.

Now…I must stop sitting here in Lost Sock Land.

I must not be like Dorothea in *Middlemarch* and spoil the plot by finding Mr Casaubon dead in the garden and falling into a fantod for several chapters. George Eliot should have been shot for that – but I don't suppose there was anywhere else for her to turn in those days when, if you weren't married, you were out, straitlaced and governessing. No.

Yesterday afternoon, instead of sketching, I googled strategic solutions for confusion and I found 1) a free trial in Islamic decision-making by the rules of the Quran and 2) toxic office management and how people who feel alienated in the office environment are over-ambitious – which just seemed to me to be posing the victim as the perpetrator all over again.

I don't give a shit about over-ambitiousness; I don't understand it – I don't even know what it means, except that maybe Phoebe was an example of it. Then again, she may have been the victim of male ambition being favoured over female. Maybe it means that there are so many people in competition with one another that you're superfluous if you don't join the fray. You might as well mind your old warrior of a mother, blind in one eye both physically and mentally. You might as well spread yourself as thin as a smear of margarine so that you can disappear without even being thought about. Except by those, like Elspeth Roach, who like to see you ooze with the Vegemite through the holes of a Vita-Weat before licking you flat with their tongues. Except that Vita-Weat doesn't have holes to ooze through anymore. After Google, I went out and bought *The Art of War*, but when I got to the bit that said that I should not encamp in low-lying ground, nor should I linger in desolate ground, I realised that the flat desert was my habitat and the advice was useless.

I can hear an old voice delivering a tirade and giving Mahni a hard time, so I get to my feet.

I climb the stairs.

I go down a hallway and off to my right there is the bedroom where Mahni is trying to subdue an old person metamorphosing, like Kafka's Gregor, into a giant cockroach with several thrashing legs. I enter the room and subdue the left side while Mahni subdues the right. We really need a third person to take up the spoon and administer her medicine, but there isn't one, so I kind of straddle the poor old cockroach while Mahni gets the lid off the bottle, fills the spoon and tries to get it past the clamped tight lips.

'She no like,' says Mahni.

'I can see that. What's her name?'

'Sultana.'

'Hey, Sultana,' I croon, 'Sultana. There, there, everything's all right.' She thrashes about for a bit, then brings her fierce old eyes round to focus on me. For a moment she freezes, but then I feel her give a bit under my grasp.

'Sultana…' She relaxes a bit more, taking me in. I smile. 'There, there…' I say. 'Easy breathing now, like this,' and I slacken my grip and show her. 'In: one, two, three. Out: one, two, three, four, five.'

'Nurr-ise?' she croaks. It's a marvellous, crackling old croak, worthy of tin-plated insides.

'She think you nurse,' says Mahni.

So I nod and demonstrate the breathing. She cackles and breathes back at me.

After a minute of easy breathing, keeping her eyes on me, Sultana eases her mouth and, in a sideways kind of way, siphons up the sticky stuff from the spoon. That done, she licks the remnant out of the creases around her lips and asks Mahni – or I think she does – who I am.

And that is how I came to inveigle myself into Mahni's home to sit out my dilemma in an odd kind of peace. I had packed my bag to go back down to the country but I won't need to do that now. I can be here, where Stella needs me and where I can be of some use to Mahni.

Over the dressing table in the guest room, I found a little mirror, hanging from a nail. I looked because I like to know how things are hung. Such a lot can ride on a nail, driven bingo, bango into a wall, fingers crossed, hope it won't fall. When we started out at Mad Meg, we thought we were smart, covering the walls with chicken mesh until one night, during an over-ambitious hang, the lot came down on top of us. The life of an artist is studded with nails: the victorious, the priapic, the loose and the droopers.

On the other side of the mirror, my face, the covering on sixty-plus years of history with two wire coathangers clanking in an empty wardrobe behind me.

The house is spick and span. There's a little woman who comes in to clean. She is a relative, newly arrived from Afghanistan and she looks like Meetra, but is utterly unlike her in mien. All she seems to do is hover on the staircase with a cleaning cloth in her hand while Mahni does everything. Everything. Her usurped afternoon tea with me was the longest break I've seen her have. She cooks, she cleans, she shops and she is at Sultana's beck and call. It's as she said, Meetra works all the time. During the day she works at the university. After work, she goes raising funds for her organisation. She gives lectures, she has meetings; she is on the go all the time. Even when she is home, Meetra is working. She is breathtaking in her stamina and more admirable than almost anyone I know.

She plays a straight game. It's easy to see what incenses her, but she is fighting from inside a situation so it isn't easy for her to see how she is seen and that is a problem for her: she doesn't say what people want her to say, she says what she thinks. I've tried, without a lot of success, to direct her attention to the receiving culture and the need to deal with humanitarian issues that arise within its jurisdiction. I've told her about dear old Beryl Blake and how she used to harbour asylum seekers.

'Doctor Blake!' she said. 'So ugly!'

'Oh, but we loved her! She was very, very kind.'

'She drank too much.'

'We all knew that.'

'She should have had more confidence in herself. She had a brain.'

'Well, we all have weaknesses. I liked Beryl. I liked her a lot...'

'Hoh! I did not really know her.'

'Well, Beryl was never going to be conventional. She was, as you say, terribly badly served by her maker but you mustn't underestimate the good things she did. She ran a public garden and hid illegal immigrants there in the time of the White Australia Policy. There was rioting in Malaysia and discrimination against Chinese Malays. They were terrorised, their homes were burnt, they were denied work. Naturally enough, if they had the chance to come to Australia for an education, they overstayed their visas until they could apply for citizenship. Beryl set up a hut for people in this position. It was supposed to be a gardener's hut, but it smelt of delicious Chinese cooking. You'd walk past and hear those stilted, staccato sounds that the Chinese make…'

She threw up her hands. 'I don't like it,' she said. 'This visa overstay. It causes too much problems for people waiting in the camps.'

'I don't think the people Beryl helped were hindering anyone in camps. It was the White Australia Policy. These people were Chinese Malays, mostly.' But she wasn't hearing what I had to say about Asian immigration in the nineteen-sixties: as far as she was concerned, in the two thousands, refugees from the camps should come before asylum seekers. 'Being in a refugee camp, you lose your human rights. You lose completely the rights. You're not allowed to go out, you're not allowed to talk and you're not allowed to eat, even, because you eat what you get when you get it. The people who run the camps decide what's to be done with the aid. Example, if UNHCR is taking shoes for children, at the door, the guards say, "Oh, thank you very much. Give it to us. We distribute to them." And they take the shoes back to the market and sell them. And poor children, they're walking without shoes. I got so many examples to give you. I'm supporting those that are in the camps. What we do is, especially Afghan refugees, they should build shelters inside of Afghanistan, especially Australia should build them. The Australian national plan, they should build shelters in different areas and take these refugees from the refugee camps, from Pakistan back to Afghanistan and resettle them somewhere, right?'

She is obdurate and in her obduracy she keeps forgetting to ring the Afghan embassy to find out whether Eli has a visa. She had forgotten come Friday and left it too late to ring and I had to stew all weekend.

I want Eli to succeed in his life, to be happy again, but his problems have been enormously disruptive. What if all this time, my hard-won support has just been feeding a habit? I want to paint without strictures before I die; I don't want to have supported a son's drug habit with money I ought to have been directing towards my career. I find myself fretting and angry at one and the same time and I'm trying to get through it by focusing on the here and now.

The mornings begin at five a.m. with the cry of 'MEEEEETRA!' issuing from The Grand Sultana's bedroom and a stream of clashing cymbals and tinkling brass in the mother tongue. Mahnaz tells me that the meaning is along the lines of 'The sun's up! What are you doing still asleep? Can't you see the sun? Start up the car. I want to go for a drive.' Sultana wraps up her things in a headscarf and attempts to rise from her bed, crying out the equivalent of 'Let's go! Let's go!'

The equivalent of 'Stop driving us crazy!' comes back. But crazy is irrelevant to Sultana. The world is at her command. And frailty is not a word to describe her. She hasn't broken her leg or dislocated her hip; her difficulty in leaving her bed is down to her shape. She is rolled up in a ball with her feet and the fingers of her good hand darting from the package.

Meetra might be the person summoned by The Grand Sultana but it is Mahni who comes, inevitably. Meetra spends her early mornings singing, out of reach (and out of tune). 'Yes, I sing,' she explains to me, 'because I cannot. I do it on my own, first thing.' And she smiles her Meetra smile, the one you wouldn't cross, an alloy of mystery and confidence. She is as steely willed as her mother. And so blinkered by her vision for her country that by the Monday evening I thought she'd entirely forgotten her promise to me. Did they give my boy a visa for Afghanistan? Why, after she told me she'd have the answer in a day, was it taking so long?

At the dinner table on Monday night, she announced without ceremony, 'Hoh! He is in Afghanistan. He went from Indonesia. They checked for me.'

Anything might have burst from my over-stuffed emotional state but in the event I spouted, 'I'd no idea he went to Indonesia first!'

'See,' she answered. 'What I told you? DFAT, bah!'

'Well, yes, it's true, Meetra, that you found out in a few days what the Victoria Police and DFAT have failed to discover in three months; you are a gem. But why Indonesia?'

'You have to ask your son.'

'Well, thanks. Yes. But I have to find him first.'

'I told you. Off-gone-istan.'

I barely know where Afghanistan is located on the globe, let alone how large or how penetrable it is. Meetra and I are wrestling with Sultana's bed linen while her highness sits in a chair, kicking the air, going, 'Hoh! Hoh!' in short, sarcastic gutturals. Just as well mine is only observer status or I would go, 'Hoh!' right back at her, loudly, in her face.

'You come with me. We are going. It doesn't cost much. Your boyfriend, your niece, they can look after your mother.'

'Come with you?'

'Sure. You come. What else you do?'

'But there's my niece's mad father…'

'Mad father, bah! People are only mad if they want to be! I know this. Mad? It's an excuse. Like Taliban. Excuse. Just want to hold on to old situation: where there are kings, there are servants. Hoh!'

'That doesn't make it any easier to deal with!'

'Look, madame, what you want? Give in to madman or find your son?'

'Are they the only choices?'

'What else? Step outside yourself? Be someone else? How possible?'

So it looks as if I'm going to go to Afghanistan with Meetra, come self-harming by Stella or suicide bombing by David. We put her 'Hoh'-ing mother in a Jason recliner with a stack of advertising brochures beside her and say the equivalent of 'Look, bargains!' which gets her avidly turning over the pages, her old eyes fairly on fire and a deep-seated desire for any variety of cut-price consumer goods burning in her breast.

It will be weeks before Stella is strong enough to go back to Redeemer. She needs close care and rehab. Soon they will move her away from her revolting companion with his festering shins and into the rehab hospital she was in after her bout of numb-onia and Audra will be turning up and kidnapping her.

Once David realised I wasn't home, he went back to hassling Wendy, who, rather than call the cops, adopted admirable, recumbent 'bugger him' tactics. She demonstrated that if you lie down, start filing your nails and saying 'bugger him' to yourself, he eventually does leave. Except he doesn't seem to do the same for me. 'Stop rewarding him for visiting!' was Wendy's advice. 'He wants you to be afraid.' Is that all? You just have to be amazingly relentless and wonderfully unrewarding to visit. David doesn't dare hit Wendy. Beyond her relentlessness and lack of reward, there seems no other reason. Or is there something else about her? When I went to their home, I found her sitting surrounded by black nail polish and punk hair spritz for her new short cut – how on earth had she managed to stun him into leaving her alone with just those defences?

An eccentric kind of neatness reigned in the house with Nin not there. The haphazard element was gone and in its place, geometry and colour. Nothing slid off anything else – all was stacked: tangerine, lime green, fluoro blue, taupe. 'I have to say, Wendy, you've got the place looking…well…'

'Neat,' she answered. 'I have to say, Isobel, you never taught that dear child neatness. You never made anyone put anything away after they'd finished with it, did you?'

'Well, you see, I don't understand "away", Wendy.'

'Weak as piss. This is away,' and she revolved a well-articulated wrist to indicate what she'd done to the room. 'The tip-up truck and a pair of handlebars with a bell rusted onto them are no longer preventing you from sitting on the couch; the tip-up truck is in the toy box and the handlebars are back on the bike and the bike is back in the shed. You should see all the things I've found since Nin and Dan have been away. You've no feeling for room, you lot. It's why you need me.'

Is that her secret? A feeling for room. Does that keep her safe while Nin and Stella and I are in constant danger of copping it because there was always something or someone else to cram in?

'But you'd have to admit, Wendy, that it's not a dominant trait. When Nin and Dan are here, it's chaos.'

'When Nin and Dan are here, I have my room and they have theirs. I'm not afraid of clutter, I just don't like to be surrounded by it, so I keep my own little study apart – it's enough for me. But I do sometimes go on the rampage and make them put things away so we can sit down, so we can have other people come in and get to the dinner table without being killed by toys.'

A feeling for room and no fear – 'It's too late for us to change I suppose?'

'And would it protect you if you did? You're soft, Sibella, you and Nin – you're play dough. By the way, David doesn't know the name of the new nursing home you put Stella in,' she laughed. 'He was threatening to go on the rampage at Broadlea and I told him, "Good luck, then. They're about to knock it down. Stella doesn't live there anymore." He wanted me to tell him the new place, jumping round like a frog in a cactus patch and I just said, "As if."'

'Did he come to see you?'

'Nope. I went to see him. Knocked on his door, barged in and gave it to him. Then I barged out again. Visitor prerogative.' She looked at the fresh coat of polish she'd put on her nails and blew. 'He doesn't know Mick's other name, either, or where he lives.'

I hadn't explained to her the situation with Eli but she let me do so without interrupting and when I'd told her about going to Afghanistan, she said, 'Well, go! If you don't go, you're as weak as piss. The trouble with you, Isobel, is you're afraid of opportunity. You're always wanting to see everybody else having their turn before you'll take yours...'

'Hey, that's not fair...'

'Tis.'

'Tisn't.'

'Tis. You've done your bit for the world, now do something for yourself.'

'But who'll look after..?'

'I will, Nin will, Mick will...We all will...'

'But she...'

'Hates us? So what? She thrives on a good old hate, does Stella, you know she does. Piss off, Isobel. Just get your ticket to Afghanistan and piss off.'

And that is why I find myself in this plane beside Meetra, pissing off. Mahni is booked in to have her womb unprolapsed when we come back and in the meantime we'll just have to hope it doesn't fall on the floor while she's chucking Sultana about.

Meetra and I have had our incipient thromboses massaged at Changi and in Dubai; I learned from a girl who sold me a nifty little tripod for my camera a stylish way of doing my headscarf. When we flew out of Dubai two hours ago, the tallest building in the world was a splinter in smog.

I have been holding my camera up to the window on our way over Afghanistan towards Kabul, filming the strange, treeless, liver-coloured landscape that for all the world looks like an ancient woman's deflated belly many years after giving birth to dozens of children. I've been looking for rivers, but I've seen none, just these gullies everywhere in what has to be run-off, I'm guessing, from the occasional yellowish pegged-out goat's skin patch of snow…But oh, oh, oh, now I see – snow. Real snow, high, mountain-smothering snow on massive mountains and Meetra and I are circling above Kabul in a plane full of white-clad pilgrims returning home from Jeddah. Home. I shall have to practise this experience as home. I've been imagining lofty tents and Bedouins, paintings by Ingres and Delacroix and the rich, coloured life of Rupert Bunny. The scents of spice, and rose and jasmine but I know it's going to be nothing like that, because that's Morocco, not Afghanistan…

Meetra's high, proud profile, against the light of the opposite window, makes a bold steady shape as the horizon adjusts against the silver sky.

And then – now – we are down on the earth and slowing and the tail of the plane next to us says Ariana, the name of the airline that flew bin Laden and his operatives around during the Taliban's time in power. For a moment I have a queasy little feeling that perhaps the chap I chatted with in Dubai airport, who asked me if I was Iranian, is on his mobile right now, telling them that a plump, ripe little Australian bourgeois is on her way into the country as he speaks. Meetra warned me to be careful and told me he was lying when he said he was Saudi Arabian. 'He look like Jew, no? Likely from Paktika. Come to Kabul to sell things and too mean to pay money to stay in hotel, so he sleeps over in the airport.'

I find myself saying to her now, 'I didn't think that man at the airport looked Jewish at all. I don't think you can look Jewish really. I thought that *you* were Jewish for a long time. I thought you were a Polish Jew.' I hope she catches my indignation, but everything is happening too quickly now and I'm talking about something that happened two hours ago as she pushes me towards the customs man, who flicks me through after a cursory glance. I don't even rank an explosives check, when I usually do at Australian airports (maybe because I look as guilty as I feel).

The Dari language squishes around me on sneakers as people juggle their hand luggage while holding their chadors between their teeth to stop them falling off. I've been told off for saying 'hijab' – it's 'chador' in Afghanistan. Whatever they're called they're a bloody nuisance and mine keeps slipping down or flopping over my eyes.

I arrive some distance ahead of Meetra in the clearance hall and take a seat – on principle – opposite the most exotic-looking people I can see, a kind of a pasha in a black turban and his fourteen wives – only there appear to be four wives and another man, an old one with a grizzled beard, someone I have picked as the family tutor, who is in humbler garb, white with a sandy waistcoat and a tweed jacket, who is chasing around after four young boys and a girl. The 'wives', if such they be, are head to toe in black, with veils across and one of them, the youngest, maybe seventeen, is sipping a can of Coke from under hers. Another, maybe twenty, is wearing huge, expensive sunglasses and is having difficulty sitting them on her veiled nose. Their clothes fall like proper wool crepe you might have seen for sale tumbling from an upright bolt on a pedestal in the days when women in Australia made their own evening clothes. One of the veils is fringed in fine gold braid and another in the kind of lace my aunt used for her low-slung necklines. These are not inexpensive garments. There is a fine gold bracelet on one of the wrists. All four women could be the mothers of the children.

Meetra is a while catching up with me and, just as I see her coming, a man beckons her back from the gate beside the passenger race. 'He wants your passport,' she says to me, coming over. 'Something they forgot to check.' So I hand her my passport, fearing that maybe she was right and the bloke I spoke to in Dubai was a plant...

But I've told myself not to be neurotic. And I will not be neurotic. I will sit here and watch the pasha and his family as if I shared his culture. What would it be like? I wouldn't want to sleep with him – he looks as if he's been perfumed and then dressed by an attendant in a Turkish bath – he's far too grand for me – you know from experience that men can't be as grand as he's pretending to be, that it's all posturing, this strolling around the premises with a silver shoehorn in his hand. Remarkable how a man can imagine that a simple silver shoehorn can grant him distinction. It's more or less the way he holds it, lassoed to his wrist by a leather thong, upward in his palm, like a fop would hold a handkerchief. And the children: the eldest is a boy of about ten, who seems to be in charge of the youngest two, also boys, about five years and a toddler. The girl is the middle child, about seven. Her head is uncovered; she is wearing a plain green smock over leggings and she is following the boys around as they dash from place to place. The eldest boy will plead with the tutor and the youngest two will dash off, the second boy, eight or nine, sticks with the tutor while the eldest has to round the youngest up and the girl follows him, lamely, as if she's been told that she should stick with her eldest brother at all costs. I'd like to live with this family for half a day – in an exalted position, of course, some kind of senior woman, maybe a begum, who is deferred to – just to see how it works. But I don't think any woman would be deferred to. They'd all be hidden away, paraded on occasions, like Stella showing Audra the hallmarks on the silverware. No, however hard I try, I could not imagine myself as part of this man's retinue or even culture. I'm not. I don't belong. And that's the point. It's why I can't see these people as anything other than exotic, belonging to Delacroix and Ingres and Bunny, but not to me. To me, they're Chador Barbies and the pasha's an over-aged boy who collects dolls.

Then Meetra is beside me. 'Hoh!'

'Hoh, yourself. What was all that about?'

'Aw, just forgot to do something. Why you sit here?'

'Just to look at that man and his wives.'

'Hoh! Hazara, rich one!'

'I didn't think they had any rich ones? We only ever hear about the poor asylum seekers.'

'Hoh! Lot of rich Hazara in Kabul. Carpets, TV – even airline belong to them.'

I'm formulating a castigation for racism, but... CRACK!

Oh no!

Oh what now?

Dive under seats, what?

No.

Not dive under seats.

Rain is pouring on the roof of the terminal and lightning flashing outside. Right when I was thinking...What was I thinking? We're off, it seems. Yes, off. Yes, the luggage is out to be collected. Meetra is charging towards...where? I've no idea where she's going, but that I must follow her is obvious. And suddenly we're in a room with an ancient luggage race that's beginning to creak into action.

'Hoh!' goes Meetra and pushes her way through a thick gaggle of touting men in shalwar kameez who are sidling up and offering to collect stuff. 'Bah!' And we're beside the race, which is moving now and every so often has a large puddle on it...I suppose it comes from the cloud break but we're indoors and it's stopped raining now and there are an awful lot of puddles. The first bag appears and a young tout tries to push in, in front of Meetra. 'Hoh!' she goes, prods the chap fiercely in the arm and makes him step back – and what do you know, he's the pasha's tout. Meetra is very quick to spot it and gives the pasha a piece of her mind. Just as I am thinking we could be murdered here, the pasha flips his shoehorn, puts it in his pocket and resumes his place in the queue. The wives are sitting off to one side, in a row, conspicuous in their black among the white of those who've been on the Hajj to Jeddah.

'No, not Jeddah,' Meetra tells me. 'They have been to Mecca. Only come back through Jeddah.' Suitcases start to come, wrapped in cling wrap. Acres and acres of cling wrap, just the handles sticking out for grabbing and then, my God, plastic jerry cans, plastered all over with yellow stickers. 'What are they?' I ask as hands reach in and grab and grab and grab again. 'Water,' says Meetra.

'So that's what's leaving the puddles. Why?'

'One of the prophet's wives, her son gets thirsty. She runs all over Mecca looking for water. The son keeps getting thirstier. She doesn't find water. God sends his angel, the angel strikes the ground, the water flows. It still flows. Miracle.'

'God! Holy water! The last time I saw holy water was when the neighbours' aunty brought home five ml of it from Lourdes. My sister dared me to drink some.'

'Did you?'

'I sneaked a sip. Didn't make any difference. This lot must bathe in it!'

'They do. They wash their head, their face, their feet, every-thing. They put it on sick people. Here it comes!' Meetra's thumbs start to fidget with anticipation. Our baggage at last. We haul, we grab, we fend off the touts from the trolleys and we barge for the exit. For a woman of her age, Meetra zips along like a skateboarder.

Portraits of Ahmad Shah Massoud beam down on us, remind-ing me that he is the poster boy around here. I hadn't realised that he would occupy such a prominent position in Kabul but I do remember Eli saying that his following was very strong in the north of Afghanistan. Oh, I wish Eli would turn up...

Here.

Now.

And Be With Me.

'Here' the word I have loved ever since Arnie left me, the word that means 'beside me'. I've been waiting my whole life for people who have delayed their coming – my mother's dead brothers, my father, my lover, my sister, my son...But it's hurry on, quickly, what seems like miles and miles of it, past the domestic terminal, through milling soldiers, slung around with guns. How silly and small I seem to be! A mother, looking for her son in hideously stricken Afghanistan!

And then there are gay umbrellas, green and white and advertising something – God knows what, May His Name Be Praised and men with more guns and walkie-talkies and people forging this way and that and Meetra, like greased lightning into every gap until I'm reminded of getting out of Flemington Racecourse after the Melbourne Cup: the running for the cars! The honking of the horns! The grass and the dirt tracks underfoot. And being charged on all sides by men – wanting to get through the turnstiles first at Flemington but here wanting to take us in their taxis for a fee! Till at last, we seem to be getting near the exit...I suppose it is the exit, barbed wire, a kind of pillbox and some sort of missile, pointed at the air, and Meetra has stopped. Phew! She's stopped. She's haggling with a bloke beside a taxi cab.

We have the maximum amount of luggage. My case is stuffed with kids' shoes, collected from friends, and clothing of many origins. In my backpack, some changes of underwear, one change of clothes, my medication and a comb. In Australia a taxi driver would have demanded a forklift, but there was Mick to drive us to the airport. Dear Mick, without whose help, none...

We have stuffed what we can into the boot and what we can't in beside us; we have slammed the doors and right away there is another cloudburst, a serious one this time to add to the torrents of Zamzam water (for I believe that's what the holy water is called) that came in with us on the plane. The taxi driver starts up. Forwards he goes. Into a gap. No. Backwards he goes because a little policeman in a drenched uniform has held up a thing the size of a child's ping-pong bat with a little red circle on it. God what a crush! And while we're in it, I notice that the entire inside of this cab is carpeted, seats, floors, dashboard, in rather nice Persian-looking carpets. 'No. Afghan,' says Meetra. And now I remember her bit of racial prejudice against Hazaras in the airport. 'Oh, sold to him by a rich Hazara, no doubt!'

'Bah!' she goes. 'I stand for ALL Afghans. Hazara, Paktia, Paktika, Kuchi, I don't care. You know what's happening here?'

'What?'

'Karzai is travelling somewhere. So everybody is carrying guns and walkie-talkie. So important. Ordinary people, they not so important. They can wait.'

'Don't you like Karzai?'

'Better than Taliban.'

'Is he Hazara?'

'Pashtun. I'm for everybody, Ms Coretti. Doesn't matter. Some people drive me crazy. Selfish. Stupid. Corrupt. Want everything while others have nothing.'

And back we go, honking. Into an impossibly small space. If I tried to get into a space like that – then, across our bows... I shield my eyes but it's our turn to honk. And we go forwards an inch. It's like square dancing in primary school. 'Allemande left with your left hand and dosey doe and a half sashay.' It almost has a rhythm and I'm almost clicking my fingers by the time we reach the gate and pass under the nuclear warhead pointed at the sky. (Who knows if it's a nuclear warhead?) Then, whoosh! It's off down a main street like a nuclear warhead ourselves, feeling on the wrong side of the road but I suppose it's right and the wipers clicking. Raindrops to the left and raindrops to the right and high street walls on either side. And metres and metres and metres of razor wire strewn along the tops of them.

Stop. First blue burqa; hand at the window, up for a tip, but it's *windows shut* and on we plough now, zip, zip, zip. Zamzam. God, I wonder why we learned square dancing at primary school. And the polka 'with Anatol and Olga, slim': I thought it was her surname, like Sir William Slim. Impossibly drenched people nuzzling up to walls and gates...Gates everywhere, some of them elaborate, most double, most shabby, mudbrick walls and the occasional tree poking budding branches through the razors. Hard to think of an enemy getting this far into the heart of a major city…Until the view is being steamed out by our breath.

'Ministry of Public Health,' goes Meetra, just as I think I'm going to suffocate and the window goes down and the diesel fumes come in and I realise she's been pointing out landmarks to me. Another policeman, this time in a yellow cape, holding up his little red lollipop on a stick as we pass the Children's Hospital and then a maimed man, up near the window, and there's the Emergency Hospital, run by the Italians…and more razor wire. And it occurs to me that we are very high up and maybe I'm feeling the altitude. Because I feel quite mad.

And I begin to wonder what I'm doing here. Why would I find Eli here? How will I find Eli, since Meetra has no better idea of where to find him than I do?

18

⚜⚜⚜

No, she has no better idea than I have, but she's braver than I am, she grabs hold of life before it flips away from her. She holds on.

We sprayed expensive perfumes onto cards in Dubai and now they have all mingled and are making my bedroom, right up the top of this high square house, smell of mothers' armpits. Lingering armpits under broken old maternal arms are what I hold on to, while Meetra holds on to hope.

We have swapped situations, Meetra and I, my hometown for hers. The suburb of her childhood, once salubrious, is now war-ravaged, broken worse than any aged arm – and it has been overrun. As we drove in here yesterday afternoon, its roads were chock-a-block with cars and every nook and cranny was stuffed with people trying to escape the rain. So many nooks and crannies! I think they are meant to be shopfronts, barely as wide as an eye.

Kabul still has some houses like Meetra's: big and square and plain and built sometime ago, but the hectic palaces of the newly returned rich are rising like sponge cakes amid the mud pies of the poor, forcing poverty further and further up the mountainous hillsides that ring the city. History has stamped with a pitted foot over what used to be.

The house belonged to Meetra's parents. Her father was a Tajik named after Babur, the Moghul emperor who thought the gardens of Kabul were as close to Paradise as earth allowed. The same Babur repudiated vows of abstinence rather than the sins of inebriation and liked to practise his sexual proclivities with the harem out-of-doors, rounding off with a bout of sunstroke – or so says Wikipedia, which I've just been searching at Meetra's desk in her office, where I am now. Yes, even this city of poppy palaces, open drains, SUVs and donkey carts is on the World Wide Web – although it has no postal service in the postman sense of the word.

I feel like a high commissioner at Meetra's grand desk with the Australian and the Afghan flags side by side. I have to say that the Australian flag was made in China and has a wooden stick to hold it up, whereas the Afghan flag is made locally of silk; it has a fringe and its pedestal is a fine thing to behold, being in the rococo plastic taste of the Middle East. The house, with no number, is down a very potholed side street with no name. It occupies a site equivalent to a 'double-fronted Californian bungalow with off-street parking' in suburban Melbourne, but this house is in the form of a compound. It has the usual high wall on the street side and a distinctive entry gate – but not so distinctive as to be unmistakable, and this has to be a good thing in a city where people are targeted once they are known.

Babur hung on in Kabul long after the rest of his family had fled – until every time he went out to the mosque or to shop, another article would disappear – a carpet, his refrigerator, his television, his radio…he was not a man to lock up, believing, in the face of contrary evidence, that his compatriots were honest. The Russians had just been driven out and everything was being looted amid the shelling of the city by the brawling warlords. There were thieves everywhere but Babur didn't want to recognise it. Once he caught a man coming out of his gate with a full sack. 'Hey, what you got in there?' he asked. 'Oh nothing, brother, just some food for mujahedeen.' Babur pointed out that the mujahedeen were hiding out in the mountains in Panjshir. 'Give me my food back. I want to live,' he said. But the man just laughed and went away, so Babur decided to go to Paris to his oldest son.

He found that he liked Paris, where he'd never been before. He developed a taste for French cuisine and breathed his last in the comfort of a hospital in a banlieue, where big houses and extended families were definitely not the norm and there was peace and quiet and no Sultana to hector him.

Meetra's employees live in a bungalow abutting the road wall. There are four or five dapper young men and an older man, of whom they make fun, who is the guard. Between the bungalow and the main house is a very green lawn. Without being prompted, Meetra's deputy, Edris, the dapperest of the young men, told me – just after I stepped out of the car into a lull in the rainstorm yesterday – that the grass comes from the steppes and stays green even under snow. It seemed an odd greeting but Edris is obviously proud of the courtyard. Since Meetra was last here, he has planted it with two apple trees, a pear, a cherry and a mulberry. He's placed them less than three metres apart in a squarish kind of arrangement so that if they all survive there'll be an arboreal punch-up for room to hang out the fruit.

I wonder if this was the courtyard where Meetra is supposed to have come into being, born into the snowdrift, with the competing forces of nature at war in her small, tough body.

The routine here is similar to the one back in Melbourne, only it is the houseboy who polishes the banisters. The polish is not one that would be known to the nostrils of Stella Motte. Stella swore by Marveer, probably because it was the most expensive. She decried all other brands. She once gave me a sideboard in exchange for a loan she couldn't repay and then insisted on sniffing out the Marveer just in case I was up to my old tricks and using Home Brand on a sacred surface. I told her she could have the sideboard back in exchange for the money but that only led to my being labelled a blackmailer.

At breakfast, we ate flat bread with Vache Qui Rit and home-made plum jam with the stones still in it. Meetra sang the glories of Kabul flat bread to me but I'm a girl who has been spoilt by sourdough and breads of all varieties cooked regularly by Mick and I found it rather tough. There was yoghurt but Meetra ordered me off it, saying that her last guest became ill on the first day after eating the yoghurt. Nor did she allow me to drink tea until I'd finished eating. They drink tea all the time and I'm thirsting for coffee, the real coffee that Mick brews. Meetra has brought Nescafé with her, declaring that 'her boys' love Nescafé. I'm dismayed. Twenty years in Melbourne and Meetra hasn't bothered with the coffee! It isn't the smell of Marveer I'm going to miss; it's the morning aroma of coffee.

The names of Meetra's staff were hard to catch as they padded up to my eardrums and knocked there with muffled fists. The language is soft, a little guttural and quietly delivered at an even pace. You wouldn't think it was the language of warmongers. I don't think you could issue a short, sharp command in it: Sultana's orders back in Melbourne were long and crackle-topped rather than explosive. I feel I should be speaking it, but as yet, I don't have the flavour of Dari in my mouth. In spite of that, I felt included in the company with Meetra at the head of the formal table, passing the food along with an almost non-stop stream of opinions and instructions.

Everything gleams. The wooden furniture gleams, the marble floor gleams, the white crockery gleams, the windows gleam, the sky gleams. Yes, the sky gleams, but not with freshness – it would be closer to say the glare gleams.

My watch says 8.48 a.m. and the computer on the desk in front of me says 10.12 p.m. – God knows what the time is. The sun is at about eleven o'clock so I'd say the computer is about twelve hours out. We must be south-facing in this hemisphere. The sun is deliciously warm at the windows above Edris's courtyard – my shoulders are basking in it. Under me is a big basement that houses classrooms for students. It's the place to go in the event of a terrorist attack, of which one is constantly reminded by the stout gates and heavily locked doors and barbed wire coiled along all the street walls and the balconies of the surrounding buildings.

Meetra's entanglements are rather conservative. Let's hope she is fiercer than Babur, who these days might find the thieves in occupation of his house on coming home from the mosque.

An email has come from Mick. He says that according to the schedule posted by the Kabul International Airport, our flight is yet to arrive. 'You have disappeared down a black hole.' Mick can be quite literal at times – when things don't turn out as written in the textbooks, he'll say, 'They should,' and look at me as if it's my fault and I immediately feel guilty and respond, 'Well, they haven't this time,' which probably means, 'What do you expect me to do about it? Recombobulate the world?'

Meetra's guard has a peephole and he is under instructions to send away anyone carrying arms of any sort. Only unarmed people can enter. Unarmed, but not unwrapped. How do you tell what's in a turban besides the head? Just before Meetra went out, two wrapped heads poked in around the door presenting themselves for spoils from Australia and went away happily with plastic jars tucked under their arms. Meetra brings fish oil capsules and glucosamine tablets to ease Afghan arthritis, and apparently they do, which is good news as plenty of folk in Australia mock the combination.

It's terribly quiet now. All I can hear is the occasional coo of the big fat pigeons I saw through the bathroom window, sitting on the aerial of the big pink poppy castle directly behind us.

Meetra has gone looking for someone to fix her smart phone – we couldn't use it in Dubai to tell the staff when we were arriving, but no one could have come to fetch us anyway because of Karzai's traffic jam. I think it's Thursday today but it seems like the day off – maybe it is a day off over here. All the blaring and shunting of yesterday has stopped.

I'm alone in the house.

I'd go out if it were Paris or London or Rome, but not here – not yet, anyway. I took a peep over the parapet on the roof earlier on and there was a mustard-coloured blimp in the glary sky; the hilltops bristle with all kinds of antennae. I understand there are loads of TV stations here – more than thirty. Meetra says that there are quite a number of female presenters on air but I also know from Eli that the mullahs in the government complain about it, saying that the morals of the young are being corrupted. Two poor things were murdered in recent years – both young – one for being too lively for the mullahs' tastes and the other, a news anchor, was done in by her family supposedly because she had ideas about whom she wanted to marry.

While I was up on the roof, I was thinking about these poor girls, one was twenty-three and the other twenty-two, when my ears were surprised by an unidentified musical instrument, possibly a flute, playing 'Happy Birthday'! How weird of Kabul to be singing 'Happy Birthday' to me while I was entertaining thoughts of the ghastly things my son has had to see and document here – an odd lure for a fat little foreigner whose birthday is still some months away…Wondering if I'd be shot at, I crept up to the roof parapet, head wrapped up well in a scarf, and stuck my eyes out far enough to look down into the street. What I saw, after all, was a conspiracy of place – a chap pushing a red ice-cream wagon along – it looked like a stunted little shoe on four wheels and while I was watching, the tune changed to Brahms' Lullaby.

Supposing I were in purdah, would there be anything to make of this existence? So peaceful, and someone else doing the housework. The houseboy, a young man of about twenty with one of the indecipherable names, is quietly cooking in the kitchen in a pressure cooker that looks like a spherical bouncing bomb of the sort the dam busters used in WWII. The scent of turmeric, preferable to and out-competing the polish, is suffusing the air. With the kitchen and the larder just across the hall I feel very comfortable in my patch of sun, even a little regal. I have asked for a Nescafé in spite of myself – 'baa shir' I have said, which means 'with milk'.

I am quite happy to be catered for on a little square portable stove by a chap who's paid to do the job. I could be a begum after all. He comes in with the coffee, a little man in jeans and sneakers with a big smile. There is another young man here who looks very like Eli, except that his eyes are dark. It's amazing how many of the young men I've seen on this trip look just like Eli; he seems to lurk behind every beard and under every beret but the eyes are never that blue/blue Arnie Russell/Isobel Coretti cross.

It feels strange to be in a house from which others come and go but you stay put. Am I a privileged princess in a tower or an outsider wanting to get 'in' – which, in this case, is 'out and normal' among others on the street? When I was a child, I used to admire adult invalids – I thought they had it made with everyone else doing everything for them. It was a life of comfort, fresh linen and pretty bedspreads. It would have done me, I used to think, and I used to practise the situation by having days off school, but by the third or fourth morning dose of *When a Girl Marries* on the radio, I'd be wondering what my friends were up to and I didn't need much prompting to go back to them.

When Meetra bustled in from her unsuccessful expedition to find someone who could fix her phone, I could smell the bustle on her and I was envious. She told me the time was 12.55 and lunch was on the table.

Bread again. And a hot dish. The young men from the staff came in from their office and Edris tried practising his English with me. Oddly, his topic was Australia's attitude to Japan after World War II! Perhaps he's already sussed out my capacity for loopy explanations.

'Well, my aunt kept a cyanide pill handy in case the Japanese invaded,' I said. And I mentioned the uncle who was killed at the fall of Singapore and my aunt's refusal to buy anything made in Japan and her avowal that she wouldn't be seen dead driving a Japanese car, even when everyone else was driving them. 'Things have changed since my aunt died, though. In the nineteen-eighties, we were selling them huge chunks of Australian soil. These days we're selling it to the Chinese. It's pushed the price of housing sky-high and now our kids can't afford to buy their own homes.'

But that's not what Edris wanted to hear. 'There was no war fought on Australian soil,' he said, like a schoolmaster correcting a wayward student.

'Well, Darwin was bombed, but no. In World War II we might have lost a lot of men in the fighting, a lot of chaps from rural towns were lost and that was bad for a country that relied on agriculture, but Australia itself didn't suffer the same damage as other places.'

'And you took a lot of immigrants after the war.'

'Yes, Edris, but only from Europe, and, to begin with, only from Northern Europe. It was supposed to be because those people would blend in with the population better. They wouldn't be conspicuous.'

'Now other people need immigration.'

'Yes. But the Australian government only takes a quota from here.'

'I would like to live in Australia. I only want to live there five years or so. Somewhere away from war.'

'But you're doing a wonderful job here. You're needed here…'

I was going to say that Australia might not be the panacea he was searching for, when 'Hoh!' went Meetra. 'Hoh!' isn't necessarily just an expression of scorn; what she's been saying all these weeks since I met her in Melbourne, is 'Khob' and that means 'Yes' or 'Okay'.

The Dari broke out again, with Meetra dominating the discourse, which was brisk and vigorous. It felt a bit like the captain and the vice-captain conversing combatively and by the time they'd finished, the table had been cleared away by the boy, whose name is easy enough, after all – it is Yar, and he was serving up tea in the sitting room.

When I went back to Meetra's computer after lunch, I realised I'd released a virus from my flash drive onto her screen: 'Sexy', it said and 'Porn'. The Web will soon be reaching out to suck in the Afghans as well as the rest of the world. At least I haven't brought over the woman with chickpea mash all over her face who comes to my computer with Facebook, advertising simple tricks to stop ageing, nor have I brought in Amy and Tina, the 'Asian Ladies' flashing their tits in the margins of serious content – so much for Asian immigration.

How shall I tell Mick about this place? The bazaar opened this afternoon and Meetra took me shopping. What comes to mind in the way of comparison is the look and feel of abandoned drive-in picture theatres. So much is boarded up. Much of the plate glass is shattered from explosions and held together by metal studs. The streets are dusty where they are not caked in mud and the road-ways are potholed. The city isn't sewered and over the drains there are pull-up concrete slabs, or grilles, but mostly they are just open and full of putrid rubbish. Surely people must fall into them from time to time.

It's 7.30 p.m. and Allah is summoning the faithful from his tower as I write – *the smells are strange: dust, shot through with diesel fumes and donkey shit and at ground level everything underscored by pungent, concentrated piss. There are some wretched people on the streets and some obviously middle class, but mainly it's chaps in waistcoats and white shirts and chaps in dun colours and berets. Not so often: you see an Afghan karakul hat, like Karzai's. Several shopkeepers know Meetra – we went to buy headscarfs – the one I brought from Australia kept falling off, it was too heavy. I bought a very pretty one, costing forty dollars Australian. Then we visited a jeweller, where I didn't buy anything, but heard the tale of the shopowner, who lived in California during the Taliban, hated it and came back. He keeps a shop in San Francisco and another in Dubai but would rather live here. He let me try on a neck hanging-cum-breastplate of beaten tin that made me feel like a member of the marauding horde until I looked in the mirror and saw a pathetic Australian tourist in a twenty-dollar top from Katies wearing a nomad necklace – a pickle in a pavlova. Then to a shop to*

*buy a couple of shirts and a gorgeous handwoven waistcoat for me —
total cost forty-five dollars Australian.*

*We peel off the banknotes and buy local money from the street
vendors, who sit on stools or squat or sit cross-legged on the ground with
their money in piles beside them or in fish tank–type arrangements or,
then again, with long wallets like the ones you used to see in the days
when bus conductors sold tickets. It's not that they don't have banks,
they do, but people are reluctant to go into buildings where there are
likely to be foreigners in numbers. A new shopping mall was blown
up by a suicide bomber recently and now the entrance is boarded up
and guarded by Afghan soldiery. You have to be searched before going
in — not that we did but some people need to get to the businesses that
are being reconstructed inside.*

*Although I saw elaborate samovars in the streets and there were
plenty of stalls selling hot food — kebabs cooked in windowsill gutters
of hot coals mostly — I saw no restaurants, no cafes, no places where
people might sit together and eat and converse. Obviously, it just isn't
the Afghan way.*

*It feels uncomfortable to be buying stuff when the beggars on the
street are so wretched, but I can see the point of supporting those who
have set up businesses in Kabul — the whole of civil life needs strengthening here. Without shops there would be nothing to drive the economy,
such as it is. I've no idea how Afghanistan imagines it will compete on
the world market — it will have to have a commodities boom to do that
because it certainly won't happen with the small commercial trade that
goes on now. I doubt if much besides carpets and jewellery is actually
manufactured inside Afghanistan. Poor people: I wonder if they could
have survived into modern times as they were in the days of the hippie
trail? Even though they couldn't read or write, they seem to have led
much happier lives in the days when Westerners dropped in for a smoke,
some rustic clothing and a meal. There were the isolated villages, the
princelings and the visitors. I wonder if the women and the destitute
were as badly treated then as they are now: there are no visible public
places where women could get together. Oh well, times can't recur, can*

they? Some things return, I suppose, but not with the ambience that accompanied them in the past.

Meetra has a system whereby she leaves stuff with shopkeepers she knows and they pass it on to the beggars. She knows the beggars too – we were greeted by a number of them, one with crippled legs sitting on a skateboard at the entrance to the jeweller's. He was maimed by a landmine in a village in Panjshir where Meetra's group supplied the local school with water and electricity.

In Panjshir, where most of the fighting against the Russians took place, Massoud's mujahedeen laid mines across the roads to blow up the food convoys. They buried their fellow jihadists where they fell and then they'd disappear. The Russians could never find them. Sometimes they existed only on the kind of grass that Meetra has growing in her courtyard. Guess they were like the Viet Cong, the indigenous enemy – a contradiction in terms.

Meetra got me to offer her guard, Hafiz, his pick of the children's shoes I brought over with me. He has six kids and he took a few pairs – maybe I should have brought him some condoms. A funny story about him. He didn't have a birth certificate – most people don't – and as part of its drive to record its citizenry, the government wanted to register him, so they gave him an age-range to choose from – he chose thirty-five and he's stuck with that, ask him how old he is and he'll say, 'Thirty-five.' He's really about fifty.

Hafiz is a gentle bloke with big brown eyes and he's rather deferential, but Meetra's deputy put tape on our doors when we went out to test whether Hafiz went into our rooms without our knowing it. It felt tacky to me to do something like that and I'm glad to say that Meetra didn't think that was especially fair either. She's told Hafiz not to take anything without asking, because it would ruin the trust she has in him. Like with the shoes – we give him first pick of the stuff we've brought with us and the rest Meetra will try to give to street children and widows. She has to be crafty in the way she gives out aid, because if she were seen to do it, she'd be mobbed. It's better, she says, to keep an eye out for the people you can help directly – like if a child has

inadequate footwear and you have something that would fit, you target
that child and give directly in private, rather than giving to someone
who would try to sell it on. Where there is poverty such as you see here,
the poor exploit the poor.

We met a little street boy on our trip to the market. He was trying
to sell us chewing gum. He looked about five, but when he followed
Meetra's instructions and turned up at our door for a pair of the shoes,
he said he was seven. We sat him down in a patch of sun in the driveway
and I brought some shoes down. He fell in love with a pair of Toy Story
high-rise gym boots that had been given to me by a mother whose child
grew out of them at age four. They fitted and when I asked if he could
do the laces up, he tied them in a knot and shoved them down under the
tongue. We gave him cake and tea and a bagful of Crocs for his little
sisters. He asked Meetra to come and visit his school. He was filthy and
had travelled a long way to sell gum in the bazaar. I hope Meetra goes
to his school.

Such a little boy for seven, a brave little fellow and cheerful to take
things home to his family.

Prayers are finished, dinner is coming, Please send on my emails to
those who are interested.

Oh, I've just realised why it's so quiet today. It's their New Year's
Day. I had no idea at all. It was a half-day holiday. I'm not so much
jet-, as culture-lagged.

Dare I ask about Stella?
love you,
Bel

In this bedroom, where I sleep alongside empty drawers, my few
things taking up a tiny space in packets that Wendy would not
believe me capable of, my thoughts, compressed by the four large
walls, could be shaped into a cube. Maybe women in purdah have
such cubic thoughts. They could be squashed flat, like cardboard
boxes on the way to recycling, stacked, like the paintings stored at
Lexie's. Maybe the women remember their childhood in the outside

world and are tempted to go in there and pull out a work to remind themselves that there is more to life than a room, four walls.

I have a friend, a noted painter, who did a series of 3D works to show the act of painting as a yearning to break through the surface and out. He strapped and buckled boxes onto boards, he squashed fast-setting plaster through meshes and made his paint so viscous he could push it through screen wire so that he was working behind the picture plane. He is a man who paints against constraint. When I paint, I want my work to emanate, to throw itself outward, like a far-reaching embrace. My friend and I have written to each other for years; we've shared books and enthusiasms and thoughts of love and life, our minds are alike: in his, the history of painting parades hand in hand with the constrictions faced by the painter; in mine, the will to express myself through the painted image parades hand in hand with the history of my life.

My cubic bedroom smells of house paint now that the Dubai perfumes have receded. It has a round plug in one wall. When you pull the plug out, there is a hole. Behind the hole is a flue. It is where the fire vent is attached in winter time. Before we arrived, Edris had the winter stoves removed to storage and he painted the rooms freshly as he does every year because they get smoke-stained. This household regimen is completely foreign to me. I've never slept in a bedroom with a portable wood-burning fireplace before – I wasn't even aware that people used such things in houses. In my early years, we had an open fireplace but only in the sitting room; early on, there was a fuel stove in the kitchen. In summer we still sat around the hearth, but it was empty and in our bedroom, the one I shared with Allegra, it was stifling. We didn't even have a fan to shift the air. At Christmas, we would go to a place that was hotter still, our Aunt Nina's property, over near the South Australian border.

Odd to be remembering that as I lie here on a bed of like lumpiness…

19

Up in the high bedstead of maple veneer with its niche for child-hood books let into the bedhead, when it was so hot we couldn't go outside, I used to cuddle up with the Brothers Grimm and read *Little Sister let me in,* and imagine my big sister stricken outside my door with the plague at her back.

Actually, she'd be down in the bathroom, having a cool bath with all Aunt Nina's unguents arrayed on the soap tray and the transistor blaring rock'n'roll, but I'd never let that detract from the book's smell of mildewed forest, its torn leaves opening up on ghoulish spectacles.

How does my child and how does my fawn? I come but once more then forever am gone. What if our mother died? What if she tried to get back to us and could only come once? Our mother! Our mother gone! It was unthinkable.

Fish of the sea, listen to me for my wife won't let me be. What if you did a good turn and as a result could have whatever you wanted for the rest of your life? Would you be tempted to ask for too much, like the fisherman's wife?

Louse is scalded, Flea is weeping, Door is creaking, Broom is sweeping, Scales are running, Dunghill burning. And the little tree quivers. And what if dead things were alive? What if there was an invisible door at which things unborn were scraping, trying to invade life?

'What?' cried the miller. 'You ask me to hew off my little girl's hands?' What if Dadda had to cut my hands off?

So terrifying were these tales that I could see why my uncle, whose book and bed it was, had got himself killed in the war. I'd imagine him locked up in a tomb with all those tattered urchins, severed heads speaking, lazy girls covered in pitch, truthful Jews murdered, abandoned soldiers, their feet wrapped in rags rescued from wicked witches by little blue lights. I tried to imagine my life as a little blue light, to evaporate myself and become an evanescent speck. The stories were unrelievedly awful. As far as I could work it out, my grandmother Euphrosyne Motte must have been a moral tyrant, bitter and begrudging, to allow her child such a fright-filled infancy. How terrible it must have been to be a child before the war! What baleful duties lay ahead! What bullet-filled breasts! I was glad to be reading them safely tucked up in modernity, even though the owner of the bed had died from burnt-out lungs after a bombing.

The war lay across everything, a grotesque obstruction that sealed the horrors of the past into the Pied Piper's mountain. My aunt wasn't inclined to speak of it. Always covered from head to foot in respectable clothes, she was taken up with good works. Letters and photographs informed us, once we were back in Melbourne, that she'd clapped rosemary to her lapel and, in hat, gloves and topcoat, taken our blind grandfather to a front seat near the bugler on ANZAC Day in rural Scunthorpe. We could see her sitting there in the newspaper photograph, forbearing to sniffle. Grief done and dead remembered, it would be on with roast dinners and solemn decorum in the house with the high, but sadly empty bed, its maple veneer bedhead and book niche.

Our aunt was very well behaved, but not our mother, and especially not on ANZAC Day. On ANZAC Days, Stella would fly into unassailable furies. Three dead brothers, one lost lover, as evil as anything the Grimms could dream up between them. Doors would slam, china would fly, we could do nothing right and the hand would slap.

Dadda would take us, until the furies subsided, to the dump to contemplate the modern apocalypse, dignified as it was by indestructibility. 'Permanence,' Dadda used to say. 'This is permanence.' And we, warm in our postwar clothing that kept the draughts out and covered over all the rude bits snugly, felt we knew what he meant. Here was our link with the past, the place that was and is always with us, the earthly, ongoing Armageddon. Here was the museum of broken hope and futility. Here lay the words Destruction and Decay, Redundancy and Ruin. A solid sea replete with gulls. The thin smell of smoke and rot.

Allegra and I romping through rubbish labyrinths, forgetful of our mother-turned-into-the-Witch-of-Rage.

The Grimms were right. There were intractable spells. You had to wait them out, anonymous in no-man's-land but safe in the attire of children watched over by a loving father.

At home there was heart quake, stomach knot, the nurturer-turned-fiend. Not even the deep, spontaneous love of children had the power – history with its awesome crush was on us. We supposed we knew why: four young men dead for a modernity that wasn't worth their sacrifice. What was there for the bereft woman but the jail of life?

That was the refrain.

The 'jang' and the 'sang'.

The war and the stone.

The jangle and the singing-over.

The petrified fist of bitterness and hate.

Here, in Kabul, where 'jang' means war and 'sang' means stone, space has been made in the debris for life to go on. It is as if children have abandoned one savage game and started over with one that is more benign. Newly planted trees look like little attempts at forest building and the houses of the rich are like plastic palaces put out by Mattel – as if every aspect of life were a plaything of history. A sign near Meetra's says 'Bright your Future at English Class'. Another says 'Gardin Dicoration' and yet another 'Beauty Paler'. There is a second-floor shop whose plate-glass window is entirely taken up with diaphanous curtains of purple, pink, yellow and green, all spangled and tasselled and tinselled like a little girl's dream of fairyland.

The wounds of war are healing over but the maimed are not disguised; they hobble on, toys from the Monster Factory whose hands shoot out, palm up.

Even the ground under Kabul is Brothers Grimm territory. It seems sour somehow, mean-spirited. Shallow, mineral rich, but humus poor. Pressing down on grass is pressing on wads of springy fibre under it. Not much digestion going on here, nothing rich and dark, no leaf rot, just a hard and ancient cycle demanding long, conservative practice by those who live here. The herders have to move from place to place to feed their flocks; the plants have to take their chances between extremes – flood followed by drought, mud followed by dust, extreme cold followed by extreme heat. Branches have to be cut back to the trunk; water has to be channelled and pooled between the times of thaw and autumn to keep it on the roots. Gardens have to be protected by mud walls to keep them from the fierce winds and dust storms that sometimes spring up here.

Rural people live in compounds. There are no forests to break the blast, not even parkland trees at this altitude; all must lie low and shelter itself. Little Red Riding Hood's wolf lives in some parts, as does Goldilocks's bear. The snow leopard and the civet cat live here, the nights of the herders are set about with flashing teeth and lightning strikes. The little human is a dun-coloured creature in the dun-coloured landscape, persisting.

Today we broke our visit to a provincial school for lunch at the home of our driver, I wrote to Mick. *His mother is a widow and, as an adjunct to their work in the local school, Meetra's group has been allowed by the local council – all men of course – to set up a centre in her home for life skills and tailoring.*

Women aren't allowed to have classes where they might be seen by men, they aren't allowed to congregate in mosques or at markets, but at the widow's home, they can relax and take off their burqas. There was a tree with doffed burqas looking like deflated personages stuck in the trunk. A blossoming mulberry dominated the garden around which they had draped the innards of cassette tapes – to frighten off the birds, they said. Oddly, there weren't any birds and it seemed a strange thing to do with tape recordings; perhaps they're obsolete, on the other hand, the ultra-religious have been known to smash up the accoutrements of easy living in this part of the world. There was certainly no music being played in the yard, which was hung about with real besoms made from the tree clippings, large harvesting baskets, beating sticks and rubber buckets that are ubiquitous in roadside stalls and look to have been made from inverted truck tyres. There was an old well under the mulberry – although I should be careful when I say 'old'. Mud structures look old even when they are new and this home has been levelled and recon-structed three times because of the war. We'd just come from the school, which is only eight years old but I almost made the mistake of saying how shabby it looked. The floor hadn't time to cure before the kids invaded and as a consequence, it is full of craters, like the road outside, down which the thaw pours itself into every crevice. There are dun-coloured men with spades wherever you look, digging deeper trenches to divert water from the buildings. Water there is, on the ground, but there is no tap water, hence the well. The government has just put in a new pump for the fields of crops between the school and the widow's house; it pumps up water from an aquifer. Kabul also relies on aquifer water; the Kabul River is dry and I imagine that if they can't manage to put in a sewer and separate the good water from the bad, there'll be some big epidemics by and by.

Our driver is extremely adept. His reflexes are sharp. On the way we flew between rapid and long-lasting halts – bottlenecks of traffic and sometimes checkpoints where armed guards peer in at windows. You approach his mother's home down a mud-walled laneway and knock at a slab gate; inside are bundles of sticks stored in niches in the wall of the covered entrance. The supply seems pretty scant; it wouldn't last us a day in the fire down at your house. I suppose they make charcoal from it to run the tandoor oven, which is an insulated pit over glowing charcoal inside a cube on which the cook squats at the rim. The women cook their bread by slapping pats of dough to the sides; they cook everything else there too, threaded on skewers. The method seems to defy gravity to me; I can't picture how it is that the glow at the bottom of the great clay pot doesn't just attract everything to it but it doesn't and the resulting stews and breads are palatable enough.

We ate with the widow and her large family in a small hall, draped in diaphanous curtains like the ones I've seen in Kabul, the floor covered with an elaborate carpet. We sat on cushions and they laid a thick oilcloth over the carpet for big bowls of cooked dishes. First we washed in a big silver dish brought around by one of the girls, who poured water from a jug over our hands. Maybe it's Zamzam water, who knows? There was bread, of course – there's always lots of bread – and a very nice meal of bolani, which is a pancake kind of thing stuffed with spinach or potato. They like to eat little green sour plums – I can't imagine why, but they seem to think that it complements salads and stews, a bit like we'd use capers.

The older girls of the house were brightly dressed and beautiful, but while they would look us in the eye and talk freely to us, they would not have their photos taken with their faces uncovered. Two of the girls are instructors in the tailoring school Meetra has sponsored at the house. The school is in a small room along the wall to the side of the house. From the yard you can see portable sewing machines in their wooden covers ranged along a lightly draped window.

We visited the sewing class where the owners of the burqas were sitting and crouching on the floor, taking notes in exercise books. A few bunches of grapes hung drying over their heads in the wooden rafters. My appearance at the low door with a camera caused a flurry of veiling, but I felt that behind the drapes, where they sat with heads down or peeping, there was curiosity and friendship. They might not like to show their faces but they do like glitter and display. They were dressed in a very tactile and highly visible way. Satins and velvets and gauzy wraps, patterned like honeycomb; some went for shyer pastels, but most were bright, rich colours, shining with sequins, and the velvets were patterned *and cut. Tassels, fringes, braids and embroidery did the work for hidden faces – that's allure for you; that's what the burqa hides.*

The widow gave me a big sprig of mulberry blossom and kissed me three times when I was leaving. Only later, when I looked at my pictures, did I see a poignantly doubtful face. It's a beautiful face, quite haunting, one of three young women sitting in front of Meetra as she held up the garments they were making to examine them. Two of the girls were looking directly up at Meetra, but the third, who was furthest away, had turned her dismayed gaze on me as I pushed the shutter. Now she is imprinted on my mind as if I myself were the camera that had stolen part of her identity. Such a face! I can hear the outraged voices of the politically correct damning me for my insensitivity. The effaced Christian saints of Spain and Malta and the destroyed Buddhas of Bamiyan all tell me that the girl I photographed feels threatened, even damned. But I cherish the photograph. It is part of Meetra's courage. Otherwise the beautiful but troubled girl has a lifetime of captivity in her husband's home ahead of her and that lovely face will never be worn freely in the world.

We left the driver with his mother while we visited the school again in the afternoon. Edris took the wheel and we nearly lost the car at a ford. Edris kept trying to reverse out of it. I got a bit fed up and suggested that he stop trying to reverse, put it in neutral and call over several blokes who were sitting in the shade by a mud wall watching. Meetra and I disembarked and approached the lazy sods in the shade. At first they didn't want to help, but Meetra gave them lip and they jumped up and got the car out in no time while I said under my breath, Allah-u Akbar, and Meetra-u Akbar and words to that effect.

It is a place of craters and jags. The Russians laid waste here, then came the southern and western warlords, along with the northern dissenters, trying to blast Massoud to kingdom come. Buildings are razed to a bit of floor and a sawtooth of wall. Holes are blasted through sturdier constructions, framing the landscape in tatters. That's the view out classroom windows, yet it doesn't deter the students; this school is fully attended. Eight hundred kids come here; two hundred and fifty of them are girls. The adolescent boys attend classes in the mornings and the little boys and the girls in the afternoons. Where boys and girls learn the same subjects, this system means doubling the burden on teachers – or halving the instruction time. Anyway, coeducation is out, so inefficiency is in.

In answer to this email, Mick sent back news about his breakfast. He was off to buy the paper. He said I should think of myself as a time traveller, like Dr Who, but to my mind, Dr Who is too recent and I still keep thinking of the Brothers Grimm.

We spend our days flat out visiting officials and academics to build bridges and initiate projects.

'Eli?'

'Wait,' Meetra goes. 'Soon.'

So I try very hard to be patient.

Edris is expanding the group's activities. I'm not told where he is off to or when – but if he is not at breakfast, I know he has gone somewhere and, in the evening, when I see him back again, I feel relieved. He is a bit of a Sinbad. His travels take him to extraordinary places such as an arcade carved through rock with caves at intervals along its sides – a long-ago centre of trade. Here, spices and textiles and foodstuffs from the Silk Road would have been traded between turbaned cameleers. He's been to Bamiyan and come back with tales of the blasted Buddhas and the thousand-year civilisation when they were worshipped. In Samargan Province, he was photographed standing under an outcrop shaped by time into a huge tree fungus and he told me that in Paktia he'd been travelling among blond giants with blue eyes who were the very frightening descendants of Alexander the Great. The mountain people of Paktia and Paktika, he says, are descendants of a Jewish tribe who hid their objects of worship in the mountains and continued, secretly, to practise their faith. This story of his grew into all Pashtun people in reality being the Lost Tribe of Israel.

While I understand that this story is widespread, Edris is a great romancer and, like most romancers, he implicitly believes what he says. At one point he got carried away with his own inventiveness and told me his solution to global warming. 'Wrap the ice and snow in aluminium foil,' was his advice, his brown eyes earnest, his small fine hand making pointing gestures at the air and his equally small, fine right foot waggling with invention over the knee of his left leg. How he would love to come to Australia! How he would love to spend five years in a country that wasn't war-torn! He would develop solar energy in Australia. He'd lived all his life in circumstances of war. He was far from his loved ones. He wanted to be married.

'You would need a bright companion, Edris Jan,' I said.

'Oh, but I am engaged to my brother's wife's best friend. All I have to do is go to Karachi and marry her.'

'What sort of work does she do, Edris Jan?'

'Oh, she is a student.'

'And how old?'

'Oh she is…' and here his foot wiggled around a good deal on the chair where he sat in Meetra's formal sitting room drinking tea with me after the others had gone to bed, 'twenty-four.'

'And what do you wish for in your companion?'

'Oh, she should cook for me and clean my house and look after me and have my children…'

'But you would need an equal partner with whom to share your ideas and dreams.'

'Oh she is equal. I will need her to tell me where I am wrong, where I have gone off track, how I could make myself a better person. She will teach me to be good.'

'How will she know?'

'Oh, she will know. She's read the Quran.'

'Will she have to be good?'

'Of course.'

'I see. And what will her work be, when she graduates?'

Here his eyes darted around and his handsome mouth fell open as if trying to taste the degree for which his prospective wife was studying…'Oh, she will be…She will be…Home Science.'

'And she is in Karachi?'

'Yes. She is living in my mother's house. All I have to do is find time to go and marry her.'

'I see. Your mother has chosen her?'

'She is…my brother's wife's friend. She helps my brother's wife look after our mother and my brother's little children.'

'And your brother is Haroon, who is the project manager here?'

'Yes. Haroon.'

'Would it be out of the question for your mother and the women to come to Kabul?'

'Oh, we have a father. He is there, too.'

'Does he work in Karachi?'

'No, he is a retired engineer.'

'But he's Afghan and so is your mother. Couldn't they all come to Kabul?'

'My mother is an invalid. They can't treat her here.'

'May I ask what's wrong with her?'

'She has diabetes.'

'Oh? Type one or type two?'

'Two.'

'Well, then, she doesn't need injections. She needs a special diet and medication. It isn't such a problem.'

But it seemed his mother didn't want to come to Kabul and that was the stumbling block. 'I want to live in a country without war,' said Edris Jan to me again before we went to bed.

In the morning, I wrote to Mick.

In Kabul, buildings are going up everywhere. They don't use metal scaffolding in this part of the world; instead, they're chopping down the forests of Tajikistan to realise the childlike dreams of those coming home from Pakistan. The enormous floors are held apart by tree trunks.

No doubt there will be entertainment rooms on a grand scale, remote controls and recliners and much to boast about to those with a lesser share of the great narcotics trade. Edris tells me it's very expensive to build in Kabul; it's one of his excuses for not organising to bring his family here. Poor man, he probably wants to keep the door open to flee back to Pakistan if the reform of the civil society fails here. He wants to come to Australia, but what would he do for a living if he did? Drive a taxi probably, certainly nothing as productive as what he is doing now. He's a romancer but he's brave and works hard. His younger brother Haroon, who is a very handsome boy, misses his wife and children terribly. He shows me photos of them all the time. His wife is lovely to look at, but she had a very glum expression on her face during her wedding ceremony. The photos of her with her children are delightful and she's full of smiles there – but there are also pictures of Edris's intended bride playing with the children and although Edris says she is twenty-four, she looks like a little girl to me! They speak to each other on Skype. Once I went into the office to use the copier and Haroon's wife and mother and children and Edris's fiancé – fifteen years old at most – were all dancing in real time on the screen. So what's the story? Who knows? Meetra says Haroon and Edris have sisters in Australia but the sisters have husbands who won't sponsor them. She tells them, 'If you want to go to Australia, apply.' But of course, it's then a question of waiting, waiting, waiting because the processing takes years and you might grow old in the meantime. People's chances just slip away.

It's all right for the wealthy ones; they can move around as they please and have always been able to, but for those without the funds, it can be a lifetime spent in futile hope. No wonder people seek asylum. How much better it would be if refugees had hope of a better life inside their own country.

What's the answer, Mick?

I suppose there is no answer and when there is no answer, people turn to religion, or sit it out, watching history unfold on the telly. Meetra and I watch the Turkish soaps on Tolo TV after dinner. There is a lot of staring between former lovers across crowded rooms. During the flashbacks to happier days, the woman starts to make little grunts, like a bear cub in training. The gent generally has a moustache and a tired, jaded expression, as if life has been hard on him since the days of fresh true love. The plots are simple enough to follow, even if you don't speak the language. Large groups of sympathetic women surround the saintly heroine, who knows he's a cad but loves him all the same. He has betrayed her, she has become frail and ill and her father is boiling with anger. The teeth grinding and eye rolling of the father are handled extremely well on Tolo: Stella could take lessons from the chaps who play the dads. In general, the dad stabs the cad in the stomach for dishonouring his daughter. The stabbing happens on a white marble staircase in one of the elaborate marriage palaces popular in the Muslim world and it happens alongside the new wife who has been arranged for the cad by his mother. Lots of lovely strawberry syrup on her pavlova gown with its pixilated neckline, but none on the stairs, as we don't want the producers having to fork out to get stains out of marble. The cad looks dead at the end of the episode where we leave him in his very best clobber in the shape of a swastika in a bed of petunias.

At the beginning of the next night's entertainment, the cad is on life support and the father has honourably given himself up to the cops.

The women are quite often streaked with blood from stabbed stomachs in Turkish soaps. They do a good line in being kicked. Bad girls, often English or American, have evil laughs. The saintly heroine may well have miscarried after having been booted in the guts by her avenging dad before he stopped seeing red after the announcement of her pregnancy, but she is still loving and pleases everybody by accepting the proposal of a clean-shaven, very upright soap-and-scent manufacturer. This means that her amazingly chinless mother and her budding beauty of a younger sister – the genetics of it are enthralling – can look forward to the release of the avenging fat little dad with his red face and the steam coming out of his ears. Bliss is on the cards for the soap-and-scent manufacturer and a life of grunting revision is guaranteed for the heroine.

On my first day here, I was hustled past a real woman, a mother in a blue burqa carrying a small, very dirty child, whose poor little fist was poking out of the bundle of her arms, palm upward, while the mother said, 'Very hard, very hard. Difficult. Please, please.' Lines she had learned from who knows where. My heart was wrung. I would have given money, but Meetra said, 'Hoh!' And I surmised that if I did place money in that pathetic little hand, I'd very soon be swamped by a legion of other little hands.

The woman and child haunted me but I soon got used to it and was soon to learn that the street beggars were probably better off than the displaced folk in the camps in and around Kabul. The poverty in the camps is abysmal. Anything in the shape of a sheet is thrown over string or cord stretched between posts or trees on ground that most people would disdain. The rubbish around the tents is not nearly as thick and complex as it was in the tips where Dadda would take Allegra and me to escape our mother's fits of rage, but that the areas are tips can't be doubted; rubbish is heaped up everywhere and people, especially children who are too small to go begging, spend their lives sorting it. We drive past such places almost every day. Edris has shown me pictures of the camps in winter after blizzards with snow mounted up the tent walls to the top. At least somebody supplies what look like army tents for the winter, nevertheless, each year several women and children die of cold. There's slush in the spring and everyone goes around wet. The summers are joyless and toyless, roasting under canvas at temperatures of forty in the shade. In the areas where the displaced people come from, the landmines might not have been cleared or there are military operations going on or the damage is so bad that no one can live there. Foreign aid organisations might erect a brick building for them in anticipation of their return, but they'll fail to do the job thoroughly. They'll omit a fence. They will not have ensured access to clean drinking water and certainly not to electricity and so the buildings are unlivable and start disintegrating before they can be used. It seems that in rural Afghanistan, Allah takes care of those who put up the buildings, but not of the people they are intended to house, just as in town the Great One takes care of those who build grand hospitals but don't equip or staff them, while He looks less kindly on those who would create the staff and the technicians. It seems that Allah likes show: it's attractive and covers over the deficiencies.

Meetra does a lot of shopping for things that she takes home and resells to raise money for her organisation. (She doesn't seem to care for the things that catch my eye, like Kuchi jewellery.) On one of our expeditions, I saw an ancient woman in a black burqa who was almost prone in the street, holding herself up on a staff made from the branch of a sapling as though she had just slumped beside the gutter. Inevitably, a brown hand was out, begging. I felt sick and had to steel myself as Meetra whisked me by. We turned off the main street and began picking our way over puddles from recent rain in some back streets. We were arranging with a Hazara in a carpet shop for the delivery of the splendid carpet I'd bought showing all the different styles of weaving in Afghanistan and with the Tajik jeweller for an assortment of filigreed silver, Panjshir emeralds, lapis, carnelian and aquamarine necklaces, earrings and bangles for Meetra's fundraising; we'd started back up the lane with its treacherous craterfuls of water and, as usual, Meetra rocketed on ahead, but I stopped to photograph a comical old umbrella outside an uncongenial room off the street and as I did so, who should climb the stairs and open the door but the same black-burqa'd crone I'd seen lying dramatically in the street. She turned her aged face to me with its crags and toothless grin and, as the door opened, I saw inside, beggars around a table, drinking tea from a tall aluminium samovar and watching the daytime run of the same Turkish soap we'd been watching the night before. There were the rolling eyes of the red-faced dad behind the metal mesh of the prison; there was the palm of the hard-done-by heroine pressed to the glass of the prison meeting room as she announced her intentions to marry the soap-and-scent guy. The tears, the are-you-sure-you're-doing-the-right-thing from the dad who kicked her guts out…

Dear Mick, I've done another Blondie – a fabulous dress: the dress of a Kuchi nomad, grey with a red front panel with mirrors embroidered into it. The front panel is all embroidered and it serves as a great big pocket – after all, they don't have handbags in this part of the world. A Hazara carpet dealer tried to tell me it was a fake. You see, I bought it from a Pashtun across the way from him. The Hazara was dropping off my carpet and he said that the Pashtun had faked the antiquity of the dress by sewing some bits and pieces together. After he left, I checked the seams and the little drawstrings it has under the arms to gather in the top and they were all of the same stitch and material. There's been no resewing anywhere; it isn't a fake.

Kuchis are a subclan of the Pashtuns. The Hazara dislike them intensely and believe they encroach on their lands in Hazarajat, but as things stand, the Kuchi have grazing rights in Hazarajat and they need to pasture their flocks there in the good weather. It's an old dispute, dating back over a century to when the Afghan monarch, Abdul Rahman Khan, dispossessed the Hazaras of the region because of their Shi'ite faith. Twenty years later, his successor, Amanullah Khan, reinstated Hazara ownership and instituted Kuchi grazing rights in place of land tenure. These days, with the cream of the Kuchi now settled and wealthy and the Hazaras very prominent, firmly entrenched and with their religious practices enshrined in the constitution, it suits the Kuchi parliamentarians to have the dispute continue, as money keeps flowing their way which is meant to go towards bridge building and peacemaking. They line their pockets while the Hazaras accuse the Kuchis of supplying the Taliban, running their guns and providing men for their militia, so justifying the blasting of the Kuchi off their lands and causing misery, as ever, to poor people on both sides.

That amazing necklace-cum-breastplate I saw in the jeweller's was Kuchi jewellery. I think I can live without it, but you never know, it could come home with the dress. I imagine when the herder's caravan *passes, it might advertise itself with a richly dressed girl on the elaborate saddle of some beast of burden, her mirrors flashing, her bells tinkling…* 'Come trade with me. My tribe is rich. I am beauty. I am what you do not have. I am mystery.' How do you think it would go down in the streets of Melbourne? We could hire a camel…*

Back came an email pronto: *Stop spending, Blondie. Your mother has now been settled back at Redeemer, but unfortunately we have had to opt for the nursing-home section as she is too weak now to cope in the hostel. I'm afraid she's moved from her cosy room to a four-bed ward. Nin is writing to tell you about it.*

Don't forget that, according to your mother, I'm only after you for your money, so don't spend all of it or I'll have to go shopping elsewhere. We are now back in Melbourne and Nin has found a place for Daniel in child care. The pregnancy progresses well. She's sending you a snap of her belly. They've decided not to find out the gender but it's due early November.

We haven't been attacked lately, but that probably won't last. Wendy has made an excellent piranha; Stella dreads the sight of her, but that's okay because Audra has turned up in the meantime and she dreads the sight of Audra more than she dreads the sight of Wendy. She and Wendy even played a game of Bingo together the other day. Stella's so blind she has to use milk-bottle lids for her counters and they've made her a specially large number sheet. Wendy thought it was a hoot.

Love you,
Mick
We're all enjoying your emails. No sign of Eli yet?

No. No sign of Eli. My eyes are glued to the TV whenever possible for a glimpse of Elias Jan on the news but he isn't there. This evening, we had a very congenial table. Some German friends have joined us, along with the Afghans of the house and another Australian, working for Oxfam. We've eaten very well, qima kebab and bolani. I told my tale of the beggar and one of the Germans said that her brother had been visiting and had given a very handicapped beggar a generous donation only to see him around the corner some short time later, counting a fat wad of money such as an ordinary Afghan wouldn't earn in a month – presumably it was one day's takings.

I've just watched for Eli again on Tolo news and failed to find him and now, on the screen in front of me, a gun has failed to go off at the temple of a star-crossed judge whose blonde English wife has just run off with a billionaire, but everything's all right, because his former Turkish wife is back, grunting, and the child of their loins is bringing tea at a trot. The judge is having his chin washed.

I'm glad the beggars of Kabul have a culture. I was once very broke and frightened myself – on my own with Eli in Sydney – and the best asset in our street was a kleptomaniac who worked in the kitchen at St Vincent's Hospital around the corner. Every now and then, the street scored half a lamb and we no longer had to choose between food and cigarettes. We knew we'd struck it lucky when our thief would come running down the street, crying 'Klepsi, klepsi, klepsi!' wielding a carpet bag with a sheep shin sticking out of it.

But just as the plot has moved on in my life and I'm still a single mother but this time searching for her adult son in Afghanistan, the plot has moved on, on Tolo TV. Yet another hero lies fighting for his life in a hospital bed after being stabbed in strawberry and spread-eagled in swastika in a bed of petunias. A beautiful, thwarted brunette is grunting at his door. I hope the beggars are also being enthralled by the pixilated décolleté and calves of our heroine as she opens the door and begins that fixed gaze so beloved of Tolo, for who knows what tomorrow will bring?

20

Today we are having a holiday. We are joining some dignitaries on an excursion to Panjshir to visit Massoud's tomb. This morning Hafiz let an SUV into the drive. Hurtling along, two steps ahead of me as usual, Meetra was out the door and down the front steps before I had my shoelaces tied. I arrived behind her, panting, still pulling on my headscarf. She was already in the back of the SUV, patting the seat beside her; on her other side was our German friend, Helga, whose brother was duped by the beggar. Helga is a teacher trainer. In front, one of the men I met on my first evening here when he stopped by for arthritis tablets: yet another engineer, whom we call Engineer Asraf – half the world here seems to be engineers. To drive us was one of Meetra's carpentry instructors, a nice, plump man called Abdullah who had dangling from his rear-vision mirror a heart-shaped silken talisman with something from the Quran embroidered on it.

We swung out of the drive and in behind another SUV, which shot off down the street ahead of us. Strings of 'Bale's and 'Khob's issued from Meetra and the engineer above a beeping from within the car that seemed to go on for blocks and blocks until I was about to ask if they could turn it off and it suddenly fell silent. What was it for? A diesel monitor? A bomb checker? I've no idea.

We seemed to be travelling in a variety of directions: around roundabouts, past enormous wedding palaces with dark green windows like sun-spoilt cellophane among new blocks of flats and huge frameworks, covered in material the colour of blue burqas, that awaited unveiling into the pink poppy palaces, those sponges with their strawberry jam filling that rise in the midst of the mud pies. Sometimes a tin dome – could it have been a small minaret, or was it an elaborate air vent for a septic tank in this city without a sewer? Gone too soon to work it out. And everywhere doors, doors, doors, doors. What are they hiding? What have they to hide? All walled off and secretive so that, in this city of engineers, insurgents attach themselves to building sites and, from high vantage points, open fire on gated communities from above, slaying foreigners, aid workers, women who work and, of course, their children. Helga is the indirect victim of an attack on the German Embassy and has had to find a new place to live. 'It's hard,' she said. 'The embassy insists on bank vault doors and razor wire all around wherever we live and so we have a space that is all door and two to a bedroom. The bathroom is bigger than the living area.'

'Who did it?' I asked.

'Pakistanis,' said Meetra, but Helga said, 'Oh, they come in from Pakistan, that's true. But we don't know whether they're Taliban or operatives for some other group bent on destabilisation. They get in with the building gangs on new projects and find themselves with a target: a foreign embassy, an aid agency, you name it. Some Aussies I know have locked themselves into a labyrinth somewhere with a bottle of Johnnie Walker Blue Label in a bolted glass cabinet with a hammer hanging underneath it and a sign saying "Break in case of emergency".'

'Guess it's hard to be anonymous.'

'Oh we manage, don't we Meetra?'

And Meetra nodded, her Meetra smile sliding conspiratorially into its berth.

Past newly planted trees on median strips, so close together that soon one half of the road will be completely invisible from the other, we went, past building yards stacked with the forest wood of Tajikistan. Meetra talked to the engineer about the refugee problem in Australia. On this topic, I've heard what she has to say and penetrated her frustrations. It starts with the massacre of the Hazaras in Mazar-e-Sharif and Bamiyan Province in 1998. Some Afghan Australians, including Meetra, begged the Australian government to bring Hazara refugees to Australia as a matter of priority. The government thought they were doing the right thing and started to bring Hazaras from Quetta in Pakistan, thinking that they were the refugees from Bamiyan – but they were the wrong people. Australia had no one in Quetta to vet the integrity of people wanting to seek asylum. When the Hazaras of Quetta heard that Australia was taking Hazaras by preference, they, whose home had been in Quetta for generations, put themselves forward. The Afghan Australians went to help them settle in, bringing clothing and money and moral support, only to find that the new arrivals didn't speak the language of Bamiyan. At most, they only had a few words. Back the delegation went to the government with this problem of mistaken identity, but the government responded by using it as an excuse not to bring in Afghan refugees at all. And sub-sequently…the boat people and a chain of illegal arrivals – people of all sorts, but not the true victims of Bamiyan, who still languish without a voice in Pakistani camps. Australia, unable to admit a mistake, blows the trumpet of righteousness and poisons every-one against the people who brave it in boats, whoever they are and wherever they come from. Ironically, the queue jumpers came in, fully protected, by plane.

Back in Afghanistan, a decade later, things are improving for Hazaras. They are industrious and well-organised people, who, through their own efforts, have good representation in the Loya Jirga, their Shi'ite religion is represented by a cleric in the upper house, they own TV and radio stations, they have very good access to university study, they occupy influential and prestigious posts and make their presence felt as an active part of the emerging middle class.

Other minorities, like the Kuchi and the Panjshir Tajik, are suffering now, or so says Meetra in no uncertain terms. In Australia, people hear what she has to say and the tone in which she says it, and immediately they say she is prejudiced – and thus, out of good will, bad will is born. As for me, I sat and said nothing while Meetra talked to the engineer. I just picked out the words and the emphases in Dari that signified where Meetra had got to in her story – brave, strong, energetic Meetra, whose country this is and whose feelings are those shaped over an Afghan lifetime. Meetra the human being, who sees the burdens and picks them up, knowing herself to be brave and strong enough to carry them.

Past dirt parks in the roundabouts, where boys rode bikes and played ball and women sat in the rubble with their hands out begging, we drove. Through traffic blare and sirens and past billboards advertising educational institutions and mobile phones. Past rubble, wheelbarrows loaded with faggots, a petrol station covered in the dust of thousands of cars and a big monument to Massoud, topped with a small black dome and surrounded by photographs: Massoud smiling, Massoud thinking, Massoud praying, fine-faced, intelligent, liquid-eyed Massoud; we dashed and we halted. Goats and sheep of the Kuchi pushed their way across the road in front of us.

Out of Kabul and onto the green plateau rolling towards us from the high, snowy peaks, we saw road stalls selling freshly slaughtered sheep and goat carcasses – occasionally a severed sheep or goat head, prosaic on the ground – and we saw stalls selling truck tyres: do they sell them for recycling into buckets, or are the tyre stacks a way of advertising mechanics at work? Behind the stacks in the fields, there were more palaces, some quite different from the big pink Karachi cakes in Kabul.

Some palaces have pitched roofs, bright as Kentucky Fried or Red Rooster outlets. They stand in the yards sending out messages of wealth and Westernisation, while inside there is probably not a single woman who doesn't have to wear full burqa on the street, should she be lucky enough to make it out of doors. The husbands of these households are probably landlords receiving rent from the Kuchi who bring their animals to graze here during the summer months; the landlords may have been nomads once themselves and are now settled and own the land by government decree, or so the conversation goes. The land-owning Kuchi are the ones with education and organisational or exploitative talents. As the suppliers of Afghanistan's meat, the Kuchi have seats set aside for them in the Loya Jirga. A push is on to register them, settle them and educate their children, but although they want their children educated, they are fiercely independent and love their way of life. They move in and move out: they stay until October or November in this area in Parwan and lower Panjshir and then go back to Pakistan, through Jalalabad and down to Karachi.

Around the growing town of Charika it was very green and very lush. Women worked waist-deep in the crops. New villages were going up by the road, the quality of the buildings was higher than in general in Kabul; there was proper glass in shop windows, but the shops were still very close to the road and would have to go if the road were ever widened. It could have been an untidy but quite prosperous suburban construction in Australia. The Afghan United Bank was operating on the ground floor of an air-conditioned shopping mall. There were plenty of opportunities for cafes or restaurants but I saw none and there were very few women on the street. Those few who ventured out were burqa clad. Outside the home, as in Kabul, there are no places for women to socialise in public.

Highly decorated mopeds sped from here to there through the up-to-date cars of Europe and Japan, advertising their businesses. I can't read the language or interpret the signs, although I'm learning to read numbers from car plates. It's easy, really: yak, do, say chahahr, panj...Panj? Panjshir – five milk? Butter, cream, cheese, yoghurt, milk? I would have asked Meetra, but she was busy talking about Charika, the area we were in, where a vast mosque stood in a field alone, waiting for the housing to catch up with it. Meetra explained that Charika was at the centre of the war between the

Russians and the mujahedeen and had been completely destroyed. This morning, it looked in better shape than Kabul, although further along the road, we saw a cluster of abandoned and shot-out Russian tanks on the former battleground.

After Charika we began to see huge decorated trucks pulled over to the side of the road. These enormous beasts, like the caparisoned Bedford in which Eli first went to Afghanistan, aren't permitted to run on the roads on Fridays. We soon came on a pro-test blockade, where we were bailed up for a number of minutes before being directed through the crush by police.

Waiting for the curfew to pass or the blockade to end, the drivers squatted on their haunches among their Metz, MAN, Mercedes, Kreiss, GE and Willi Betz V doubles and triples, amid scenes painted along the sides, mythical birds coiling their necks around cabins and front bumpers fringed with sheep bells and zigzag valances. People had been busy with tin cutters making elaborate perforations in side panels and spare-wheel covers and those wheel whisk holders whose brushes are like large false eye-lashes. Peacocks and horses, silver stars and diamonds showed under red and blue and green tarpaulins. Above some truck cabins were high decorated prows, embossed with shields as if they were battleships of the ancient world. What comes into Afghanistan on these? Goods, I suppose, returning people and fuel? One day it might be meat, doing the Kuchi out of their way of life.

As we climbed from the plateau and began our ascent of the Hindu Kush, we crossed a fast-running stream with high banks and entered the mudbrick and shipping-crate shop territory familiar from along the roadsides of Kabul. There were samovars and petrol for sale in a very damaged village, its houses shelled out and broken. A factory run by the government that once exported high-grade cement had been wiped out here: Pakistani insurgents of the type who shot up the German embassy came in and sabotaged the fac-tory, looted it and took the equipment to Pakistan. 'And now they sell it back to Afghans,' said Meetra, turning up her palm.

A young woman walked by in a burqa, her spring skirt billowing out in front of her, and behind her came an ice-cream vendor pushing his little red boot-shaped wagon, playing the ubiquitous happy birthday and lullaby songs. There were nomads' sheep and tents on high, rocky ground, dominated by a bombed-out shelter, stacked with sandbags – does someone live there now, or are there still gun muzzles nestling down behind the barrier?

New building was going on, a mosque and a huge school and a field fluttering with green flags that marked the many, many graves of the men, women and children who'd been killed fighting Massoud's war or just getting in the way of it.

Engineer Asraf comes from Nangahar Province and he began to voice his distaste for Massoud. He called him selfish and egoistic. Meetra translated. 'He caused a lot of instability, the engineer Asraf thinks, bu-ut,' she continued, thrusting her proud Tajik profile high, 'he was a national visionary. Engineer says all he brought was for the betterment of Panjshiri. He was Tajik Panjshiri – Panjshiri people are Tajik. So he did a lot and still helps the people; they are enjoying what he left for them. Engineer Asraf thinks that he was selfish like all warlords; he was selfish, a self-determined person. He didn't want to move from what he was thinking.'

'So he was very stubborn,' said I to the Tajik Meetra.

'He was very stubborn man.' Meetra's chin was getting higher. 'He had made up his mind about something and wasn't prepared to change his mind.'

'Should he have?' I asked.

'Well, most warlords are like that.'

'So really, they're fighting for the survival of their group…'

'No. He was fighting for the country. He didn't want Afghanistan to be a part of anyone. The Russians were not supporting him.'

'Because he was a nationalist?'

She drops her voice. 'Then they started to have a good relation.'

'Yes,' said the engineer, who must have been listening and understanding the gist of our talk, and he said *yes* as if to say,

You see, Massoud was a bastard after all. I wasn't sure whether this meant that Massoud had actually courted or been courted by the Russians at some stage, but I didn't get a chance to ask.

There was a wedding going on around the car. No bride in sight but a car decked out in red and white flowers and four men, obviously of the wedding party, walking briskly towards it…

Helga broke in. 'He had good relationship with France.'

And Meetra. 'Yeah. The best relation that he had was with France. And during his relationship he sold emeralds from Panjshir, exchanged it with guns and arms from France.'

Helga said, 'He had a talk in the European parliament. They invited him to come. He actually announced the terrorist attacks on the World Trade Center a few weeks before 9/11 and he asked for help, asking Europe because there would be very bad attacks. And then he died himself two days before the attacks.'

'I know,' I said. 'People posing as photographers and journalists killed him. They asked for an interview with him and blew him up at his hideout.' But I wish I could have curbed my know-all tongue to elicit a response from Engineer Asraf, because this seemed like something very significant in Massoud's defence.

'We will see the hideout,' said Meetra.

It was now very mountainous, a green grass and white rock-mosaic along the slopes that fell away quietly, surrendering themselves to the clear rushing water of the Panjshir River.

Awesome grey mountains rose in tiers; here and there, there were shell craters and war debris, the upturned cabin of a truck stuck out like a giant's skull as if it summed up all the men who fell here, leaving the women and children to pine in the rocky landscape – or to die their own little flagless deaths.

On our side of the river, new trees started springing up and houses of better quality than those you see in Kabul climbed the gentler parts of the slopes. Across the river, an entire village that was ferociously razed has been left as a monument to speak for itself.

We were in a string of daytripping cars and I couldn't tell if the car we'd been following was still in front or not. In fact, I'd forgotten what it looked like. There were fewer and fewer habitations and cars coming the other way. We had climbed very high. A few men passed us, carrying spades, and I marvelled again at the intense greenness of the grass.

At the tomb, Massoud lies under a slab of black granite surrounded by blood-red carpets of intricate design. Over his head a grey marble dome rises high with inscriptions all around the inside of the rim. Outside, a formal Islamic garden, austere, colonnaded in the same grey marble, might hold a thousand people at a time. The mausoleum occupies a copious plateau of its own, enfolded by grey mountain tops, a sombre, elegant and reverent place bespeaking a great martyr who died for a whole country. There is no ostentation here. Care and judgement have gone into the construction.

Even the Engineer Asraf walked slowly and appreciatively as, by silent agreement, we each wandered off on our own to think and photograph and wonder.

Massoud's office, a small shabby pink building, hovers unassertively behind the mausoleum, left as it was the day he was assassinated. It will stay like that. We grouped with the rest of the party on the balcony outside the room where he worked while Abdullah, our driver, took our photographs, then we went downstairs to the back of the office and peeped in the windows of three black Mercedes cars parked end to end, as they were when the assassins arrived, in a modest sunken drive. The only ornamentation was an elaborate plastic tissue box between the front seats of the middle car with a tissue half out of it as ready to pull.

Yellow and orange graders stood idle in the act of smoothing a roadway up to the parapet around the edges of the park. An amphitheatre was under construction on a level below the mausoleum, its arms subtended by the tanks and armoured cars and field guns with which the war was fought.

Now we have left the tomb behind us and we are driving down a branch road edged with blossom and pollarded trees close beside a river with a rusted jeep chassis sticking out of it. They pull over among some parked motorbikes so I can take some photos and I'm clicking away through the car window, when someone from the first car walks up alongside and suddenly I'm looking into blue/blue eyes. The Arnie Russell/Isobel Coretti cross and a voice is saying, 'Hello Sibella.'

'Eli!'

'What I said?' says Meetra.

'Eli!'

'Meet you down at the hideout.' There are tears on his cheeks. He wipes them away with the back of his hand, his fine-boned, taper-fingered hand and he runs it down my cheek and kisses me.

'Eli!'

'Bah!' says Meetra, and for good measure, 'Hoh!'

But he is already up by the other car, giving me a baby wave as he climbs in.

How beautiful is the world! Although I saw the people from the first car at the tomb, I'd forgotten with all the looking that we were in a convoy. 'Was he in there all the time?' I ask Meetra.

'Yes,' she says. 'You just didn't see him.'

'How could I miss my own son? I've come all this way...'

'He keep out of sight. He ask us not to tell you.'

'So he's been watching me?'

'Of course. But you lost in your dreams and you don't see him.'

'I was thinking of Massoud.'

'Of course. We all do.'

'What's Eli doing here?'

'You just have to wait to find out. But first we are all going to Massoud's hideout.'

Then I realise that there is not only an SUV in front of us, there's also one behind us. I can see in the side mirrors that it has a policeman and three armed guards in it.

'Have they been with us all the way?' I ask Meetra.

'You didn't see them at the tomb?'

'I took a photo of one of them looking in the window of the mausoleum when I was inside and another one at the amphitheatre. I didn't realise they were with us.'

She shrugs and says, 'Doesn't matter,' as Abdullah parks the car.

As I step from the car, Eli is coming over at a trot. Right away, he hugs me to him, saying, 'Come on Mother, we're going to see where the great Massoud hid out. Come and I'll show you.' And he takes my hand.

Over a stretch of gravel, nestling in under a steep mountain-side, there are two nondescript rock and mudbrick cabins. They are run-down and the windows are broken but they have sheets of plastic over them. Behind us comes a personage, the dignitary whose excursion we are part of: long, crisp black suit coat over white shalwar kameez, stepping out smartly ahead of his entourage. He heads for the humble mud building where Massoud was quartered in hiding, but he is soon out again with one hand behind his back, as if he'd been disappointed in the middle of a bow. No, Massoud wasn't there to meet him, nothing to see…

Eli and I take our turn. Inside is a decrepit memorial to a great struggle. The room is small, render cracked and fallen from the walls, two small windows stuck open in their frames, a ceiling of tin and beams, rubble piled high in the corners. To me, it is a monument more fitting even than the stone mausoleum; it speaks of work and hope and time passing, whereas the mausoleum pits itself against time, the expression of a high and mighty grief.

The soldiers precede us into a dark little covered porch linking the two cabins and seem to dissolve into blackness in front of us. They are the bodyguards following the personage. 'Who is he Eli?'

And Eli does the same thing to me as Meetra has done and says, 'Doesn't matter, Mumma. Not for now. I'll tell you when the time's right.'

'But you were travelling with him.'

'Yes. I was even driving some of the way. I could see you all the time with your little camera on its tripod at the window and I was thinking, "That's my mum!" You never miss a moment, do you?'

'Can't see the wood for the trees, you mean!'

It isn't a door into which the soldiers and the personage disappeared ahead of us. It's a hole in the mountain. A cave. A soldier gives us a smile and a nod as if we are in on some wonderful conspiracy.

'Gosh, it's pretty dark...' I mutter as Eli's grip on my arm tightens.

We edge our way in with the feeble light of a torch being shone behind us. Eli starts crooning softly and his voice comes echoing back, wrapping me in its warmth and joy. Then he says something in Dari to Meetra, so I have to ask, 'What are you two saying?'

'Massoud was coming and staying in here,' Meetra says, 'when the Russians were bombing.' Every now and again the walls light up in the beams of the torch and I can see that this is a big place. Meetra translates what the guide is saying: 'It was only for Ahmad Shah Massoud. For the rest it was bigger and longer.' She means there is another one of these somewhere close.

Eli hugs me close. 'What about that, Sibella?'

'It's wonderful, wonderful. Did they dig it out by hand?'

'Some of it is natural, but I think they increased the size a bit.'

It feels very big in the dark and we feel for the walls, little embryos trying to attach in a mysterious womb.

As we passed to the outside, sunlight gleamed on Meetra's crown ahead of us and we came out into a great shaft of brightness. We stood on a small arena of flat ground above the tumbling Panjshir, surrounded by stupendous clarity. Rocky peaks encircled us, clear air entered us and the light picked out the details down to pebbles.

Pushing its way up through my joy is the horrible weed of what happened in Melbourne. Eli has joined me in the middle SUV and we are on our way to lunch. Meetra says we are going to eat at the house of one of Massoud's relatives, which is not far from here. The relative isn't there but connections of the VIP in the leading SUV have made the arrangements.

'Eli.' I am holding his hand. I lay my cheek on his upper arm and look into his bearded, very tanned, blue-eyed face. 'Can you tell me what happened to your unit in Melbourne? It looked as though a violent crime had been committed there. You hadn't paid your last bill and there was money outstanding and the landlord came after me for reparation and an explanation. Please tell me what happened.'

He sighs and squirms on the threshold of a mental space he doesn't want to enter. 'Well, to start with, Mum, you have to believe me. *I* didn't commit a crime, but I do know what happened.'

His tone has changed abruptly and I try not to snap in reply, but I'm so fed up with the devious tangle that our relationship has become over the years! 'There was a pool of blood that someone had tried to remove with bleach…'

'I know. I wish you didn't have to be involved in this but let me tell it from the beginning so you will understand.' So he takes a deep breath and adjusts his face, his eyes losing the immediate view as he arranges what he has to say.

'I didn't live there a lot of the time I was in Melbourne. There are Afghans in Melbourne who are in a lot of trouble. It's a very small minority of them, mind you, but there are a few. I'm known to the Federal Police as a person who speaks Dari and who has been back and forth to Afghanistan lots of times. And I'm in contact with ASIO and people in DFAT, so quite often, when I come home to see you guys, I'll be asked to do a little favour for one agency or another. This time it was the feds who approached me.

They asked me to look after an Afghan woman who wanted to go into drug rehab. She'd been in Australia since the nineties with her husband and children and her husband's parents and she had citizenship, but it hadn't protected her much. For all that we tout Australia as the land of mateship, she had no mates, didn't speak the language and lived like a prisoner in her own home. The family's very conservative and wouldn't let her work and she was so depressed, she was on the verge of topping herself. She'd turned up out of the blue one day at St Vincent's casualty with a baby on her lap and she was very agitated and acting as though the baby was sick. Well, a doctor looks at the baby and the baby's showing all the signs of narcotic poisoning. It was about a year old.

'So, baby on narcotics…Doctors at St V's see it every so often because there are a lot of heroin addicts in and out of their rehab. Turns out, as it generally does, that the mother's addicted too and she's been breastfeeding it. But there's a special problem in this case because no one speaks her language and she won't tell anyone who she is. It's a case for social workers. Well, they're pretty savvy and they have her picked as a Dari speaker with a drug problem and they know it's a matter for the Federal Police not the locals.

'The feds know about me, knew I was staying nearby at the time, and they got hold of me to come in and interpret for this woman. My work with the feds is the reason it was hard for you to get hold of me and why I had to lie low. I'm only useful to them as long as I remain anonymous.

'Anyway, turns out this woman has heard somehow, possibly the SBS programs in Dari, or from the telly, of the methadone program at St V's, and is desperate to go on it. The family won't let her out of their sight and they hold her drug supply over her head to keep her from doing what she's just gone and done – come to the notice of Australian social workers via the medicos. Social workers means police, police means getting busted, getting busted means jail. She was too scared to stay in the rehab because the family would almost certainly trace her there, so it's Eli to the rescue.

Well, it's one thing to harbour an Afghan woman in your home but another thing entirely to face an infuriated Afghan husband. He's likely to kill you and his wife, so I agreed to set her up in my flat so long as I wasn't going to be caught living with her. Meanwhile the feds could investigate the family and see where they were getting their drugs from…It turns out that the husband's become a supplier of alternative medicines and they've built themselves a castle in Coburg. Obviously, something's going on.

'While they were investigating, I shaved off my beard and became the clean-cut Charlie you saw at your opening…'

'Oh God! You turned up in your *gym* gear.'

'Well, that was part of it, Mum,' he exclaims, suddenly irritated with me. What he thinks of as my pettiness is a bone of contention between us, but he will do things – like turning up to my grand opening in his gym clothes – that I'm certain are meant to slight me. Sometimes I think he does it to draw attention to himself – what as, though? My protector? My absence in his presence? His humility versus my pretentiousness? He isn't humble!

But it isn't the time to go down this path so I pull my horns in and listen.

'I was being a gym instructor for an outfit in Fitzroy and living in a room in someone's house while I was keeping an eye on Samia – that was the woman's name – taking her to her methadone program and making sure the social workers went to visit her and the baby. The family were out looking for her, of course, but they weren't about to report her disappearance to the police for obvious reasons.

'She was around thirty and that family's doings had been the story of her life since she was sixteen in Afghanistan. They're Shinwaris. She told me that her father sold her to her husband's family to pay off a debt. He owed the family for sixteen sheep. Sixteen sheep, one woman; you get it. She'd been a nice-looking girl at some stage, too, you could tell that. Since being sold, she'd had six kids. Anyway, that hardly counted. She was good value as far as the family was concerned; they treated her like a slave. She did all the housework and looked after the kids and her husband's parents as well. They were quite wealthy as far as wealth in Afghanistan goes. Well, of course they were: they were in the heroin trade.'

'But the blood...'

'I'm coming to that, Mum. That family has extended connections with other communities, Vietnamese, Lebanese, Chinese, Thai, Cambodian, Europeans too, who are into sports medicine. They know people everywhere, all over Melbourne, and they found out where Samia was within four days. After all, it's only a long tram ride from Coburg, Samia couldn't drive, she had no money to take a cab and no access to money. She was toting a kid around. You can't hide in this world if those are your credentials. We knew they'd find her and were hoping for a drug bust before they did. So I've stocked Samia up with things she needs for herself and the baby, including stacks of disposable nappies and bleach. Why bleach? Well, I remembered you always had a supply of bleach around when Nin was a baby and it didn't occur to me until later that the point of disposable nappies is you don't need to wash them. Anyway, no harm done, just four redundant litres of bleach stored up in her en suite. I'm living in a room about three doors away from Samia's. She's using the phone I had on there and I've got a mobile – any trouble, she rings me right away. About a week before your opening, I'm pounding away at the gym when there's a call on the mobile. She's seen one of her husband's brothers skulking in the driveway of the units – you had to go down a driveway to get to my unit as you obviously know by now. So, not quite knowing what I'm going to do, I'm on my way in my tracky daks and singlet, sweaty, tough-looking, I hope. It takes me about ten minutes to get there, about twelve minutes from the time of the call. In that time, the brother has got into the garage and opened the piss-weak door into Samia's kitchen – the doors were done on the cheap; you could lock them but they were hollow inside and bendable. Only the very front door has a bolt so anyone with a picklock is home and hosed and doesn't even have to do damage to get in. By the time I get there, he's upstairs with Samia screaming and kicking and being held against the bathroom wall. I came through the front door, using my set of keys.

"'Hey, hey, hey, what's going on here?" In a deep voice. He lets her go, the poor little kid's squalling and suddenly Samia starts to haemorrhage. And I mean haemorrhage; she's having the mother of all miscarriages. It's pretty bad, blood everywhere, she goes unconscious, I ring the ambulance, the ambulance comes. I just didn't think it out. There wasn't any time. I got Samia into the ambulance, I phone the feds from the ambulance. They tell me they've got it under control and I'm not to go back to the unit under any circumstances because the bastard of a brother is probably armed. Then suddenly I remember the kid, phone them again, but I get put through to voice mail, in the back of my mind I'm reading, "Siege in Collingwood, Kid held hostage" and I'm trying to morph into fifteen versions of myself to be in all the places where I'm needed, not to mention the one place where I want to be – with my mother and my gran and my cousin and her kid.

'Poor Samia's very, very sick. I call them up in the rehab and ask if a social worker from there can come and hold her hand while I go back and see if I can get the kid, because I'm buggered if I'm going to take the advice of the feds and leave well alone when there's a little kid involved. Besides, the bloke from the feds is an immature young cock and I don't know why they've hired him. He thinks he's Rambo. He's really, really up himself, half my age and what would I know about anything, I'm only a journo. I haven't got top-secret clearance. He's got top-secret clearance. Some people are so infatuated with their job descriptions they can't do the job for playing the part.

'Nobody's free right away at the rehab, but they're ringing around the hospital and as soon as there's a social worker available, they'll send him or her up to where we're desperately waiting for an operating suite to become available – I don't know why they bother mentioning a "him", because I've yet to come across a social worker who isn't a "her". Well, another hour goes by, Samia's still bleeding, there's no operating theatre available, and, bugger it, they have to move her to the Women's where there is a theatre. She's getting mighty desanguinated by now and it's a matter of the Women's or death. So, off we go to the Women's and she's rushed into theatre. New hospital, new staff, who am I, what am I doing here? Where's the husband? I don't know who the husband is, she knocked on my door and was in trouble, I called the ambulance and there's no way anyone can ask her who her husband is. "Lovey? Lovey?" Bent over an unconscious woman as the theatre doors swing shut. And then she's on the operating table fighting for her life. I can't go in to be with her and I can't go and get the kid, because she might not make it. I ring St V's again. Can they send someone over? I've got to go check out the little kid. What about a policewoman? they ask. Well, no. There's a drug bust on and I need a social worker who knows the history to come. Please. It's urgent, she might die and I should go and get the kid if I can. Luckily, at St V's they know the routine. So, half an hour later, the social worker from St V's comes over – more bloody hospitalese, what's one of *their* social workers doing on our patch? While all that's going on, I skedaddle. Back I go to the unit. No yellow tape, no crime scene, so I let myself in. Nobody home. Upstairs the basin in the bathroom's been broken and some idiot has poured the bleach I bought for the putative baby nappies all over the stain of Samia's haemorrhaged blood at the entrance to the bathroom.

'My heart sinks. I'm in a fury. I ring the fed guy whose name's Jason. "What the fuck, Jason?" "Don't worry about a thing, mate, you're in the clear." "What've you done?" "We're getting you out. We're sending you to Bali, all expenses paid because your life's not worth a pinch of shit in Melbourne right now." "What about Samia?" "We'll get her and the kid into a refuge." "Have you got the kid, then?" "No?" "So the fucking brother's got the kid." "We thought you had him." "Don't you ever listen, Jason…" "Now, don't speak to me like that, my friend." "Are you threatening me?" "We know all about you, Elias Jan of Tolo TV." "What?" "Yeahhh!" he chuckles. He's heard that I've reported things on Tolo.

'I was just so angry and frustrated, Sibella, that I flung the phone across the room and broke it. The ignorant little puffed-up bastard. And anyway, I don't work for the Federal Police, I'm a journalist and I didn't set out to be roped in. I've done this type of thing before and beyond having my expenses paid, I got bugger all out of it. I was furious.'

Eli sits there in the car beside me, blinking and fuming as we jolt along. 'I tried to think it out, Mum. But it was just some concocted situation. As it happened, I did go up to Indonesia. They gave me five hundred dollars spending money. Big of them.'

'What happened to Samia?'

'She came out of the operating theatre in a bad way. The St V's social worker decided to drop the pretence and they contacted the fucking family so she could see her children. They all came in and sat around her bed, weeping the true tears of crocodiles while the poor, poor lady died. Her fallopian tube had burst well and truly, her womb was ruptured. She was just too weak from loss of blood to take the hysterectomy and, in any event, there was muck in her body cavity.

'They put the husband and his father on surveillance and two weeks after I left Australia, the feds busted them on drugs charges. They were part of a pretty big smuggling ring but it wasn't just heroin they were bringing in. It was ecstasy and ice and the makings of growth hormones for gym freaks and sporting heroes. They've been in jail for some months now waiting for their case to come up...or so bloody Jason tells me. I'm so, so sorry Mum. What a thing to put you through! They've informed the state police about what happened to Samia now, I believe. At least, that's what the latest email says. I'm so sorry, Mum. Down the track I'll try to get reimbursement for the damage to the unit.'

'And Mr Liu, the owner, has he been told anything?'

'Only that someone had a bad miscarriage, there was an accident with the sink and that I botched the cleaning. God I hate that! I hate lies. Why Mum, is the world built on lies? Why can't people be honourable, fair and reasonable?'

21

We were wrapped in a cocoon of two, which now had to break again and spill us out because we had arrived at the relative's house with the Panjshir galloping along beside it like wild white horses. We crossed a couple of yards and passed through low stone walls without noticing anything except where to put our feet.

The bodyguard has climbed up onto the roof. I don't know whether that's a good thing, because it advertises our presence and potentially spreads messages to people further away: Important Personage on Premises. But there isn't time for worry, only time to be with my son.

Eli has been travelling abroad with the important personage. They've been in one of the Gulf States – not allowed to say which one – talking with former leaders of the Taliban and trying to gauge what demands are going to come the way of Afghanistan before a peace accord can be signed. Because Eli now has a large compendium of knowledge about the country and has all kinds of contacts, he is able to put people in touch with those they could not meet under regular circumstances.

'But why is it necessary for the Taliban to be at the peace table at all?' I ask as we take off our shoes and progress into a spacious foyer with a large, ornate fountain in the centre at which we wash our hands. Neatly dressed and turbaned serving men hand out towels.

'Gosh, quite a house, isn't it?' says Eli. We follow the rest of the party into a plain but commodious hall whose extensive windows give onto the river and we settle ourselves into a corner where the windows meet and there is a fresh breeze coming in. 'The Taliban?' he continues. 'They're part of the fabric of southern Afghanistan by now. They're guerilla fighters and they've infiltrated deeply into the Pashtun regions. In that way they're like the Viet Cong and can't be defeated. They also make up the single largest political group among the Pashtuns. If they are not involved in the peace process, they'll just keep up the sabotage and murder that have been their hallmarks since NATO came in. They're very well armed and will never agree to an armistice so there'll have to be local truces or something. We're not sure how firm their support base is but sympathy for them is widespread in the south. I don't know that too many of their sympathisers would also harbour and help them, but they'd follow them if they had significant military victories.

'And then there's Pakistan,' he says, swiping up almonds from the entrée bowl at the low table before us and chucking them absently into his mouth. 'The Taliban have formed a Pakistani branch and they are all over northern Pakistan, too. In the Swat Valley and places like that. The border between Afghanistan and Pakistan is often more theoretical than real and the Taliban are deeply involved in the border culture, so amelioration would be a better outcome for Pakistan than exclusion.'

'You know a lot, my boy.'

'I have to, Mum. Or someone has to. The West doesn't understand this area as well as it might.'

'But who are you collecting the information for and where does the money come from to keep yourself, Eli?'

I've made him squirm now. He sighs. 'I was asked to set this last thing up by the UN. They paid me and I'll get a lecture tour out of it. I'll be talking in Geneva and Brussels and Paris and London and then I'll be talking in the States to some congressmen. It's all right Mum. I know it's been really hard on you but I'll soon be able to reimburse you for everything you've had to hand out.'

'Well, it's problematic, you know. Deeply problematic now. I am at the bottom of the barrel. The house is falling to bits and I'm going mad for want of space to work in.'

'I know that, Mum. I'm very conscious of that. I can only say wait a little longer, just a little longer…'

'I've already waited, honey. You can't promise what you can't give any more than I can live in expectation of plenty. I know that.'

'I'm afraid it's keep a low profile or be killed, Mum. Sometimes I think it would be easier to be killed.'

'Oh don't say that! It's just as well you've always been a master of disguise, eh?'

'Odd bunch, the Coretti family, and forced by our talents to live odd lives.'

'Do you think anyone lives smooth, unworried, joyful lives, Eli?'

'I've never met anyone who does,' he says with his mouth full, and gobbling. He's eaten all our hors d'oeuvre and I've had two nuts.

They have put on a large spread for our lunch. No sooner have we started one dish than another arrives. Eli and I are together in a corner of a great table at which there is much passing to-and-fro of specially prepared food. There is lamb, of course, okra and chicken and bread. Yoghurt and bolani. Lentils, salads…all the usual fare that there is at an Afghan table but lots of it and well prepared and there are the people of the house to wait on us. Eli eats as if new to it, so much so that I feel reassured in having told Dan that this is the life where everything alive has to eat something else that's been alive.

Although the house is plain, it is on the scale of a baronial hall; maybe it works like a barony with Massoud's family as the barons. It is hard to hear each other talk but most of the noise is coming from the VIP's table, where the VIP is informing people of what he has been doing in the Gulf. He seems a little bit loud and boastful to me. 'Yes,' says Eli, between mouthfuls. 'Sometimes people like him like to let off steam and blow their trumpets among potential supporters. I had to keep telling him to cool it when we were talking to the Taliban blokes: he was bursting out of himself with his own importance. It's something you have to learn not to do, although you do get excited and almost everyone does it, especially politicians. They just can't keep things to themselves until they've had gestation time. It's one thing I've learned , Mum. You have to let information mature in the vat alongside everything else you know before you go making a hero of yourself. It's better to lie as low as you can and never make a hero of yourself so you can develop a continuous picture and learn to predict. Guess it's why there are secret police.'

'There are other ways of drawing attention to yourself, dear, apart from boasting.'

'What do you mean?'

'Well, you're obviously very hungry and unused to dining in high-falutin' company.'

'Still drinking, Mother?' he taunts. This is the barrier we're up against: I'm not allowed to have any wisdom of my own. He's the bloke, I'm the bird and I've never yet been able to open the door to the legitimacy of my own thoughts in his adult presence. I can't think how to do it here, in this dramatic and utterly extraordinary situation, so I ask. 'Are there lots of secret police in Afghanistan?'

'You bet. You would have been followed from the time you arrived.'

'Who by?'

'Government spies. They wouldn't have wanted you to get into trouble – or to cause trouble, for that matter.'

'How would I cause trouble?'

'Photographing installations, that kind of thing.'

'Really?'

'Sure.'

'And you're followed?'

'Sure. I'm well and truly known by now. I've had the third degree on my Taliban contacts. I'd be dead meat if I didn't come and go frequently.'

'Oh don't say that!'

'Don't worry Mum, what's the use of worrying? I know how to look like a local. I'm gone even when I'm there.'

'Do you?'

'Sure. I've even been a woman sometimes. I make a good woman. I've got tiny hands and feet. You did well there; they came from you.'

'Believe me, you wouldn't make a good woman.'

'Why do you say that?'

If I say *never mind* the way he says it to me, he'll only take offence and we'll argue and I can't let that happen here, so I say instead, 'You're the wrong shape.'

'Not wrong enough to be a standout. I've been a Sunni mullah – not a very good one, but good enough to hear the crap they go on with, particularly the guys in the south – they'd love a Taliban takeover and the proclamation of the Sunni Islamic State of Afghanistan. They're all puffed up with their own self-importance – and the people they control, the henchmen they want to send up north to gain control of northern provinces, they're even more puffed up.'

'What are their chances?'

'Not great, but not absolutely negligible. Sometimes they manage to put in one of their boys, but the people up in this region, Kabul, Panjshir, hate them. What the conservative mullahs really want is for the Taliban to gain control of the Afghan Army.'

'Will they?'

'I don't know. The army is getting better at behaving like a national army, but there's a long way to go yet. As things stand, the Taliban would be defeated if they tried to overthrow the Afghan

Army today. They haven't got the firepower or the technical skill. They know they haven't, too. The Taliban operate in a way similar to the Mafia. The Mafia were a great help to the Yanks in the Second World War and they could put themselves forward as a great help to them again in this situation. I reckon that would hinge on drugs; it wouldn't involve the Pakistani Taliban, who are right into drugs trading, but the Afghan Taliban under Mullah Omar are dead against it. If the Yanks or the UN paid them to get rid of the crops in their bailiwick, they'd do it.'

'I thought that the opium trade accounted for most of Afghanistan's GDP.'

'It does as things stand, but that's probably about to change.' He reaches across me to grab salad. 'This country is sitting on huge deposits of rare metals. If they don't develop the minerals industry themselves, you can bet your boots someone else will be in here doing it for them. If they do manage to capitalise on minerals, they'll be able to pay their way for the first time in history. They'll have to start from scratch, of course. They'll have to import technocrats and train up their own. But if they succeed in doing that, there'll be a bonanza.'

He eats absent-mindedly, dropping stuff on his clothes so that I reach over to blot his lap with tissues…He follows my hand, left and right, bemused.

'But the completely insurmountable problems of the moment are Taliban zealotry and their abominable attitude to women. They don't credit women with will and intellect,' he says as I wipe his lap, 'they equate them with prestige goods. Either a woman is worth something because of her birth into a desirable family, or because of her skill as a carpet maker or embroiderer or cook, or she is worth twelve sheep, like poor Samia. Or worse – she's a scapegoat for everything that goes wrong and she's punished to the point of wanting to die. I've seen some terrible things here. Once I saw a sixteen-year-old wife who'd had her tongue cut out by her husband for telling a lie. She wouldn't even have been worldly wise enough to be able to concoct a decent lie…' he pauses for a moment, mid-chew, and then shudders.

'Oh that's terrible!' But of course, it's just like Eli to tell me such a thing. He constantly buys me off with abysmal stories and the need to combat the dreadful things that happen. But I seem to pay for half the combat. If I keep on having to fork out there'll be nothing left for me. He knows that but I'm always coughing up in the name of some greater goal.

'But that's the detail,' he continues, almost as if advising himself. 'You have to overcome the detail, curse it, put it aside. It used to enter my dreams and wreck my sleep, but not now. You have to stand up tall, Mum. High, but invisible. You have to look out over all the heads, count them and know that among them there are good people, right-minded people, people who will dare to be educated and dare to change things without reaching for the switch that turns off the lights and stops them from seeing. You have to locate those people in the anonymous crowd. You have to follow the chains of association until you find yourself in enemy territory but with a way out. Ariadne's thread, as you used to teach me. I thank you for that. It would be a poor world without Ariadne's thread.'

Well, that's true. I always have stressed that. Without the thread you're in the labyrinth forever, with the Minotaur's wrath at your back: it's just that all I can afford at the moment is Ariadne's string and even that's frayed.

Ariadne's thread, he tells me, has taken him among Taliban high up in a plush hotel in the Gulf where everything works and the food is served on silver trays. Where there are smart phones and flat screen TVs as big as a wall. Where the swimming pools are made of marble and each one has a fountain far more elaborate than the one in the foyer here. Far, far from the recruiting grounds where people are so poor they sell themselves for a gun and some hope. 'Imagine what the Taliban saw in that hotel,' he says. 'The sort of luxury they despise on one hand, certainly, but on the other, the fabulous communications – news and knowledge on tap, distances shrunk and goods and information at everyone's fingertips. Those advantages they would envy and wish for themselves. If they had those things, I think it would be transformative. New information would have to seep into their consciousnesses. For instance, they would see that acceptance of women playing powerful parts in world affairs is widespread.

'There is a mighty chasm as things stand. They are putting draconian demands on the peacebrokers. They're insisting that Karzai and his clan are ousted and have nothing further to do with politics. They see Karzai not as an intermediate step towards a peaceful Afghanistan but as an archenemy.'

'And what do you think?'

'Well, one of Karzai's brothers is reputed to be hugely involved in the drugs trade and there's no knowing how corrupt that family really is. I guess they're stacking up the wealth against the day when they'll have to get out. They're just like the old Romans, I guess – a quaestorship in Sicily and then pleasant banishment to an outer province with your ill-gotten gains. There aren't too many saints. The women of Afghanistan often feel betrayed by the Karzai government but not for the same reasons that the Taliban do. Women of both sects think that the Shi'ite Ayatollah in the Upper House has too much power over the marriage laws. They don't want Karzai to enact Shi'ite exemptions from Sunni legislation, like women having to agree to sex with their husbands on pain of not being fed.

'The women politicians have won the case for the legal age for marriage to be set at sixteen for girls and eighteen for boys and they've won legislation against forced marriages. But those laws are widely flouted. They're not properly policed. No one outside Kabul seems to adhere to the rights enshrined in the constitution. It's very frustrating for them. The country is lagging way behind where their minds are. They're educated women, of course, and as such they are still a small elite. Some of them had their education within Afghanistan, but most not. They've come back from places like Pakistan and the USA. They're very vulnerable. If you want to live a long life, don't be a female politician or journalist or police-woman in Afghanistan.'

'Poor things,' says the humble parent of the over-achiever, but I find myself listening in spite of myself. I'll never get rich.

'Yep. And even the rights they have won so far, which, when you hear them are considerable enough in words anyway, are likely to be ripped away by the Taliban, given half a chance. The Taliban are saying they won't come to the negotiating table unless the constitution is discarded. They insist on being part of the rewrite, but if you ask me, the constitution as it stands is not too bad. It gives all citizens standing. It stipulates a certain number of women representatives in the Loya Jirga, more than the number of women politicians you'll find in the House of Reps in Australia. The law runs according to moderate Sunni precepts and there's some allow-ance made for the Shi'ite differences. But the Taliban want it all scrapped. My guess is they will refuse to sit down with women to do the business of government.'

'Is there a way around that, do you think?'

'Well, they're going to have to sit down with women or exclude themselves from the peace process if the Americans are involved and there aren't going to be peace negotiations without the Americans. At least they're coming to their senses about their ability to over-run the country. They can't: they haven't the military strength for a start and they certainly haven't a skerrick of support in the north-ern provinces. I mean, up here, they're hated. They'd never govern these people.

'As far as the south's concerned, they don't want civil war – at least, not all-out civil war. They aren't the only militia in the south. There's Al Qaeda, and they're not fans of Al Qaeda. They weren't fans of 9/11.'

'I didn't know that.'

'No. The Taliban – at least the ones who follow Mullah Omar – are not pan-Islamists like Al Qaeda and the Haqqani network. They want their own-style Islamic state in Afghanistan, that's where their focus is. They don't like heroin traffickers and so they're only tolerant of the Haqqani network when it's tactical to be so.'

The custard dessert has arrived. Eli woofs down one plateful and then reaches over my head for a second. 'I wish you didn't bolt your food,' I say and he laughs.

'I'm hungry, Mum.'

'You've always had a weird pattern of eating: stuffing yourself, then starving. I was hoping you might develop regular habits one day.'

'It's a reflection of my life, Mother. I'm an adrenaline junkie. I love to slake a deep thirst.'

'What about your poor stomach?'

'Doesn't seem to cause me any problems.'

'Surely there are things the Taliban can see women doing in civil life?'

'Yes, there are.' He reaches for a third plate of custard. 'They can be female doctors and midwives dealing exclusively with female patients.'

'And you can't be a female doctor unless you're taught by females?'

'You follow. What they hate is coeducation after puberty. Might fan the flames of illicit love, you see…'

'How things have changed for you, son. You're a very different person from the chap with the hookah in the days of Peshawar.'

'Oh God, that makes me cringe. I'm so lucky to have been able to shake it. I'm sorry to have lived in such a haphazard way.' He's scratching his head now and then looking at his fingertips as if he's caught some nits. 'But it's the way of an investigator. I've always been curious, needed to know and to go where it takes me. The trouble is that now I know more than I can put to use. I have to suppress a lot of it.'

'You and Phoebe never talked of a different kind of life?'

'No. Phoebe was, and probably still is, the complete party girl. No one has ever wanted to impress as much as Phoebe. After all, she was a stunner! And I have to say that sometimes, even often, she did impress. Her whole life was one great, dangerous party at which she sparkled. I was allowed to applaud and to be her husband but never her soul mate. Soulless parents, soulless child.'

'Charles Green is a nice man.'

'He had a different mother,' he sighs. 'But yes, you're right. Charles is a brick.'

'Do you keep up with him?'

'I'll see him when I go to Geneva. He's always pleasant. We'll go for a drink somewhere, talk for a few hours and then go our separate ways. It's nice.'

'Do you talk about Phoebe?'

'Not really.' He pulls his hands across his eyes and down his face as if to get rid of his thoughts, then suddenly asks, 'How is my grandma?'

'Oh God. I don't know. I haven't had her on my mind recently. She's back in the home but the nursing home section of it, unfortunately. Do you know, it's the first time in years I haven't had to spend any time at all during the day thinking and worrying about her. I just haven't thought of her at all since about a day after I arrived here. Mick just says she's okay, or that she's settling in to her new accommodation...'

'Has she been in hospital?'

'Oh, I haven't even told you, have I?'

So we talk about the old lady for a minute or two and about Nin and Dan and very briefly about Checkie's case against me but it all seems a very long way away and Eli and I are about to be parted again.

I take his small, shapely hand, 'I love you so, so much,' I say to him, my complaints stuffed somewhere way down in my socks as we reach for the shoes we took off inside the door.

'I love you back.' And off he goes, over the stone-walled yards, waving, to the SUV with the VIP's entourage on board. The door shuts on him and he jolts off in one of the passenger seats, his beloved palm on the windowpane until I can't see it anymore for distance and tears.

'Hoh,' says Meetra at my elbow. 'Come.'

We drove back to Kabul, arriving in time for the evening prayer which Meetra performed in front of me.

I sat at her desk as she made her bows and prostrations towards Mecca. Over and over, she reminded herself that there was but one God and that Muhammad was his messenger.

I'm not sure if she believes or if this is ritual. She is, after all, a proud Muslim: it seems to be a good deal more than custom. At the very least, it's exercise, but Meetra seems to have a deep gladness in her that comes when God acts in her favour. She seems to be a fatalist and to believe in her mission. Maybe her morning singing amounts to chatting with God. I think she has faith; I think her performance of her prayer in front of me was an act of inclusion.

I do not resist Meetra: I accept her completely.

In the absence of God, there was nothing for me to do but watch and think and enter the idea of continuance as a companion in hope.

One day I hope the worms will feed on me and transform my body into good earth that life may feast on me.

My soul? I am myself in the chain of selves. Dan will carry some small part of me out into the future, whether he wants to or not.

There might be a component that will surface again as me-ness in another life. For now, I am who I am and it cannot be otherwise. Perhaps the mind is a continuous, and continuing, invention. Perhaps it has no bounds, but is always growing, emanating away from its source.

22

The journey to Afghanistan was over. We spent the last day hurtling as usual from place to place. At the tail end of a Turkish trade fair we hunted for preserving equipment for Meetra's agricultural projects but we found none. What we did find was a ten-year-old boy picking some women up at the entrance to the exhibition hall in the family car. Meetra strode up and ordered him out, while the women grew hysterical with laughter in the back. He drove them everywhere, they said, he'd never been pulled over, he was a good driver, what were they expected to do? Stay at home and wait till he grew up? Meetra's head was craning for a policeman while little children crawled all over the car's interior. 'Meetra!' I called, laughing myself. 'Meetra, you can't reform everything...'

'But this boy, this boy...'

'Meetra Jan, it doesn't matter.' She'd said it to me often enough and now I said it to her. For once I won. She's a wonderful, forceful creature, Meetra – a Mad Meg out to reform a hellhole. She has done a lot. The evidence of her work and the work of others like her is everywhere. Of a hellhole, they have helped to make a city of hope, a seed in a country's heart.

Abdullah, his silken talisman hanging from the rear-vision mirror, drove us to the airport. Edris and Haroon squashed in beside him in front. They dropped us without ceremony at the women's checkpoint and I was hard put to it then to keep up with Meetra, who, once checked, was through the door before I had time to rezip my flash drives into my backpack. I called, 'Slow down!' but she didn't. She had something on her mind and wasn't listening. We didn't see the boys again. Maybe they were touting for a car park, I'll never know, but obviously there was more to their quick disappearance than that. Perhaps it was that Meetra didn't want to grant Edris the time for his marriage to his very young arranged bride. I know they argued about Edris not taking responsibility for his own choices and not having a more mature outlook about women. It was hard for the boys being so far from home and the customary way of doing things, but Meetra's situation is easily as hard, running an aid organisation from the other side of the world and needing to be able to rely utterly on her staff in Kabul. Imagined feats and exploits have to be matched by real ones. She doesn't say no to the boys but she does say, 'Consider what you are doing.' And she makes it known when she disagrees with their choices.

The long journey home was reflective and much quieter than the journey out. There was space to lie stretched out on the aircraft seats, just sleeping and watching movies and sorting out the images I'd taken. We wandered around the airport in KL and snacked on French pastries in the patisserie; I was glad to wrap my mouth around some real coffee. We straggled into Melbourne in the early hours. Mick was there to meet us and somehow we managed to pack in all the purchases that Meetra had made to sell for her fundraising.

As we drove out Chadstone way to drop Meetra home, I saw that she was trembling all over. I put my hand on her upper arm, tenderly, but she just said, 'Hoh! It doesn't matter.'

'Are you sure?'

'It's nothing.'

But it was something. Not anger, I felt, but exhaustion. She had never paused in all our time away. Apart from visiting bereaved families – of which there were too many – she had visited officials in refugee agencies, food-distribution centres, educational institutions and women's centres. We had met female judges and politicians, female principals of schools and directors of agricultural centres. We'd met women hosting the projects of Meetra's group and women in NGOs. We'd also met men, plenty of them – senators, vendors, teachers, instructors, mechanics and, of course, engineers. How many engineers does it take to run Afghanistan? If you want to impress, stick 'Engineer' in front of your name. Once I stood on Meetra's roof and watched while a man who might have called himself an engineer laid tarred material on a neighbouring roof: he set about burning any obstructing debris out of the gutters with an acetylene torch then set the bolt of material alight with it and kicked the bolt out with his foot until it was all played out. Then he sealed the edges. Meanwhile five possible engineers stood by watching, not raising a finger. It reminded me of the men at the ford when Edris got the car stuck, all contemplation and no action – engineers, the lot of them.

Meetra's resolve is enormous; at every encounter she risks rebuke, but she handles it all with such mastery and such certainty in her manner that she is rarely challenged. She knows she is a person who gets her way and is unused to refusal. These are the qualities needed to rehabilitate a nation after the guts have been torn from it by war.

Meetra's Australian household was asleep as we sorted her banners and carpets and embroideries from mine inside the huge front door – an Afghan door to be sure, not a weakness in the fortifications, but a portal strong enough to keep the enemy out and wide enough to let in family and friends. She had brought home far more than I had and my bags were stuffed with her things. At last there were the Kuchi dress and the carpet and the little knick-knacks I'd brought home for my family at the bottom of my case along with my scant supply of personal things, and we left, but before we did, I took her trembling hand in mine and held it steady so that the warmth of friendship and admiration would

reach her. I hugged her. 'You're very, very brave, Meetra, and tire-
less. I wouldn't be surprised if you were trembling with fear and
emotion now you are home. Be soothed. I appreciate everything
you've done and all the work you will do. You're more stubborn
than a warlord.'

And she is. Meetra is one of the truly brave women of the
world. She could well be targeted and killed doing what she does,
but she will do it, she will press on, believing that there is a right
way to do things. The cow will jump over the moon. It's in her.

When we opened our front door, little feet came pounding down
the hall to meet me and a curly-headed boy flung himself at my
middle. 'Sibella!'

Nin slid out of my studio, where there is a spare bed, and
slipped her loving arm around my neck. A laden lump of humanity, we squeezed our way down the hall to my little sitting room and
fell in a fond heap. Then there was hot chocolate and cake and…
JOY! A big whisky and soda. 'Return to normality,' said Nin, as
she balanced a Kuchi herder girl's very large neck ornament on her
swelling belly.

'Everything going all right there?' I asked.
'All good.'
'Know what it is yet?'
'Yep.'
'Are you telling?'
'Nope, you'll just have to wait to find out.'
'How are Princess and Lightning going, Dan?' But Dan was
asleep, an embroidered Afghan hat pulled down over his eyes.

David had been active while I was away. Once he realised that
Nin was back in Melbourne, he began terrorising her, jumping

on trams she was on, and following her till she had to escape into a women's toilet, where she rang the police and told them she was being stalked.

'He was still standing outside when the police arrived,' she said. 'They rang me inside and asked me to come out and identify him, which I did. Then they arrested him, but he got sick in jail and now he's in hospital. I'm not going to visit him. Even if he is dying, I'm not going to visit him. He lobbed rocks at your house and, I don't know whether you noticed it on your way in, but he's broken your front window. Don't worry, I'll pay for it to be fixed.'

'It's not the money, Nin…'

'I've got a job.'

'What!'

'Well, if you can go to Afghanistan, I can get a job. It's a guest event at NGV Australia. I'm going to organise a big drawing show of the postwar painters – Reg Sorby, Leslie Hallett and…wait for it…Henry Coretti!'

'How?'

'Oh they know me there. I'm not as stupid as I look. They know I'm Henry's granddaughter and I know quite a bit about him. Not everything's in the bloody Siècle Trust. A friend of mine has just received a big promotion to Curator of Drawings and I went in to see her and she took me down to the store and we went through the collection and reckoned there was a really good show in there. So I'll be working on that until the baby's born in November and the hang will be in March.'

'That's marvellous!'

'Yeah. Checkie'll be spitting chips,' and then there was a change of tone. 'Oh…there's a letter for you from Raven and Barratt in that pile. Guess it's about the case. I've been out and finished all the documentation with Lexie. I think we should say we own it jointly and then Checkie will have to sue me as well.'

'But what if she wins the case? It's our bread and butter.'

'You need to paint and teach, Bel, that's your bread and butter.'

'Well, that's right, but I still haven't much faith in my capacity to make money at it. My last show didn't give me much more than what it cost to hang.'

'Enough already.' She sounds just like Allegra. She never used to. She bundles up Dan and carries him off to his loft bed in the studio. We squeeze past the door, beckoning Mick to come and hand Dan up. The bed is flying a pirate flag and has the plastic rib cage from Dan's kit skeleton hanging over the side on a piece of string. 'That's the anchor,' Nin nods, 'and that's some hair from your hairbrush tangled in it: that's the seaweed.' She lies Dan down and a hail of binoculars, toy compasses and maps comes over on top of us.

23

Yes, the trip to Afghanistan is very much over and, with it, the clarity of thought I had away from Stella.

'I'm sorry I can't seem to die,' she says, catching me in my hangover of other emotions. I fear there will be no graceful death, no choosing. All will go on being silly, crabbed and half lost. She will have been the Midnight Knitter, the madwoman who passed long years just knitting anything, driving needles into stitches, turning corners, making heels in God-knows-what-garment; she, whose hands became too crippled to go on; she, who saw the light briefly, long enough anyway to chuck out the garmentry in favour of mowing down the populace of Hawthorn East in a motorised buggy; she who must surely be at the end of the road, surely… Please God, she can't be so unpleasing to your gaze that you'll never take her in.

She looks up at me with those hazel eyes of hers – eyes that have sunk a thousand ships – from the chair where she now spends most of her time. 'You'd better bring a brick in a sock next time you come.'

She shares her new ward with three other very old women – although none of them as old as she is: she is ninety-nine. Wendy, Nin, Daniel and Mick came in with birthday cake and had a party to celebrate while I was away. 'Where's *she?*' she asked. 'Afghanistan,' they said. 'Oh yes, I'll bet. After-man-istan, you mean.'

After the great lengths taken to retrieve some of her hearing, what she hears now is others saying, 'Ner-erse, ner-erse,' and

'What do I do nee-ow?' and a trembling mumble with a silvery refrain that sounds like beads being said over and over again along a strident chord.

Liz, the heroine of the Christmas-cat disaster, is looking after her. 'She is *so* funny! We just adore her in here,' she says.

In the common room, from where Liz and I have wheeled her to the ward, there were blackbirds chirruping at the windows. Had we not been quite so far away we could have seen the children's playground and the parklands where tall white-trunked gum trees play the summer wind gusts like fiddlers in an orchestra farewelling a ship, a kind of Edwardian weatherboard liner, bound for the ultimate destination, trailing red-brick wings.

The old claw points towards me and she strains her head so much turning to look over her shoulder at Liz that a bloodless stripe forms down the bridge of her nose. It's a fine little nose, elegantly shaped, one of her best features, although she wishes it longer because, among Mottes, short noses are synonymous with syphilis.

'She's a research fellow,' she enunciates very carefully out of the blue as if she'd read my wish for more decorum. 'You know, Sir Macfarlane Burnet and all that.'

'Really?' says Liz, smiling at me, her soft, brown eyes deepened by acceptance. She is trying to coax Stella's foot into a new slipper.

'Not really,' I say. 'I'm a painter; it's a long time since I worked at the university and I wasn't a research fellow, I was helping one of the scientists with a hobby of his. He was the Research Fellow: capital R, capital F mind, Liz. Important personage.'

I've liked Liz from the start for her diplomacy. 'Your mother's very proud of you,' she says. 'It's Isobel this and Isobel that. Science *and* art. There must be some clever genes in your family.'

'There are,' says my mother, who normally wouldn't have heard that. 'I'm related to the Edinburgh Gregorys. They were surgeons and mathematicians.'

'You've bucked her up,' says Liz. 'She's been rather down in the dumps since you went away. She's had one or two good spats with your nice gentleman friend but apart from that I think something's gone out of her.'

'She loves a good skite. She loves having something to skite about.'

'The older we get, the less there is of that,' says Liz, 'but she's been winning a few games of Bingo lately. Wendy's been coming in and helping her. She plays by her own rules – when Father O'Brian calls out a number, if she hasn't got it, she puts a milk bottle top on an empty square – if she has got the number, and realises that she has, she leaves it up to whoever's playing with her to put a lid on the right square and somehow or other she gets to call out "Bingo!" all the time.'

'You think I can't hear, don't you?'

'Well, what did we say then, Mum?'

'You're talking about Bingo.'

'Have you had your ears cleaned?'

Liz says, 'Oh yes. We have a lady who comes in with a Jobson Horne and she does everyone's ears.'

'Jobson Horne?'

'Yes, it's a probe in the shape of a loop. It gets in under the mass of wax and lifts it out in one piece. It doesn't seem to worry the old folk much. She just stands up beside them with a light and in she goes. And out…come some awful globs. Sometimes they're black!'

'You mean to say that all this time that Stella's been deaf – I mean years – they could have just fished out the wax with one of these loops?'

'Sure. Unless her ears were infected.'

'Mine wasn't black,' says Stella. 'Mine was golden.'

'Oh, so the lady had the Midas touch, did she?' I ask. 'Or was it just that you had superior wax?'

'It was your bloody Indian audiologist chap who had the Midas touch. How much did those hearing aids cost you?'

'Oh, far too much…'

'And I hate to say it,' whispers Liz, 'but I fished them out of her cup of tea a few days ago.'

'Well, I can *hear!*' goes Stella, crossly.

'That doesn't mean you can chuck your hearing aids into a cup of tea.'

'I didn't. I don't know who did that.'

'Probably the same boy who used to use your phone at Narrowlea on his way home from school.'

She looks up at Liz, her brow in a tangle. 'Are you going to get those slippers on or not?' she says crossly.

Liz laughs. 'That's more like the old Stella. Sister Colleen calls her Our Lady of Mischief.'

'What's so well-behaved about her?' says Stella. 'She says haitch. We were never allowed to say haitch. It was common.'

'Sister Colleen comes in sometimes to sit and talk with her. And you'll have noticed that Sister Colleen got her way with the bishops. We've had air-conditioning put into these wards. It'll be great for the summer. '

'Well, hooray for the good old different.'

'Different?'

'Sister Colleen. I'm sure that's the euphemism that Mother Oldmeadow uses for her.'

'Oh, you're a wag, just like your mother.'

'No. I've just got ears. I have to say on Mum's behalf, though, that I'm glad the plasma telly lobby failed.'

'Conscience,' says Liz. 'At least the old folk here will be cool. It was terrible last summer, just terrible. And this summer it's tipped to be even worse.'

'PUT MY SLIPPERS ON, DAMN IT!'

'Well, Liz is trying to, Mum, but your foot's a funny shape.'

'Huh,' she says, disgusted. That's a 'huh' that expresses a whole swag of sentiments. It's the huh that delivers a knockout blow to good intentions. It's the hardening up of resolve before a tantrum. It's the whole mangled history of stuff about little feet being thought desirable among the Mottes, while big feet on a woman attracted ridicule. It's the huh that scoffs at my generation being convinced in the long run that it's better to have shoes that fit than to have small feet – to her generation it was a case of the smaller the feet, the closer the palanquin of privilege and serving girls whose feet were unimportant.

Her mouth comes shut in an ancient pout and the steam seems just about to start rising from that bashed-cat head of hers. 'You remind me of an old bloke I saw fuming on TV in Afghanistan,' I say.

'Huh!'

I am about to comment that he'd just kicked his daughter in the guts but that might set off the leaping and the bounding of Righteous Indignation. Be patient, I tell myself as I've been telling myself for years. Surely, at my age, I ought to be over having my buttons pressed. She can't still be capable of driving me crazy. All the same, it's as if she's the person who is at the controls – she will not let me be myself, I must be who she 'knows' me to be.

I have to put a stop to this. I am a painter, not a fucking research fellow. Being a painter is what is important to me. I've striven hard to put good shows on gallery walls for years. She remembers the names of the shows that did well and pretends to be able to plumb the depths of individual works and has claimed paintings for me that she's seen hanging here or there that I haven't had anything to do with at all – and wouldn't have wanted anything to do with. I suppose it's just the behaviour of a proud mother and I should be thankful and titter at her mistakes but she hasn't any grasp on art and in her habit of putting it down reveals to me a genealogical history of rock-solid ignorance. I can hear fucking Audra's voice, saying, 'Why don't you paint something people would want to have on their walls, Bel? What's the point of spending months and months and months doing all this stuff if no one wants to buy it?'

But why should I let Audra's opinions oppress me? Audra isn't someone I'd bother to trample in a stampede.

The old claw is pointing at me again and she is saying to Liz with a special note in her voice, 'She dabbles, you know. Like her father. You must have heard of Henry Coretti?'

'Stop breaking my heart!'

'Well, it's true. He was famous for his dabbling.' Then to Liz, 'You must have heard his name?'

'Lots of times,' says Liz, smiling, 'but I have to admit I hadn't heard it before I met you.'

'Coretti, everybody knows the name Coretti. Or they *ought* to.'

'Well, it's *your* name,' says Liz, who can't feel the sharpness of that surname and its existence like a perilous needle of coral in the sea onto which all Stella's psychic coracles founder.

'You know I'm Rh positive,' she says to Liz.

'Well, I'm Rh positive,' says Liz. 'Most people are.'

'What have you been up to? It's a disease of homosexuals. It's terminal. Her father gave it to me.'

'Oh, for God's sake!'

But Liz is splitting her sides, 'Do you mean AIDS, Stella? You haven't got AIDS!'

It's time to take a stroll. I can feel my inadequate guile being sucked in by the mighty tide of doom.

'Are you *going*?' she croaks, suddenly frantic.

'Not yet,' I manage. Although Dadda has been dead for thirty years or more, she still thinks he's capable of spiriting me away. That's why the tide about her is so strong. She is in need of endless reassurance.

I head out of the ward for the common room to see that playful wind again. I need inspiriting.

Dadda, why couldn't you have lasted? Why were you so brief and transient? Why couldn't you be doing what I have to do now so that I could get on with my life?

In the common room, the windows are large and you get the feel of being on a cruise. Outside I can see palm trees, their crowns caught in sunlight, waving their fronds as if it were the Riviera we were cruising along. When I first saw Redeemer, the palm trees and the big tank of reef fish by the window made me think of Matisse, wheelchair-bound in his last years but still scissoring shapely colours from the exhalations of the Mediterranean gods at his shutters.

Would that I were as certain of my talent and as single-minded as Matisse. He wanted to paint pictures that charmed and heartened people and he did just that – his was as true a gift as was ever bestowed – he was the right person and his genius was sufficient unto itself. Whatever the griefs of his private life and his slice of history, he lived his talent right through to the end. How seldom we can say that of somebody.

The closest I can get to Matisse in my baby-boomer middle-class milieu is to look at fair reproductions of his work and mentally paint the interior of Mick's house in his colours – my own house is too encumbered with everybody else's junk to think of painting it without spraining my brain and I have to move the junk into spaces that won't obstruct my view through rooms into other rooms so I don't go mad with claustrophobia. Down at Mick's I've done the imaginary paint job on the house so thoroughly I'm trying to extend it to the outside so that shots of yellow daisies with dark foliage can be framed in aquamarine and grey when you look through the windows in autumn – but autumn is over so quickly and then it's winter and I want to have crepe myrtles making snaky skeletons where once I wanted daisies and then I want tremendously promising green shoots of flowers to come up and bud purple and orange and blessed fresh white and blue. Matisse did it all so fluently and I don't suppose he had to do more than adjust his jalousie for the inspiration right there in front of him.

Ah, Matisse, give me strength. She is ninety-nine, I am sixty-three: I might have thirty-six years ahead of me.

When I walk back into the room, having taken in a good draft of genius at the windows, Stella is muttering curses about cheap footwear.

The new slippers I've brought in still won't fit over the bunch of bunions and hammertoes that masquerade as her foot. Liz has twisted the felt every which way and there's nothing for it now but to widen them with scissors. Her last slippers were smart, expensive and made of purple plush: they were bought by a Motte relative, whose husband, before she killed him off, sold luxury cars, which somehow made the slippers worth boasting about. Unfortunately, they were lost in transit from hostel to nursing home. I suppose it's easy to lose things in a place like this, but when she went into Narrowlea, she was convinced her belongings were being stolen and, for all I know, they were. I asked around, but although other things turned up, like somebody else's nightie or old cardigan, her 'disappeared' articles, generally new, never seemed to resurface. I got so sick of asking about them that eventually I doubted my own memory. One of the losses, sadly, was a little golden ring with two love knots on it. It was given her by Geoffrey Latimer, her lover, who went off to the war and was killed. He loved the name Isobel, and that is how it became my name. Stella always said that Dadda didn't call me Isobel because another man had chosen it, but I don't think the reason was that at all; being Italian he couldn't make his tongue stop at a final L, so called me Sibella, which, after all, is close to Isobel in sound.

There've been one or two mix-ups here at Redeemer but I think there was a thief at Narrowlea. Here, they're a bit more conscientious about what they do. It may be the fact that most of them are Catholic and Catholics are against euthanasia, so you're alive and owning stuff until you're dead. What's more, thieves are accountable in Catholicism, though not as accountable as they are in Islam: no one cuts off their hands. Liz is certainly no thief. She has what they call 'a vocation' for aged care. A calling. God is calling Liz to look after the likes of Stella. The organ through which He calls is the Christian church, Catholic branch. Why, of all possible outcomes, was this the one that landed face up for a pleasant patient woman like Liz?

Jesus and his bloody cross! Why couldn't he have done something else for a living? You think of him being hauled down with the Last Supper still being gobbled up by enteric bacteria in his belly – unless, that is, the Last Supper already lay in a squalid mess somewhere in Gethsemane. You think of the one true cross being prey to the degrading organisms: slugs, snails, slaters, centipedes, millipedes, mites, spiders, worms, fungi and bacteria and you know that wood disintegrates when left to their depredations. Yet, there are all these people and institutions who swear they have a piece of the one true cross intact. You think of Veronica's veil and Christ's shroud and moths and myriad things that feed on cloth and the lengths folk go to to 'prove' that the bit of fragile warp and weft they are in possession of once touched Christ's body and it makes you wonder why people cling so hard to the resurrection of the particular, when resurrection goes on around them all the time: the earth regenerates, things grow, combine with one another and everything born dines on something else, has its day and becomes again the earth, the air, the fire, the water.

How bizarre to think of the expenditure of effort and life in the name of a mangled corpse. Just one. When you think of the endless millions: the good, the bad, young, old, innocent and corrupt: the fresh and decrepit; prey, predator, furred, feathered, shelled or slimy. A weird world indeed in which for two millennia people have been ignoring soil organisms in favour of arguing about whether Heaven is selective when it comes to souls and whether the wine through which they believe they commune with God *is* the blood from that one corpse or just the *symbol* of that blood.

Or is it that the body and the blood are the fruits of the earth and that's what Christ meant by resurrection all along?

'I know what you're thin-king,' sings my mother.

'Do you?'

'You're thinking, "How can I get rid of her?", aren't you?'

'And how can I get rid of you, Mum?'

'There, I said that's what you were thinking!'

'No one can get rid of their mother. You're built in. I've got your rib cage. I've got your knees. I've got the same age spots on my hands as you have. You're unget-riddable of.'

'He, he, he! Heard any good stories lately? I need a good story to cheer me up.'

'David threw a stone at my window and broke it in such a beautiful shape I can't bear to have it mended.'

She screams with laughter. 'He would!'

'Did Nin tell you, Mum? He's angry because he has cancer. He thinks you're going to outlive him.'

'What did you say?'

'I said, if you call a crowd of Irishmen Paddies and a crowd of Welshmen Taffies and a crowd of Englishmen Poms, what do you call a crowd of Australians?'

'I don't know, what?'

'A vacant lot.'

And she laughs so much her top teeth flop down and make her dribble.

'But wait a minute, wait a minute, what did you say about David?' she drools. 'Didn't you say something about David?'

'He has cancer, Mum.'

'Cancer? Poo! Audra's always getting cancer. What makes him think he's got cancer?'

'I don't know, Mum. Perhaps it was the operation on his lung.'

'But you're a research fellow.'

'That doesn't mean I know everything. David used to smoke a lot, that's probably where it came from.'

'Did you say he broke your window?'

'It doesn't matter, you know what David's like. Can't even throw a stone without creating a work of art.'

She thinks that's hilarious and her entire body gives over to laughing. She pauses in between spasms to wipe the tip of her nose with a Kleenex.

Meanwhile, over the other beds in the room, there are signs that Mary is on the watch for the hour of death. Christ has just one corner of a photo shelf to desiccate further upon. There was none of this stuff in Narrowlea, where inmates displayed their football colours and digital clocks – Stella insisted on keeping her clock upside down because it interfered with her television reception when it sat the right way up. And, after all, time was standing on its head. Just like her furniture when it rose up and punched her lights out. It was all that's left of Stella's 'Mottean' inheritance, a conjunction of peculiar items that has accumulated over the generations going back to the Maori Wars to which a Motte Forebear ran away when threatened with life in the church – the Church of England, of course – although the Forebear scarpered from Beyond the Pale in Catholic Ireland. There are letters in the family from his absentee landlord of a father in Leicester.

Dear Son,

We last heard of you on board the X, engaged in the battle of so and so, and since then, no word. We pray that you have made landfall and that this letter will find you safe... and so on, including the death of Dear Mother, at whose bedside the scarperer was missed. He was here, buying up a cattle run and siring enough long-lived children to make me related to half the original British settlers.

The laughing spasms have stopped. 'Do you want to go and play Bingo?' I ask. 'There's a game starting up in the common room shortly.'

'Oh no,' she says. 'I can't be bothered.'

'Are you sure?'

'Bingo, what's bloody Bingo? I didn't win anything last time. I used to win all the chocolate frogs.'

'Yes, you've been hoarding them. Let's polish some of them off, eh?'

'Well…if there's a Caramello Koala I might have a nibble.'

And I rootle around in her jar for a Caramello Koala. 'There,' I say and settle down with a peppermint frog myself.

Liz is off doing the medications and finding a decent pair of scissors for the slipper enlargement and another nurse trundles by. Stella raises her claw as far as she can (not far) and calls out around her mouthful, 'Hey!' The nurse looks around. 'This is my daughter,' and she points at me vigorously, 'Isobel. She's a *research fellow*!'

'Gosh, Mum, that'll keep disaster from the door – a *research fellow*.' And I say to the nurse, 'Fall on your knees at once; prostrate yourself before me and have a chocolate frog.'

The nurse, an Asian girl called Melissa, who also loves her, comes up, waggling her finger at Stella's nose. 'You're so funny, aren't you, Numpa One?' She calls herself Number One because she's in bed 1A, a Distinguished Destiny. It has a dip in the middle so she doesn't fall out at night.

She is living proof that we are nothing but mountains of genetic material that keep on idly coordinating for no reason at all. If in the past we were wont to provide continuity with our ancestors by embellished storytelling, what in the world to come will carry the memory of before into the future now that word of mouth has proven so faulty?

Richard Dawkins thinks it will be 'memes' – replicable pellets of social practice. Presumably these pellets, however organised, will make a coherent, if plastic, whole.

In the beginning was The Word and the word was GCAT. And the book was the endless Guanosine-Cytosine/Adenine-Thymine ladder, twisting itself into this shape and that, living in this or that agglomeration of cells and it matters not where we came from or where we are going – only that we are. We are nothing but a list of instructions to get the job of life over and done with. As David Silver says so often, 'We are what we do.' Amen.

Liz is back with the slipper, refashioned. 'There,' she says, 'That's better.' And she eases in the bundle of bunions and hammertoes.

'Cheap and nasty,' says Stella. 'Where are the other ones?'

Liz winks at me. If my husband sold luxury cars, she'd have worn them even if it had killed her.

'I think they'll be very nice,' says Liz, 'very comfy. And they look smart.'

'H'mph,' she waggles her foot around but can't see it. 'Let me see, let me see!' And testily she shoves at the invalid table over her legs.

Big rearrangements.

'They're lined with sheepskin,' she snaps. 'It's summer!'

I snap back, 'Spring, actually, and your feet hurt you so much you can't wear leather on them. You go into shrieks of agony over your corn whenever I try to put on your sandals.'

'Well, I don't like these, they're hot.'

'So what are we supposed to do, Mum, stand around here praying that God sends down ideal footwear? I traipsed the bloody shops looking for those. They were the only ones I could find that were soft enough on top for your corns.'

And suddenly, I'm out of patience again and out the door.

Yes, I am strolling now, up and down the corridor to cool off. Blessed Mary MacKillop is keeping her eye on me.

Liz comes up to me and pats my arm. 'Never mind,' she says. 'We'll leave them on her until she gets used to them and then, I dare say, we won't be able to get them off her.'

'I don't know how you've got the patience.'

'Oh we love her around here. She's so funny, so naughty. She's a real bright spark but I know it must be hard for you.'

'It's the years, Liz. The years and years and years of her having it her way. She makes me feel like a bit player in my own life.'

'Oh, I find her terrifically interesting. She has such stories. Sometimes they don't quite make sense but she tells them with such passion. I suppose you've heard them all a thousand times.'

'And then some.'

What else is my life imbued with but her tales?

When I return to the bedside: 'You got another chocolate?' she asks, slittering brown stains over her bosom.

'You haven't finished that one yet.'

'Aw. I don't think I want one anyway. What time is it?'

'Late afternoon,' I say.

'Yes, but what *time!*' Her chimerical old anger is going for a joy ride today and it isn't even ANZAC Day. She thumps her chair arm so hard she hurts herself. 'Ow!'

'Serves you right,' I say. 'It's nearly five. I'll have to go soon.'

'You're always going.' Melancholy now – little frowns hitch themselves up briefly all over her brow. Nearly dead, but so alive!

And inimitable.

And funny.

'What are you laughing at?' she goes.

'You.'

'Why?'

'You've got such a funny old head,' and I plant a kiss on the wide white skull under the hair – Allegra inherited that hair, dark, fizzing and thick. Hard to believe that it's still pretty dark at ninety-nine, that it still stands up of its own accord no matter that she's dipped a comb in water every morning for nearly a hundred years to flatten it.

'Bye,' I say, 'I'll be back tomorrow.'

'What?'

'I'll be back tomorrow!'

'Oh.' And her head falls forward, forlorn. 'What a waste of time,' she says – and it is a waste of time, this waiting and obeying the rules until someone calls 'Bingo!'

24

✿✿✿

I generally excuse myself from Mum by saying there's work to be done; then, when I get home, I read my emails and play endless games of cards on the computer. If I were a Catholic, I'd probably be beating my brow about sin – I would have beaten my head off well and truly by now. I'd be a roaring drunk, probably, whereas I'm just a mild drunk as things stand and an obsessive player of patience.

I cheat, of course, because there's nothing like the luxury of being able to reverse wrong decisions – would that I were as obsessive about my art; wrong decisions in painting make it a waste of time finishing. A painter has to ask perpetually how can I instruct the viewer in the way I see? Do I do it with a literal instruction or with an emotional connection – a reflection is no more than a puddle of paint. The humiliation comes when someone else does it so much better or achieves it with so much greater ease than you can yourself.

Science works in a similar way, except that in place of landing the image, there are facts of the universe to bring to light and facts have real contours, not just ones that rely on your imagination. Where the imagination comes into play is in the recognising of the contours – the making known, the greeting – yes! I know what you are. An artist doesn't have the luxury of knowing what it is.

I suppose mine is a singular life. And when I look at my mother, I see that hers, for all its tattiness, is singular, too. I think her life mission was primarily to raise the name of Motte to the level of past glory. Allegra and I fully believed in that glory because it was so vehemently expressed by both our mother and our aunt but the longer I live the more I realise that Stella and Aunt Nina were repeating stories concocted by past believers who were venturing into a world that no longer believed. Now the stories can no longer be established as true or false; they have taken on the trappings of Chinese whispers. My mother tells the tale of her family as if it were the flowering of poems by Wordsworth and novels by Walter Scott. She has sown her fragments along with isolated quotes from famous men into the biopatch, where they will prosper only by dint of chance resurrecting them in a future time.

The early path-finding lessons of my life have led me down a hotchpotch way, although it's no more crazily paved than the paths I notice other people taking. I find myself at a place where I teeter in three directions at least – there's the silly version of myself that I have to concoct for Stella's benefit, then the pathetic version of Isobel that has been constructed by David and Checkie to wipe me out of their lives and, underneath these struggles, the feelings of authenticity that won't be denied but still aren't adequately realised, on the cusp of elderly life, to provide the will to be unassailably me.

While Mahni was having her operation after we came home from Afghanistan, I was able to help Meetra with Sultana, and Meetra, in turn, came to visit Stella. While Sultana imagined that I was a nurse, Stella, feebler by the minute, thought Meetra must be a Very Important Personage. After all, my professional contacts were only ever Very Important and reflected glory on the fabulous Mottes. Meetra, Mahni and I had a great laugh about this pair of ancient mothers. 'We are who we are,' said Meetra. 'It can't be helped that we aren't the ones like they think.'

It is nearly the end of summer and Nin is due. She has been working hard on the exhibition she is organising for March and so we have seen a lot of Daniel. David has not been harassing us because he has been very ill and now he is gravely ill. Jeremy of the bookshop came to see me yesterday to say that if we wanted to see him it would have to be soon. Jeremy came out of concern for me. He was not under orders. He sat with me in my studio and put it to me that there were ends that needed tidying up. David hadn't behaved very well during his illness. He'd turned on Checkie as if the illness had been her fault and she wasn't going to visit him again, nor was her home available for him to return to for his final days.

'But it's all being taken care of, Isobel, don't worry. He'll die in hospital before they can get him into a hospice.'

'What about the funeral and so forth?'

'All under control. You needn't worry about them. I've been talking to him. Sometimes he's bitter and twisted and in a lot of pain. I don't admire the way he carries on but there are things that should be done.'

'Are you talking about the pictures?'

'No. Not the pictures. Personal things. Personal things of yours and personal things of his. You should see him.'

'Are you angry with me for the way I behaved at the launch of Bronwyn's book?'

'No. Of course not. Elspeth's a sniper, snipers get hit – touché. He's a very odd man, David. Very talented, but he lives…kind of like the skeleton of a leaf – enduring, but fragile.'

'I never said anything about his talent.'

'I know you didn't. Of all the people who've known David, you might have been the one who best appreciated what he was capable of. There'll be a big show of his work at Siècle after he's gone. He's left his estate to the Trust. That won't surprise you. In my opinion, it's a valuable bequest.'

'Did he make it of his own accord?'

'Yes. I helped him to do it properly.'

'It wasn't because Checkie leaned on him?'

'No.'

'She wouldn't happen to have changed her mind about suing for those pictures, would she?'

'No. She hasn't changed her mind.'

'I wish she'd leave us alone.'

'I'm sure you do.'

He patted my shoulder and got up to leave.

'It's not as if he's leaving the world without heirs, one way and another. Nin's expecting another baby.'

'Yes. I know that. Go and see him, Isobel.' And he left and I thought of Eli and his words about letting what you know mature in the vat alongside the other things you know before you act. It's no use racing off the moment you are bid. I thought if David dies before I get to him, so be it – in the meantime...

David used to ask us, 'What do you think I'm thinking?' almost as if he didn't know his own thoughts, but maybe he meant that no one else could read his mind – that he was the only one privy to his thoughts. It's a strange attitude. Of course, we are the final arbiters of our own thoughts but that doesn't mean we can't deceive ourselves – somehow, David does not believe he can deceive himself. He believes his own estimation of himself is the only valid one. All I can say to that is that I'm the person who best knows what it's like to be me but I'd never say I was incapable of self-deception. David thinks that you cannot deceive yourself if no one can read you because the deception is in their eyes and not in yours. I think I make mistakes and that it's awfully hard to admit it. I have encountered very few people who are capable of dismantling a mistake. A simple error is easily brushed aside but most people find difficulty even with forgetting to put the garbage out. If more than one person lives in a house where the garbage hasn't been put out, the guilt is usually spread by way of a diverting excuse made so that the blame is shared.

We can't anticipate the future, so we're bound to make mistakes – what's to blame for them? Maybe no more than the condition of living through time.

Interesting word, mistake: miss plus take – a failure to understand or an inappropriate reaction – yet mistakes are the engine of change. Mutation is nothing more than the coming to light of a mistake.

David sees his actions as part of a great world of guilt and blame – anyone can live in that world, anyone can magnify the trivial to make it fit among the gross crimes of mankind. Just about all of us do it these days, that is, just about all of us who live in middle-class residences in the heart of the democratic dream. The walls we purchase on the never-ending mortgage serve to hide yesterday from today and to reduce the promise of tomorrow to a fashionable colour chart, over which there are bound to be wrangles when the time comes for decorating. The idea of more choice meaning more freedom is a wondrous illusion that leads us further and further away from considering life's ledger.

As for that stone – that sang – that David hurled at my window, whatever it was that motivated his elbow, only David could make such a gorgeous shape with his missile. It is a Miro bird with a heavy round head that tilts down and forward like a toy. There's a little beak, quaint in itself, accidental, and the shapes are brown, black and vivid yellow, unified by a subliminal haze of turquoise, reminding me of Matisse. I am holding this vision in my head and I want to land it but I don't know how. I just have to store it along with the other images I've never managed to land – or I've avoided landing by doing the shopping or the minding or the cooking or the laundry or going to Afghanistan instead. You can't believe such a person as David is possible. He is so dismally unpredictable that when goodness and intelligence shine out of him, even accidentally, it's like divine revelation.

It's as if his outward displays of misogyny are in direct proportion to his inner capacity to love what he professes to hate. He was incapable of bringing up a child, but it was too dangerous for me to sue him for custody after Allegra died so that the situation would have legal standing. I did not sue, but, by a default that was predictable, Nin came to me. I am Nin's mother in deed, if not in fact. It would have been so much simpler all around if he'd acquiesced to custody and agreed to whatever level of support he was capable of giving. Instead we've been victims of his capriciousness.

I've been seeing the psychiatrist now for donkey's years, having depression kept at bay, being told that David is the cause and that I should get him out of my life as thoroughly as I can. But I have been saying, right at the start, that I suffer from legitimate recurrent depression because I'm thin-skinned. I feel things more than other people do. All I can do is live with it – by now it's getting on for thirty years of psychiatry and I think the psychiatrist has matured enough to agree with me. Dadda's leaving, followed by Allegra's death, cast me into the pit where I'd seen my mother raging against her grief, bringing herself, her mind and her dependants down with her. I'm not much of a rager by nature; I need to paint my way out of the pit of rage that is not mine, it's my language. Meanwhile, I have listened to indignant advice from the psychiatrist that suggested the law actually acted as a preventative to the people like David. How can the law prevent a person? It can only censure acts and therefore it can only ever have limited effect as a corrective. There has to be susceptibility to correction. David exists and to provoke him is to promote a metastasising misery while, on the other hand, handling him carefully can bring rewards you never knew existed. But who has the luxury of making a life work out of David? He can only be borne through non-engagement or in small doses with long rests in between.

As for David's talent, the psychiatrist seems to think that an artistic *idée fixe* such as David's is an ineradicable neurosis. I haven't had the words to tell him convincingly that the hypothesis with which the artist is stuck is the lifelong nub against which talent writhes, a cat possessed. You have to stick with the nub despite fashion and fortune – or never produce a body of work. Too bad if your idea is bad or infantile, or proves to be a cul de sac or something that happens before its time. Art is a never-ending fascination with perception. It's facile to say all people are artists; artists are those who embrace the nub and never give it up.

I understand why people are surprised when they meet artists, expecting to adore them only to find they don't like them at all. No one can be a rebel against the status quo and be in all ways lovable.

In the public mind, artists are famous faces at a distance – surely they must live exciting, liberated lives? Well, some have the strength, energy, wealth and momentum to carry all before them till they drop. But such people never have time to be self-aware. They don't look in mirrors and those who don't die young have to race against the death of their idea. Exciting, liberated life? No – interesting and sometimes liberating, but not a middle-class life of choice, not comfort laid on, not 'niceness'. Sometimes David catches himself in a mirror. He sees helplessness and self-hate – not because he lacks talent, but because he feels unworthy of the talent he has.

I'm sitting by his bedside. He's small and compact, nicely shaped with skin like new caramel in spite of all the tubes keeping him alive. He's well known in the art world, but not outside it: nevertheless, he's so distinctive that people assume they've seen him before. People will say to me, 'Oh, you know him! He's so interesting! He's so nice! I've always loved David!'

They like the idea of David – a person who makes original, exquisite objects. They think he is at home in himself, that it's peace and beauty that stimulate his output. But it isn't. It's despair. And from despair the most delicate beauty flowers. He does so much so doggedly because every time he looks up he reads his own failure in the world. He is tormented and elegant, graceful art is his heaven, the place where there is harmony, joy, innocence and love. He wasn't made to live forever and he reads that as 'doesn't deserve to live forever'. If you ask him 'who does?' he'll cut you off with rage. You're expected to know that he should live forever: there's something about him that's special and sacred – he ought to be given the chance to be with it and stay with it.

His voice that has always had a velvety timbre, even when he abuses its pleasantness in anger, has become feeble now. He has said hello. His eyes are very dark blue and his lashes are long. I can't deny that, even at death's door, he's beautiful. His head moves on the pillow so he can see me and a smile slips up one cheek. How dare it be so precious?

How dare it remind me of the poems he used to read us to foster our feeling for words? Tendril, neck curl, pickerel smile?

But he will surely break it – and he does – 'How old is your mother now?' he asks.

'Ninety-nine,' I answer. Such a question to ask at the end of his life!

'That's old. That's very old,' he says as if Stella's life were neither deserved nor undeserved, nor to be compared to his sixty-two years.

'Did I ever tell you that you have ugly arms?'

Why that? Why now? 'Yes, David, you've told me that.'

'Why do you think I told you?'

'I can't read your mind.'

'It was *tenderness,* Isobel, *tenderness.*' He has strained forward, as if it is the most earnest thing he has ever said...

'But it was so very odd, David...I had the feeling it was tenderness but it was such an odd way of expressing it – tenderness in a hurtful statement.'

'Ugly is beautiful. Ugly is unique. No two ugly things are the same.'

'That's a fine thought, David. But why are you so bitter? Why do you act so appallingly towards me? I've done my best for you, my level best...' and I feel the tears rising.

'*Listen.* I want you to *listen* to me.'

'I'm listening.'

He runs the back of his fine hand down my ugly arm in the most tender of gestures, just as he did on the day he married Allegra. 'Nin...' He starts coughing. Everything starts to crack up with pain, to derail. Water doesn't help. Soon he is screaming and a nurse comes. It's a male nurse. He quietens him down. 'There, there,' he says. 'There, there.'

'*No. No. No. No, don't give me morphine yet. Isobel?*' the voice squeezes past the iron grip the illness has on his throat.

'Yes.' It is terrible to see so much pain, but my breath keeps going in and out.

'*Nin is not my daughter.*'

'Oh for God's sake, David! How could you? How dare you say that?'

'*No. No. You don't understand. Isobel. Nin is Barrie Bull's daughter.*'

'What!' Barrie Bull was the painter whom David belted up in the fight that wrecked my show.

'*You don't understand. I was cruel to Allegra. She went off with Barrie Bull and got even with me.*' He is spluttering and in agony.

Once again at his expense, I feel the withdrawal of my blood cells from my capillaries. 'You melodramatic bastard!'

'*She did, Isobel. I was cruel and she hurt me. I suspected – and when Barrie Bull mocked me, I hit him. Nin isn't mine. I didn't realise. I didn't want to realise.*'

'I don't believe you. You're making it up. You're saying that to spook me. You wrecked my show out of straight-out jealousy. You've never owned the pain and harm you caused.'

'*Oh, I've owned it. I've owned it.*' And he sobs, deep, body shuddering sobs. '*Nin isn't mine. I wish she was mine. I wish that Nin was mine.*'

'Oh David!'

'*I can't go on,*' he wheezes.

'No, you can't go on.'

'*My muvva came to see me,*' he says. '*She thinks that Nin is mine. Please don't tell her. Please.*' David has always had a childish speech impediment, his mind has never found its way around the words 'mother' and 'father'.

'You ruined me,' I say. 'You ruined my show.'
'Please don't tell my muvva, Isobel.'

I sat with him an hour or so longer, too emotionally played out to move. He hardly spoke again. Sometimes I stood up and looked out the hospital window. I saw the old street where Mad Meg was and the old house still is, though not visible from where I was standing. Further up the hill were Miles Turner's Figments, a dark, plain front and right at the top, the building that housed Siècle, its roof a splash of red in the afternoon light. I thought back to the time when David flooded us with his excited and clever ideas on art and introduced us to painters we hadn't heard of and to ways of looking we hadn't known. Part of me wanted to thank him for those days and the gifts he gave before the first manifestations of his violence but the violence got in the way.

How could he pretend that Nin was not his child? Or if she were not, how could he have pretended all her life?

I went back to the bed and said above his body, *'Are* you telling the truth?' and from the centre of the place where he was lying, he said, 'Yes.' And there was no apology forthcoming, even on the brink of death. If there were to be an apology, it would have to come from there; I was not going to coax it: without an apology I could not forgive. If he was too small, then he was way too small.

It is hard to be at a deathbed and to find that there is no graceful exit. There was no way away from that last impression, a breakfast tray pushed to one side with nothing eaten, the smell of illness, then of warm piss when he wet himself and let out a cry. The nurse came in to clean him up. I had to go. I could not stay.

Out on the street again, it was still and hot and Sunday. Some big event was on in town and the streets were deserted. I waited a long time for the tram with my eyes closed, listening to the sound of the occasional indifferent passing car. Eventually the ringing of tram wheels, the sigh of the opening doors at the stop, the sound of my shoes on the steps as I climbed inside, and the emptiness within.

Later, when Mick had roused me with food and coffee, I found the strength to call Jeremy and he asked me to come into the bookshop for a talk. We sat in his office. He held my clammy little fist in his dry, warm hand.

'Is it true that he isn't Nin's father?'

'Yes. And when Nin had him arrested, he just let it all hang out.'

'In front of Nin?'

'Yes.'

'How can I take this?'

'As a fact of life, Bel. Nin knows. She is blood group B, David and Allegra were both A.'

'Why don't people tell the truth?'

We sit in silence, his enveloping hand a comfort. At last it moves gently away, my eyes come open and he sits back in his chair. 'Nin has taken it well,' he says.

I ask, 'You don't mean flippantly? Ninny has a tendency to flip…'

'No. She has spirit and courage. You brought her up. She's resilient. And she has Wendy and Wendy is resilient. Now you must be resilient.'

'He is a wound, that man.'

'But he's not your wound. You mustn't wear him.'

'He's taken so much from my life.'

'If it's any consolation to you, Isobel, you were the only person who ever looked deeply into David and found what was there.'

'What do you mean? I never picked his work up, showed it, promoted it, held it up for people to see.'

'None of that matters to David. What you did was coax it out. You pulled on a thread and he felt it and spent the rest of his life following that thread that you located. You can take hold of your life, now, your thread.'

'Funny you should use that metaphor. A thread…' It is true that his art started to develop when we painted alongside each other, he at Figments, me at Mad Meg. We thought about work then, what it was to be painters, what art was. 'Oh, I have hold of my thread. Yes, I still have hold of it, just that my thread is made up of so many different strands, I'm not always sure I can hold it without its unravelling. David told me that his mother came to visit him. Did you meet her?'

'His mother?'

'Yes. He has a mother somewhere. I've never met her. She's the sister of Miles and Bart Turner.'

'Odd. Miles Turner told me that David's mother died a long time ago. She lived in Terrigal or somewhere and had two or three other kids. I think she died while you were living out of Melbourne…'

'But he said, "Don't tell my mother."'

'Could he have meant "your mother"?'

'Hardly. He and she hated each other. But it's funny, he asked me how old she was now. Isn't that weird? What a thing to ask on your deathbed – hello, Isobel, how old's your mother now?'

We've resorted to the whisky bottle.

'And how old is she now?' asks Jeremy.

'Ninety-nine. What the fuck?'

'Well, here's to Stella!' And we drink a toast to her.

'Their birthdays are within days of each other. She's a Taurus and he's a Gemini.'

'Well, here's to Mad May,' he says.

'When's yours?'

'Christmas Day,' says Jeremy.

'Well, here's to the Christ Child as well. Have you known or suspected for a long time that Nin wasn't David's?'

'Quite a while.'

'Did anyone else suspect?'

'The only person I know who did was Barrie Bull.'

'Really? I thought I could see characteristics of David in her. Her beautiful hands and feet. Her thick hair.'

'Allegra had those. Your hair's thick and straight, like Nin's. That comes from your side. David's neat.'

'God, Ninny's not!'

'No. And there's a stiffness to David, you know. He strides, he jerks, even when he's being eloquent, there's a staccato element to it, a kind of prissiness. Nin isn't prissy. Not at all. But she is limber. She can turn a somersault. Her thumbs turn back, yours don't. David's don't.'

'Gosh. No. When you think of it…'

'Barrie Bull's do. And he's an athlete. Used to do gymnastics.'

'And would he want to know about his daughter?'

'He's never suggested it to me. He already had two daughters by the time Nin was born.'

'Oh Christ! It's sounding like our family story all over again. Does Checkie know?'

'No. To my knowledge only Barrie, Nin and I are in on it. But Barrie hasn't shown any paternal interest in Nin. David has. You can't reject David as Nin's father, except genetically. For all intents and purposes, he's as much Nin's father as Wendy is Daniel's mother.'

'I suppose; although Wendy's a caring and supportive parent.'

'David cares. He's just completely inept.'

'I guess that's right. I'm going to have to come around to all these new concepts of parenting that are abounding. I have a friend who calls them "modern arrangements". And so they are.'

There's half a bottle left and half an hour to go before Mick comes to pick me up.

'So many genes in the world,' I say, 'that we're all pretty closely related.'

'Yes,' says Jeremy. 'Like you and David. If you ask me, you're David's mother, the one he didn't want you to tell. You've divided

yourself in half for David and now he's expecting you to keep something from yourself. Can't be done, Isobel, can't be done. You'd
better tell his mother what you know.'

'Crikey. That's the most modern arrangement I've heard in
all my life. Why do you think David never felt moved to apologise
to me?'

'I don't think he allows himself to feel guilty for the way he's
treated you. He'd be overwhelmed if he did. He can't repay you
and can't restore your work or your reputation.'

'Then it doesn't matter that I told Bronwyn about the brawl
at Mad Meg. Why did you say at the book launch that I shouldn't
have brought it up?'

'David was using me as his confessor, Bel. I was thinking of
it from his point of view. He was terrifically hurt and angry about
Allegra's affair when he picked the fight.'

'It was wanton and wrong.'

'Yes.'

'I didn't deserve it.'

'No. I know you didn't and I'll never forget what you said to
me that night. "I don't want to be known as a feminist test case.
I want to be known for what I do. That's not too much to ask for
a lifetime of trying." I might have jested about you going broke
because you didn't keep your books properly but I understand the
rightness of the wish to be known for what you do. Keep doing it,
Bel.' And he smiles a smile that's been carrying good cargo between
us for forty years.

25

Such news isn't taken in in a moment. I hadn't fully absorbed it by the time David died four days later. I might never take it in completely – that from sheer, desperate desire to belong, he could keep this information from us. I felt deep pity for him, so deep that it overrode my own despair at having been used.

Used is one way of looking at it, proven is another. For I have also been proven.

The funeral was an odd affair, organised by Checkie before she and David fell out. Apparently he wanted Catholic rites because his mother was Catholic but in the event it was done in the High Anglican manner with a rather beautiful sung introit. She did turn up – indeed, she played chief mourner. It was a chance for her to resurrect the black onyx cross that she had worn after our father died. Her allies were all there, including Elspeth Roach. Jeremy was good enough to give the eulogy. He spoke of the Turner uncles, Bart and Miles, and said that nobody would pretend that David was an easy person to get along with. He was an artist of original-ity and his contribution would be celebrated at Siècle where he had worked for many years with his one-time sister-in-law, Cecilia Laurington. He left a daughter, Nin, and a mother to whom he'd recently been speaking – I let myself smile at that.

Nin and I came late, while the singing was on. We sat at the back. Checkie sat in the family pew. She held her head high and pretended not to see us. She is older than I am but has no wrinkles on her face. 'Never goes out in the sun,' Nin whispered. 'Lives all

her life in the dark.' We stayed in the church for a while afterwards, then we went to the altar and lit candles.

In spite of the pomp, he was cremated and stuck in a wall at
Fawkner. 'Cheap,' said Nin.

A few days later, Nin and Wendy welcomed a daughter into the
world. She was called after her grandmothers with her great
aunt stuck in the middle. Gorgon's name is Georgia and Georgia
Isobel Allegra took the surname Coretti, as Nin had always done.
Thinking back on it, Allegra chose Coretti, saying that a daughter
should take her mother's name. It was a feminist statement.

It is January. My mother has gobbled her last Christmas dinner
and sung her last carol. She is being handfed and refuses anything that isn't ice-cream or chocolate or some other kind of treat.
She's failing.

Liz has arranged for us to go into a pleasant room that was
about to be renovated when Stella stopped taking food. 'You can
stay over with her here. I think it would be best. In my experience, people have been brought back with drips from this point but
really all that does is put a great pocket of saline under their skins,
makes them uncomfortable and gives them bruises. We do it when
relatives are coming from far away but in Stella's case...'

'Well, we want her to be comfortable. No point in suffering
now.'

She isn't speaking anymore. The room is big and light and
has its own bathroom. There is a little garden outside the window.
The last word she said as she swung by my head on the patient
lifter was 'Sibella'. Perhaps she recognises who I really am at last.
She has never called me Sibella. Never. It was Dadda's name, his
special address for me.

There is an old priest who lives alongside the hospital in an
independent residence. Liz has called him in to give the Last Rites.
He is a nice old fellow with white hair and a pleasant manner.

He puts the stole around his neck and removes the holy oil from his bag.

'In the name of the Father, the Son and the Holy Ghost,' he says and makes the sign of the cross on her forehead. 'Through this Holy Oil and through the great goodness of His mercy, may God pardon thee whatsoever sins thou has committed....'

'Ththththt...thrup!'

She has blown a raspberry.

'Oh Lord! I'm so embarrassed, father. I'm sorry but I'm going to have to run for an Anglican.' But the poor old father is already out the door with his pyx back in his bag and his stole folded. Liz comes in and holds me by the shoulders. We look over to where she lies, her eyes wide awake, staring at the ceiling, fuming, the Anglican breath still in her.

I pause on the steps before the church, hoping that the Anglican is in. I can see an office through the glass. The sunlight is warm, not to say blazing hot, on my back. I am struggling for wording. 'I wonder if you could help me...' yes, that seems the right way to begin and soon I am in the office and the next moment standing before the vicar, a tall, unrumpled, grey-suited, dog-collared, bald chap, saying, 'Um. I wonder if you could help me? My mother is dying. She's an Anglican but she's in a Catholic home nearby and this was the nearest church. She has just refused the Last Rites from the priest there and I was wondering if you would come...'

'Is she a practising Anglican?
'Well...'
'I mean, does she go to church?'

'She's ninety-nine and not quite up to that, I'm afraid.'

'Was she a regular attender?'

'I wouldn't say regular but she did go sometimes with her cousin.'

'And what was her parish?'

'Well she didn't go in her own parish. She went in her cousin's.'

'And where was that?'

'East Melbourne.'

'High or Low?'

'I don't especially know. But she was christened in Scunthorpe. Her uncle was the bishop there, actually.'

'I mean Catholic or Evangelical.'

Not liking the connotations of Evangelical, I say, 'Well, we always used to say, "I believe in the holy Catholic church, the communion of saints, the forgiveness of sins, the resurrection of the body and the life everlasting, Amen," so I suppose Catholic.'

'No. I don't think you follow. There are two Anglican churches in East Melbourne. One follows the Catholic procedure.'

'Really? I thought Catholic meant inclusive and Evangelical meant...well, bible bashing.'

He laughs, almost. 'Catholic means observing the original rites of the church.'

'Does it? I'm sorry, I'm out of my depth.'

'We don't give Last Rites.'

'What! What do you mean?'

'The Anglican Church doesn't administer Last Rites.'

'What do you do, then?'

'Oh, don't misunderstand me. We call it by another name. Extreme Unction.'

I feel I am going to lose my temper at any moment. 'Look,' I say, 'I don't really mind what you call it but my mother is at death's door and she wants the Anglican rite, whatever it's called, to see her out of the world. I would be devastated if she could not go with the rite she so desires. She no longer speaks and yet she has managed to make it quite clear it is you she wants, not the priest who is at the home. If I go and get her cousin to explain the nature of her faith to you, perhaps that will clear things up.'

'Well, I need to be satisfied that she is a true Anglican.'

Jesus Christ, he is as autistic as my dentist! 'I see. Well, I have a postcard in my possession that was given to her by the Bishop of Scunthorpe when she was confirmed.'

'Oh. Does it affirm that she was confirmed?'

'It says, "To Bunny with love from The Bish". I'll go and get her cousin. Wait here.'

'I have every intention of doing so. I'll be here until six p.m.'

It's about midday, I suppose, sun at its hottest as I trundle past the Mercedes Benz showroom around the corner from Audra's. I turn left, then left again and park outside Audra's house at the back of the Mercedes dealer. Audra's house has a high wall around it, not like something out of Afghanistan, but high because the house has been made much of. She has broken it into her own home and a flat at the back that brings in rent. Her garden is cut off from the flat's. 'It's for privacy,' she's always said, with a short 'i' in privacy – upon which, Stella has always retorted 'pr-eye-vacy, my mother always said pr-eye-vacy.' For a while there, there were lavatory-toilet wars, Audra declaring that she must be right because they said 'lavatory' in England – and she'd *been;* but Stella stuck with *We have a mulberry tree, We have a persimmon tree, but we do not have a laver tree,* no matter what the English said – the English, after all, had outlawed the use of Scottish surnames and she was a descendent of Rob Roy's, as were all true relations of hers. Then there'd follow the tale of 'Dig 'er wide and dig 'er deep' and the making of the toilets at the family property with a six-foot drop, a toad at the bottom and three different sizes of seat: gentlemen, ladies and children.

Why am I doing this?

So an old heathen, who never so much as trod on a treadmill at a gym, let alone visited a single psychiatrist, can live out her fantasy of high birth and God having his eye on her to her very last day? Here I am, knocking on blasted Audra's door in need of help!

And I'll swear she's been watching and waiting for me behind that front door for weeks. Whoosh! goes the door. 'Come in, come in!' *Come into my parlour, said the spider to the fly.* And here I am, sitting up on her genuine Octaloctapus sofa, 1836, drinking lapsang souchong out of Impelimpetus china, stirred by a Frippatippenny solid silver spoon from Sklutch and Brothers, asking for a favour and thinking, Fuck! Daniel has left his 'let's-recycle-this' innards of a Ben 10 Omnitronix-cum excavation of Pharaoh's tomb with budgie grit for sand on the front seat of my car and it has leaked and I've got to get Audra in there and up to the demon vicar and then get both of them over to the ancient heathen before God…but God will wait. Fuck it! God will wait.

'So, may I ask you to take over this bit Audra?'

'You certainly may.' And she has clapped her rhinoceros-hide handbag to her forearm and, like the chatelaine that she is, is going briskly from door to door, locking up with keys that dangle from a ring that would do justice to a bull's nostrils. Even the tantalus she locks – that is to say, she locks the little antique decanter holder where masters and mistresses of the great house of Motte would lock away the liquor from the servants and she says, 'You can't be too careful, can you?' while I race out ahead of her to put Daniel's construction in the boot, saying, 'No,' a word I ought to have learned to use a great deal earlier than this and in answer to some very different questions.

As Audra rides beside me in the car, there's something I notice – like Stella, Audra has no neck. But unlike Stella, she has obedient hair. She *Is-she-very-ill-dear*s all the way and I refrain from saying *Isn't that obvious* and decline to mumble.

'Yes.'

I talk to her as if she were human.

Audra and the vicar are one. I might have known. Away we bowl now in the vicar's spick-and-span black Holden Commodore to the unrenovated but comfortable pink room at Redeemer. Once there, I park them with Stella, pretend to have a deep turn of grief and to be unable to look on and I take to prowling the corridors, again. Under Blessed Mary MacKillop's gaze I go, past the chapel where Mother F. Oldmeadow is on her knees breaking her own appeal for group entreaty by dropping a private one at the feet of the Saviour. So you lost out to sanity over the air-conditioning, and are you now asking what you did wrong, Mother F.? I walk into the common room with its Matissean window gods.

I know those gods quite well, having strayed as a schoolgirl deeper into Catullus than was permitted, trying to find out what his lascivious allusions meant and finding, to my excitement, Cybele, the Earth Mother. She preceded Zeus in the pantheon. Cybele had history years before the Romans got hold of her. In some cultures, she was androgynous until the other gods castrated her – I can't remember why, perhaps they were envious that here was a woman who could inseminate herself; perhaps they discovered early on that such practice leads to inbreeding and monstrous offspring. Anyway, with her male parts, these envious, super-rational or just plain cruel gods grew an almond tree. A ripe almond fell off and struck the river nymph, Nana, in the breast and she fell pregnant with a boy, Attis. Strange way to fall pregnant but there you are: technically, Attis was the child of Cybele mothered by Nana, but when he grew up, he returned to Cybele as her lover. He was a flirt; he got about a bit, notwithstanding that Cybele was a bitter, vengeful woman after having had her bloke's bits cut off. She drove poor Attis out of his mind with guilt-inducing hectoring – I've been guilty of such behaviour myself a number of times but my victims did not then castrate themselves in a frenzy as Attis did and die from their wounds. Nor did I resurrect them, as Cybele did Attis, in the form of a woman, with all a woman's ferocious longings. (Although I wanted to – I wanted them all to suffer as I had suffered: I thought it would be instructive. I thought they would learn from it. I didn't know that bitterness and vengefulness, when paired, have bitter and vengeful offspring because they can't have anything else.)

Some say Cybele morphed into the Mother of Christ, whose name, Mary, means 'the bitter sea' – there's vengeance in waves and salt spoils water for slaking your thirst. Of course, some say that's nonsense: Mary is so named because she came from the Dead Sea, whereas Cybele was from the mountains, but I say Mary is Cybele brought down to sea level and civilised by Navigation and Trade and all their heirs. It's my guess that civilisation couldn't have arrived at the great middle class we know today without a Mary straitjacketing libidinous behaviour.

Mary will find you a lot less troublesome if you shop for a decent house in a respectable neighbourhood and stock the house with name-brand white goods than if you let your mind wander. If you just think of the buy-and-display cycle (behind which sits Womanhood holding the stakes), you'll have a single-minded, coherent world and everything else will take care of itself. Right down to the pictures on your walls. Which almost certainly won't be mine.

I wish that David had broken Redeemer's window in the beautiful way he broke mine. Then I could throw myself out – right through a charming, bird-shaped hole, fly up high in the blue and be a tour de force with a brush that went for miles.

When Audra asked if she could join our vigil over Stella, I did not say no. And I asked the vicar to oversee the proceedings at the funeral home when the day came, even though he had difficulty accepting that Nin and Wendy were the parents of Daniel and Georgia. 'Two women cannot parent a child,' he said.

'I know that.'

I didn't say 'Your Grace', although I was tempted to.

'Not in the biological sense. Nevertheless, they both parent the children. They live together in the same house with the children and sleep in the same bed. If that is distasteful to you, please don't undertake to conduct the funeral. If you can accept that Nin and Wendy co-parent Daniel and Georgia and that Daniel and Georgia are Stella's great-grandchildren, then please conduct the funeral as the person who delivered Extreme Unction. It will be a simple funeral and I ask you, please, to say the words with which my mother has been familiar all her life as an act of respect to her.'

Thank God I'd organised the occasion long ago as part of the business of moving Stella into Narrowlea. Audra began to nag me to have it at what she called 'our church'. I was, at last, able to say the word, 'No'. I was able to say, 'It's all arranged.' And when I got the hangdog look and the whine, Meetra's visage leapt into my mind and I said, 'It doesn't matter.'

We took it in turns to sleep beside the bed. During the days we listened to the tennis in the roasting sunroom of the nursing home to which the blessing of air-conditioning was not extended. A mad old former priest called Father Michael kept whizzing into the dying room in his wheelchair to see what was going on and we had to hunt him out. Relatives traipsed in and relatives traipsed out. Stella did not stir. We moistened her mouth with water and administered teaspoonsful of cold ginger ale. A week passed and fires broke out near Mick's country house. He and I sat watching the telly, horrified in the sunroom. 'Go,' I said to him. 'You have to go and bring back what you need to.'

So he went. The spotted pardalotes, the cockies and blue wrens were burning. The country was cracking open. Trees split open of their own accord before the tempest reached them.

Stella passed quietly in the night. She was still warm to the touch when I found her, her little nose high and beautiful, rose in her cheeks, a smile on her face. 'Numpa One!' wept the little Asian nurse. 'Oh, goodbye Numpa One.'

Mick came back. The fires had stopped just short of the town.

On the seventh of February, 2009, the relatives began to assemble at the funeral parlour. As Mick and I were driving up the street, we saw a phalanx of them, streaming sweat as they made their way up the road from the train station. People's clothes clung to them the way that old Beryl Blake's used to cling to her. I was glad for having chosen the parlour over a church. We had air-conditioning.

'The Lord is my shepherd,' we said. 'I shall not want.'

But everything changes. The vicar said the international version.

'The Lord is my shepherd,' he said. 'I lack nothing.' Obviously, if Stella had truly been a regular attender, they were the words she would have known.

A relative brought a portable organ and didn't know the tunes. 'Hallelujah! Hallelujah!' we sang, all off-key. Sweat dripped from every pore. Babes mourned loudly. The Nations assembled: the Vietnamese, the Indians, the Islanders, the Somalis, the Russians, the Czechs, the British, at least one with Aboriginal forebears and another with Chinese. Australians all and all, at some stage, sheltered under the eaves of the Hawthorn cottage, drinking tea or something stronger with the Queen Mother's cousin, twice removed. The sandwiches were good. Audra and the vicar were one, solid and irreproachable in the sight of so much sin.

Afterwards, we went to the pub where we used to take her for seniors' lunches. The rowdier elements came with us and those relatives who couldn't take the train home because the rails had buckled in the heat during the service. On TV screens where usually they had the races on a Saturday afternoon, there were walls of fire. The countryside was going up. A return of the summer horrors was upon us. We were downing beers – 'Gosh,' someone said at my elbow, 'nearly didn't make it!' I looked up.

'Eli.'

'Mumma.' His was the last plane in before the airport closed. 'It's horrific,' he said. 'It goes for miles.' And he shook his head in slow, sad disbelief.

We were going to bury her at Scunthorpe among her relatives on the Sunday but the roads were closed. Along the route we were to take fires were still burning until late Monday, and so it was on the Tuesday that Mick and Eli, Wendy, Nin, Daniel, baby Georgia and I sat up in a small cavalcade of two black cars behind a hearse and made the slow, sad journey.

We hardly spoke. We played no music. Where the fires had been, creatures lay, legs-up beside the road, bowled over by the flames. The air was thick and grey. The land, black. Where, in Afghanistan, it was a shelled-out landscape, here in Australia were the jang and sang of nature – the war and the stone – shattered trees, split scenery, all black or ashen. No birds. No green.

We carried our little sparrow of a mother, grandmother and great-grandmother to the place where her people lay waiting for her in the family grave. I farewelled her at the graveside with *Fear no more the heat of the sun*, from *Cymbeline*. I love the line that goes *Golden lads and girls all must, as chimney sweepers, come to dust*. We brought with us the oddest flowers we could find, a box of chocolates and a bottle of sherry for luck. So she went down with truffles, oloroso, pineapple lilies and waratahs, there being no monkey orchids at the time of year.

Then back we drove to our mourning city through the ruined scenery under a sorry sky.

26

There has been rain in the weeks since.

There were long shining puddles across the floor of the Yarra Valley when we drove out to Lexie's this morning. We have driven through the blackened acres and the thorny profiles of burnt-out mountains, past the black and jagged memories of its forest trees around whose bases the green is already sprouting but not with the promise of survival. These shoots are the last hurrah of the eucalyptus. It's only when you see the green high up that it signals continuing life. Grand European requiems on the tape deck were wrong for this journey; what it needed was a dirge of didgeridoos and clap sticks. We didn't have any, so we drove in silence. Where there is no thread to pull, you must make one for yourself.

We have followed Vance and Suzanne down graded tracks to their patch and felt, under our feet, the depth of cinders. Lichen, gold and green, has begun to lace the top of the powdery ground. There are trunks burnt through, like giant keyholes. The trees on the ridges seem to have writhed and cursed in their death throes like the people of Pompeii. Here is Garibaldi's statue in the piazza in Milan, its outline impossible with pigeon shapes; there, two trees have fallen together to make a Chinese dragon whose remains rear up, powerless before the greater dragon whose annihilating breath so recently passed this way. Yet it's our land, whatever our cultural memories. 'I've found one!' calls Suzanne from where she is crouching in a nest of skittled logs. 'It's a purple wax lip!' We've already found white spider orchids and blue Caladenia and greenhoods. They are small and easily overlooked but our eyes are becoming better at searching them out and they are beginning to be everywhere. It makes us feel as if we are bringing them to life and, in their life, they are transforming the way we see.

Under the ground the mycelia are delving, finding the seeds, and the seeds are sprouting, their alluring ladies waiting to come out and loll around to fool the native wasps. This is what happens in our midst – here, now and with me no longer waiting.

Lexie is a kilometre away up the hill doing small salvage jobs around her house. The double glass in the windows stayed intact but the guttering melted, as did most metal things, leaving holes and planks and flaps of masonry behind. Lexie and her family were safe under the hill and were able to go back twenty-four hours afterwards. They lost the solar panels off their roof but their generator helped them in the meantime. The water in their dam is covered in fire debris but it was effective when they needed it, filtering water down to the bunker through underground pipes. It won't be very long before their systems are back in place.

Yesterday I was at Raven and Barratt's, signing papers. More than once the lawyer has said to me, 'Keep your powder dry.' It seemed stupid to say that during the drought when you would have had a hard time getting your powder wet. It seems to me that the law exists only to feed lawyers: having spent hours bending my mind around ridiculous, entrapping questions put by Checkie's law-yers, and even more hours bending it around the changes of mind and the shifting of the arguments, my insurers thought the best way out of the mess was to offer Checkie compensation. I objected stren-uously but there was no point. If I didn't accept the insurer's terms, they would go ahead without my agreement. They did just that, offering twenty thousand. Apparently, it wasn't enough. Checkie wanted three times that sum to drop the case. It was between her and the insurers then. There has been an out-of-court settlement. Thus do those who fish with a long line between the cracks of fortune reach the bottom to land the flounder.

Dadda's paintings are still down in the store but they won't be there for long. Some day soon, Nin and Lexie and I will bring them up the hill along with all the other art and craft in the store and hang them in the house for an exhibition to celebrate their survival and ours.

On the day, we shall reopen Lexie's restaurant in the large, airy house. The restaurant has a very long wall, and on it, in train, is a very large triptych. On the first panel is a crouching, naked woman, pressing up against the glass pane of the frame, her palms white with effort, her cheek and hair also pushed hard into it. Reflected in the glass that will go in front of her will be the flames of the centre panel which leap through the devastation we can see stretching forever through the restaurant windows – but there will be people in the painted version. The centre panel will remain unglazed. Through mayhem and conflagration, the world will go tumbling in a revisitation of Breughel. The Shi'ites, the Sunnis, the Protestants, the Catholics, the Liberal and the Orthodox Jews are taking shape. Crosses admonish, Stars of David hang around people's necks and bear them down, Crescent Moons are wielded like cutlasses. Ayatollahs race to-and-fro, women in burqas beg, nuns advise their acolytes with their backs turned, bishops preen before mirrors while choirboys adjust their raiment and kiss their shoes. Death meanwhile is not some striding black-draped figure with a sickle over its shoulder, nor Mad Meg with her reforming zeal, but a tiny woman, lying in a tiny bed on an island in the very centre: her tiny expression is amazed, because it isn't God or a band of angels she sees hurtling over her deathbed, but a stone, a sang, headed out of the picture plane for the third panel, which overlaps the second and is in the act of breaking open in the shape of a bird.

Instead of having the broken window mended, I lifted the glass out, piece by piece to preserve the shape and, with Mick's help and much swearing, I've remade the window, frame and all. It is to swing against the scene of the blighted forest as it is now with the orchids proliferating and as it will be, real and changing through the restaurant windows. Money? Oh well…Cost? Well, I can't put a price on it, I can only put my life into it.

"Sgreat, Mum,' says someone at my elbow, his mouth full of sandwich. He's talking of the triptych. God knows what he'll get up to next, but he's stayed around since the old girl's funeral, playing with his littlest relations. He came out with us this morning and has been up helping Lexie and seeing the painting for the first time. Now he has joined us on our orchid hunt, bringing a champagne lunch. He holds a bottle aloft and calls out to Mick and Lance and Suzanne, who come on over as the cork pops and the liquid fizzes into plastic glasses that George Green wouldn't have drunk from had his life depended on it.

Acknowledgements

I have written this book, as I always do, for my family and friends and this time also in hope for peace and prosperity in Afghanistan following their first democratic elections. I was in Afghanistan in 2013 with the Afghan Australian Development Organisation and its redoubtable inspiration and leader, Dr Nouria Salehi. I thank her from the depths of my heart and also her sister, Gulalai, who made our meeting such a special and pleasant occasion.

I also thank, with much love, my husband, Robert Hind, who supported my efforts during the three years of writing. Robert also read for me, as did my friend, Jenni Pearcy, and my brother, John Morrison.

Many thanks also to my editor, Bruce Sims, and my publisher, Rose Michael at Hardie Grant.

I write in memory of those who are gone: my parents Laura and Charles, my many aunts and uncles and other friends and companions.

I dedicate the book to Robert, Jane, Jonathan, Rachel and James, all of whom were in my thoughts as I wrote.